DON'T STOP

ALSO BY

BONNIE FRIEDMAN

Writing Past Dark
The Thief of Happiness
Surrendering Oz

Bonnie Friedman

DON'T STOP

Europa Editions
27 Union Square West, Suite 302
New York NY 10003
www.europaeditions.com
info@europaeditions.com

This book is a work of fiction. Any references to historical events, real people, or real locales are used fictitiously.

First publication 2026 by Europa Editions

Library of Congress Cataloging in Publication Data is available
ISBN 979-8-88966-174-0

Friedman, Bonnie
Don't Stop

Cover design by Ginevra Rapisardi

Cover image: Ramon Casas, *Tired*, oil on canvas, 1895-1900.
Photo: incamerastock/alamy

Prepress by Grafica Punto Print – Rome

Printed in Canada

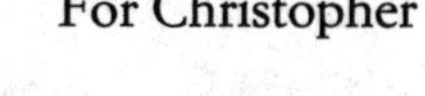
For Christopher

DON'T STOP

Part I

Chapter 1

When Ina discovered sex at the age of forty-one, her whole life turned upside down. She found that she liked things that she didn't know she could like. Or, to be more precise, she found that she craved to do certain things, and to have certain things done to her, that before this time she would have regarded with mirth and incredulity.

Her entire personality had apparently come spring-loaded with a secret compartment in which all sorts of desires lay hidden. Most people didn't know their whole character, she now believed. She certainly hadn't, and she was highly educated and with a wide circle of friends, married at the age of twenty-eight and with a normal dating life before that. Now events that had once struck her as cartoonish or pathetic—a politician caught with a prostitute sucking on his toe, women who wanted to be handcuffed naked to their boyfriend's bed—didn't seem so strange. Now she withheld judgment. And it worried Ina to think that she could quite easily have lived her entire life without discovering this hot, disorienting aspect of herself, as if she'd occupied a dim apartment without ever realizing there was a light switch.

It all began late one October afternoon when her friend Janie invited her to a networking event for writers, an open-invitation party for literary types. "You're home too much. You're missing all the fun," said Janie, gesturing toward the city which, from where the two friends sat on the Brooklyn Promenade, resembled a jagged steel honeycomb, the cells of which were brimming with a clear sweetness. The brake lights on the FDR were just starting to show raspberry in the gathering dusk.

Ina smiled. Naturally she didn't think going to a networking meeting sounded fun. "If only I didn't have a deadline."

"Life too has a deadline."

Ina laughed. "You sound so macabre!"

Janie merely raised her eyebrows in response. "I think working too much has narrowed your vision," she said, speaking far more slowly than she used to. "I think that's part of your problem."

Janie was just back from three months in Nepal. Subtle things about her had changed. The spring before she left she'd dashed about—playing bass guitar, an instrument she was still mastering, with new friends in a weekly gig off Avenue C, dancing many nights in a row at clubs that closed just as the cobblestones of Gansevoort Street caught the first light. It was as if she'd hoped to exhaust the city before her pilgrimage. Ina was relieved that now, back home, Janie hadn't surrendered her old joys, although she sensed that they meant something different. Janie had an ascetic, otherworldly appearance—whether from hours in meditation halls or her prolonged bout of malaria, it was hard to say. She had also acquired a new way of listening; she seemed to be hearing echoes inside echoes. It was disorienting.

"I don't have a problem," replied Ina, touched however that her friend wanted to diagnose her.

"You seem a bit dogged. A bit too sequestered."

"It's called focus." Ina winked affectionately at her old friend, wondering if Janie would change back soon.

"Sweetie, you are starting to say odd things."

"I've always said odd things." Nevertheless, Ina tapped the Post-it pad in her pocket for reassurance. If she didn't have good judgment, her project would come out wrong. The instincts she relied on would mislead her. She had to be able to identify the shifting emotional valences of the Eugene O'Neill plays she was studying—and to do that she must progress into the indeterminate, the not-yet-named, without losing her grounding, the common sense that every literary critic needs. She lowered her gaze. Through the bottom of the cast-iron grillwork before them, someone had woven the grimy felt stalk of a yellow cloth tulip. The scent of a cigar reached her, expansive and deliciously acrid, as if offering the whole elliptical promise of the metropolis. She was conscious, too, of an almost audible giddiness emanating from across the river, from Wall Street, whose shadowy length she could practically see, and from which came incessant reports these days about Masters of the Universe and new IPOs whose values leapfrogged by fifty percent week after week, inducing crazed states of greed and joy, as if the very rules of reality had been suspended, as some people believed they had. Some very credible economists were saying that not every market that goes up must come down. She and Simon had just moved back to New York last year. "Okay, tell me," she said with a sigh. "What have I said that's odd?"

"If you don't talk to your sister before eight in the morning you get tense."

"I can't have Violet calling later. I've got to be able to immerse."

"Yet a small interruption—"

"Not odd," she affirmed with relief. Her friend hadn't discerned a secret something that was amiss, if indeed anything was.

Janie turned toward her. Her blonde hair, which she'd worn in joyful cascading ringlets all summer long, had been shorn into a pixie cut. "Complaining to your landlady about a faintly buzzing doorbell."

"It's always going." Still, Ina again tapped inside her pocket because Janie wasn't wrong. It would be better to be able to ignore it, the alarm deep in the wall, steady and soft. But she had to attune to the nuances of moments in the texts and that made her susceptible. Chapters were due in less than three weeks. Post-its were stuck all over her study walls and they formed no pattern. Without a book she couldn't continue at Quincy.

"Ina," Janie said. "One almost has the sense you are running away from something. After all, life should be bigger than a desk."

"And when I submit my book, it will be."

"It's not either/or."

"You've transcended dualities," Ina said with a smile.

In answer Janie looked at her with her probing gray eyes, her gaze sad and unnervingly steady, and just said her name. Ina suddenly felt like weeping. Janie actually truly cared about her! This wasn't a game to her. A clang rang out—a shopping-cart banging a light post. Time abruptly seemed real, as if someone had snipped a ribbon with a shears. After a moment, however, time had started up again, spooling forward with its dull, monotonous churn. All the while her friend had continued to regard her with that compassionate expression. And for that reason, and in deference to Janie's newly winnowed, almost haggard appearance—as if all the paraphernalia of life had dropped away—Ina murmured, "Fine. I'll go."

After all, what was just one evening? Still, another voice inside her declared, *You shouldn't stop. You can't afford an interruption. You'll lose the organizing idea that was just starting to emerge.* And for an instant she glimpsed the dozens of Post-its stuck higgledy-piggledy to her wall. They seemed to be desperately trying to communicate something to her that she was on the very verge of hearing.

The two friends walked further and further west on Bethune Street, advancing ever deeper into the blur of the fog and the scent of the sea. Where the hell was the bar? Well, it was probably good she'd come, thought Ina. This was O'Neill's own terrain, after all, and she should know it better. As a young man he liked to spend his days in sailors' saloons with other alcoholics and the criminals known as the Hudson Dusters, who treated him as a kind of honorary member, even a mascot. He hadn't discovered writing plays yet. He didn't think his life was worth much. "I'm surprised you're over your jet lag," she said.

"I'm not. But I didn't want to miss tonight. I might meet a magazine editor. Or someone who knows a magazine editor." Janie had studied writing years ago but had given it up. Traveling had gotten her to start again.

A man and woman stood in a townhouse doorway, kissing. Handsome, the man wore a dark suit and loosened tie, a knapsack at his feet. The woman stood in a T-shirt and sweatpants. Ina felt numb for an instant, transformed into wood pulp. That appealing man found that woman attractive.

A big white poodle stepped out of the milky air, hauling along a slender woman. A man with a chain-link choker around his neck appeared, mascara raccooning his staring eyes. He passed so close to Ina that she caught a breath of spearmint and sweat.

Soon the fog closed around them. She and Janie were swathed in separate cocoons, affording a deep privacy. "Why did you go?"

"My life was going fast. I was missing too much."

"Were you?" From her perspective, her friend had reached almost sybaritic heights before she'd decided to go to Nepal; she'd made the most of each long day and night.

"Yes," said Janie, and pushed on a door Ina hadn't seen, opening a dark loud rectangle in the fog.

Horrible music banged. Were people singing to it or just yelling? She couldn't tell; it all melded into a muddy cacophony. Ina hovered near Janie while they waited to order. A counter ran the length of the vast dim hall, and beyond it lay a jammed narrow room, but the crashing, throbbing music was everywhere. She asked for a Heineken; Janie requested just tonic water. Ina was so nervous her arms seemed threaded with a tingling electric current, and as if they would drift up if she didn't root her hands deep in her pockets. She became aware, however, that this gave her a rigid, robotic appearance. She hadn't been in a bar among strangers in years. A woman in black vinyl pants reflective as aluminum strode by. Could that be a writer? Another woman followed, enclosed between exquisite, shellacked boards of elbow-length stick-straight hair.

Janie tipped her chin toward a man in a rumpled overcoat. "Going to say hi to that guy. I just heard he's some kind of at-large writer for *The New Yorker*."

Ina nodded, curious. What would Janie say to the man? How did you introduce yourself to a person from whom you wanted something? "Qualcomm's valuation," shouted a voice near her, but the sentence was swallowed into the roar. A woman tottered by wearing a candy necklace that had smudged her throat in sherbet colors. Ina saw that Janie was just standing near the *New Yorker* man, beside a few other people, not intruding. She was shy the same way Ina was, after all.

"Planes are going to be falling out of the sky," a man with an unpleasantly resonant, bullhorn voice was saying. "Bank assets'll vanish. I mean, it's going to be fucking bloody. What I'd like to know is, what the hell were those supposed geniuses thinking?"

Ina's gut tightened.

Across the crowded space there sat an empty chair, floating in a kind of no man's land. It was adjacent to a table where a woman in a raspberry cable-knit sweater sat with an overheated-looking fellow with a dense beard. Ina maneuvered her way across the room, inserting herself into momentarily empty spaces, and politely inquired if the chair was occupied.

"Help yourself." The woman had long blonde bangs and her hair was pulled back in a braid. She offered her hand. "Mary."

The overheated man was Jack. He wore a silly tan vest with

foot-tall blue argyles beneath a thick earth-toned sports jacket. "I write music," he said. "I'm a composer."

"Isn't that kind of a cheat?" exclaimed Ina, relieved to have thought of something to say. "I mean, yes, writing music is technically a *form* of writing—"

"Maybe I'll find a lyricist here," he replied stiffly.

Her face stung with embarrassment. Perhaps Janie was right: she had become too cloistered. "Sorry."

"I'll forgive you this time if you promise to be good from now on."

Ina laughed. What a pompous twit! Yet she was grateful he was so easy to talk to.

"Mary's writing a book."

"It's called *How to Get to I Don't*. It's about how to avoid getting married. Did you know that in seventy percent of divorces, it's the woman who files? Unmarried women live ten years longer than men."

"Do they?" Ina leaned toward her. "Marriage is that unhealthy?" She'd somehow surmised as much from certain aspects of her life with Simon—the secret sense she had of something ersatz in their life. Last week in a restaurant the couple at the next table started making out and she suspected that she was looking at them too long. Their kissing made something rasp inside her, as if her inner self was being scraped. A desire overcame her simply to go to sleep—if only she could sleep right then! So that she could spring awake the next morning for work. Which was confusing because she loved Simon. He was handsome and funny and kind. When she saw him walking toward her on the street, her heart squeezed with joy, and she would snatch his hand and kiss it. He looked startled then, as if love was a surprise, he didn't expect to be noticed and cared for.

"Marriage certainly is unhealthy," said the woman. "People ought to go out in groups. To forestall the possibility of getting too serious. They should never meet in gatherings smaller than three."

"Are you married?"

"Goodness, no!" Mary lifted her braid and let it drop, and her silver bracelets chimed.

"What do you think of that argument?" Ina turned to Jack. He had intelligent, warm brown eyes below dark hair that jutted attractively like the visor of a skipper's cap.

"There's some problems with it."

"Like what?" Ina pressed.

He held himself stiffly, glanced away. "It just doesn't seem likely to work."

"Exactly!" Yet why was this slightly pudgy man so elusive? For it seemed to Ina that he was, since she could find no worthwhile reason merely to be pleasant. She even wondered irritably if it was beyond his powers to be clear. Individuals should express themselves forthrightly. "People want to go on dates," she heard herself announce. "They want to get together for drinks and flirting and whatever. Are you going to change thousands of years of human nature?"

Voices rose up around her in a whirl; a fuzzy bass throbbed over the sound system. It occurred to her that she was no longer talking about marriage, unless she was.

She swallowed her beer fast. She wanted to drink it all before it got warm. It was thrilling to be out with new people. It loosened one from constraints, although she also felt a sharp mad envy of Mary in that exquisite cable-knit sweater which seemed to signal an ability to have adventures, to be self-possessed, to do what she wished.

"People change when they have to," said Mary.

Ina burst out laughing. She saw Mary's face harden. Oh, Janie was right; she'd gotten odd. It was from focusing on O'Neill, remaining stationed on her hard chair beneath a poster of the playwright looking typically dour, his cheekbones jutting at angles reminiscent of a slingshot, his eyes sunk in their sockets. He was an unbudging visionary truth-teller on the order of Aeschylus, and she'd grown increasingly bewildered by his steady glare. The mid-career experimental plays on which she focused had masks and life-sized puppets, and she claimed that they created a reality for the audience that in fact had a greater truth than was accessible by conventional means. Recently however, something weird had happened. The plays had taken on an increasing inscrutability. It was as if they were arguing on their own behalf for their actual obscurity, in opposition to the argument that she herself was making.

But then, just a week ago, as the October dark started to come on noticeably early, the atmosphere around her work had shifted again. Something was assembling. It was like the ion-charged moment before a storm, when the leaves fling over, the green showing silver. She had the sense that she would very soon see whatever it was behind the plays' enhanced mystery. She'd waited on edge, expectant. But the effort, the keyed-up receptivity she'd maintained, had evidently eroded her ability to be in normal society.

"Besides," Mary continued, "to some extent this book is just a sellable concept. It'll be like *The Rules*, only the opposite. Remember how popular that book was—until, actually, one of the authors got divorced. By the way, are you married?"

Ina nodded.

"Then you're not the market for this book."

How at liberty Mary appeared to be in her cable-knit sweater, like some girlhood heroine—a Heidi, an Anne of Green Gables. Her blonde hair was woven into a glinting long braid. A chill emptiness swept through Ina as the thought occurred: Jack is attracted to Mary.

"Still, why not be as persuasive as possible? Maybe all people should *do* is date," said Ina. "Instead of going the Puritan route, go the decadent one. That's what people really want!"

"Advocate old Mel Tormé records," proposed Jack. "And pink lightbulbs with a drop of patchouli oil."

"Beaded curtains!" added Ina. Maybe a sellable concept wasn't so bad.

At once her smile faded. No—it gave her a lousy feeling. The sellable concept was the opposite of her own exacting, note-taking method, her piecemeal way of pulling the world into focus. For all its impracticality, for all its spiritual cost to her, at least hers was a sincere attempt to determine what was true, rather than what could pass for truth.

"Beaded curtains," echoed Jack. His words seemed to carry a second meaning.

"I'm going to get another beer!" Ina abruptly announced, standing. She wanted this fun to continue. But there was nothing in her glass. "Can I get you anything?"

"Michelob," said Mary.

Jack shook his head.

Chapter 2

Jade, ruby, amber. The bottles glowed, backlit, a periodic chart of intoxicants presided over by an elfin woman with brushfire hair. She clanked down the Michelob bottle on a thin napkin on the bar but poured Ina's Heineken into a tall glass. Froth ascended toward the brim. Whitish yellow, it manufactured more and more of itself beneath Ina's blank gaze. "Do you ever think of having children?" Janie had asked earlier as they walked over to the gathering.

She'd replied curtly: "Yes."

"I think Simon would be a terrific father," said Janie. "Don't wait too long."

People said this to her a lot these days. In fact, she'd visited a fertility clinic the previous spring to understand how much time she had before she must decide. For she felt that there was something that needed to happen between her and Simon before they might possibly have children. There existed a murky place in their marriage. Intimacy between them felt haunted by odd burrs, even during their first years together, when the sex had been naked and friendly and quick. Simon had a cheery frankness about his own body that made any other attitude seem like nonsense. It had to do with his evangelical upbringing, she suspected. Nevertheless, after sex with Simon, she sometimes lay on her side, dull with melancholy, coolness pooling between her legs as she gazed out the bedroom door and down the corridor. It was as if he'd done something mean. In any case, now wasn't the time to have children: she had a manuscript to deliver.

Across the room, the *New Yorker* writer was opening his wallet. He plucked out a card and handed it to Janie. How did her friend manage it?

"Monastery drinks are the strongest," a voice murmured. Ina turned, and there stood Jack, of the too many clothes! How distinctly pleasant! It seemed to her a great coincidence that he had appeared beside her, although she knew of course he'd merely decided to come up to the counter, too.

"The strongest?"

"Oh, yeah." His direct brown eyes held bemusement. "Benedictine. Frangelico. I guess those monks needed something to do for fun." He ordered a B&B, and they both surveyed the illuminated drinks. "Chartreuse is supposed to be excellent."

Chartreuse. That contained wormwood, didn't it? Which was the operative force in the young Eugene O'Neill's favored drink, absinthe. A Princeton classmate of his had marveled at the "fantastical excursions of the mind" it induced in O'Neill. Ina had never even thought to try it—which now seemed distinctly strange to her. How incurious she'd been.

"All the Chartreuse in the world comes from one place, a monastery in Grenoble," said Jack. "That sounds like marketing, but it's actually true."

"How do you know?"

"I read it on the internet."

The man had a Terry Thomas smile, with that same gap between his front teeth as the old charming British actor. Jack's eyes on her made something shimmer within her. She held her cool drink to the back of her neck. He asked: "Which do you think it is?"

Cerise and Aqua Velva blue bottles shone in the display. One clear vessel contained what looked like swollen apricots, peeled, upside down, the fruits nestled atop one another to compose a tree of yellowish-orange hearts or babies' bottoms.

She shifted her gaze away. Beside it stood a slender bottle of liquid the green of fresh spring grass.

"If you drink Chartreuse, you're drinking a color." Was this an obvious thing to say?

He smiled approvingly. "Let's try it." With a decisive nod, he signaled the bartender. Heat was radiating off him. How uncomfortable he must be in his wool jacket, she thought. The bartender stood up on a stool and came down clasping a bottle of gold-green liquid which she wiped with a rag. She set out a very curious, squat drinking glass. It was square on the outside but curved within, as fascinating to Ina as a goat's eye. She poured. "Go ahead," urged Jack.

Ina drank a little. It was blindingly potent, scalding her throat and seeming to do something to her on a molecular level. Would it be rude to get out a piece of paper and take notes? But she felt too drifty to do so. What fun it was to be in a bar tonight. It was good she'd come out. If she'd remained alone at home—as she often did now that Simon was more involved with his acting—after finishing work she would have wandered up to Barnes & Noble. There she had taken to reading books about common if bizarre female maladies—hair plucking, self-cutting, kleptomania, bulimia. There was a nonfiction book about people in a therapy group; she read all their stories, night after night, thinking that the journalist's style both admitted her and kept her out. It was breezy, conversational—it seemed to hold the truth, but a truncated truth.

Ina lifted the glass again, and a delectable aroma rose up, sweet and clean. She sipped, and after a moment the mirrored wall of bottles appeared to swing into place. "Nice."

He took a sip, too. "Yes."

She tried another. Exquisite. This was in fact the most delicious thing she'd ever tasted. She wasn't being hyperbolic. It absolutely was. It possessed a vegetative fragrance (chamomile, she proposed; he thought basil) and imparted to her mouth a fiery, bright sensation. In the corners, the room was a misaligned four-color print, surging yellow-greens, blue-reds.

"It tastes, it tastes . . . " she searched for the right word. "It tastes—like stripping!" Heat pricked her cheeks. "What I mean," she added stiffly, "is it strips the inside of your mouth. Like turpentine. Doesn't it seem to remove a whole layer?"

He smiled kindly. "Yes."

Ina took another probing taste. First came the briskness of peppermint schnapps but without the peppermint, then a kerosene heat followed by a sweet aftertaste that resolved into nothing. This made you want to try it again, to establish if the flavor was really there and follow where it went. It was like stage charisma: there's more than you can grasp so you keep watching. Last week she'd seen an Irish Rep performer with just this trait, playing Hickey in *The Iceman Cometh*. In every scene there was more going on than one could absorb, due to a coolness the actor maintained with his eyes. He was holding something back, even as he smiled in welcome. Ina picked up the glass and just wet her lips, but even that felt wasteful because she wanted the drink never to end. "How did you come to be here tonight?" she asked.

Jack gestured toward a portly man seated in the middle of the bench that extended along the rear wall. He wore a turquoise shirt printed with palm fronds and toucans. "A friend."

She rubbed her chin hard. She felt, oddly, that she didn't deserve for Jack to look at her; it made her self-conscious. She almost resented his gaze. He was actually quite handsome.

Ina liked standing close to him and conversing amidst the throng. He was easy to be with. "I should bring this beer back to Mary," she said regretfully. "Not that I really want to go back."

He offered no opinion.

She turned toward their table, clasping the shot glass in which a few last delectable sips remained. Disappointingly, however, the people at other tables were already putting on their jackets. She discovered it was past midnight.

Janie appeared through the dispersing throng and wordlessly hugged her, then gazed into Ina's eyes lovingly—(had she become more loving during her Nepalese journey? Ina thought yes), then departed to say goodbye to a few others, whom Ina noticed she also looked at quite directly. Ina worried about making her way home. It was foggy out and she didn't know this ancient part of Manhattan beyond the grid, where the streets traced the route of cow paths and submerged creeks. "Anyone else going to the 1 train?" she asked in a loud, carrying voice. A few suave-looking people glanced over, startled, and she resolved to be unconcerned if she was being uncouth. If she was, so be it. It was late and she did not care to be lost. Mary offered that she was walking toward Sheridan Square.

Jack turned to her. "I'm going to the subway."

The hush of the street came as a surprise. And yet tucked into its silence as they walked was the clamor of the bar, echoing. She, Mary, and Jack progressed down the avenue and then at the corner crossed into a narrow side street. Red brick Federalist homes rose behind black-painted railings. A haze permeated, swelling the yellow lamps with nimbuses—though it was otherwise a mild, unremarkable autumn night. "The narrowest house in New York—isn't it around here somewhere?" She and Simon had seen it on a walking tour. They loved to go exploring together, Simon reading from a guidebook, the city a treasure map.

"I used to know that ferry poem," said Mary. Not a non sequitur, because Edna St. Vincent Millay had lived in the narrowest house, around the corner from the Cherry Lane Theater. Millay and her two sisters had performed in O'Neill's *The Moon of the Caribbees*. They'd been the sirens, singing softly from the beginning of the play to the end. It occurred to Ina again that

Jack liked Mary more than her. After all, Mary was available. And had that raspberry sweater and thick blonde braid, both of which indicated a certain self-possession and freedom.

He asked, "When was the last time either of you took the ferry?"

"Years ago," said Ina. "There was a wedding couple on board. They were having their picture taken with the city behind them."

"There's always a wedding couple. The ferry can't leave without them," he remarked.

"And the bride has to wear a great big white dress!" cried Ina. Then she fell silent. This was precisely what she'd worn at her own wedding, with a long train that got wrapped around her like a maypole.

"Here's my turnoff." Mary swept an arm toward an adjacent street.

"Goodbye then!" Ina said, pleased by her good fortune that she should be alone so soon with this friendly man and yet at the same time afraid she'd miss Mary, as if the space she had occupied would be alarmingly empty.

"Ciao," called Mary, striding off into the fog.

Ina was about to tell Jack that she wished she herself could say "Ciao" without it feeling artificial—but the mood had abruptly changed. They walked in silence. She had the sensation that a level of frivolousness had dropped away and that they were both acknowledging that life itself had a certain gravitas, although out of politeness one generally acted otherwise. He lit a cigarette, which surprised her. Nobody she knew smoked. She was aware of his warm body. The jangle of a dog collar came from somewhere, and from an open window issued the urgent male monotone of an announcer broadcasting game scores. The sidewalk angled like an elbow, jagging to the left.

There, set behind a chain-link fence, rose a row of yellow private houses. They seemed transported from a small town, along with their swath of emerald lawn. A lamp glowed in the window of one of the homes. "Imagine living there," remarked Ina.

"I actually knew someone who did," said Jack. "A kid in my junior high."

"Really?"

"Yeah. His dad was a writer for *Superman*. The TV show."

"Heavens to Murgatroyd!"

Jack laughed. "It was actually dark and crowded inside. And his mother said it was really hard to keep clean. But it was an actual house, so that was nice. Where did you grow up?"

"Co-op City," said Ina.

"I wonder if anyone ever actually said 'Heavens to Murgatroyd.'"

"My sister did," said Ina. "Learned it from Perry White."

"No kidding. Were there other ways she was like him?"

"Lots." Even as a young girl, Violet's girth imparted an authority that at the time seemed embarrassing, defeminizing. She'd been high school valedictorian, a brilliant young woman in a cherry-red silk scarf with impeccable diction. She'd never found her place before her life became constricted. "My sister reminds me a little of Julia Child, actually," said Ina. "Awkward in that same way." She added, "Did you know it wasn't until Julia Child was forty-nine that *The Art of French Cooking* came out? Before then, she was just a gawky woman with a plummy voice! Can you imagine what her life would have been like if she'd died before her book was published? She'd never have been on TV!" Ina felt sad, telling this, for Violet hadn't had her full chance. Her multiple sclerosis was diagnosed when she was just twenty-six.

"Aw," said Jack. "She probably had other things she was happy about before then, even so. Private but real things."

Ina studied the little window where a lamp was burning. A moment passed. "That's true." She recalled seeing a girlhood photo of Julia Child on a seaside vacation, when she was one of several radiant passengers in a posh convertible car on the beach. Violet too must have had important pleasures that Ina didn't know about.

And after that it was easy to keep talking.

Chapter 3

At the Christopher Street station, the arriving local made the tunnel reverberate. They rode the train two stops and then were on the platform again. Jack was talking about an opening number he'd just finished. It was for the musical of *Goodbye, Columbus,* his first major commission. It went: "Welcome to the country club, but for just one day!"

"His horrible cousin Doris!" Ina exclaimed, tickled that she'd remembered.

"Yes!"

"She invites him for one day each summer because her parents make her. And for him it's like going to heaven. From the hot, squalid Bronx. That's the movie, of course. In the book it's Newark."

He nodded.

"I love that novel." She grouped it in her mind with *The Graduate*, stories about making it in materialistic America during the post-war boom.

"It's good," said Jack. "I see the opening number as having all these women in 1950s bathing suits and sunglasses. Remember those three-part reflective silver cardboards? Or are you too young? They'll be holding those under their faces or, you know, putting on Chapstick, and they're singing 'Welcome to the country club,' with horrible Doris, as you put it, booming out: 'For just one day!'"

"And at the end of the song Brenda walks over and asks him to hold her glasses."

"Exactly. Shouldn't we cross over?"

"What for?"

"This is uptown."

She stared into his face. Then, bewildered, peered about. Across the rails lay an extraneous set of train tracks. Strange! She had the feeling a huge mirror was reflecting the tracks behind her. She spun around. Brick wall! She'd grown up in the city and had never once mistaken uptown for down. She must be extremely drunk.

They mounted the stairs and walked the short length of the overpass. "Maybe we should just stay up here," she proposed. "That way you don't have to climb back up when my train comes."

He stepped forward and was kissing her. She stood rigid, arms taut. Screeching sounded in her ears like metal-on-metal brakes. This was wrong. She was married. He knew she was married! Yet she avidly wanted to know about this. Oh, please, please, begged something inside her. She was for once the girl being kissed on a street corner as she and Simon drove by—for it had happened frequently, very frequently in the city, that they passed some couple making out, and Ina had felt neutered, almost sick with envy. Others were alive; she was made of sandpaper, gritty and plain. Now she made a decision and leaned toward Jack. His mouth was surprisingly warm. She opened her lips and his thick, soft tongue slid in. An inner self collapsed inside her, folding, slipping down. She hadn't been kissed by another man in over thirteen years. And with Simon, it had never been like this. She felt desperately curious and at the same time subsumed by languor.

And then the stairs were whooshing up around her, pixilating. "I have to sit," she said. It would be ridiculous to faint! "I feel dizzy."

His tone was matter-of-fact as he said, "That sometimes happens. But should we sit right here?" he added with obvious dismay.

But she had already sat down hard, on the grimy topmost step. She lowered her head between her knees.

Geometric mosaics jumped behind her eyelids. The air was thin and almost burnt. It was hard to draw enough into her lungs. After a moment or two she was able to lift her head. She gazed straight out, telling herself to breathe evenly.

The subway lines were sunk deep into their tracks. They were excavated very low into the earth and were astonishingly, miraculously straight. Staring at them made the world calm.

"I suppose I ought to apologize," he said.

"Why?"

"I know you're married."

She scratched her elbow. How sexist. "If I didn't want to, I wouldn't have kissed you back."

Yet his action had been a marvel. There had been empty space. And then he'd had the bravery to cross it.

He leaned forward and they were kissing again, and then she pulled herself away. She stared at the silvery blue rails. They appeared strangely static in their long iron grooves while everything else swam: the stained gray cement stairs, the plaster walls scraped with striations, the wood benches on the platform. She'd had two beers and a green liqueur; he was wearing cologne but of course that wasn't what made her head spin. "Do you want to go out for a drink?" he asked.

She laughed. She was doing a lot of laughing. "It's twelve-thirty!"

Sadness crossed his face.

"But it's fun talking with you," she added quickly.

"It's fun talking with you, too. You're smart."

"Oh, that," she said dismissively. Her hand waved as if to say, I didn't mean that to sound arrogant; ignore that. She studied the tips of her shoes. They appeared oddly rounded, gnomish. That past summer Janie had explained to her that people just started out to go clubbing at one in the morning. Through the wall of Ina's own apartment she'd heard the breathy pennywhistle of her stockbroker neighbor's modem—three shrill notes before a plunging electronic bass—rousing her when he got home from dancing, the sky already seeping light.

"Also, I think you're cute."

She regarded him.

"We have the same hair," he continued.

His was lustrous black with a stiffish, straight texture she liked and that held the cut of a scissor, like the hair of some Asian men. Hers had some strands of gray. "You're too young for me," she observed.

"How old do you think I am?"

"Early thirties?"

"Thirty-three. How old are you?"

She turned her head away.

"What kinds of things do you like to do?" he asked.

She shrugged, not able to understand the reason for his question. "Read," she reported factually. "Go to museums. Walk around Manhattan. Talk."

"We can do those things. I'm good at talking!"

She smiled. She had Simon, and she wasn't lonely. She and her husband had terrific adventures, especially now that they were back in the city. They visited artists' studios together, rambling around subdivided warehouses in Chelsea, and often stood on line for cheap tickets at TKTS. Simon was insightful and pragmatic, and she understood things more deeply from talking them through with him. Sometimes they just watched old movies on TV and discussed them. Last week they'd happened upon the black-and-white 1940s production of *Great Expectations*. Although it was three in the afternoon, they lowered the blinds and, while the movie played, took turns hugging the cat.

"Can I have your number?" he asked.

She opened her wallet. A gold ticket stub the size of a Hershey bar stuck out—from *Aida*, her parents' birthday gift last spring. She scrawled her phone number on the back but then her fingers stopped. Was it 6659 or 6689? There was simply a blank where the third digit should be. She kept staring. Weird not to recall her own number! She let her pen make a guess.

He in turn produced a card. A black serif font with sills and cornices. Jack Salmond. The raised type flashed bluish-silver as if something on the surface had gone skittering.

The station walls started to thrum and Ina went quickly down the stairs. He stood on the platform beside her. "Can I call you?" he asked as she was stepping aboard.

"Please don't," she said. "I need to see how I feel when the Chartreuse wears off."

The doors shut and she was sitting. Her eyes inclined themselves toward the floor, which happened to be filthy. An empty root beer can rattled all the way to one side of the car as they traveled. It paused, then after a silent moment began its clattering, jangling journey back. Her cheeks pulsed. She felt unable to look up lest she meet someone's eyes.

Finally the train tilted down and began its long passage under the river with no stations shedding light. At last she could lift her head. A woman in a dark blue slip-dress and twinkly heels that seemed twisted out of pipe cleaners was scanning the *Times*' stock pages, the rows and rows of initials in tiny type. She circled an item. An upright older woman was crocheting with a hook as tiny as a hummingbird. Ina's world was indeed too small; Janie was right. Look at all these idiosyncratic people in the nighttime world—part of life! The crocheting woman met her glance, and Ina smiled, but the woman looked steadily at her without smiling back.

The fog was thick in Brooklyn. The marble bank building on Montague Street appeared to be dissolving; its bottom portion slumped toward the pavement and the rest of it stood vaporous.

How astonishingly light her legs felt. They seemed to have become sleeker and more bare. Beyond Henry Street, the open door of an establishment across the road displayed a woman on a distant stage. Karaoke blared. The woman wore a leopard-skin dress and clasped the mic close to her lips. She belted, "It's up to you, New York, New York!" She sounded terrible but happy. The people in that bar seemed vibrantly alive. She'd never fully noticed before that she'd felt this way about them. In the past she'd always quickly tugged her attention away, as if it were on a leash. And she'd told herself that it was stupid to feel jealous of vulgar, crass, and probably unintellectual people, that of course such people contented themselves with cheap thrills. Now it came to her in a sudden rush that she'd actually spent years feeling only half here, an ashen person. She'd known but hadn't known. She drifted along Montague Street in her tall stiff nubuck shoes, on legs smooth as clothespins. The hazy air seemed an extension of her expansive mood; she felt enfolded in an opium dream. An aroma floated up—spicy cedar from Jack's aftershave permeating the fabric of her shirt. Darkened shops lined the street: Best French Laundry, Klein Optical, the Pakistani laundromat. In Key Food the big round white clock indicated 1:15. She noticed an odd sensation: it was as if there were a braid between her legs that wanted to be touched, a strange thick red braid.

She descended Hicks, then turned the corner onto her own street. Quiet reigned. Gardens stretched away behind freshly painted black railings, the grass blue-green under shepherd's-crook lamps. Behind the gardens, brownstones presented faded faces. A banged-up yellow dumpster stood opposite her building. The real estate market here was crazy. Wall Street was just a few subway stops away. Sales and renovations were happening up and down the block. Last year, when she and Simon had moved to this neighborhood located midway between their jobs, the house next door had been a ramshackle multi-family dwelling. Now it was a five-story mansion.

Ina hauled open her building's heavy front door, then spiraled up flights of battered red carpeted stairs. She and Simon often spent evenings apart with their separate friends, getting home by midnight. Tonight, though, she was later than usual. The quick, even telephone dialing of the downstairs neighbor's modem came through the wall, followed by three breathy whistles and then a deep electronic bong. She repeated the melody as she climbed, feeling for once in tune with the euphoric city.

Upstairs, Simon was already asleep, with the door of the bedroom open. She shut it as quietly as she could.

At the kitchen sink she drank glass after glass of water. A milky glow saturated the room. Outside, in the graphite sky, the dilated moon leaked light all around. At the corner, the Bossert Hotel glowed, squat and muscular and faintly fascistic. She was reminded of a painting by de Chirico of a barren streetscape under siege, with its austere plaza traversed only by the elongated shadow of a riderless bicycle.

Ina lay down on the couch. She was too aroused to sleep. Had she ever been this aroused in her life? In the diaphanous lit air, everything in the room appeared swollen. She touched herself, and this both intensified the feeling and yet, in an unprecedented way, made satisfaction more distant. The place between her legs became something enormous and half-numb. It needed to be pushed on very hard. This had never happened before. Soon the muscle in her arm ached. The area that needed to be stroked—or rather pummeled—stretched. She sensed that if she wasn't careful her fingers would slip and her whole hand would fall inside. At last she came with a concatenous obliteration that gripped her throat but also brought regret for she instantly realized she'd remained as aroused as before. How could that be? Her two legs had been parted and that new braided part had been added. Legs still apart, she stared into the haze. She fell asleep under the illusion that her eyes remained wide open.

Chapter 4

The red light blinked. It was a message from her sister, but she couldn't move yet because the room was unsteady. An upper corner kept springing like a page trying to be flipped. Her memory offered no trace of Simon leaving or of the phone ringing. She wondered how O'Neill had endured waking up like this morning after morning, feeling like an ashtray dirty with stubs. He'd been a black-out drunk when he was young. She felt a surge of compassion for the young man. No wonder it took him so long to straighten himself out in life.

She hauled her body vertical. It was already, astonishingly, after ten. Half the morning gone! Normally she was awake by six. Yet how wound up she still felt! A spring inside her had been over-cranked even as her limbs remained deliciously indolent. Across the street the retired history professor sat already stationed in the window of the top-floor apartment, working. She wore a crisp white blouse with buttoned cuffs. Her era was the Weimar Republic, Ina knew, because she and Simon had sublet in that building for a month while they waited for this apartment to become available. Once when they rode the elevator together, the professor opened a book in German to a photo of a clerk using a sheaf of Deutschmarks as a scratch pad. "A loaf of bread rose from three marks to 80 billion marks," said the professor.

Ina had nodded. "1923. I'm interested in that time, too," she explained. "Eugene O'Neill was very inspired by the German avant-garde. I'll come interview you." But the old professor stiffened forbiddingly.

Which was too bad. It would have helped Ina to discuss Weimar aesthetics with her: *Caligari*'s funhouse angles, *Metropolis*'s regimented workers marching underground, Marlene Dietrich in satin hot pants, and curved-walled houses whose first floors floated in midair. And, past the thrill of innovation, the awareness that the repressive forces were gaining power, a terror O'Neill also registered. He often set the visionary against the militantly conventional. Ina wondered if the professor felt any of this strain in herself between the liberated and the lockstep. Once, waiting for the elevator, she overheard her chatting in German with a slender man who resembled her. Ina had wondered how old they'd been when they came to the U.S., for them still to speak together in their native language.

Ina got herself to her feet. At the sink, she poured herself a tall glass of water and drank it. Then set a pot of coffee to brew, and dialed.

Violet picked up on the first ring. "If it isn't the sitzfleisch scholar."

"Reporting!"

"It's the middle of the morning, Ina."

"I know. I'm sorry."

"I've already been out in the ambulette. Out and back."

Ina didn't want to say that she been up late at a party. Violet no longer went to parties, if she ever had. Even before Violet got sick, when they were growing up, Ina hadn't told her much. Six years older than Ina, Violet had been an imposing girl who carried herself with the aplomb of a town mayor. She pronounced the h in "white" and complained that Bob Dylan couldn't sing. She referred to Ina's friends as "your little pals." She told one brother that his greasy hair should be washed a minimum of once every three days, and the other that he grinned too much.

Violet had been the fat girl allowed to say blunt things. The bossy child nobody could correct. "If the truth be known" had been her favorite phrase. It made Ina love her even more because she was so touchingly odd, so frighteningly easy to mock. When they were girls together, and even now, Ina didn't dream of trying to convey her own experiences to Violet. They simply lived utterly separate lives.

"I was thinking about that wonderful salat gadol we once made," said Violet. "With purple cabbage. Why don't you come over this Sunday and we'll make it? You can pick up some of that lovely Bulgarian feta on Atlantic Avenue."

"I'm sorry, this Sunday we're going to Simon's parents." She couldn't quite reach the coffee, which was done brewing. "I'll come soon." She stretched a tiny bit further, the wire taut, and then a deafening clanging crash burst out. Behind her, the heavy yellow phone receiver lay on the floor, the metal disk on the bottom having swung askew. "One minute!" she called, leaving the handle to grab the receiver.

When she returned she said, "Hi. I'm sorry."

There was a silence. Then, eventually: "That hurt my ear," reported her sister starchily.

"I'm so sorry, Violet!" To have added to her sister's physical pain! It was the last thing a person should do.

"I told Mom when you were in junior high," said Violet, speaking with slow precision, "that she ought to enroll you in dance lessons. They might have helped with your clumsiness. But: water under the bridge." Violet sounded bitter.

"True." A pressure tightened Ina's scalp.

"Do you remember that comment your Spanish teacher made your freshman year?" asked Violet.

Why had she ever shared this? But she knew why: to make Violet feel better. "'Speak more carefully,'" recited Ina, blushing at the memory. "'Everyone here is intelligent.'"

It was a Spanish class, but she'd been so excited by her ideas that she'd spoken urgently, sloppily. She'd forgotten that the entire point was the correct use of Spanish. She'd lacked common sense. She feared she still did. No, she knew she still did. It was as if she stood too close to the pointillist painting of life. By some miracle she'd managed to become a professor anyway, hiding her severe limitations. "You know me well," said Ina now, speaking softly because her head was splitting.

As soon as she hung up and set off down the hall, an unsteadiness asserted itself again, as if the floor itself were billowing.

"I met someone at a party last night," she told her best friend, George.

She'd called at the stroke of noon, which was just nine California time.

"Did you?" He had a smile in his voice. "Ina met someone?"

"Yes. He writes music."

George was silent. She pictured him knotting one of the funny narrow ties he bought at the Salvation Army for a quarter; his clothing these days was a cross between the ironic and the sincere.

"He kissed me at the subway station. It felt unbelievably good. I really had no idea a kiss could be like that."

"It's about time you found out, girl!"

She laughed. George had been a star at grad school in Chicago until, like Janie, he discovered that he needed something different. Now he interned at a mental health clinic, helping street kids. He was working to get credentialed as a psychologist. He wore wrinkly button-down shirts and wingtip shoes already down-at-the-heels, with a stud in his ear that was like a wink.

"I don't know whether to see him again. He's younger than me."

"What does that matter?"

Ina pressed the receiver hard to her ear. "Oh?"

"You're getting yourself confused."

Ina's hands gathered up the phone cord's pink rubber curlicues, neatening, straightening. She compressed them into a stack of *o*'s. It was always helpful to get George's perspective.

"What you need is a fling, Ina. That's all."

She felt slightly dazzled and frightened by his words, as if she'd set something dangerously effervescent inside her.

"You have a marriage. You don't need another marriage. You love Simon and he loves you, and what's missing has nothing to do with love."

"True." George was entirely correct, and yet—she gazed troubled at the emerald rug with its pattern of mauve and russet leaves that seemed to lie atop the rug's surface like real leaves on a lake. She'd often felt antiquely maternal with Simon, or like a pal. Occasionally, at the start of making love, she'd had to bite her tongue, resisting an urge to push Simon's too careful hands away from her breasts. Once or twice she actually had shoved his hand. Lolling, lewd, fleshy things, her own breasts had seemed to her then. He'd gasped, wounded, and withdrew.

Still, at other times sex between them went okay. He and Ina cherished one another; he didn't give a hoot about the way she looked. She was a gnome, a monkey, a funny face. So much of their life together was good that she waited for this one aspect to resolve itself.

"A fling is a fling," said George. "It's a little gift to yourself and then you should forget it. It's useful only insofar as it provides information about yourself and what you want to be getting from Simon."

A phrase came to her from O'Neill: "Sex, the philosopher's stone." She'd always taken that line as the playwright merely being droll and clever. He loved to provoke, especially when he was young. Now she wondered if she hadn't misunderstood him. Did she really know why he'd called it the philosopher's stone? Could it be that he wasn't being sarcastic? She contemplated the gold paper fan in the fireplace; George himself had folded it. The pleats concentrated the available light in a way that seemed magical. Even on overcast gray days, it shone.

"Be strict."

"What do you mean?"

"Don't tell this guy secret things about yourself."

Ina burst out laughing. "There's no danger of that! I have *you* to tell secret things to."

George was the perfect person to tell secrets. On their very first evening together, after a graduate class, George had said something surprising. She'd gone to his apartment, and they drank red wine out of juice glasses. "You carry your smile before you like a big hoop skirt, keeping others at a distance." Nobody else had ever thought to tell her this most obvious thing. He'd handed her a key to her own character. Over the years he'd handed her many others. There were times she felt that, without him, she would be locked away from herself.

"It's just that this man kisses so well."

"Kissing is important," George agreed. During a recent visit to Los Angeles, George had spread on Ina's lap a gigantic photo—the novelist Colette sitting cross-legged on a Paris stage, hands crossed over naked breasts, a silver dagger-ribbon skirt just covering her thighs, and her hair cropped into an Egyptian helmet. "Isn't that the way to live?" George exclaimed. Ina had been wearing a baggy sweatshirt, her hair a rat's nest. Yes, she'd thought, it absolutely was. That self-possession. That erotic liberty. George often regaled her with tales of his sexual adventures. He and his boyfriend Charles allowed each other great freedom. Now he said: "Just stay clear about what you're doing."

She rolled her eyes. "Of course!"

How could she not stay clear, she thought as she gathered Simon's shirts from the closet floor to take to the drycleaner.

She adored Simon—the fuzz between his eyebrows, the cozy nubbly surface of his brown plaid robe, the way his voice was low and scratchy in the morning. His loose-limbed, vaguely abstracted walk down the pavement, his feet kicking slightly, as if, as a tall man, he couldn't be bothered to keep track of those distant extremities. He opened his wallet and donated to panhandlers, even the bristle-chinned woman stationed on a wood crate outside the bagel shop, who irked Ina. "God bless you," the woman always told him, and he answered, "And you, too." He had taken the teachings of his childhood church to heart although he became uncomfortable if Ina drew attention to it. And he was charming. This past Sunday, when she asked him for an orange from the kitchen, he'd supplied her with two, one an unsheathed moist round lantern and the other still in its rind. As she took them, the round unpeeled fruit burst, uncoiling to reveal an empty core—she'd cracked up. "You nudnik!" He laughed. This was pure Simon.

Last November when they still occupied a house in Connecticut, they'd come down with the flu together, and lived on Dayquil and stale yellow Easter Peeps, while he plucked on the banjo softly, playing the old Girl Scout songs she'd grown up with, giving the simple melodies the soulfulness they deserved. He was a terrific musician. Their heads hurt from sneezing, and, late in the night, Simon said, "I know just the cure!" handing her her coat and boots even though she wore pajama bottoms under a robe.

Snow glazed the ground; the entire world glowed bluish-white. How cool their foreheads finally felt. He was right: it was a cure. So often what Simon proposed turned out unexpectedly well. Even his plunging into business reflected Simon's basic optimism. The future was in high-speed connectivity, he'd decided, and so he chose to switch careers and go into cable marketing, despite his being an engineer. As it turned out, this gave him an advantage over the other marketers, who'd attended business school. His boss often came to him with questions.

That night they walked the long road, and it felt thrilling to stroll in their pajamas. Simon fell asleep as soon as they came in and she could see the lonely boy she'd first met, a lean figure in snap-button shirts with downturned eyes. She couldn't help but kiss him on the lips although they'd made a policy not to kiss while they were ill. When they woke up in the morning they were both well. Not long after that he proposed they move to New York City, where he could get a better job.

They moved that very winter. And at first she felt enormously lucky. They traveled up to Symphony Space for Gilbert and Sullivan, Simon enrolled in acting classes, and Ina spent sweet evenings with her parents and afternoons with Violet because they no longer lived far. But in the spring something shifted. She couldn't say why. There followed inexplicable afternoons of weeping on the couch. She felt quite unmoored, as if there were a blankness that hadn't been there before. It wasn't that she missed Connecticut, where she'd had only acquaintances, not friends. She was weirdly overcome by the impression that there was nothing in life to look forward to. She'd never felt this way before. And she became addicted to listening to a certain radio psychologist who had intuitions so great that his callers often exclaimed after five minutes, "How did you know?" The radio psychologist had a warm, juicy way of speaking, and a slight lisp. She sometimes stood right over the radio as he spoke, gazing through the little holes into the dusty interior, listening to the caller's stories, noticing a wisp of the cat's fur drift about in there like a slow-motion globe in a pinball game. She seemed to be waiting for someone with the exact same problem as hers to call in, and then she'd recognize exactly what it was.

It had certainly been a mistake for Ina to go out last night. The apartment still brimmed upward and subsided, over and over, although it was already mid-afternoon, the October day angling toward dusk. She seemed to be reading *A Touch of the Poet* on a boat riding the swells. And things she understood yesterday were quizzical today. Why did the mother journey far from home to speak to her poet son when she was sure it would do no good? Why leave the sequestered garden in which she lived? She shook her head, and her eyes sought an index card taped to her wall:

"As a boy I saw so much of the old, ranting, artificial, romantic stage stuff that I had a sort of contempt for the theater."

And beside that, on a Post-it: "*Theatron* = viewing space."

It always motivated her to be reminded of O'Neill's quest. She'd tried to articulate it to Marguerite Nelson, the department chair, and to the half dozen committee members who interviewed her for the position at Quincy, all of them crowded into Marguerite's office, their keenly intelligent eyes examining her with interest, their pens jotting an occasional note.

Of course, she began, O'Neill was one of the great American dramatists of the 20th century, with his four Pulitzers and the Nobel. Only Tennessee Williams and Arthur Miller were of his rank. And he was far more revolutionary, far more interested in continual formal experimentation, than either of them were, although his best play, one of his last after the nearly fifty he'd already written, was an absolute breakthrough in realism, *A Long Day's Journey into Night*.

Where did his innovative grit come from? She posed the question to the committee, and then answered by telling about how he'd grown up with a father who starred in the melodramatic, grandiose theater of his day and a mother who, in daily life, was also a kind of actress. O'Neill discovered, when he was fifteen, that his entire life she'd been a morphine addict, almost from the day of his birth. He'd assumed she suffered from dementia. He was the only one in the family who hadn't known the truth. So: he'd grown up in a world of illusion. The realization changed him, embittered him. As an adult he committed himself to portraying the truth of experience. To cleaning out the fraudulence. He possessed the seriousness of purpose of a prophet.

Across from Ina, a slender man with a thin strawberry-blond ponytail scratched something into a small spiral-bound book. Other committee members regarded her with a cordial but noncommittal air.

Which brought them to Ina's own work, she explained. She was interested in all those experimental midlife plays—the ones that were four hours long, the ones with robotic movements and continually swiveling heads making asides. "What they're actually trying to do," she said, "is to give the audience an experience of the true felt sense of things. People's actual emotional reality. Which we know, in its essence"—here she glanced around the tiny room, in which the judicious, assessing faces seemed momentarily to overlap and meld into one another beneath the towering green curtains—"is actually quite weird."

"True," said the department chair. She was a dignified, friendly Black woman in a khaki pantsuit.

Ina concluded by explaining that she was examining the imagery in those plays—the significance of something that is "beyond the horizon" or a "dynamo" of power. What does it mean for the sea to be a "devil" or for an Anglo woman to call a sooty coal stoker a "beast"? Her working title was something like *Levels of Language in Midcareer O'Neill*. "With a subtitle, of course."

"Of course," replied Marguerite with a joshing twinkle in her eye.

Ina almost laughed at her own pomposity. What a nice boss Marguerite would make! A man in a frayed blue blazer set down his pen. Ina surreptitiously wiped her palm on her trousers. In a moment they would be shaking hands.

"But why is O'Neill important to *you*?" inquired a woman in the corner, who Ina later discovered was the creative writing professor. She was festooned with bright necklaces, her dusty hair piled high with pins.

"Oh, I saw Kate Hepburn in *Journey*."

The committee members laughed and started to gather their papers. Ina smiled, relieved. They were done! But the woman in the corner said, "And?" A few pins glinted, as if she wore a cloud of lightning.

Ina curled her toes in her shoes, a trick she'd learned to secretly ease tension. She mustn't share what came next. It would make her look unprofessional. O'Neill seemed to know something about Ina's own family. There was a shadowy resemblance. She'd read *Long Day's Journey* in her parents' walk-in closet, sitting atop a step stool, her father's jackets on one side, and her mother's padded-shoulder dresses on the other, the arms brushing her as she turned the pages of her high school textbook. So much comprehension of the family seemed compressed in the lines of dialogue. She couldn't say what the meaning was but it seemed as palpable as the sleeves that stroked her whenever she moved.

"O'Neill understands the way that people take possession of one another," she said slowly.

"Ah," said Marguerite. "So it's the psychology that attracts you."

"Yes," said Ina, relieved to have her thought clarified. "That's exactly it."

Two days later, Ina was surprised and delighted when Marguerite phoned to award her the Visiting Assistant Professorship. It was a plum position, but nevertheless the department chair went out of her way to say there was also a good chance that, when her appointment was up, the school would create a tenure-track line in Modern Drama. "We have the need, Lord knows, and the money's there."

"That's very good." Ina purposely spoke with sangfroid.

"Yes, it is," said Marguerite in a tone that was almost affectionate, as if she understood and was charmed by Ina's ploy of nonchalance. And again Ina nearly laughed.

Her first year at Quincy College had been excellent. Days she wasn't teaching she spent in her study, clad in big green Michelin Man thermal pants that were once Simon's, and hand-stitched shoes from Denmark that her mother had given her and which looked as if they had been sewn out of catcher's mitts. The main thing was to maintain engagement with the manuscript. She didn't hurry. Her mentor at Chicago had said, "Your first major publication needs to establish your presence. Hold back until it can." Her dissertation had been able grad student work, he'd said. She needed to press further.

Sometimes she worked until the tint of her page altered, turning apricot, and she looked up. The walls flushed a golden pink. Out the window the sun was a sunken ball slipping behind New Jersey. But it was only, what, not quite four! Fear tingled painfully through her: she was deceiving herself. Life itself, with all its passions and textures was catapulting past. Other people had children. She'd returned to grad school after ten years working for a small, funky publisher. She'd lost a decade.

Still, if she remained perfectly still for four or five anxious minutes, enduring the discomfort, patient—for patience was her secret, she believed, more than intelligence—color drained from the room, she then pressed a button on the table lamp, and a door she'd been trying to jimmy all day suddenly sprang ajar. Insights overtook her, profuse as pollen. She scribbled them fast on the yellow Post-it pads. Some of these ideas were good and a few, she suspected, were distinctly excellent. She wrote until the Verrazzano Bridge twinkled in the dark and New Jersey had vanished.

Which had all been lovely until the day last spring when Marguerite stopped her in the hall and said, "On the Q.T., Ina, we need you to have that book in hand before your appointment ends. That is, if you want to continue on here. The new dean wants us to become a Tier One research institution."

Ina smiled, feeling sick. "That makes sense."

"But no worries," said Marguerite, registering the concern on Ina's face. "You've been chugging away for so long, you can certainly finish your book this coming year. Just put your mind to it."

An awful feeling had lodged in Ina's stomach, as if it were full of sticky, raw dough. She didn't have enough written—or even conceived—to draw together a book significant enough to be accepted by a top-tier press. Steeling herself, she asked "Could I possibly have the fall semester off? Without pay, of course."

Marguerite tilted her head, studying Ina's face, making calculations.

"I think I can arrange that," she said ultimately, with a sigh. "Have the manuscript to me by next April, please, and a list of where you plan to submit, and we'll take things from there."

But Ina had still felt uneasy. "Do you think," she said, pressing her luck, "that I could have a single course release in the spring, just in case I need that extra time? So I'll just teach two courses instead of three?" A look of concern flashed across Marguerite's face. Ina held her breath.

"We want you to succeed, of course," said the chairwoman, sounding a little tentative. "But it would mean significant sacrifices by others." Her face had taken on a surprisingly maternal expression. "I'll see if I can arrange that. But you know what? It would be best in that case for me to expect your outline and two sample chapters by November, okay?" She held her hand straight up as if to forestall any expressions of gratitude. "You can thank me in your acknowledgments."

"I thank you now!" exclaimed Ina. She was actually quite excited by the opportunity to focus singlemindedly on her book, but her boss was already moving away in her rumpled gray skirt suit, shoulders sagging beneath a burden of papers and books. Ina admired Marguerite. She ran the department with a sense of fairness and good humor, an achievement even greater than one might imagine. On Marguerite's desk stood a photo of her daughter, the young woman's expression dreamy, large-eyed, gazing rapt at something just outside the frame. Zoe had been pre-med at Princeton when, in the spring of her senior year, a car opened its door into the path where she'd been quickly biking, and she'd gone flying and slammed her head on the pavement. Now instead of attending med school, Zoey bagged groceries. Sometimes she sat in Marguerite's office, headphones on, staring at a tiny TV. Marguerite was always gracious to others when she could be, as if she'd made some internal vow of kindness.

Ina had worked all summer long beneath the photo of O'Neill with his glowering oracular eyes, and by late September the walls and floor of her study were cluttered with Post-its.

At some point, she understood, there would come a galvanizing concept that would attract and structure all her sundry bits. She could almost see the giant magnet of the central idea. *Come on!* she urged. *Get here.* She recalled the kiss from last night, and shook her head. She sharpened her pencil again although it was already sharp.

That evening, Ina stood with Simon's gym bag at her feet. Each time a car turned onto her block, she prayed "Please be Simon!" She was stationed across from their own doorway. She hated his long commute. An hour going, and often an extra half hour returning. At the corner, each driver at the wheel presented an identical gray silhouette. Each could be Simon. Then the car rolled under the streetlamp, and the light swept down, illuminating the features of a distinct man or woman. No. No. Not Simon.

And then there he was! *Simon!* He was driving toward her in their little blue Jetta. She grinned and stepped into the gutter. "Hi, baby!" she called. What a relief, to see him! He'd made it. He leaned over and pushed open the car door, and she climbed in.

"Hi," she said again, and leaned over to kiss him. He slid his pursed lips all the way over to the side toward her—he made his mouth have a comical, independent life of its own, quite at liberty—while his eyes remained on the road, driving. He was a decidedly good-looking man, with backswept blond hair that needed to be cut, and a thin nose sunburned simply from being in the car, and brown eyes that carried a look of slight surprise, as if he hadn't known that you liked him. Last night? No, she did not feel guilty about it. It seemed to have happened on an unreal plane of existence, like the rushing-away reflection in a revolving door. Still, she turned and gazed out the window, her leg bobbing, as they prowled the streets for parking.

They found a spot on Joralemon Street. Out of the car, they kissed swiftly, as if merrily checking off an expected item. Yes, I love you! Then Simon began to lope quickly, almost mechanically, down the block. He was several steps ahead of her. He had a great deal on his mind, she knew. Shaking her head with affection, she rushed up and grabbed his arm. He half-turned, swiveling, as if he'd forgotten his arm behind him. She kissed him again, harder than she'd meant to, landing her lips clumsily half-off his mouth. He laughed and squeezed her hand, an abrupt pneumatic pressure. She snatched his hand and held it. It wasn't fair to him, this judgment she felt. In the past she hadn't been tremendously bothered when he walked ahead, which he often did. But now it stung. She tilted her body and leaned against him in a way that was clownish, pressing into him as they walked. "Ekshu-sh me!"

He laughed, and she was disarmed by how perfectly even

and white his teeth were. He'd just finished having the last ones capped.

"Slow down! Please walk with me."

"Well, hurry up!" he replied good naturedly, with that new bright smile.

That too felt like a rebuff, as if he'd have some reflexive retort to whatever she said.

But then he asked her about her evening with Janie, if she was happy to have her old friend back in town, and he noticed the marmalade cat that they loved but wished wasn't allowed out. It lived on a side street past the church that had been celebrating its hundredth birthday for the past two years, according to the dusty sign lashed to the building's façade. The cat let Simon rub its head. "How you been keepin' yourself?" he asked it softly. "I see you have a hitch in your gitalong. Never noticed that before. Is that new, girl?" and a very soft squeaky purr came out of the cat. Ina sighed with relief and tenderness. She'd been judging him too harshly.

On the StairMaster at Gold's Gym, Simon let each pedal sink until it was an inch from the floor. Then he switched to the other leg. It was a grueling workout. Ina climbed beside him but didn't let the pedal drop nearly so low. Soon Simon was drenched. His T-shirt with the Catskill Game Farm logo clung; his face flushed pink. And then, Ina noticed, it was turning a darker red. "Don't overdo it," she said before she could catch herself.

"Don't undermine me!" he exclaimed.

She nodded, and sucked in her lips. His comments were sometimes barbed but she reassured herself that this response was simply a reflex. She rarely saw his sharp-tempered remarks as having anything to do with her. They were like old splinters that came out now and then, having been embedded long ago by his bullying stepbrother—and quite distinct from Simon's usually kind, actual self. And she respected his commitment to lose weight, and the strain it took. He'd been admitted last week into Scene Study II at the Stella Adler's studio after only a few weeks in Scene Study I, and he was already preparing a performance. The people in the new acting class were all trim.

On the way back from the gym they stopped into a bodega for Simon to buy a Gatorade Zero. The young man ahead of them in line pointed to an item he wanted behind the clerk. He was buying condoms. Condoms! The man was planning to have sex that evening! He wore jeans and black canvas sneakers, and as she stood beside Simon she felt denatured. The sadness remained with her as they walked back to the apartment together, Simon sipping from the blue drink that seemed to make a virtue of its flagrantly artificial color. He told her about a book he was listening to on tape, *A Brief History of Time*. Every ten minutes there was another railroad car full of ping-pong balls orbiting the moon. He laughed. Ina had the unreasonable sensation that Simon was aware of how she must feel, how ugly and undesired. Madness, of course. And she was struck by a crushing curiosity about sex, because there was something that she actually didn't know about it—in fact, a great deal she didn't know—as if it were a language she'd once understood the rudiments of but hadn't spoken in so long she'd half forgotten. Strange. She sometimes even wondered if Simon was actually attracted to her or if he were just inhibited due to his upbringing. She waited for her bad feelings to depart. And they did. At home, she and Simon shared the oregano chicken she'd broiled, and then split the last of the rhubarb pie that Simon had made that weekend. He'd used a bag of the frozen chopped red vegetable but the pie was still delicious.

"Amazing it came out so well, even without strawberries," she remarked, finishing the last bite of crust.

"The humble rhubarb is underestimated," he declared. "Like okra."

She went to bed before Simon, as usual—he staved off sleep

since the very next thing would be heading to work the next morning. She lay in bed with the exultant party of late-night TV carrying across the apartment.

But tonight after a few minutes the TV clicked off and after a while banjo music carried through the night, muffled, very soft, a song she used to play with her third-grade class on her recorder in the Bronx: "Red River Valley." The mattress swam upward. She recalled the man's gaze. The sensation when his tongue entered her mouth.

Chapter 5

She didn't call him on Wednesday or Thursday. A mysteriously good feeling enveloped her. The walls of the study seemed to subtly spread and contract, as if attached to the mouth of a drowsing giant. What was the half-life of wormwood? Obscurely inspired, she wrote a record fourteen single-spaced pages on Friday morning. She told herself she might never call Jack. But early that afternoon, taking a break, half idly, impulsively, she plucked the card from her wallet.

The first ringing tone seemed expansive, a cat stretching. Silence. Then the long, purring ring again. At the start of each ring, her stomach contracted with anxiety. During the fifth there was a click and an instant's quiet. "It's Ina," she announced. She hated her name. It sounded like "heinie." Why had her parents imposed such an odd, old-world moniker on an American baby?

"Hi, Ina!" He sounded delighted.

Immediately, she was at ease. They each sipped coffee, gabbling wildly. He was an accompanist twice a week at a performing arts school on the Upper West Side, in addition to working on *Goodbye, Columbus*, he explained. "The kids are terrific. But the voice instructor drives me nuts. She's always turning to me at the piano to agree with what she's saying, and I feel like some kind of Charlie McCarthy dummy."

Ina laughed.

"You know, I was a little worried, letting you walk home with so many intoxicants in you."

There was a pause, and then he said abruptly, "Hey, do you want to go to a movie later?"

The breath was knocked out of her. She could do that. She could go to a movie. She'd been planning just to go over and have sex, but she could certainly go to a movie. That evening Simon had class. They agreed to meet at four-thirty. Then she exclaimed, almost irritably, "I don't know how I'm going to get anything done this afternoon!" Her body had started thrumming, shivering almost. "I'm not used to going out like this."

"Right. But you want to."

"Yeah. Although you know I'm married. There's only one thing missing from my marriage." It was important that he not delude himself.

"I'm not sure I believe that."

She let a silence fall, then stated flatly, "You ought to because it's true."

"I don't believe that that one single aspect can be separated from the entire rest of the relationship," he answered. "It's a kind of intimacy. It shows a lack of intimacy."

"Maybe in other people's cases," reported Ina dryly. "Not mine."

She heard a brisk intake—he was smoking. "I don't want to *debate* you," he said. "But it seems sad, to miss that aspect of things."

A shimmer caught Ina's eye—the yellow legal paper of the retired Brooklyn College history professor across the street as she swept another page under the bottom of her pad. She wore a black turtleneck, like a 1960s existentialist. "It is, I guess," conceded Ina.

"Frankly, I find it incredible!" he blurted. "I mean, is your husband in good health?"

She laughed at the non sequitur. "He works out every evening."

"It doesn't add up." He paused again. "But in any case, it

would be nice to see you again. Why don't I check what's playing. By the way—" He hesitated. "The number you gave me may have been wrong."

"That's unlikely." She recited her number.

"You put down one number differently," said Jack. "On Tuesday."

Then it came back to her—the strange inability to recall her contact information, the odd blankness where a central figure should be.

She remarked briskly, "Well, it's a miracle I could find my own address."

She couldn't work. She simply couldn't stay put in her chair. In the living room she set an old record on the spindle: Astrid Gilberto. She sprayed the windows with cleaner. The paper towel she wiped against the glass came away dark, so richly coal black it was almost iridescent, although the windows themselves had seemed only clouded with old rain. When the last chords faded, Ina immediately lifted the needle and set it down on the first groove of the song again. "Why should I have spring fever, when I know it isn't spring?" The voice had a driven monotone; breathy, private, girlish, fixated, as if the singer were murmuring to herself.

There were five hours to fill until they would meet. It was all wrong, of course—seeing this man was wrong. But all she intended to do was have sex with him, nothing more. She wanted to know what sex was like. Because although she'd had sex before, it had come to seem almost as if she had not.

"I'll just have sex. I just need to know about sex," she now said aloud. She noticed an enormous crimson flower opening in the window of the Asian woman's apartment on the second floor, and that the man on the third floor was playing his guitar shirtless.

CHAPTER 6

Shoppers labored along the broad incline of 86th street, many of them clasping oversized rattling plastic bags that skimmed the pavement. Cars inched, their basses so loud that each boom made her skin jolt. Stadium lights bleached down although it was still day.

The neighborhood had changed a great deal since she'd been here last. It was dominated now by electronics outlets and a giant pet supply emporium. Ina found the movie theater—a battered-looking old Loews just off Lex—and waited in a nearby doorway. She wore black jeans and a black T-shirt.

When Ina was in junior high school, she'd visited here with her sister. It was then a Bavarian district of pharmacies scented with bath powder and shops that practiced specialized arts—you could have the seat of a pair of suit trousers rewoven by hand, Violet explained, or a doll repaired, its limbs reconnected inside with rubber thread. Violet had said that her favorite place in the city was there. Her sister led her to a store with marzipan peaches and Granny Smith apples the size of gumdrops. There were also minuscule pigs and lions, and even a trumpet telephone the size of a chocolate kiss—each confection testifying to a vision of the world in which nothing was insignificant.

Violet had bought them each a high-stepping white Viennese horse, using careful schoolgirl German. She planned to sing opera one day. Ina nibbled her marzipan immediately while Violet saved hers in a frilled paper in a hard-sided box, cradling the little box on her palm so it wouldn't get misshapen. That shop had vanished, along with the aproned ladies who'd cooed over Violet.

Jack appeared three steps away. She was as surprised by his sudden appearance as if they hadn't in fact arranged to meet. Again he was overdressed, wearing a different snug wool vest and a houndstooth jacket. Disappointment shocked her: he was a squat man with a round face. He reminded her of her ex-brother-in-law, an eczema-stricken rotund figure with the same bright-eyed imploring eagerness.

"Guess where I just came from!" he announced.

"Where?"

"Circuit City!" As if this was a surprising marvel.

"Ah."

"I needed to get certain connectors for my USB port. And also something called an Orb Drive." He grinned. Orb Drive sounded like something lewd out of *Sleeper*—like the Orgasmatron. She nodded rigidly.

He leaned past her and pressed open the heavy door of the movie theater so she could precede him in.

Ina wasn't used to being treated as if she were delicate, and felt almost ridiculed by his gallantry. The triangular prow of the candy display dominated the center of the lobby like a glass sailing ship. "Get anything you want," he announced, flinging his arm in a broad sweep.

"That's okay."

"I mean it. Anything."

His grandly solicitous manner embarrassed her; it made her feel as if he desired her to be someone more traditionally feminine than she was.

Jack held open the door to the auditorium. Stepping in, Ina stumbled forward in her wedge-heeled shoes on the angled floor. She caught herself with a mortifying trot. "I like to sit up close. D'you mind?"

"Up front is good."

So there they sat, in the third row in the empty theater, and pretty soon the movie began, and he kept talking. He spoke out of the side of his mouth, emitting clever-style slings about the credibility of the dialogue, the quality of the acting, the predictability of the situations. She laughed or nodded. It was tiring. The side of her body beside his felt irradiated.

At last he subsided into silence. At one point one of the men in the movie said, "I'm still alive, you know! I still have blood in my veins! I still want to fuck!" A sad shock went through her. The man—Jack—squeezed her hand. She glared. A few minutes later she noticed him peering at her. She felt like putting a hat over her face.

When the lights came on they were back in the theater. Unoccupied blue plush seats extended in rows around them. The place was nearly empty. She stood, and the chair bottom flipped up with a loud, awkward bang. She waited for him to collect himself. Then she strode briskly up the ramp toward the propped-open doors, past the attendant with his gray rubber garbage can and broom.

On Lexington, a noncommittal, impassive, seasick light flooded down. A semi-truck swept past, releasing a flatulent roar. How could it not yet be dark?

"I know a kind of fun cowboy bar," said Jack. "It's usually quiet, and there are booths."

She managed a smile. "Sounds good." Perhaps being in a bar would summon what had been wonderful on Tuesday night.

It was a long walk up First Avenue. A sticky glare fell from the sky, seeming to obliterate all subtlety. They passed a sports bar and a bland, corporate-looking pasta restaurant and a diner with a sheet of oily yellow translucent celluloid over the windows.

"You don't mind walking, do you?" he asked. "We could have taken a cab but it's such a nice afternoon."

To Ina the afternoon seemed overheated, dull. She was almost always inside at this hour, working. It surprised her how slack and arbitrary things could seem, and for some reason melancholic, as if a pulverized meaninglessness permeated everything. This had been the characteristic sensation of her early childhood, she recognized with surprise. She hadn't felt it in decades. She quickened her walk.

At the bar she drank her beer fast. He leaned across the table and kissed her. It was awkward. She hunched forward, and then came around the table and slid in beside him. And though they were kissing again, it was just two mouths pressed together. Was this because tonight she hadn't drunk as much? Or was it because the other time they'd kissed—on the subway platform—had been the first? Maybe sex was like that, really wonderful only at the very beginning of a relationship.

He asked her if she wanted another drink, and she did. Later, when he kissed her on the lips again, it was a little better, and she had more hope.

He lived in a neighborhood of bodegas and decaying walkups. As dusk deepened, gray curtains seemed to be dropping through the air, one behind another.

"What?" he asked, smiling, because she'd gestured surreptitiously.

"Women in house slippers, walking dogs." She was charmed by the women's casualness. Although this was First Avenue in Manhattan, they treated it as just an extension of their home.

He slipped an arm around her waist.

They turned onto a side street of low grimy houses and catalpa trees hung with leathery, brown leaves. Curled leaves lay on the pavement and they reminded Ina of the skin of a mummified Egyptian she'd once seen in college.

"Already!" she remarked, pointing to a Christmas tree leaning on a second-story fire escape. "It's not even Thanksgiving."

"I'm like that," said Jack. "You wouldn't believe how early I start looking forward to Christmas."

"But you're Jewish."

"What does that have to do with it?" he said, offended.

Revelers hurried up the street, various couples on dates, the women in short skirts and the men in shirts of a special hue, cobalt blue, creamsicle. A feeling of loneliness seemed to hover over the pavement. She supposed it was due to the people on dates rushing up the street. Jack ought to be on a real date with an available young woman, someone with whom he could get close.

"Here," he announced. He set his cigarette between his lips and turned the key of a glass lobby door.

The stairs were covered with gray carpeting. On almost every landing it looked as if something filthy had been spilled. "These walls!" said Jack, exasperated. Watery white paint had been splashed over the cinder block, and now it was blistering. "The management company does such a terrible job."

Ina gazed blankly at the cracked bubbles of paint. She climbed the steep stairs ahead of him, self-consciously wondering if he was looking at her derriere. At the top level she stood aside and he threw open the door on a series of narrow rooms that bloomed eccentrically off one another, reminding her of a diagram she'd seen in a Bronx Science textbook of the digestive tract of some small woodland creature. She wished she were more drunk. His living room was the size of a service elevator, with a lolling blue futon couch. Where was Simon at this moment, she wondered with a stab. She'd told him she was attending a talk at the Mercantile Library. What if he left work early and decided to surprise her before his acting class?

"Would you play something of yours?" she asked. An upright piano stood against the wall in the tiny living room.

He shrugged. "It may sound old-fashioned," he said. "This isn't from *Goodbye, Columbus*. It's from before that."

She sat in a corner easy chair. The music was strange, with odd progressions up the keyboard, and an aura of being improvised and almost inadvertent, like the work of Erik Satie. It had an autumnal, melancholic mood. It was as if he'd summoned that sense of the arbitrary on York Avenue, with the sooty sunshine washing over and even through people, and had built it into something. On a walking tour that past weekend, Simon had read to her that the merry-go-round in Central Park was originally propelled by a horse and a donkey treading around and around under the earth. A real live horse propelled the pink and yellow and blue icing-colored parade. The animal had gone blind in the darkness. At least it had the comfort of its donkey companion.

When Jack stopped, she didn't lift her eyes.

He tapped his cigarette into the ashtray. "Maybe one of these days you'll let me read part of your O'Neill book."

"Oh, it's not art," she said, her tone pointed, as if in a retort, although she was also wondering what he meant by "one of these days." She'd never be back.

"It's your work."

He got up from the bench and she stood, awkwardly, and they were kissing again, and this time was different. Her knees wanted to buckle. Vertigo overcame her, as if she were being tipped backwards in a lake. There was a momentary stab between her legs, half pleasurable. So it *could* be the way it had been before.

His hands slipped upwards under her T-shirt. Her entire self was at the periphery of her body, which now blurred, ecstatic, the molecules of her skin spreading apart, yet concentrating sensation. She wished she didn't have to breathe. Every time she inhaled the feeling dissipated.

After a while he murmured, "Do you want to go inside?"

She nodded, hanging her head. She was frightened, miserable, thrilled. She would be with him just once, see what it was all about, and be gone. The sliding pocket door rumbled along its track as he rolled it open. Revealing a barren, stark room. Two or three metal items hulked in a corner: gym equipment. On the NordicTrack an invisible angled stick figure seemed to be striding. Rectangles were carved through the six-inch-thick walls: windows. They had no shades or curtains, and offered lilac-blue images of the city.

"Do you want to take this off?" he asked.

She pulled her T-shirt lightly over her head. Instantly, she was embarrassed, but he was kissing her again, and touching her through her bra, which seemed suddenly preposterously thick, layer after layer of slippery, obdurate linings. She loved his swatch of dark hair as he lowered his head to suck through the bra. Then he cupped her breast with his warm broad hand and the sensation traveled sharply and pleasurably throughout her whole body, as if her entire being rayed in lines from there. He sat and the bedsprings creaked. He began to undo the button of her black jeans. "We need to deal with these."

She liked the nonchalant, dismissive way he put his cigarette between his lips before he attended to the business of her pants. She felt—ridiculously—that somehow she did not deserve his attention. He had a mature, unsmiling, focused, forthright manner. Whatever he looked at was important, and now he was looking at her. It made her woozy.

"I'm going to take off my shoes," she announced.

He nodded, and she sat beside him on the bed, and pulled out the tight bows of the plasticized laces, then pushed the shoes off with her toes. Her husband's blue socks covered her feet. Should she take them off too? No, that would be too forward. She stood, and pulled her tightish jeans down—he watched. If only she were more drunk! She felt painfully awkward; the fabric bunched. By pushing hard with her toes, she removed the last crammed denim folds where they clasped at her ankles.

He had a hairy chest—so extremely hirsute, in fact, that his chest was almost mutant. She decided she would try not to notice it. They lay down side by side. He held her face in his hands and licked the outside of her lips, and then thrust his tongue into her mouth in a way that made her flush, and which convinced her that he was doing this for his own pleasure, that he was actually aroused by kissing her. She had the sensation, when they were kissing, that he was drawing her deepest raw emotions up out of her and revealing their carrot-thick roots. Simon kissed briefly and pulled back. Jack did not. He breathed in her ear and a tremor swept down her. "Oh," she moaned aloud. "This is so nice."

"D'ya think so?" The tone was conversational. "Isn't it strange?"

She nodded.

"Isn't it strange," he continued, "to actually get to touch another person's body? So often I see a woman on the street, and I wish I could rub myself against her. It's amazing to actually be with you here, to be able to touch you."

She just loved that he was so conscious of women. Still, she became aware that a metallic light was shining on them from the bare windows. "Do you think anyone can see in?"

"Not as long as it's dark in here." His voice had a bit of gravel in it.

He kissed her again. She started stroking him but encountered an alarmingly cool, slick garment—satin boxers! Her eyes widened. Gold? The garment seemed autoerotic, like a feather boa he might have swept across his own shoulders.

A diesel truck heaved past as if trying to pull the sidewalk along with it. A skein of laughter billowed up. *Couldn't* people see in? She was acutely cognizant of the blank windows, oblong chunks incised out of the fortress-thick wall. He pulled her over until he lay on top of her. He thrust toward her. "You feel so good."

Everything happening now was unreal. It didn't actually have anything to do with her. Her true life was calm and steady, was with Simon. All of this was all the equivalent of an epileptic fit.

"Do you want to have intercourse?" she inquired. It sounded rather formal, even to her own ears.

He covered her lips with his finger. "Let's take things slowly. We don't want to get ahead of ourselves."

"I don't mind speed," she said, smiling. She didn't plan to return.

"But it's better to stretch things out."

"Okay," she said. She'd come back once.

"It's hard going out with someone who's married," he declared, suddenly turning and lying flat on his back.

She was silent, concerned he wouldn't want to see her again. The word "married" seemed like something antique pinned to her, a bustle or snood.

He said, "Does it mean that you'll never be able to stay over for the weekend?"

"Yes." She had no intention of impinging on her weekends with Simon.

"Can you ever stay over during the week, then?"

How perplexing. She'd taken pains to be crystal clear about this.

"I went out with a woman once—" He glanced away, out the window. "She was married but managed to stay over. She had a girlfriend who knew about us, and she told her husband she was there."

She shook her head briskly. She was surprised at him. Childish, to sneak around! "I couldn't do that."

Still, she lamented that the sexual interaction with Jack was over or seemed to be over—almost before it had begun. Yet how fine, beyond fine, beyond even pleasure, even this amount had been. She suddenly understood that it must be one of the great things on earth, this sort of experience. She was a latecomer to the party. Only, it wasn't a party; it was more serious than that. She said, "There's only one thing missing from my relationship with my husband."

Jack lay on his side and gazed at her. She pulled her shirt over herself. He said, "If you're not intimate physically, it has to affect all the other ways of being intimate."

"You said that before, but it doesn't." Jack had never been married, so he wouldn't know about marital intimacy.

"Then why weren't you wearing a wedding ring?"

"It fell off, swimming." A funny tapping had jiggled against her finger and then the gold ring had gone somersaulting into the Caribbean depths. She glimpsed the figure eight of orangish metal tumbling. She and Simon had been snorkeling off a boat with a group.

"When?" Jack demanded. "How long ago?"

"Half a year."

"And you never asked for another. Your husband didn't get you another."

True. She'd liked the sense of greater—"spaciousness" was how she expressed it to herself—of not wearing a ring. "I told you on Tuesday that I was married."

"Yes, but your manner was that of an available person. People who are happily married have an air of self-sufficiency about them. They don't seem to be searching for something else."

She looked away, into the city, where towers blurred in the gauzy light. Was what he said true? It suggested that some long-married people—many perhaps—were actually fulfilled by one another. Did they go home after seeing a movie together and make love slowly, the way people did in the movies themselves? She'd seen a performance of *H.M.S. Pinafore* where the male lead looked at the female lead while she spoke, looked at her with joyful interest, and had felt such a pang. She would have liked Simon to look at her like that. She'd wondered if such a thing happened only onstage.

Far in the corner of the room hung Jack's diploma. A yellowish document the size of a business envelope. It was tilted slightly askew. "Where did you graduate from?"

"The University of Albany. After Curtis."

Albany! she thought with relieved disdain.

His clock flashed 12:21 in long red digits. Her body went hollow, suddenly made of corn husks, and she sat up. Simon must be home. "I've got to go."

"But we just got here!" he moaned.

She glanced over, surprised. She thought he despised her! He was so critical.

"Are you going to walk me to the subway?"

He nodded, and they dressed in the semi-darkness. Although she suspected she wouldn't see him again, she enjoyed walking beside him through the empty streets. He wore a brown leather jacket and black fabric basketball sneakers, and the scent of his aftershave came to her, calling to mind the nice things they'd done in bed. She had the odd feeling of living inside a daydream she didn't even know she'd had. Or rather, she'd occasionally glimpsed these desires, but they seemed ephemeral as the doorway of blue on a soap bubble. She wasn't interested in macho-seeming men, although of course she'd noticed them. Men who stretch their arm along the back of the passenger's seat in the car when turning their head to go in reverse, men who rode bicycles with curved handlebars wrapped with surgical tape, men who were good at baseball or who could confidently jack up a car, men who held the door as you preceded them in—they'd caught her awareness. Jack seemed to be a man like that, capable and independent in that same way. She felt almost embarrassed at how much his presence pleased her.

He waited silently beside her at the station. She had her card ready to swipe. When the train came in, she said an emphatic "Goodbye."

During the 4 train's long uninterrupted journey underground

between Wall Street and Borough Hall, she recalled the sensation she had had of Jack looking at her as she stood close. It was odd to be so very moved simply because he paid attention to her. It dawned on her that she had been so touched because she'd believed females to be somehow beneath the notice of men. What a nasty surprise, like discovering a secret bruise she didn't recall acquiring. Her father had certainly prized her brothers more, or at least differently. As did the TV shows of her youth, tinged as they were with the eroticism of female subservience. A voluptuous bikini-clad Playmate sprang out of a giant cake before a boardroom of besuited, ogling men; a harem girl called her husband master and resided in a vase like a bottle of Windex.

And, she considered, when Jack kissed her at certain times, she had a sensation of tumbling, telescoping to the ground, as if her outer self were mere sheath. She knew some women cried after sex. She'd thought them silly. But now she understood why they did. She opened her pocketbook and groped among the sticky pennies and brittle, crumpled receipts, but there wasn't a single yellow Post-it. She slid his card out of her wallet—Jack Salmond—and on the back scribbled, "Being wanted to one's bones." She jammed it back behind a Bronx car-service card.

Then took out Jack's card again: "Nipples erect. Pinched." She paused, and set beneath that. "His lips sucking."

She tucked the card away for good. This singular evening was exactly the kind of thing living in a metropolis allowed. She pictured the beautiful revelers in Florent where she'd gone with Janie at one in the morning the evening before Janie flew to Nepal, people's eyelids or entire faces sparkling with glitter and freedom and joy. How alive they had seemed! Ina had smiled at them but told herself these extrovert pleasures were not for her. She recalled, too, the silent midnight streets near the Café Gitane where she and Janie often turned a deserted corner and found a movie set whose lights cast an oceanic shimmer that made the air porous, effusing molecular brilliance, so that everything in the hyperkinetic daytime that it created was both pasteboard and real, exposing the essence of life under the guise of the fantastical. It was the same with Jack: he existed but was mostly make believe.

Simon was already in bed.

"How'd it go?" she asked softly, standing in the bedroom doorway, testing if he was awake.

He stirred, and yawned. "Fine." He rearranged the pillow beneath his head. "Redmond gave me permission to go straight into Acting III."

"Wow!" she burst out with a laugh. "You must have been amazing!"

"Was okeh," he said in a gruff Boris-and-Natasha voice from the Bullwinkle cartoon.

"Acting III already. You were scarcely in II."

She could see his grin in the semi-darkness, as disembodied as the Cheshire Cat's. "Yup."

All was good. All was glorious.

It was excellent that they'd moved to New York.

Chapter 7

"You were out late," Simon observed the next morning. He sat in the living room, in his bathrobe. Ina sat down near him on the couch. She was surprised to discover that a clear, hard Lucite wall now separated them. It had never been there before, and terror prickled through her that it might never go away.

Simon was watching a real estate show on local access TV. Slouchy moguls in suspenders discussed construction projects. Simon enjoyed their gruff, insider manner. "Game over!" said one of the men. "Trump's got the air rights. He took his time, and was quiet about it, but they're his. *The Times*, Cronkite, the UN across the street can squawk all they like about ruining the tone of the neighborhood. It's going up, and it's going to be the tallest residential building in the city." "Yeah, but who's going to lend him money? He's filed for protection from creditors too many times." "Oh, he'll get the money," said the first man. "Maybe not from the U.S., but somewhere. I heard the Russians like him." Another man said, "You think?" and they laughed. It was almost noon, and even so she'd had to struggle to lift herself into consciousness.

"It *was* late," said Ina. "Janie invited me to a dinner party after the reading." She glanced down. She was trying to clamp shut the stretched-out waistband of her lavender sweatpants, doubling the extra fabric and employing a bunch of paper clips she kept tucked on the waistband.

"She was at the reading?"

A cool flicker went through Ina, who nodded. She frowned. These stupid clips were made of extremely skimpy, flimsy material.

"What time exactly did you get in?"

Ina stared at her fingers. They seemed swollen and clumsy. "After one. I didn't look at the clock." She often went out late with Janie. Was something different about her that she couldn't tell? "There's a whole brilliant group she hangs out with." Her tongue felt numb. "It's surprising how many psychiatrists want to be artists."

Simon smiled. "I suppose there are secrets they hear that they need to transmit in their own coded way."

"I suppose."

They spent the afternoon watching the old movie *Laura*, Ina wanting just to zone out. Simon was tired as well. She was aware that the Lucite wall was still there. In the movie, a minor-key tune evoked for the characters an unreachable memory. She recalled how she and Simon had first met, as undergraduates. Her roommate had had a crush on him, although they'd never spoken. He'd been a skinny banjo player in a bluegrass group, standing on the side of the stage, with round, blue-tinted John Lennon glasses and scraggly hair that often fell in his face. Sometimes Simon strolled forward to do a bit of a solo. He had a shy, sunny smile with teeth that were a little discolored because, she later learned, he'd chewed his father's tobacco when he was young. His playing sounded like two banjoes at once, he was that good. Afterwards they and the rest of the group went out. He'd ended up sitting next to Ina. Everybody else was drinking liquor but he ordered tonic water. He had an appealing accent, his vowels as pleasantly softened as butter on a summer afternoon, and when she asked, he told her that he'd begun college in Texas, a religiously affiliated place where he studied engineering. But then, he said, the event happened that every parent in the fundamentalist community most feared would happen at college:

he discovered theater. And also Buddhist art and modern architecture, and philosophy classes that led him to question the dogma in which he'd been raised. And so he'd transferred to the northeast last year.

She found him to be a gawky, appealing young man in a faded snap-button shirt, gifted with voices. He told long funny stories, able to hold the table spellbound. She didn't yet know that Texas was famous for its talkers. He explained to Ina as he walked her home that he believed his evangelical work had helped his acting: he'd become familiar with all sorts of people. Most individuals he knew hated knocking on strangers' doors. He'd liked it. He enjoyed hanging out even with the older folks who wanted to keep him there all afternoon, drinking sweet tea. "I'm still in touch with a few of them," he said. And in the week that followed, when she visited him in his dorm, he showed her the cards, some dusted with glitter, some embossed with manger scenes, most with very few words penned beyond "Good wishes" but nevertheless a strong feeling of actual love coming across. He seemed to Ina as sweet as a sugar cookie. When he was unhappy his eyes took on a childlike wincing sadness that made her feel desperate to comfort him.

Ina's roommate took her courtship with good grace. To be kind, however, Ina stayed over at Simon's room rather than bring him to hers. He had a bunch of instruments propped against the walls, and they seemed like a substitute family, a ukulele, a fiddle, a guitar, the banjo, all mementoes of the town where he'd grown up. He helped pay for college by working an afternoon shift at a brick factory, and she was impressed by that, too. A fresh brick was tossed down, still hot, from the top of the pile and he caught it between two other bricks. The air was pink from dust, and he wore a bandana over his nose; even so he still got nosebleeds. She'd never known anyone who supported himself with that kind of tough manual labor. He shrugged. "My parents can't help me out." They lived a hardscrabble if holy life.

He'd known almost immediately that he wanted to get married. She was hesitant. His family was just too alien from hers. His father especially, a dour, taciturn man, seemed almost spooky to Ina. The brother played deafening acid rock all day long in a room whose walls were painted black. Only the mother seemed normal. Then, too, Ina had recently dated a man—a senior—to whom she was more forcefully attracted. But she found herself speaking inanely when she was with him. And he'd been so insistent and forceful about physical matters that in bed she internally withdrew. With Simon she held onto her full intelligence, and this had seemed like feminism. Besides, they had a very good time together, and she wanted that to continue. They lived together after college and she loved the coziness and joy of it, the special way he fried eggs on weekend mornings, with cream cheese, while she juiced oranges, and the way he made her alert to the world, always able to spot, walking by the Prospect Park lake, if a turtle was poised immobile on a log in the sun. She loved the way his body threw off heat when he slept—and they had an affable relationship in bed. The second time he proposed, which was six years later, she said yes.

When the movie ended, Simon hummed the *Laura* melody, yearning, painful. It was so lovely. "What?" he said, startled, for her eyes had teared up.

"I'm thinking about things that get lost."

"You're thinking about Violet?"

"And us."

His brow wrinkled. "Us?"

"I met you when you didn't even have hair on your chest," she said in confusion.

"And I'm a he-man now."

She laughed.

"It's okay that we're getting older," said Simon. "That's nothing to be sad about." He took her hand and started to dance with her, moving slowly around the living room to "Moon River," which she'd never understood before was a waltz. When he sang the line about the drifters on their journey, she pulled him closer. He pivoted her past the bookshelves, past the windows, around the entire circumference of the room, which strangely seemed bigger. The cat started to trot beside them, meowing, and Simon scooped her up and changed the words so that now he was singing about not two but three. Looking in Ina's eyes, he sang that her direction would be his.

She smiled, her throat feeling thick, and wondered if the wall between them would ever be gone.

In the waning light the brownstones held a rosy glow. They were walking around the corner to the Polish diner. Living someplace beautiful made everything easier, Ina understood, even if she and Simon could barely afford it.

He ordered boiled pierogies and chicken and broccoli, and she had babka with coffee, that was all she wanted. Over supper Simon discussed with her the opening of *True West*, which he was preparing for class. He was going to be the writer brother. The other character reminded him of his own real brother. "Ugh. Gideon." Ina shook her head. "Your parents were just not equipped to handle him."

"And the church fathers weren't much help. They didn't want my mother to send him to therapy."

"He might end up an infidel?"

"Uh-huh. They worried more about his soul than the rest of him, I guess."

Ina nodded, not venturing an opinion. Sometimes when he was doing a chore she overheard him softly singing one of the hymns he'd grown up with. Once she'd tried singing along, and he fell silent, as if offended.

"You seem born to play Sam Shepherd," she said.

"That's the problem."

She nodded. This was part of his training, not being a cartoon. His classes focused on an ability to be non-clichéd in each moment. To study this, Simon sometimes attended the same play two or even three times to see what changed, to see how actors made the scripted into something spontaneous. When he returned home, he regaled her with stories of black box theaters stuck beside wig stores and electrolysis cubicles, and once even a bowling alley, Thornton Wilder punctuated by the smash of the pins. His companion was Kate, a classmate in her early sixties who'd been "the diva of Houston." They had Texas in common.

"I think you can find your own way to play the brother in *True West*," said Ina. "He's the more sensitive one. You have your own inner world to draw from."

"Thanks, darling," said Simon, his golden-brown eyes like worn suede, beckoning and comforting, yet also keeping her remote, as if he were already thinking of what he might draw on from that inner world for his performance.

The phone began to ring as they climbed the steep apartment stairs. Something jolted in her stomach. It was around ten. Who would call at this hour on a Saturday night? Her legs were very heavy, as she slowly advanced upward toward the phone. She entered the apartment but stopped on the living room rug. "Aren't you answering?" asked Simon. He went in.

"Hi, Violet. How you doin'?" he said. Relief sank through her. She shook her head. Her stomach hurt. She didn't want to talk.

"Yes, she's here." Simon held out the phone, and mouthed, "I'm sorry." If she'd been behaving normally, Ina would have hurried to the door and stood on the landing so Simon could say she was out. He could not lie, a legacy of his religious childhood.

"There's been a development," said Violet. "Everyone at the MS Society is talking about it. Everyone hopes they're a candidate."

"What are you talking about?"

"Beta interferon. It's the first proven treatment ever. It slows the progress of the disease, Ina."

"Oh, Violet, that's wonderful!" It certainly was.

Before this, there had been no recognized medical treatment for MS. Some people took laetrile or traveled to Mexico for expensive infusions at a spa. Violet herself once proposed doing that, going for the laetrile treatments in Mexico. They cost $10,000 and she was going to ask a loan from their parents, but in the end she didn't.

"The beta interferon only helps people with a certain kind of MS," said Violet. "Relapsing-remitting. And only if the disease isn't too advanced. I don't know if I'll qualify."

"It seems to me you have the relapsing-remitting type. You had those exacerbations."

"We'll see. I called Zimmer's office this afternoon but didn't get through. All his patients want to see him now."

"I really, really hope you can get the medication."

"It has to be okay if he says no." Her voice was giddy, though.

"I'm knocking on wood." Ina banged the door frame so hard her knuckles felt split.

"Heathen."

"Shhhh. Simon is standing right here."

"Heathen," Violet whispered.

Ina hung up, forbidding herself to have too much hope, but it seemed many things might be different in the new millennium.

The next morning in the car, Ina slouched low in her jeans with her knees bucked up against the dashboard and a joyful song playing in her head. She felt slimmer than she had in years, an aftereffect of seeing Jack. They were traveling to Simon's parents, who had moved east a few years after Simon and she had married, relocating to an offshoot of their sect near Newburgh, in upstate New York. On her lap she set the stiff blue corduroy pants with a high waist that were a gift from Simon's mother. They lay folded atop her battered old pocketbook. Simon frowned.

"I'll change at the rest stop."

Normally she would have worn the ugly slacks. But she didn't want to revert so soon, to leave behind this attractive feeling.

"Did you ever think about how there are a lot of important invisible characters in O'Neill's plays?" she mused. "Characters whose force comes from them never being onstage?"

"Uh-huh."

"You did?"

Simon didn't answer.

She found herself describing how the young man who has "a touch of the poet" is sick upstairs and could come down one flight at any point in the play but O'Neill never has him do that. She pointed out other missing characters in O'Neill plays. Simon replied with a quick "Uh-huh, uh-huh," nodding briskly. It made her feel ordinary. Finally she pressed, "Do you think this is an interesting angle?"

"Yep."

"You do?"

"I said so!" he shouted, his face suddenly red.

Shocked, she didn't respond for a moment. Then she said, "Well, it felt like you were hurrying me, like you knew it all, already."

"No-o-o," he said slowly, "I was *agreeing* with you."

Did he really believe that?

He was usually so affable that it surprised her when he was explosive or abrasive with her, as if underneath the smiling banjo-playing man lurked someone with a bruised spirit. Sometimes, when they argued, he stalked off all afternoon or evening. She had the feeling that he assumed she'd recalibrate while he was away, and in fact that was often what she'd done.

Ina turned and gazed out the window. A column of trees flung themselves past in a swift, dull iron-stiff procession. Each seemed like a metal pillar, rigid and resolute, like a person emanating a cold force-field. Seeing that man, going to his apartment, had changed the emphasis of everything.

"Y'all made it!" cried Simon's mother with a laugh as she approached through the dark of the latched screen door. She had a big round easy chair of a body clad today in a hot pink blouse and black trousers set over pristine white tennis shoes. She wore her hair in a varnished updo. Mrs. Kirk was her husband's second wife. The first had died in a car accident. And it seemed that, after the loss of his demure first spouse and a period of mourning, Mr. Kirk had wanted a festival time, for he'd courted this bubbly girl who worked as a clerk in the town hall, someone not from his religious community. She'd been seventeen when they met, a chatty high-school graduate attracted to the impressive sobriety of this resolute man, but who never grew to feel at home in her new community. She remained giddy, restless, not quite able to fit.

Mr. Kirk approached across the floorboards, a newly slender figure tucked behind his wife. He'd recently begun dialysis. The entire time Ina had known him, he'd been portly, taking second helpings of his wife's cooking as if to show her how much he appreciated her. Simon looked stricken at his father's gaunt appearance, but then immediately his face assumed a cheerful bland expression.

"Any trouble on the road?" His father shook Simon's hand roughly, patting him on the upper arm. He smiled at Ina, gave her a nod.

"Naw, it was a good trip," said Simon, assuming a bit of his family's way of speaking.

"How are you *do*-ing?" asked Ina a bit more loudly than she'd intended, looking him in the eye.

Mr. Kirk replied cordially, with a shrug, "Good days and bad."

Two guests sat in the murky kitchen—the father's younger cousin, Laurie, who was a grammar-school teacher, and her new husband, Frank, a nattily dressed textbook salesman who gave the impression of having just scraped a razor over his cheeks. Like many of the men in this community, he seemed almost preternaturally scrubbed and neat. They wore freshly washed Wrangler jeans or creased trousers and white button-down shirts over clean undershirts.

"Sit. What can I get you?" asked Mrs. Kirk.

"Just coffee, thank you." Sleepiness had overwhelmed Ina the instant she set foot in the little house. A soporific pollen mingled with the gas scent of the stove.

"Ina, sit here," said Simon's mother. "No, not near Simon. By me, honey. The coffee will be ready in a jiff, you don't have to go looking in the pot. Take yourself some French toast, Simon. No, more than that! Go on! I know you're hungry after your trip. And some eggs. No? Really? None? Okay, suit yourself." She shrugged expressively. For once, ignoring Mrs. Kirk's instructions about where to locate herself, Ina sat beside Simon.

"Tonight there's going to be chicken-fried steak," Mrs. Kirk announced. "You'll drive back to the city after, so don't tell me you were planning on leaving a minute before we're done. I was up at five this morning making that chocolate pudding pie you love."

On these visits after the first few minutes Ina often felt groggy. She forced herself to sit straight, biting her lips sometimes to stay awake. Still, afterwards Simon usually complained she'd been rude by yawning. Nor could she herself understand why, at his parents' house, drowsiness overwhelmed her.

Today, for the first time, she eventually simply allowed

herself to settle her hay-filled head against Simon's rigid shoulder. And the answer came to her: she felt superfluous. An item of furniture. His parents asked her no questions. She let herself think about Jack's bedroom, the two uncurtained windows, the strange way it looked as if there were a snowstorm outside although in fact the air was clear. The appearance of a snowstorm made being inside cozy.

Mr. Kirk was softly explaining in detail his attempts to buy an abutment of land, a strip the width of a driveway adjoining his property. Certain factors involving taxes were involved.

Simon chewed, and nodded. He'd finished the French toast. Three big squares of cornbread rose in a column on his plate.

"I feel a little tired," murmured Ina. Then, in a normal voice she said what she'd been longing to for years on these visits: "I'm going to lie down for a little while."

"Ina!" Simon exclaimed.

But she was on her feet.

"You know where the boys' bedroom is!" sang Mrs. Kirk. "I've been cleaning up in there. You wouldn't believe what I found," she added in a murmur. Laurie leaned toward her. "An athletic cup! At the back of a drawer. I remember the day when Simon came home and told me he needed a cup for gym class." Simon glanced over at his name but kept chewing. "'You need a *what*?' I said. 'An athletic cup,' he told me. 'Oh, come on,' I said to him. Ridiculous!" Mrs. Kirk was already laughing. Mr. Kirk remained impassive. "A peanut in a peanut shell!" she roared.

Laurie shook her head, blushing. And Ina, ascending the stairs, pondered why Mrs. Kirk would give such a misimpression of Simon's quite normal endowment.

"I just call 'em like I see 'em," said Mrs. Kirk, behind her. And then, with a comic tone of reflectiveness: "It's a strange thing, raising boys."

*

The thin foam mattress in Simon's old bedroom crackled when Ina sat down. Warmth soaked the room in airless sunlight. There was a childhood photograph of Simon and his stepbrother Gideon that seemed snapped through butterscotch, both brothers with dreamy, angelic expressions on their faces, as if drugged. The bookcase housed burgundy-bound books, all religious. A talcum scent hung in the air. Ina stretched out, and almost immediately seemed to be sinking within herself. She imagined a hand clasping her waist. She kicked out a foot, and shook her head. Again she started to drift, then Jack's hand parted her legs.

"Too noisy?" inquired Laurie when Ina appeared in the dining room doorway quite soon after she'd left, fleeing the intrusive thoughts of Jack. Laurie peered at her kindly, blinking. She had gray eyes behind large gray plastic glasses. She seemed as straightforward as a person could be. Ina liked her very much.

"I got lonely." She sat beside Simon, who absentmindedly draped his arm over her shoulder. It seemed a shame that he was undoing his hard work, all that dieting.

"I used to let both kids dress themselves," said Mrs. Kirk. "When Simon came down the stairs as a child, if he was dressed all in blue I used to say, 'Blue, blue, blue. A vision in blue!'"

"And if he came downstairs wearing all brown, remember what you'd say?" said Mr. Kirk, smiling, obviously trying to please his wife. It seemed to Ina that perhaps this was how he made up to her the ill he'd done her bringing her into a community where she never blended in.

Mrs. Kirk grinned. "'I didn't know they piled it so high.'"

A stricken look flashed across Laurie's face.

"It was a joke," said Simon's mother. "Didn't you know we were joking, Simon?"

Simon just took another bite.

"Please show some respect," said his father softly, tapping his son's arm.

"Sorry. Thinking about work."

"Well, think about family."

Simon turned. "You're right, Dad," he said, looking troubled, and it seemed to Ina he would have taken his father's hand at the end of his newly gaunt arm, if they hadn't both been men.

The steak was bland but pleasing. Ina let the conversation transpire around her. It came to her that it would be a relief to be back in the city, where Jack was. She had something of importance yet to learn from him; the entire somnolent day seemed to be gesturing toward what. She slipped her hand around the side of her chair. Then she twisted. "One minute," she said, and hurried out of the kitchen and down the front steps, and across the hard earth to the car.

But no, the handbag wasn't there.

She ran back in and surveyed the living room, and then the mudroom with its lolling raincoats and dog-scented wool jackets on pegs. Her bag held keys, wallet, debit card, checkbook, everything. Her heart had started pounding. Racing now, she dashed up the creaking stairs to the old boys' room. No handbag. Madly, she even crossed the threshold of her in-laws' room, where she'd never set foot. Of course it couldn't be here, but nothing made sense anymore and she had to check. A vast slumping bed covered in pink chenille lay close to the floor. Against the wall stood a laminate wood bureau with knobs the size of grapefruits. There was a faintly acrid, alarming scent in the air. The bag wasn't there.

"I must have left it in the rest stop when I changed pants," she said to Simon. Whoever found it would have both her keys and address.

"Why can't you keep track of things?" said Simon heavily, without rising.

"Don't I usually?" she asked, frightened. He had entrusted his happiness to her.

Simon's mother clasped Ina's two cheeks and slid the flesh

upward, then planted a kiss. "I bet it turns up." Facilely reassuring, thought Ina.

The drive back was silent. When they finally arrived at the rest stop, Ina's hand was on the door before the car halted. The Pizza Hut and Burger King were deserted. In the bathroom, she flung herself into the first stall and swung the door shut, almost hearing the pocketbook careen around and bang. But there was no bag. Blank impassive shiny plasticized beige faced her under a bare hook. A blurry reflection of herself lay on the glistening surface like something that could just be peeled off and thrown away. She hurried out to the next stall. But each closed door was equally empty. Finally Ina wrote out her number for the ponytailed girl in the Pizza Hut, which doubled as the Lost and Found. Simon and she continued their trip. No radio; any distraction rankled. On their block, Simon stopped in front of their building. He worked his apartment keys out of the brass clips inside their leather packet and handed them to her, then drove off to park the car.

In the apartment, everything seemed slightly altered, as if someone had been there and examined all the objects. She knew this likely wasn't the case. Then she stopped moving. She stood still. Was someone here right now?

A creak sounded, electrifying the hairs on the back of her neck.

Miss Marple strolled in, and Ina laughed.

She started searching, picturing the things in her bag: her key ring with its trapezoidal tongue of battered leather on which hung a tarnished brass 'I,' which was a gift from her father, the wallet bloated with ATM stubs and yellowing receipts. The card from Jack. At the end she looked under objects she'd already looked under, and was constantly surprised when the handbag wasn't there, even though she recalled using it at the rest stop.

Yet she slept blissfully. At some hour of the night she was

provided with a trial-sized bottle of a green liquid—Scope. She swished the liquid, and an expert at her elbow (a doctor?) urged her, "Swallow!" She protested, "You're not supposed to drink it," but did anyway.

In the morning Simon dropped a kiss on her cheek and went off to work.

At about eleven, three young men appeared at her apartment with a new Medeco lock that they bolted to her door. They carried their gear in a white bucket. One of the men, with gold-rimmed front teeth, set the old lock in her hand. It was as heavy as a pistol. "$269.00, ma'am," he said. He wore a black nylon pantyhose cap and three small gold ascending earrings. Ina carefully inscribed the top check from a brand-new pad—the fresh brimming stack of checks itself seemed so spongy and pristine it felt unreal, a prop. She would advertise for editing work. Soak beans on Sunday morning to cook with during the week. She'd done that back in Chicago; she could do it again. She was without pay this semester and the new lock had cost a shocking amount. Simon shouldn't have to pay it. The young men went thundering down the stairs. Their laughter drifted back up.

She waited a few minutes, then pressed the checkbook down into her front jeans pocket, where it couldn't possibly slip out. In fact, it jabbed reassuringly with each step as she walked purposefully up Hicks Street and along Montague. But at the hanging blue plastic Citibank sign, she stopped. She had no way to prove who she was! She turned, inhaling a sip of air, and walked back briskly, unconsciously shaking her head. At her own corner a fear she'd been staving off overcame her, and she ran the last block.

In her office she wrenched open the file cabinet, and everything flew forward. Her hands dove in. Bank statements were stuck together with an occasional rusty coffee cup ring. Old onionskin essays of hers offered up British-sounding phrases (she winced) and there was a clump of yellowish-green Polaroids featuring her sister Violet grinning in a floppy hat, with Miss Marple as a kitten on her lap, clutched firmly by the throat—when a rectangle of deep martial blue winked. The passport. Her shoulders sank.

"There is an unconscious," she murmured as if to placate a god. She took the booklet with its familiar but still imposing insignia of eagle wings spread above the words United States of America, and clasped it all the way to the bank and home. Nevertheless, even as she filed the passport back in place she had the sensation—most worrisome—that it would get itself lost and she was helpless to prevent it.

Ina had fifteen days to sort out her work and get at least a précis off to Marguerite. All Monday morning she kept thinking about the way the playwright was mirrored by his great creation, the uncannily discerning salesman Hickey. "I can size up guys and turn 'em inside out," the salesman says. O'Neill seemed the same, preternaturally observant. She was copying out a description of the bar owner Harry Hope (O'Neill was famous for his knowing, novelistic portraits), and wondered why some people's experiences of the world change them while others remain innocent all their lives, when the phone rang. She snatched it, seeing the ponytailed Lost and Found girl in the Pizza Hut.

"It's Jack." His voice sounded shy, like an intimate form of teasing. The blood sprang in Ina's veins.

"It's nice to hear from you." There seemed to be a second meaning to her words, as if they were very special words rather than ordinary ones.

"I thought a lot about you."

She was surprised, and admitted, "I thought a lot about you, too." She added, "I was always thinking about you." She spoke in a wondering tone. For it was true that even when she had another thought in her mind, it was a semitransparent thought through which she was still considering him.

Chapter 8

On Wednesday morning Ina scribbled Jack's address in the margin of the *Times* and headed out. Downstairs, an exquisite marble countertop—faint peach in color—advanced toward her on the street, held by two workmen. A second dumpster stood lodged behind the first. On the train she read in an editorial that the country was in the midst of the longest economic expansion in history. The surplus stood at 86 billion dollars. The cover of the Business Section reported that on its first day of trading, Alkami Tech stock rose 458 percent. She patted the paper, excited, as if she somehow stood to benefit from this extraordinary fact.

She got off at 79th Street, found Filene's Basement, and roamed the aisles. But nothing pretty caught her eye. In fact, most of the garments looked to be stitched from bright stiff glazed cotton and were too generously proportioned. They would impart to women's bodies a cheery but mountainous appearance with the head popped out on top. Others, made of polyester, draped like dolorous, humid flower petals.

The clothes called to mind her sister Violet and also Simon's mother. Each had a portly body that seemed to have erupted and then subsided. They wore these very styles, which—Ina now realized—she found just heartbreaking, as if the sunken shoulders and clown colors were meant to distract attention from some abiding sadness.

She had just enough time to go into Supercuts, which was across the street. Unfortunately, during the trim, her face seemed to grow rounder and rounder. Hanks of wavy black hair slipped off fast; her remaining coif became increasingly short and chunky. This was a bad duplicate of other, excellent cuts she'd received at this same salon, but how to explain the difference? "Excuse me, do you think you could cut into it to make it less thick?"

"No scissors here," replied the stylist.

A militaristic flop of hair framed her face, ugly as an earflap cap.

Still, Ina overtipped the stylist, who wordlessly tucked the money into the horizontal slit pocket of her white jeans.

He stood outside his lobby door, bemused, smiling, wearing a brown leather bomber jacket, hair draped over the back of the collar. "You bounce when you walk," he told her. "Like you're excited about life. It's fun to see you approaching. I could tell you from a block away."

He pulled her to him, and kissed her, and as he kissed her his mouth opened. The world went beautiful, although her eyes were shut. Her hood fell back.

"Oh," she heard him say.

She stepped back. "Can we not talk about it?"

"In a moment. Why did you do it?"

She crossed her arms. "It was unkempt."

"I don't like short hair." He seemed to be deeply upset. In a way, it touched her, that he cared so much. He grabbed her arm and began pulling her down the sidewalk, apparently embarrassed to be arguing on the pavement. "I like unkempt," he elaborated. "Women who cut their hair short usually do it because they dislike men."

"That's ridiculous!" But then she thought, what does it matter, his Neanderthal ideas? This is just an affair.

In the window of a card shop, a silver glitter skeleton danced, the wind of a fan fluttering its bones. A witch's hat sat on a stool. They passed a woman in a grimy beige puffer coat pushing a shopping cart, feet in vast black rubber boots although it wasn't raining.

He brought her to an Indian restaurant. It was late afternoon and they were the only patrons, seated in the back of a room with enormous smeary glass windows. "Hey," he said gently, "you know, the way women look *is* often about men."

She smiled, no longer caring to argue.

They ordered, and, after a short while, oval dishes arrived—chickpeas in a dark green spinach sauce, red saffron-studded rice on a shallow platter, and his dish, a brilliant red tandoori chicken. They didn't have much to say. She looked at the arrangements of glasses and blue silk flowers lining the ranks of empty tables. Their table was swathed in a slick white cloth.

"I'm not in a very talkative mood today," said Jack. "It doesn't mean anything."

She nodded. The clack and swish of the push broom was audible. The waitress returned and sloshed water into their glasses from a tin pitcher. She was a heavyset woman with oiled black hair twisted in a heavy braid, a sky-blue embroidered blouse that clung over her hips, and stretch slacks. A musky feminine scent drifted from her as she padded around. She seemed to Ina almost extravagantly female, as if perhaps her size had increased her production of subliminally odiferous hormones.

After she left, Ina leaned toward Jack across the table. "That woman reminds me of my sister." It was the combination of ponderous, forthright, unbudging femininity and daintiness.

"It's so hard for a girl," he said softly. "Appearance counts for so much."

"Yes." Her sister had made being female appear almost monstrous.

"She must have been jealous of you."

"I suppose. I never really had a weight problem."

Violet had been an eighteen-year-old girl afflicted with

toppling breasts like gallon milk jugs, a line of dark hair wandering down from her navel, and an easily wounded and defensively sour nature. Ina, at the age of twelve, vowed never to become such a creature.

Early in the morning Violet would sit in her underpants on the bed opposite Ina's, and carefully work the six hooks and eyes of an inverted bra prior to turning it around and hitching it over her shoulders. Ina didn't need to leave the apartment until a full hour after Violet. "Don't turn on the overhead light!" she begged. "Can't you use just the lamp?"

But Violet dressed with precisely the amount of light and noise she would have required had Ina not existed, no more but no less. She had an air of wounded justice. She thrust her hand into the sock drawer and pulled out a ball of knee-highs, which she unfolded and drew up slowly, then doubled neatly at the top. She pulled the laces of her Hush Puppies tight and formed careful bows. Then she tromped around Ina's bed, flicked on the overhead light, and yanked out of the closet whatever dress matched her socks, setting the hangers ringing. Violet's pitiful but stubborn manner wrung Ina's heart—the care with which she straightened her socks and tied her shoes paired with her aggrieved fury. Ina couldn't help feeling that Violet was like an enormous hole covered with a vast doily, as were many women.

Ina herself had been the thin daughter, quiet and obedient. Even when her body developed and her breasts became, to Ina, embarrassingly large (although nowhere near the size of Violet's), she and her mother had slenderness in common. They sat up late together, sipping black coffee and reading. Sometimes a particularly mournful expression lay on her mother's face, and Ina asked what she was thinking about. Usually her mother flashed a smile and dismissively shook her head, and Ina had a sense that there were experiences too painful to set into words, and she worried that her mother would pass away before she knew what they were. If that happened, she would likely continue as a simpleton in life.

Ina set down her fork although much remained on her plate—the crunchy, stuck-together rice, the watery spinach.

Jack insisted on paying the restaurant bill, and they left. It was only about six-thirty, and the sidewalks were bright. A boy on a skateboard sailed past. "I'm sorry about how I reacted to your haircut," said Jack. "It reminded me of other things, very personal things. Would you mind letting me know before you cut your hair again?"

She shrugged at the request. "Okay."

He smiled. "I have plans for you." She toppled a little on her heels and he caught her arm, glancing brusquely in her eye. "Sorry," she said.

"Don't apologize," he said in a flat tone. "Come here." He pulled her around the corner from the restaurant and pressed her against the wall, kissing her, and all she could think was *Thank you*.

It wasn't so much Jack she was internally thanking, as life itself. She leaned into his collar and inhaled. She'd seen the bottle of Gillette aftershave on a wicker shelf in his bathroom in its squat drugstore bottle, swimming-pool blue. On him, though, the cheap stuff was an aphrodisiac; it was as if an ineluctable aroma lay buried in his skin and if only she could inhale along his throat deeply enough, all the while licking or kissing, she would ferret it out and end this excruciating pleasure. The sky glowed the identical shade of saturating, solvent blue, like something invented across the river in New Jersey, at the International Flavors & Fragrances lab. He kissed her again. Something warm washed through her, a kind of brandy that reached to her fingertips, to where her legs came together, to the soles of her feet; it was something strong he was giving her that would do her good whether she wanted it or not. It was as if she'd been issued a new body, simply by being near Jack. He was a sort of Midas, who made things near him sexual. She felt she'd been a kind of potato before she'd met him.

They resumed walking back towards his apartment.

"It's open!" he exclaimed, indicating a corner shop. "I've been wanting to show you." It kept surprising her—that he'd thought of her while they were apart. "I hope you don't mind a tiny delay."

It was an antiques shop, empty of people. Spindly highboys held themselves imperiously erect. A diminutive drop-front secretary revealed narrow wood compartments for sorting envelopes. Out of the corner of her eye an odd painting snagged her attention. Four dull birds in a grid. Pigeon, chickadee, sparrow, crow, each in stark silhouette, but with an eye that gazed with the hauteur of a marble god, icy but full of knowledge. The canvas kept attracting her attention as she wandered around the shop. Finally she made her way over. Such beautiful, haunting eyes! She bent close. Thumbtacks.

"Isn't this shop nice?" Jack breathed in her ear.

She shivered, laughing. "Yes," she said. "If a little offbeat."

He frowned. But in fact, several objects were quite *Twilight Zone*ish. There was even a blue-eyed dummy surveying a landscape of wood objects, including a one-armed chair and several gaunt shoe trees holding lachrymose expressions. Under the murky lights the objects had accrued a kind of vestigial humanity, as if they'd appropriated the personalities of passersby. "My neighborhood has lots of terrific aspects," said Jack in her ear.

"Most neighborhoods do."

The bell tinkled as they stepped back into the city. "Mine really is special," he said. "You'll find out."

Inside his apartment, he pushed a button on the lamp on his desk. This lamp had a round base topped by a long shade, and resembled a plump gnome wearing a conical wizard hat.

They sat down on the squashy futon couch. Everywhere he touched her jumped into life. It alarmed her to think that her whole life could easily have gone by without her ever experiencing this. By *this* she meant the way the room swung around her, and the way his warm tongue entered her mouth, blurring her entire being, and the way she felt wanted down to her bones, to her impulsive mineral core.

"Let's not be in a hurry," he told her. But she longed to know what it would be like to feel him inside her. He seemed happy to caress her through her clothes.

"I don't understand what's wrong with your husband," he said. "You look fantastic."

"Oh. You do, too," she moaned. "You really do."

In bed he stroked her nipples, looking at her, then he pinched them, and lowered his mouth to her. She groaned. He caught her by the wrists, held her with her hands clasped over her head, kissed her again.

Still, quite soon, he said, "Let's get up and sit on the couch a while. So your leaving isn't so abrupt."

She regarded him. They still had not had intercourse. Her body felt alive, wanted, beautiful. She almost didn't mind that they hadn't consummated things sexually yet. She assumed it was because she was unavailable, and that seemed fair.

She sat and hooked her bra, then reached for her T-shirt.

"Do you have to put that on?"

She let the shirt drop, recalling something her mother had said when she was fourteen and told her she felt bad because her breasts were so big. Her mother had replied, "Men like them."

Now, with Jack, for the first time in her life she felt the joy implicit in that statement.

The TV was an old portable with rabbit ears, the top of its screen distorted with bands of orange and blue. An old *Frugal Gourmet* was on. The Gourmet sautéed eggplant in olive oil. In an overhead shot, two slices of eggplant were separate islands laying side by side, surrounded by a frothing sea. It was good just to sit next to Jack. Her whole body felt languid and alive. Five more minutes, she told herself. But when those minutes had been cut away like a sliver of halvah, she told herself: five more. At eleven, a stab of worry went through her. At eleven-thirty, her nerves ringing from tension, she jumped up. "I better go."

"Okay," he said gruffly. He combed his hair, and then slid open the small drawer in which he kept his keys and wallet. She enjoyed watching him do these things. Even his writing on envelopes on his desk pleased her: the decisive, bold hand, the strokes casually slashed.

As they walked down the street to the subway, she leaned into him. "I feel like such a little girl around you sometimes."

He rubbed the back of her head. "I've read that women often feel that way with men," he said. She was surprised both by the observation and by the fact that he valued knowing how women felt. She pressed her cheek against his chest. Her eyes stung. Her childhood self, a clumsy girl in a red vinyl beret and white trench coat who didn't feel she deserved much of anything and whom Ina thought she'd long ago obviated—when she found studying, when she earned Phi Beta Kappa, when she taught college classes—why, that little agonized girl was *still there*! Still inside Ina! And full of craving. Was there any ending her?

Jack laughed. "You're practically running!" He pressed her head again to his chest.

"You live a long way from the train," Ina muttered.

"You're just not used to letting someone see what you need."

Ina nodded, a decisive hatchet-like chop. Sophomoric drivel!

Still, she sensed that it was that agonized girl who wanted to run away down the pavement. It was that girl whom she couldn't bear for Jack to witness—the girl who ate lunch alone in the schoolroom, dull-witted, squinting through round tortoiseshell glasses. Ridiculous, to have a doctorate and to still feel negligible and ugly!

"Shh," murmured Jack, pulling Ina back. He stopped still on the sidewalk and smiled down at her.

"I'm sorry about my hair!" she burst out urgently.

He took her hand in his and tucked it inside his coat, near his heart. "Shh, that's okay," he said. "We all make mistakes."

Chapter 9

The clerk in the Club Monaco was dressed in a tight suit like a vixen banker. She took care as she folded crisp white tissue over the separate purchases of the customer two ahead. Shifting from foot to foot as she stood in line, Ina wondered why her physical sensations were more powerful than ever before. Her pages to Marguerite were due in just over a week and yet she couldn't remain at her desk. It was utterly impossible. She kept leaping up whenever she sat down.

A siren approached from far up Fifth Avenue. She should have eaten. But food was counterproductive—like burdening herself just when she was on the verge of levitating.

Ina didn't remember sex *ever* arousing the feelings it did now—she shuffled forward in line—not even when she was in her twenties. Back then, sex had been something good and salutary. Ortho-Gynol jelly seemed as buoyantly healthy as Herbal Essences shampoo, and her diaphragm as wholesome as a loofah.

Earlier, at college, while many of her classmates were enthralled by sex, Ina had devoted herself to her books. She'd loved discovering the scaffolding of her own mind. When she was a child, Ina's mind had seemed like a piece of silverware forever slipping from her grasp. She stared in horror at the red 60s and 70s emblazoned atop her tests. No wonder she sat merely blinking during conversation at her family's dinner table. What a doofus. But then, her last year in high school, she'd learned how to study. She was far more motivated by the possibility of intelligence than of boys. She'd needed to find, not lose, herself.

"Cashmere!" said the clerk, glancing up with emerald eyes. She tucked a crackling sheet of paper around the sweater. "Good choice."

"Thank you," said Ina, wondering when clothing shops had become like restaurants where you were complimented on what you wanted. Her debit card flashed, a bolt of sun flaring across it. She signed fast, not bothering to focus her eyes, and shoved the flimsy receipt into the little trash bin. It made no sense to spend so much on this gob of fluff, but the sweater fit almost magically well, identifying a certain delicacy in her throat and neck. Holding it, she'd been overcome by the impression that there really were a sparse number of truly beautiful things and if you stumbled across one, you'd regret forever if you lost it.

A moment later she was out on Fifth with her purchase in its smart red plastic bag. 12:27. She'd been, it seemed, transformed into one of the sexpots in the *Playboy*s she'd read as a girl while babysitting. Sexpots! The word evoked a brain as smooth as a breast. She'd seen, in her childhood, young women in crinkly white raincoats and go-go boots. They held clear plastic bubble umbrellas that descended to their waists so that as they walked they appeared to inhabit transparent disco cages. Ina had yearned to be one of them.

Carefree was the name of the gum they chewed. They lightened their hair with Sun-In. But when Ina grew to be their age she wasn't free, nor was she free in college or even after that; somehow she'd never discovered the secret to possessing that champagne-y liberty—until now, really, when she'd become a sexpot. Ina stopped on the pavement, poised on the corner of Fifteenth. No, how she felt didn't correspond to that word.

Traffic rushed past. A truck with Hebrew writing, with the word ECNALUBMA across the windshield. And another truck, which she recognized from her own neighborhood, hand-painted with saws and scissors: the blade sharpener.

Ina couldn't describe what was going on with her, even to

herself. Every attempt to name the force that now governed her degraded it. She approached the corner of Fourth Avenue, slid her hand into her jeans pocket and touched a Post-it. "Why did so many recorded spells refer to the sexual organs as the psyche?" She'd copied this from an article about ancient Greek and Roman magic.

Why *did* magicians refer to the sexual organs as the psyche? Furthermore, why did her soul live in what—for lack of a better term—she now thought of as her cunt? (She stumbled back as the tide of people retreated hastily from the curb. A biker whizzed past, blowing a whistle.) It seemed to her now that this sexual aspect of life was somehow sacred. She'd cracked a mysterious code and a thousand nuances she'd never grasped suddenly made sense. It was an open secret, sex, but one she'd never understood. She waited for the light to change. And, when it did, she went racing, clutching her red plastic, resentful almost to the point of bitterness of how silly she must appear.

Chapter 10

"You're getting way too involved," declared George. "It shouldn't matter to you what school this guy went to or how he feels about your hair. And it is, by the way, absolutely ridiculous that he commented on that. The arrogance—telling you how to wear your hair!"

Ina leaned forward on the couch. She often pressed the phone firmly to her head when they spoke, not wanting to miss a syllable, but today she shoved it so hard against her ear that her arm ached.

"It's sexist of him," said George. "And infantile. Don't listen to him, Ina. And *please* don't get so intimate. I've made that mistake—and then the angry emails I get! It turns into a horrible mess."

"Really?" Ina was surprised. George had always spoken with glee of his liaisons. "I didn't know you got messages like that." Her gaze rested on George's pretty gold paper fan in the fireplace.

"Haven't wanted to mention stuff like that, I guess. But it's happened. And it's horrible. It's much better not to let people mislead themselves. Quit seeing this guy right now."

People felt misled by George? But he'd never wanted to say? People got angry because he misrepresented himself? She felt bewildered. She told George *all* her secrets even if they didn't make her look good.

Across the street a man sat in his window playing a guitar with a big round steel lid riveted to it like a sundial. Light glared from side to side as he strummed, and it made something jab and wince within her. It was November 1, her due date. But the pages and chapter outline were not at all ready. Well, surely the department chair had better things to do than track what particular day or even week Ina's work arrived. She'd be focused on the applications for the Americanist position the school had posted. Its close date was October 31. Marguerite would greet Ina's pages if they arrived right now with a groan, and have to set them aside for at least a few weeks. Ina was glad she'd thought of this.

"Obviously he wants a relationship," said George. "You don't."

Out of her mouth leapt the words, "But who else is ever going to want me?"

"What do you mean?"

"Well, what man would want to be involved with a married woman?"

"Honey, you're crazy! New York has about a million men who would love to fuck you. Choose somebody who's also married or who doesn't want a relationship."

"I don't think I'm misleading Jack."

"Even seeing him one more time would be misleading him."

"I told him I'd see him tomorrow!"

George was silent. Then he exclaimed abruptly, "Look, darling, you asked for my advice. I take a risk in telling you what I really think."

"I appreciate that," she replied.

But she needed to find a certain thing out. Once she did, she'd know why the Greek poet Cavafy, even when he was old and able to focus his mind on contemplating the span of life, ultimate things, nevertheless wrote aching poetry about handsome, elusive young men. And she wouldn't register, when reading *The New Yorker*, the pain and muffled terror that she felt when the short story ended up being all about sex, as if this proved that sex was crucial whereas she'd almost succeeded in convincing herself that there were more crucial things in life, things in fact so very crucial that sex couldn't actually be crucial too.

"Don't you get it, George?" she said. "Things are wonderful for the first time in a long, long time. Years maybe. It's easy for you to be sadder but wiser—you've already had your experiences!"

George was silent. The phone transmitted a tense, brittle restraint, as if he were primly angry.

She sat quite still because she'd just understood that she hadn't actually been happy since last spring. She'd deceived herself that things had gotten better over the summer. In fact, that wasn't true. But she so valued peaceful days that she'd fooled herself that all was fine. The depression had begun when she visited a fertility clinic back in April. That much she knew, had always known. At the clinic, the specialist had explained to Ina, "If you're going to have a baby, you need to get aggressive about it. You're over forty. There's no time to spare." He swiveled toward her a drawing of a stairway. It was a chart: every five years a woman's ability to have a baby plunged. Ina now stood on the next-to-bottom step. She'd delayed because she'd begun her academic career so late, but also because having children had depressed her own mother. Ina didn't want to be submerged in the same morose state. It was during this time that she'd begun listening to the radio psychologist. His voice, empathetic, low, with a slight lisp, made her bend close. Sometimes she wept, but felt no relief afterwards, as if she'd just had a spasm in her torso.

The first therapist she saw was a woman in a Rubik's-cube sweater of hot pink and yellow and spring green squares, who said crisply after listening for ten minutes, "The question is, will Simon help out if you have a baby? Since a baby is a lot of work."

Ina was surprised. She'd spoken about many different aspects of her life with Simon. It was true that the crisis pertained—or at least appeared to pertain—to her having a baby. But that didn't really seem the cause of her depression but rather the focal point of a predicament that was ambient and that she'd been living inside a long time. If she had a child with Simon, she could never leave? Sometimes she went so far as to wonder if Simon was gay. Could that be the problem?

The next therapist was a serene, elderly personage in a gray wool sheath. Her office was embedded like a necropolis vault into the side of an edifice on the Upper West Side. Oat-colored cloth blinds created an anesthetic haze. "I can help you explore those issues," she murmured when Ina finished speaking.

Ina's gazed into the gentle face. "But I need answers, not an exploration."

"We can locate answers too," replied the soothing woman, "with enough time."

In the waiting room of that therapist, Ina had opened an *Atlantic* magazine to discover a poem by an old classmate who'd gone off to earn an MFA at Columbia. Excited, Ina flipped to it, truly happy for her friend.

"Lost Parrot" was about a bird who has flown from the child who loved him. The parrot now sits "in the topmost fronds" with the other "flashy runaways." The child is heartsick. The poem's final line, "But what's / love compared with wild red fruit, a big / gold moon, and an evening that smells of paradise?," made her blink back tears, as it reminded her of Simon, the lonely, yearning child. She didn't mention the poem in her session with the therapist, perhaps because the session already felt dilatory enough. She had the feeling that if she returned to that anodyne gray therapist, together they would explore and explore but never arrive.

No, she needed someone who registered the nuances but was also unequivocal. Pragmatic.

Once home, she dialed the radio psychologist. It was a marvel, what he could do in five minutes. What might a whole hour with him bring? Yes, the receptionist said, he saw new clients and had an hour available. He cost a very great deal, but Ina had assumed that would be the case. She went early and sat downstairs in the office building where he worked, stirring a cup of coffee, waiting for just the right time to go up.

He collected her from the waiting room—a burly, grandly confident man in a black tie patterned with big white piano keys. To her surprise, most of their hour together was devoted to diagnostic tests. At one point he asked her to twirl before him while she counted to sixty. She spun, silently reciting numbers, and then planted her foot down hard. He spawned doubles and triples of himself, an array of playing cards, all kings. "How did that feel?" they inquired.

The floor swung up; she gazed into a dozen blue-gray eyes. "Humiliating. I was at a disadvantage. I didn't like that you were in control and I wasn't."

The faces nodded.

Peeved, she added, "Isn't that how everyone feels?"

"No," came the answer. "Some people enjoy it. It feels tingly and thrilling to some people, actually."

She sat down beside his desk again, and the therapist said, "I hate to disappoint people who come to me for advice." He sighed. "My advice is: Don't have a child right now."

She held her breath, abruptly nauseated. A feeling of loss went through her.

"But I have an offer to make you," he continued.

"Yes?"

"Usually I see people for just a single consultation and then I recommend another therapist here for them to work with. But I'll make an exception in this case. You have an internal abyss, Ina. And you need to experience it. I'm willing to have one extra, private session with you during which I let you experience this abyss. The session will take place in a room we have here that's padded and soundproofed, and where the lights are low. As I say, this is an exception I'd make for you. Would you like to do it? The cost is $325."

She contemplated the psychologist's wild, silvery hair, his enormous, shrewd eyes so dramatic they looked outlined in pencil.

"Yes," she answered.

He lifted a black phone that stood on his desk. "Please book Ina for an additional hour-and-a-half session with me. Yes, yes." He used her first name with the receptionist as if she and everyone there were already friends.

She descended from his Midtown tower and practically danced through Central Park. She scaled a jutting, gray outcropping of Manhattan schist. Such stone provided the foundation for all the skyscrapers, she'd learned during a walking tour with Simon. Blue hieroglyphs patterned the hillock before her, curving figures sweeping across rushing grass. Looking up, she saw birds winging.

The radio psychologist had aroused fantastic hope, she understood, despite his resemblance to a charlatan. Or perhaps because of it. Con men see into people, after all. O'Neill's genius salesman Hickey was like that. She recalled the psychologist's dozen eyes, the way he'd fanned out into an array of selves. Just that week she'd heard Ray Bradbury at the Union Square Barnes & Noble. He wore a stark white suit and spoke about how he'd run away from a funeral when he was a boy and escaped to Mr. Electrico, a sideshow magician he'd met the day before. Mr. Electrico touched a sword to the child Bradbury's shoulders; electricity banged through him. Mr. Electrico whispered, "Live forever." Every now and then one encountered a Mr. Electrico. The best psychologists probably had some Electrico inside them.

Yet for that very reason, she thought, stopping under a maple tree hung with tiny pointy lime-green leaves, there was a problem. To have this man acquaint her with an intimate emptiness and then hand her off to someone else . . . wasn't that a recipe for heartbreak? Wouldn't she always wish she could continue with the radio psychologist, who possessed her answer, who understood about her internal abyss? And didn't everyone, after all, have an abyss, a hungry core of desire? She rushed out of the park, found a phone booth, and canceled.

But that night during supper, she felt increasingly desperate, hope gone. She told Simon about the radio psychologist and then, for the first time, about the despair she'd been experiencing all spring, the not knowing what to live for.

"Hmm. Sounds rough!" said Simon emphatically. He stared at her with anxious bright eyes.

"Yes," she replied, waiting.

He faced her a moment longer and nodded a few times encouragingly, but seemingly at a loss. Then, still nodding, helped himself to more brussels sprouts.

She had felt heartsick, and had gone into the back room and phoned George. He'd understood—not just about Simon but also about the piano-key psychologist and the blue cliffs that underlay the soaring city, and the waiting-room poem—as if George could decipher even the shadow alphabet cast by the flying birds. "Thank you," she'd said, grateful, wondering what her existence would be like if she didn't have George.

When she came out of her office that evening, Simon had finished his supper and was washing all the dishes. And then later he played for her on his banjo, a merry-sad tune that for some reason made Miss Marple yowl. She and Simon burst out laughing. He tried again, and the same thing happened. "No music tonight?" he asked the cat, who continued to stare at him solemnly. "Okay," said Simon, and set down the banjo. He picked up the cat and kissed it, and she came over and kissed it too, the cat still in Simon's arms. She was glad not to have music that night, although she understood that Simon in his own way wanted to help her.

"George, I'm not going to stop yet."

"I don't know what you want me to say." He sounded testy, for once.

A shock of fury went through her. "Don't you?" After all the support she'd always given him.

She set the phone down into the receiver.

She'd never hung up on George before, or even been really rude. *Apologize! Call right back*, implored a frightened voice inside her. Instead, she snatched up her new keys on their twisty-tie and descended the corkscrew stairs.

From the landlady's apartment came the sound of a child toiling at the piano. It was a melody from the red Thompson book that Ina herself had struggled through once, about swans. Only Ina had never actually believed she was capable of music and so she hadn't been. She'd never been appreciably better than this laboring child. She heaved open the glazed wood front door. The painstaking melody pursued her.

She'd misunderstood the point of her own lessons, it came to her as she rushed beneath the Korean pear trees. She'd assumed that the aim was to do excellently what she was doing poorly: being a student. But the lessons were meant to give her *music*. She'd never seen this basic fact. They weren't meant to amount to some grueling, endless chore! The swans were meant for her—her mother was paying so that she could have *beauty. Pleasure*. She stopped still on the street.

A man with a gigantic black dog high as a Shetland pony bounded past. How did he fit that beast in an apartment? She continued on, noticing the minerals set in the sidewalk, their glinting reflecting surfaces like tiny pools. At the promenade, she mounted the three steps and passed the row of green benches set perpendicular to the water where people sat reading or minding children. It scared her not to go back and dial George. Yet she was also aware of a continuing stab of anger, as if something under tension had sprung, releasing the poke of a sharp wire. The sky through the branches held a beautiful jagged cracked pattern. A helicopter made the heavens reverberate like a plate shaking atop a bowl. Breadcrumbs flew through the air, tossed by an elderly, babushkaed woman who stood inside a whirlwind of wings. Ina pictured George's gold fan. She had often admired the magical way it shone. But now its even, straight folds seemed as domineering as the rayed bars of Japan's imperial flag.

As if to escape it, she broke into a run toward the famous bridge with its pointed blue vaults of air.

An hour later, hot, still uneasy, she opened the door to the apartment and went straight into her study, resolutely not calling George.

"So glad I caught you in, Ina!" The voice boomed out early in the morning over the phone in an authoritative but jovial manner like a gruff, kind TV boss. It depressed her that her sister felt she had to do this—to resort to this joking bonhomie so as not to feel embarrassed to call again.

"Oh, Violet! I'm so sorry. I've been ridiculously busy."

Half awake, she'd been recalling Jack's hand stroking between her legs. They'd met at a party in her dream, and he'd drawn her into a corridor where he slid his hand under her skirt.

Then Ina exclaimed "Marguerite!" for she'd realized who was really on the phone. She thrust her dream away. "Hello. How *are* you?"

It was indeed the department chairwoman. Ina shoved the quilt aside and sat straight up, although a sheet lay tightly coiled around her legs. 9:04, said the clock, but she felt groggy.

"Work going okay?"

"Yes. Quite well." She nodded as if Marguerite might see. "That's why I've been so busy." She was eight days overdue.

"Mm-hmm." Marguerite was noncommittal. Ina's progress was her own business, her tone implied. Still, Ina's furniture—the bureau across the room, the chair beside it—seemed light as balsa wood, almost floating off the floor.

"I've discovered another level to the project that I hadn't anticipated, and I want to do it justice." Her stomach clenched into a hard ball. "I'd like to get it to you on December 1, if that's okay."

Marguerite didn't speak for a moment. "Get it when you can," said Marguerite, as if refraining from playing games with deadlines.

"December 1, then."

"Now let me explain why I'm calling. It seems Sybille's stopped coming to class."

Ina was concerned, but bewildered. What did this have to do with her? "That's too bad. I hope she's okay."

She felt kindly toward the professor who had asked why in particular Ina was studying O'Neill. Colleagues often referred to her with a laugh, Ina discovered, skeptical of the fact that her acolytes lingered for years, stalling graduation. Once last spring Ina stepped past her classroom and glimpsed silhouettes around a flame. A Renaissance melody—Palestrina?—wove out. A pair of eyes met Ina's, and a moment later the door landed shut with a loud, humiliating bang.

"Luckily she had just the workshop this semester. You'll cover for her, yes? I'll need you to start next Monday."

"But I'm on leave." The coiled sheet bound Ina's legs, and she kicked at it. Would Marguerite request this if Ina had met her deadline? In any case, Ina couldn't possibly turn up at Quincy in her current disordered, feral state. "I really need to focus on my writing now."

"I know, but it's a small department. Everybody's got to chip in. Life isn't always reasonable, alas. It would be an indication of your collegiality." Ina pictured Marguerite in her gray Totes and rain-sheened wool coat, shoulders slumped, her daughter lagging a step behind. Of course Ina should contribute.

But she felt so irrational, so unmoored! What if word of her disorientation reached Marguerite?

"I understand," said Ina softly, "but surely there's someone more appropriate, with more expertise. I wouldn't know where to start with creative writing." She added: "You know how Sybille's classes are."

"No worries," said Marguerite a bit coldly, as if surprised that Ina had continued to object. "The students will teach you."

Ina flung a leg up savagely against the sheet. A scalding sensation flared as her leg leapt free: a toenail had sliced her shin. If she'd just submitted those pages! She shook her head, and kept shaking it, as if she had palsy. But replied, "I'll be there."

"Thanks muchly," said Marguerite, and was gone.

"I'm not vastly surprised at his disapproval," said Janie, handing Ina a bag of old writing textbooks. She wore white tai chi pants and a faded sky-blue T-shirt bearing a single Asian emblem that was a word or concept, Ina surmised. "He doesn't want anyone to have sex but him." Janie smiled. "He wanted you to have a fantasy of being Colette."

"That doesn't sound very nice."

They shared a narrow teak bench in the temple vestibule. Beside the door were dozens of neatly set sneakers and gummy-soled sandals. There came a whiff of rancid orange peel. "You think he wanted me to torture myself with a fantasy of being Colette without ever having the nerve to do it?"

Janie shrugged. The figure on her T-shirt looked like a tree, running. Janie no longer listened as if hearing echoes. She mostly spoke normally. Still, she looked haggard.

"So you don't think I should stop?"

"You're at the beginning not the end."

Oracular sounding, but Ina no longer had an impulse to tease her friend.

"Imagine if I'd shut my own thing down too soon," Janie continued. She'd lived with a partner she loved but who made her morose, in a pretty house on the island of Rehoboth. Then she'd fallen in love with a summer visitor from New York. The romance with the visitor ended but the one with New York did not.

"You weren't fully alive," said Ina.

"Yes." A bell rang, and Janie rose.

"I think you're spending too much time here," blurted Ina.

Janie regarded her with surprise, her fair eyebrows lifted. "How would you know what the right amount of time is?"

The question seemed almost insulting. The bell rang again, and Janie bent and kissed her lightly on the cheek. Ina caught an odd scent. Sandalwood? Being unbathed? Then Janie vanished within. After a moment came the sound of chanting, a soft murmur. Ina paused a moment in the doorway, listening to the steady monotone, the droned syllables evenly weighted, trying to pick out the voice of her friend but could not.

Chapter 11

Although it was essential she calm down before appearing at Quincy, she saw Jack two nights running. The first night was glorious. On the second, though, as soon as he lifted off her shirt, he remarked, "I recognize this."

But it was *not* the same white bra she'd worn the night before. It was a different one. Mortified, she was unable to speak. She lay on his bed, which was covered with a faded tan comforter. She looked away. "I wish you had curtains."

"Don't worry. Nobody can see us."

It occurred to her that he *wanted* people to see in. Who doesn't have window coverings?

"You should get some other bras." Propped up on his elbow, he reached for the ashtray and his cigarettes. "Do you mind if I turn on the lamp?"

"Go ahead."

He'd aroused her so much that her panties stuck and she'd felt almost demented with happiness. But now came a click. Light struck off the walls. A weight bench stood beneath an empty bookshelf. The NordicTrack's beam sloped before the window. Where was Simon? At home? Still at the office? "Men like lingerie," said Jack. "Underwear that isn't cotton is sexy. At least what you have on now has some interest to it. It's much better than what you were wearing yesterday."

She was shocked. She was currently wearing baggy white cotton underpants stamped with blue flowers the size of cabbage leaves. That he *enjoyed* this decoration! That he'd even somehow registered it! She'd always assumed that underwear itself was negligible. Designed to come off. And oh!—that he recalled the pinkish-white underpants she'd worn yesterday! With the memory of an ancient brownish stain in the crotch! Her face stung with shame.

"Cotton is boring," he continued. "Satin or silk shirts are sexy, and dresses are too. Dresses with stockings are always sexy. Although—you'll laugh—I hate fishnets. I suppose it's because it makes the woman seem too available. You want to know one of my favorite things to see a woman wearing?"

"Yes," she said flatly. She did want to know.

"A suit. Isn't that surprising?"

She was indeed surprised.

"It's the desire to make a conquest." He inhaled luxuriously on his cigarette and then slowly released his breath. He was lying on his back in blue flannel boxers. A square glass ashtray rested on his chest like a warlock's medallion. Outside, above the rooftops of 77th Street, the air glowed the white of a blizzard, although in fact the weather was warm. Still, the fact that it looked like it was snowing made the room they occupied seem a protected, warm, lofty corner of the city. She wished he would touch her again.

"I once went out with a girl," he said, "she was just nineteen—this was a student at the school, an actress."

"A student?"

"The semester was over. So I asked her out. We were going to a movie and supper. I was looking forward to seeing her and bought a new shirt. But when she showed up she was wearing jeans and a T-shirt." He exhaled cigarette smoke. "I thought, she doesn't even want to be bothered."

Ina nodded. She'd worn jeans every time she'd seen him. Her bra was a stretched-out white Warner model with straps as yellow as dogs' teeth. Her mother bought her undergarments, ordering from J. C. Penney's certain resolute brassieres that a battlefront nurse might wear, all sturdy straps and underwire, with fabric that creaked when new. She never threw any away. Her bureau drawer swirled with baggy ancestral cups (her mother wore the identical size and brand), and glittered with tiny bent-back claws. Yet bras were, she'd always believed, essentially invisible! Certainly unspeakable.

"Why don't you buy a silky one?"

She shook her head. Wasn't the naked body erotic? Wasn't he in fact asking her to supplement herself with prostheses? His comment made her feel ugly, exposed.

"Shiny things are interesting," he continued. "Satin is great. Men like curves."

"Oh." Of course she knew this but somehow it hadn't seemed real.

"Look," he exclaimed. "Half of all Victoria's Secret catalogs go out to men. Did you know that?"

"No," she responded, finding this information quite wonderful. On some level she'd never quite believed that men were attracted to women. Of course there were certain conceits everyone pretended were true—and that men were always interested in sex was one. Yet now she was with a man, Jack, who was just like a man in a textbook. "I think about sex all the time," he'd said recently. "I see a doorknob and I think of sex." Ina had been delighted.

Now he said, "I like really long hair. And you never wear makeup."

She nodded. She'd worn makeup every time she saw him. But apparently not enough. For she applied it and then wiped most off, a technique learned when she was a teenager from a woman for whom she babysat.

During this entire conversation he did not touch her. Last night he'd touched her for hours, and everywhere he touched her had grown alive, wanting. She'd worn a black-lace shirt—she'd had it forever; nothing special—and he'd stared at it and through it, and her thighs and legs turned into warm butter. In the dusk the edges of objects sifted into one another, pastel blue and lilac, and even the sirens, blurred in the distance, added to the intimacy. Afterwards, he'd played her something he was working on for *Goodbye, Columbus*, the melody for when Brenda shows Neil the old furniture that her father saves in the attic, just in case the family falls on hard times again. It was an exquisite melody, remembering the old place, remembering how things were.

"You should go out with a girl who already wears that stuff," said Ina. "New York is full of girls like that."

"I've tried. It never works out. Look, what I want is totally normal."

This was too unfortunate, she thought. I can't come back. I can't wear the clothing he wants.

He plucked her underpants out of the crack of her behind, distractedly. "Grooming is very important," he said kindly. "It reflects how you feel about yourself."

Obviously he didn't know about academics. We dress this way *because* we respect ourselves, she thought. Did Susan Sontag wear rouge? "We're hardly touching each other tonight," she observed.

"I think maybe you have some fantasy of how it would be between us. But it can't always be hot and heavy."

The air outside resembled cloudy faucet water. Far away, on his desktop, stood four lit candles. Their blue plumes thinned into transparency, each with a disconnected crown of orange floating above.

She got up, feeling grotesque, and started to dress.

"Are you going already?" he asked, surprised.

She kept averting her face, as they walked together to the subway. It was long after midnight. A drizzle softened the air, not falling from the sky but ambient, saturating.

At the station, fluorescent bulbs cast a harsh light. Suddenly a deafening noise erupted, roaring like a gigantic dental suction device. Women in white jumpsuits descended into the stairwell, walking backwards. The whooshing grew louder. The women were steam-cleaning the stairs with high-pressure machines strapped to their backs. In her entire life in New York Ina had never seen this.

"What time is it?" she asked.

"Almost two."

A moment's dissociation made her woozy. "Oh." Her arms were faintly trembling. Had she ever come home this late from an evening with Janie? No. Not ever. The cleaning crew entered the station and started hosing down the walls. One of the many surprises of seeing Jack was discovering the late-night life of the city, its previously invisible maintenance systems. The working women employed hoses and brushes, and cascades of soapy water. The walls thundered.

"Ugh," said Jack close to her ear. "I don't want to stand near that. It must be bad to breathe in."

She turned away from him, looking down the platform for a train.

"I could tell you about a thousand things wrong with this scene."

"I'm sure you could," Ina replied.

She thought, I'll never see him again. Yesterday he'd gazed down at her where she lay with an expression of absorption while he stroked her through her bra. He'd looked at her body with a rapt, lost expression. The heat of her cheeks had made her eyes fall shut, the pleasure was so great, and she had to remind herself to open them.

But now she happily anticipated ending the terror of this period of her life. What a relief. The world would assume a comprehensible, moral shape. She thought, he is punishing me, he will punish me, he can't help punishing me, he is deeply,

deeply fucked up. I can't possibly see him again. Sex can't be that important.

The train rumbled, far off, sounding like an urgent parade one must join now or miss forever. Service at night was sparse. Miss a train and it could be forty minutes until the next. As you waited, tired, you had to avoid glancing down at the tracks or you'd see rodents with long stringy tails, their bodies pink, indecently bare. Sometimes a train reverberated in the distance but what materialized might be a clanging orange-and-white wood vessel devoid of people.

"That sucks up rats and garbage," explained Jack last night when the strange vision churned past, gongs ringing. "Gross, huh? Imagine being the conductor of that!"

Ina had told him about Anna Christie, whose father pilots a coal barge. Jack smiled at her, eyes glowing with pleasure as she explained how at first Anna says it's too filthy for her to ride the barge but then agrees to try it, and eventually feels purged by living at sea. "Is there a movie of it?" he asked.

"Garbo's first talkie. The first words America ever heard her say." And here Ina broke into a sultry, Swedish-accented voice, "'Gimme a whiskey. Ginger ale on the side. And don't be stingy, baby!'"

He laughed. "Don't be stingy, baby!" Then he added, "We need to see it."

He'd have liked it, too, with his strong aesthetic sense: the New York harbor clogged with steamships and ferries, all captured in a pearly mist as, in the background, they passed Garbo's barge. Too bad.

Lights flared along the track, bluish-white, illuminating the lengths of steel. The train sprang into view, but looked stuck in place. No, it was floating toward them in slow motion. Ina thought of the pilot Charon with his cloak of rags, and how the Greeks interred their dead with a coin on their tongue. Buried without payment, you waited a hundred years on the riverbank between the world of the living and the dead. Ina fixed her attention on the train, which flew toward them with lightning speed and yet hovered in place. What about those unable to pay? A hundred years is longer than most people are even alive, she thought with a touch of panic. The train came hurricaning in.

"Goodbye!" she yelled. She pressed her way through the turnstile and the doors shut behind her.

Relief arrived immediately. She fell into the hard gray metal seat, rejoicing that it was over.

The apartment lay quiet. The bedroom door hung open. It was almost three in the morning. Standing quite still, she listened to Simon breathing. Thank God, she reassured herself.

Miss Marple curled around her legs in figure eights. Ina leaned over and stroked her, and to her surprise encountered the old cat's spine. The creature had lost weight. Ina caressed her ears, soft as rabbit fur, then went into the kitchen and shook some kibble out onto a plate, and topped it with cat treats. The cat sniffed around, head dipping and rising as she approached the food. She ate a moment, then paused, ears tipped back, startled, and stared up at Ina with round gold eyes. But there was just silence, no intruder. She started to eat again. "It's nice to be home," Ina whispered to the cat. She was glad that the whole thing with Jack was over. She'd be able to focus on her work again. She'd be able to sit and think.

In the living room Ina flipped open Simon's *Time Out New York* magazine, which was on the couch. A woman in a clingy red satin dress swiveled around a chain riveted to the ceiling and floor. Her blonde hair was set in waves, her mouth lipsticked a Chinese red. On the next page a woman in a snug gold leather dress unzipped to her navel bent forward to light a cigarette, her head lowered but her gaze fixed on the viewer. Ad after ad showed women in clinging clothes. Somehow Ina had always dismissed the fact that many men like this look. She turned the pages, fascinated, feeling uglier and uglier.

Of course, she'd known that certain men were attracted to this style of woman. A naked blonde pinup in red cowboy boots, her breasts enormous, grinned in a photo tacked up in the service station near her grad school. She'd wondered why the mechanics put that picture up, to be seen by anyone who walked in. Was it to make women uncomfortable? To broadcast this was a male domain? Did the mechanics actually like breasts that big, or were the massive lolling boobs an object of the men's derision, as if the woman's body was parodying itself? Certainly the men didn't want to walk around all the time in a state of arousal, did they? And did the familiar picture even still arouse them? It was years old, from the looks of it.

Ina had never thought she'd be involved with a man who liked this look. But now she saw that the magazine pages constituted a manual of what regular men wanted. How extraordinary. It was there *all this time* and she'd never seen. But I don't look like this, she thought, flipping the flimsy pages. And with each picture she became more upset, as if a boy she liked was calling her cruel names.

Chapter 12

She slid from bed before dawn the next morning, went into the kitchen and pierced a sweet potato in several places with the prongs of a fork, then set it going in the microwave. She sliced a Red Delicious apple into eighths and started to scrape a cucumber. She hadn't been up this early in many weeks. Simon had recently shown her a diet plan he thought might be good for him. It let you lose weight while filling up on vegetables and fruit. She'd been only mildly interested but now she cranked open a can of pumpkin and mixed it with ninety-calorie blueberry yogurt.

And then there was Simon in the doorway, smiling. "That's nice."

His suit trousers bunched over swim trunks. He'd begun swimming at the St. George Hotel.

"Just a minute," she said, and hurriedly set the many food tubs into a plastic bag she handed to Simon. They kissed perfunctorily and he turned. "Bye," she called out behind him, for some reason suddenly blinking back tears.

He didn't answer.

"Bye!" she called out again, louder. "Bye, Simon!"

"Oh!" he cried, surprised. "Bye, sweetie. Have a good day."

Ina followed him out onto the landing and watched him disappear down the corkscrew stairs. He wore a blue-striped button-down shirt and slacks and black loafers, and he seemed very young and unblemished, as bright-eyed as a rubber doll. First his legs disappeared, and then his waist, and then his chest. He went to an office and when he came out it had been dark a long time. An entire day had gone. Then he had the drive home, another hour and a half. Whole years were passing like this. Soon he would be an old man.

She knew that for Simon work was at best pleasant incarceration, at worst a grueling place of disrespect and even mockery. Her heart hurt as she watched him swivel his way down the stairs. She felt that with each step he was erasing her, like shaking an Etch A Sketch. After a while his blue legs flashed past as he crossed the bottom landing. She retreated into the apartment.

Then suddenly ran to the window, and peered down and waited. Blank pavement presented itself below; gray-dusted cars lined the street. And there was Simon! He walked with a loose gait, and he set his oxblood leather shoes down at a wide-turned angle; his back was bent forward. Poor man!

And then she ran dashing down the stairs in her lavender sweatpants, clasping the extra fabric of the stretched-out waistband.

"Simon!" she called when she reached the pavement. "Simon, wait! HEY, SIMON KIRK!"

He turned at the corner, surprised.

She ran up, panting. "You have to give me a better kiss."

Resting his fingertips on her shoulders, he kissed her lightly, dotingly on the mouth, with the weight of a butterfly landing. Her nails dug into her palms. "Not like that," she blurted.

He winced.

"I'm sorry, but I had to tell you."

"That's how I kiss."

"You can kiss differently. You really can."

"Look," he said, perplexed. "I have to get to the gym, then work. I can't stand here and discuss this."

Her heart ached for him, but something also snagged in her, and she said, "There's always a reason."

"If you had a full-time job you'd understand."

She walked up the street beside him, neither of them speaking. He strode swiftly, with his usual springing step. The air held an early morning chill; it was almost mid-November.

She wished she'd brought her coat. The brownstones of Grace Court showed complacent facades, serene ginger and cocoa.

"Actually, would you mind if I talked a little bit about work?" asked Simon.

"Of course not. Please do." He looked worried. She clutched her lavender sweatpants. There hadn't been time to position the paper clips. She was aware of how eccentric she must appear, and wondered why she hadn't previously understood that appearance mattered.

"Suzanne changed my assignment," Simon told her. "It doesn't make sense." He explained that he would now oversee the Connecticut portion of the rollout of high-speed internet. But with the rest of his time he'd consult on the on-demand television product, although the actual responsibility for the business was given to someone else. "I'm supposed to think about it but the other guy gets to run the operation." He shook his head.

They'd arrived at the car, and she stood beside him at the door. "Maybe she wants to free you up for this more strategic thinking. It sounds like she values your perspective."

"I suppose. I liked the sheer hands-on aspect of the old assignment. Just getting to completely focus and have a measurable effect." He laughed ruefully. "You stand a better chance of staying employed that way—if you're the one who's actually cranking the wheel." He asked: "How's *your* work going?"

She didn't tell him she'd missed the first deadline. She had twenty days until December 1. "Hasn't quite come together yet."

"I think you have to make it." He gazed down at her

sympathetically, and gently brushed a few strands of her hair away from her eyes. "You've spent time pulling your ideas together. Now bang them into shape. You can do it."

"That's not how it works." Her voice was tight.

"Isn't it? Obviously you think I'm being a clod. But at a certain point it's not about the perfect idea or chapter. Time is real. You have, what," he paused. "Four-and-a-half months to get your entire book to Marguerite?"

Her skull throbbed. She felt somewhat frantic. "Simon," she said softly, "you can't just bang ideas into shape. That's like banging a light bulb. Even tapping ruins it."

Besides, lately something was shifting in her understanding. O'Neill's characters were no longer figures that enacted concepts. They were taking on a rude, almost demanding palpability. It seemed misguided to focus on O'Neill's language. "Ideas emerge from within the material," she said. "They aren't superimposed. If it's not the right idea, then it's something else."

"I could never get by the executive board with that attitude! I have to form an argument. Decide what things mean. Ina, there's an opportunity cost to not taking action. I can't ask my company to pay that."

"But you have to identify your thought accurately," she said. "Otherwise it's wrong, and a distortion. You can't approximate it." She was nearly weeping.

"I could not disagree more." He extracted his key case out of his pocket and slapped it into his other hand. It had been a birthday gift from Ina's mother, alligator skin, an envelope the size of a calling card, from Brooks Brothers. "Write a draft. Revise. Just lock yourself in."

The look in his eyes turned empathetic. "You're wasting your energy running around. You might want to stop that."

"You're right," she said softly. "Done."

They were standing beside the Jetta, which, she could see, needed to be washed. The city had encased it in metallic grit.

He shoved the keys back in his pocket and rubbed her back. "Good. You might want to lay out what you'll do by when."

She nodded. It had been three weeks with almost no tangible work, three weeks since she'd started seeing Jack.

"It is nice to get some extra time with you in the morning," he said. "Less lonely." She smiled back, half miserable. She squeezed his hand. He kissed her on the nose, and then pressed his mouth on hers emphatically, pushing her teeth against her lips as if pressing into sealing wax. Oh, he was trying to do what she wanted! She thought of a child's messy, heartfelt gift to its mother.

At home she pushed open the study door. Post-its on the wall curled upward, faded gold the color of hay. She stepped in and noticed that the writing on one of the notes looked faint. Another had gone blank. As had the one beside it, the ink drunk up by the sun. All that lost work! And yet it was just as well, wasn't it? The slips of paper had carried just prim neat schoolgirl observations. There had been something inauthentic about them all, aiming, as they had, for an approving pat, a dog biscuit. They had one eye on the audience, trying to establish her intelligence. They didn't come from the right place.

They derived from when she didn't know that how you looked mattered, that the body mattered—and that what was growling up from deep within you didn't deserve to be ignored. She leaned toward the wall and lazily flung her arm upwards. Slips of paper clicked onto the floor. Good. She languidly swept again, fingertips skipping on the plaster. More pattering. Thrilling! In fact, it would be excellent to scrape the entire room right down to its shell. Ha! She'd do it! Laughing, she touched the wall again but her arm sprang back as if electrified. Was she mad? *She had twenty days.* There was no time to start over. Even though it was true she'd been misled, the whole time she'd been working, by the need to prove her intelligence. She carefully lowered her hand. It came to her now that she knew nothing about life in a barroom. Or with sailors. And that, astonishingly, she'd never thought she needed to learn! She'd treated O'Neill as if he was writing just to win awards. To win approval, to get high grades in the school of life. Like her.

She sat down on the floor. The dust, struck by the sun, was more plentiful than she would have imagined—an even field of glittering infinitesimal breadcrumbs. She'd acted as if, if she got enough rewards for intellectual work, she could convince herself that she was smart. And then maybe she'd even become smart. She'd been faking it, a celluloid girl in a land of make-believe, thinking that with enough validation, she'd feel worthwhile. She'd had a secret agenda. And she'd assumed O'Neill was the same way. But if anything was true of him, it was that he was in it for real. He wasn't playing games. That was actually his singular trait.

She'd thought he said certain things just to be provocative, for instance when he claimed that Nietzsche was the best thinker concerning the subject of tragedy. She thought that O'Neill had just liked praising someone who was scandalous. And Nietzsche *was* scandalous on this as on so many other subjects. He'd lauded the satyr, whose song was the origin of tragedy itself. To Nietzsche the satyr—half leering man, half goat—wasn't a vulgar grotesquerie, but rather, oh, what was his phrase? What? Right: "A prophet of wisdom." A prophet of wisdom!

How Ina had raised her eyebrows at that.

She ought to look it up. See what actually O'Neill had been so impressed by.

She rose onto stiff legs and brushed her pants. Then she searched her bookshelves. So many plays, old journals, books of theory. At last she found it, her paperback of *The Birth of Tragedy*. The pages had turned saffron, and had an almost pitted surface, as if they'd suffered from the hormones of adolescence.

A sarcastic, tilted exclamation point stood beside a passage: "Dionysiac stirrings arise either through the influence of those narcotic potions—"

She paused.

"—of which all primitive races speak in their hymns, or through the powerful approach of spring, which penetrates with joy the whole frame of nature."

Penetrates with joy. How beautifully put.

"There are people who, either from lack of experience or out of sheer stupidity, turn away from such phenomena . . . These benighted souls have no idea how cadaverous and ghostly their 'sanity' appears as the intense throng of Dionysiac revelers sweeps past them."

Ina took up a scissors and, although she'd never cut a book before, thoughtfully snipped out the passage and taped it on the bare wall. But there was something she'd almost successfully forgotten. What was it? Her stomach plunged with anxiety as she recalled. Simon's disappointing kiss.

"Please," she said softly.

"You sure you want to know?" said George.

She'd phoned him after she taped up the Nietzsche quote. She'd apologized for her rudeness, her face feeling as if it had been shrink-wrapped; it was still stinging and tight. "Yes. Please tell me."

Even if it meant, on some level, being further lost by having the explanation supplied.

"Simon wants to remain inviolate," said George.

She picked up a pen. Then immediately dropped it. Note-taking was her old way.

"You're not just asking for a kiss. You're asking for a moment of communion, a moment of being present together. And Simon doesn't want that."

"I do just want a kiss," insisted Ina. "A certain kind of kiss."

"Well, you can't order it."

She'd actually rather believed that you could—that if you loved the other person and they you, you could teach them to kiss in the way you liked. Besides, she'd never strongly objected to Simon's kisses before. Of course, there had never been any "wow" in them. His tongue had a certain granularity, brushing hers, as if stippled with poppy seeds. But surely she was distorting the true value of things, because of her involvement with Jack. Once again she tried to reassure herself that there was something mistaken in how she was currently viewing Simon, and that once the affair was over, her old serene life with him would resume.

"You're right!" she exclaimed abruptly. "I agree with you."

"Then why do you sound so happy?"

"Because I'm going to see Jack. Just once more."

But she'd do it differently. She'd give him exactly what he wanted. If he wanted certain clothes, so be it.

"*I-na!*" groaned George.

She silently studied the dark trees with their bare branches, jagged now that the leaves had fallen. Why did George permit himself that tone? She said, the words sounding dragged out of her, "I. Am. Figuring. Something. Out."

"I don't know what you want me to say."

"Then let me tell you. Say, 'I'm happy for you. That's wonderful. Be alive! If there's something that you have to find out, then find it out. This is your one life.'" The words she'd said to George many times.

Silence.

Her chest hurt as if someone were shoving a door open against it.

"You know I'll love you whatever you do," he said.

She stared at the spindly tree limbs. "Thank you." It sounded sarcastic. She added, "I really mean that." Also acidic. A curse had been laid on her tongue. Mad thought: O'Neill approved. The eyes of the playwright on the poster gazed at her with pride. Outside, a scraggly crow had sagged onto a branch. The beast looked heavy as a child. It kept rummaging in its feathers. She had the crazy worry that whatever was perturbing it might crawl in through the shut window. It sickened her to be estranged from George. Everything he said was reasonable and yet somehow mistaken.

Chapter 13

Ina checked her watch as she hurried upstairs. Seven minutes late. If she was lucky, she'd arrive and leave Quincy without encountering other faculty members, especially Marguerite. She was acutely aware she looked different from the last time she was here. Her blue teaching slacks sat balanced on her hipbones even though she'd bored a new hole in the faux leather belt. Her face felt as narrow as an index card and she had the sense that something in it might be askew. Climbing, she noticed scuff marks on the wall that should have been scrubbed. It was more than midway through the term. The building itself was a neat two stories, neoclassical, compact. She never entered it without feeling heralded to do something humane and enlightening. A slight hubbub came from the classroom. She checked the number. Yes, this was it. She always had a slight flutter of nerves as a teacher before entering any classroom, even her own. She walked in, buttoning her blazer with one hand.

Several of the students continued talking, shooting her just a glance. Many looked older than usual undergraduates. They appeared to be in their late twenties and a few seemed older still, including two unshaven men with stud earrings, and a solidly built woman in a dark blue NYPD windbreaker. Ina's own students were usually open-faced and obviously young. It came to her with a start that there was no guarantee of Sybille returning. "Hello!" she called out. "I'm Dr. Rosenbluth."

She felt distinctly odd being here. Her forte was scholarly analysis, not the expressive arts.

Impassive expressions. She noticed that most of the students had an idiosyncratic notebook before them; one was decorated with tarot cards and another taped with fortune cookie slips, probably ironically. A few had a child's wide-ruled marble notebook (also ironic?) and one had a battered leather logbook that a naturalist might carry into the field. "Nice!" said Ina of a book bearing an angel clasping a lute. The young man whose notebook this was gazed cooly at Ina in a manner that seemed almost insolent. Had her remark somehow been inappropriate?

"Where's Professor Leopardi?" called a walleyed boy positioned directly across from Ina. His blond hair stood on end, a gelled crew cut. He wore a jacket from a military academy reminiscent of the kind advertised in the back of the Times' magazine, for recalcitrant boys. It occurred to Ina that he might be taking this class simply because Sybille was a famously easy grader.

"Away this week." She clunked her heavy tote bag down on the desk. "You'll have to put up with me."

"You teach writing?" He eyed her outfit. The white square-shouldered blouse with its big buttons, the blue blazer.

"Literature." Dust caught in her throat and she coughed.

"Lit'rature?" asked the young man, to Ina's amazement.

Someone laughed, then suppressed it. Another student shifted her legs. Had she stumbled on a code word?

"American drama," said Ina. "And I've discovered certain things about how the greatest playwrights worked." She glanced at a serious, dark-eyed man sitting beside the bristle-haired boy. Were his eyes circled with mascara? "You might find it useful.

"When he sat down to write, Eugene O'Neill sharpened all his pencils," said Ina. To her relief, she could feel interest intensify. The woman with the fortune-taped book even sat forward. "He liked to get them needle-thin. Can you guess why?" She hadn't planned to talk about this.

"To stab someone?" asked the walleyed boy.

"Yep," said Ina. "Himself. He wanted to pierce through to the unconscious, is what he said." Ina pulled her notebook out of her bag. "Which is interesting, because his mother also liked to use needles. In her case, though, it was to escape life."

"Maybe he was also escaping," proposed the walleyed boy.

"Very likely," said Ina. "Also, another physical trait of his work: he wrote his manuscripts in a tiny handwriting. It was literally the size of a skein of waxed dental floss. Can you imagine that? Like the bits of tobacco chopped in a cigarette." She held up an invisible smidgeon and squinted at it, and at that moment the pleasure of teaching rushed back.

"Lots of what he wrote was indecipherable to anyone but him and his typist."

She told them about going to the Beinecke and holding in her hands the original manuscript of *Long Day's Journey*. The writing was infinitesimal crests and slurs, a pattern often as unreadable to her as Cyrillic. "He wrote about a thousand words a page," she concluded. "Why so small, do you suppose?"

An older, rumpled woman was bent forward, listening closely. None of the students answered.

"Many scholars think he wanted to be unreadable, almost secret. Others say that he was trying to overcome the tremor in his hands. He ended up having a kind of Parkinson's," she added. "But most agree he was writing small so he could go super-fast. Get ahead of the censor. Ahead of whatever restrains. Can you imagine going so fast you're ahead of whatever holds you back?"

One of the students, a man in an army surplus jacket, nodded slowly. He'd gone that fast, he seemed to indicate. Where had he found himself, she wondered. She turned from him, and shoved her shirt into the back of her trousers. It was a shimmery blouse, and also too big. She suddenly felt that the O'Neill book that she'd been writing this past summer was one anybody could have written. Her reconceptualized book, whatever it now was, would be her own. "Tennessee Williams—you know his work, right?"

"*Glass Menagerie*," said the older woman in a loose sweatshirt.

"Yes. Well, these playwrights—O'Neill, Williams—each had a favorite book. When they traveled, they took it with them. Even if they were going just a week. It was a totem. Gave permission. Reminded them of who it was possible to be."

The older woman nodded.

"Williams' was a book-length poem by Hart Crane. O'Neill carried philosophy. *Thus Spake Zarathustra*. It's an absolutely iconoclastic, wild book. Full of a gleeful spirit. It challenges all sorts of orthodoxies—Christianity, any kind of otherworldliness, bookishness, and even virtue, even what we mean by virtue itself."

Ina felt confused. Was she preaching getting rid of virtue?

She had an idea. "I want you to hear it, to hear how strange and inspiring it is, like a tarot card, like a series of fortunes, or like an angel singing to the accompaniment of an ancient lute." Maybe she might persuade them she wasn't such an outsider, that she could possibly understand them. "It's written in parables, like the Gospels. I happen to have the book with me." Her hand groped deep into her tote and located the chunky corner of her hardback. She pulled the book out, and it fell open to a passage. She read, "For this is the truth: I have moved from the house of the scholars and I even banged the door behind me."

She flipped backward to a place where she'd drawn a star: "There is more reason in your body than in your best wisdom." Her eyes skipped backwards further still: "But the awakened and knowing say: body am I entirely, and nothing else; and soul is only a word for something about the body."

The students stared.

"You see, this was all very different from O'Neill's strict Catholic upbringing and the very proper upper-middle-class notions his mother had. Zarathustra was like a secret friend who could reassure O'Neill of his own beliefs."

"A secret friend is always good," volunteered the older woman.

Other students nodded; they were respectful of one another.

"Well, who among you has a favorite book, I wonder," Ina asked. "A magic book. A book that opened a door. What the writer Edith Wharton called one of your 'inseparables.' Petrarch carried St. Augustine. The singer Patti Smith used to have a volume of Rimbaud in her pocket when she was a young woman. It told her something she needed to remember in her own little town in New Jersey. You're writers. You each have to have one." She'd come planning to assign an exercise that Janie had given her, not this. The room itself seemed to have provided this topic.

"I'll give you five minutes," she said. "Write the name of your book and why it is important to you. A book you might want to carry around because of what it says, because of what it tells you that you can be."

"What if we don't have a book?" asked the spike-haired young man. "Can we put a movie or a TV show?"

A few students looked up, eyebrows lifted. The class was a mix of older, committed writers who'd taken the course before and younger undergraduates.

"Please list a book"—palpable disappointment in one or two quarters—"but if you can't, if no book has really spoken to you in a special way, then a movie."

Their pens began to scratch. Out the window, a plum hue spread across the horizon, above a charred speckling of boulders. When Ina began teaching in Chicago, she'd had a hard time lecturing. Every bob of a restless leg called her attention. If eyelids drifted shut in a lax face, or a student got up to use the bathroom a second time in one class period, she froze. She was inhibited by any gesture that might indicate boredom. She would be a better teacher, it was obvious, if she could speak with greater ease.

It had to do with her father, she knew, and the childhood dinner table. She'd seemed to exist in her father's peripheral vision even when she sat directly across from him. Violet wove compelling tales out of the events of her day; her brothers spoke to their father about their science and math studies. When she, the youngest, talked, he glanced at his watch or even obliviously spoke over her to ask a question of Martin.

It wasn't that her father was mean, she understood. He just knew how to talk to males and not little females (Violet occupying a category of her own, being preternaturally mature). He also appreciated that her brothers had to make their way in a world full of other smart boys. In fact, once her brothers had left for college, something in her father eased. At that point only Ina was still at home, and their father seemed almost to become someone else, a dear careworn soul. She was in high school then. They went for long walks in Fieldston, identifying trees. They attended the Met, and he whispered to her, "This is a very famous aria" (other patrons exploded: *"Shhh!"*). Once, between the acts, they had dessert on The Grand Tier, waited on by men in tuxedoes. He'd arranged it all in advance. She had chocolate-covered strawberries and strong coffee, and felt as if the glittering chandelier was somehow a crown her beloved father had set above her head. It no longer mattered to her that he'd been distracted when she was a child. Still, she'd had to train herself to accept attention, and it had taken years of teaching to become the more confident speaker she often could now be. Although Sybille's students seemed unusually guarded, in some kind of private cabal.

"One more minute," said Ina. She'd given the students five but most were finished in three. "Put your pen down when you're done." All pens clattered down except for one, that of a pudgy girl in a grimy white sweater. She was writing with a plumed pink ballpoint. The creaking of her pen crossed the room. The girl kept working. Abruptly, she looked up, and blushed. Her clear green eyes were rimmed with pink, as if she had allergies. And something was stuck to her eyebrow. No, her eyebrow was pierced. She set her pen down, too.

"Would you please begin?" Ina said, turning to the pallid girl beside her, who simply lifted up her book and waved it. A pear-gold glazed volume: Dover Thrift edition. *Selected Poems*.

"Emily Dickinson," said Ina. "Can you say why?"

The girl shrugged. "It's haunting."

"Yes? And?"

"She talks about stuff like mortality and infinity. What's all around us but we don't talk about. Also," the girl added, "it seems like the book's got answers."

"Does it?"

"Sure. Just not ones I can paraphrase." Her expression remained unsmiling.

Ina nodded, impressed.

"*The Glass Castle*," said the next student. "For its portrait of resilience."

"*Girl, Interrupted*," said a young woman and then a second. "For its resilience."

"*Jane Eyre*," said the woman who had written in a plumed pink ballpoint. "Resilience. Also, it's romantic." Ina glanced at the sign-in sheet for this student's name. Aurelia.

"But you wrote more than that," said Ina.

Aurelia's skin stained a deep strawberry. "I just wrote that it carries you into another world."

"It does," said Ina. "I feel like reading it right now."

The class laughed, easing up.

"*Rocky*," said the crew-cut man across from Ina. "Resilience?" she queried.

"Yes."

"*Titanic*," said the woman beside him.

"What's your book, Dr. Rosenbluth?" asked Aurelia.

Ina was startled. She hadn't actually thought about it. A book she'd read over and over. "*The Voyage Out,*" she said to her own surprise. Not O'Neill. She'd read the Woolf before she'd even considered graduate school, when she knew she loved theater but also knew she couldn't make her life in it. The Woolf had been helpful somehow. "Actually, the book is kind of a mess," she said. "And you could hardly say it's about resilience. The heroine gets a fever and dies!" The class laughed companionably.

"Then why?" interjected the army jacket man. He had a beaklike nose and his thick salt-and-pepper hair was combed straight back. He was disturbingly attractive.

Ina looked away, at the sweatshirted woman who appreciated a secret friend. "It's about coming of age," she said, "The protagonist starts out very dreamy and unsocialized—her mother died, and she's been raised by a sea-captain father."

Ina glanced back at him. "She's introverted and strange, overly intense." She felt almost defiant, describing these nearly inarticulable things to him, things she'd never clearly formulated. "Woolf found a language for peripheral thoughts, all the thoughts that you think in the background but that you don't really know how to identify. So: your life feels more possible, from reading her novel. More *likely.*" It startled her that she could state this to a man whose attention, in the past, she would have found jarring.

"So in a way, it *is* a feeling of resilience that it gave you," the man said gently.

Ina nodded.

The walleyed boy shrugged. "Whatever."

She didn't respond. Instead, she turned to the assignment she'd prepared, suggested by Janie. Write a page of beginnings. The first time this, the first time that, including a few details after each. "There's a lot of power in beginnings," she quoted from Janie's textbook.

Again Ina sat still as the students wrote. At the horizon the scarlet of sunset flared upward. Across the quad, the trees massed in a dusky violet although the sky above glowed bright—a Magritte effect.

After she called time, a hand went up.

The girl in the grimy sweater, Aurelia. "I want to finish this at home. May I mail it to you?"

"Show Professor Leopardi, when she's back," said Ina.

"I want *you* to see it. You talked about needles."

"Please save it for her," Ina replied with regret.

She needed for Sybille to return. She didn't like the apparent lack of structure of the class. The absence of an authoritative master text seemed to loosen something, made personal associations slide forward alarmingly. She felt embarrassed to have so obviously taken heart from Virginia Woolf's first and highly imperfect novel. Although, come to think of it, Virginia Woolf took heart from it, too.

She dismissed the class ten minutes early. Then stood by the door. No other class was dispersing right then. She rushed downstairs, head lowered.

Outside the air was cool and fresh, and the man in the army jacket sat cross-legged on a picnic table, smoking a cigarette. He regarded her, then lifted a hand in greeting. She did the same, blushing, and quickened her step.

Chapter 14

In Ina's closet, a shawl of dust had accumulated across the shoulders of an oversized black silk blouse identical to one owned by her mother. Voluminous skirts daubed with Day-Glo turquoise and scarlet clustered together—in vogue a decade earlier. It was Friday afternoon. What could she wear to see Jack? The broomstick-thin dowels bowed under the weight of Simon's shirts, trousers, and suits, and Ina's clamped slacks. In the back of the closet, tucked behind her synagogue dress, her hand touched something slippery. She pulled out a length of silk—a snug sleeveless black cocktail dress. Her friend Alexie had held it aloft in a shop in L.A. "Simon will go nuts for you in this! You've got to buy it!" That night however, Simon had merely said, "Very nice!" and nodded in a bright, rigid way.

At 4:00 P.M. she sharpened her brand-new jade eyeliner with the box-encased razor she'd also bought the day before, and carefully rimmed her eyes. For once she didn't blot off most of her lipstick. Around her neck she tied an Hermes scarf, a gift from her sister. She curled and uncurled her toes in her high heels—even her feet seemed slick. She pulled on her black cotton jacket and stowed a purple chenille sweater in her tote bag.

Climbing the cement stairs at 68th Street, Ina recalled a pair of plastic sunglasses that might be in her tote. She fished her hand into the bag and located a jutting sidepiece, and out came the glasses. Walking down Lexington, she saw something flash: mirrors lining an express sushi shop. She stepped inside. But the mirror reflected just an assemblage of pieces—red lips, green-and-black geometric scarf, short dark hair—not an attractive woman. Ah well. She left the shop.

And there he was! Standing across Lexington. He was—why, he was grinning at her. When she was halfway across he yelled, "You look great!" She couldn't help but smile back.

He stopped often to kiss her. It was wonderful. It was beyond wonderful. She hadn't understood that she could actually *make herself more attractive* and that the results would be this positive. She'd believed that beauty was something one either possessed or did not. But now, in her black dress, Ina could scarcely draw breath.

After a few blocks of silence and intermittent kissing, she said, "Isn't it beautiful out?" The texture of the dusk was like luxurious dark pollen. "Crepuscular," she said. A regal word, nice to share. They made their way along 75th Street, walking farther and farther east. The apartment building bricks shone peach gold in the low sun. That past spring she'd gone to Victoria's Secret in another attempt to interest Simon. It was an embarrassing, tawdry store. She'd brought home a little white silk sailor outfit consisting of satin "boy shorts" and a spaghetti-strap top. "I hope you enjoyed buying that," was Simon's response. It had suddenly seemed a ludicrous, comical outfit.

A walkway covered the FDR Drive, with its racing roaring traffic. They crossed it, and on the other side it was surprisingly quiet. The East River's surface kept shuffling the mosaic tiles of a blue tugboat hauling a long, flat, open orange platform. The platform, too, was transformed by the shifting water into lozenges, furrows, three-card-monte strips. Above, in the world of whole objects, cobalt powder suffused the air. "Crepuscular," said Jack softly into her ear. She shivered. He laughed, and kissed her.

She told him, "On the promenade near where I live there are always couples kissing. I've envied them so much."

He nodded, looking her in the eyes. "That's terrible."

She leaned forward and kissed him again, and his warm mouth unclasped her from the inside. She sat back. "Look at all the bridges." Several were visible: two sides of the Triboro directly across the water, as well as the frilly 57th Street Bridge, and, far away in the gauzy air . . . could that be the Kosciusko? In the long oblique rays of the setting sun, the various webworks and extensions burned orange.

Then she and Jack were walking back across 72nd Street. "Hurry up!" she wanted to say—although at the same time she didn't want to lose an instant of this. This, this, this, she thought, as if the walk along the moist pavement with her heels faintly scraping was also sex, as if his hand holding hers, not letting go, was sex too, as if the trees were sex, and the chalky moon leaking all over the moody sky was sex, and the taxis, and the rumble of the subway far beneath their feet, and the high floor of a nearby apartment tower shimmering vaporously in the air, floating aloft in the mist.

"Do you mind if I just look at you for a while?"

She stood just a foot away from him, in the shadowy quiet of his living room.

"This is really such a nice dress," he said. "You look terrific in it." He took a drag on his cigarette and exhaled.

He straightened the waist of the dress, and then tapped out his cigarette in the ashtray. He ran his hand up her leg to her waist. She could shatter with joy; it was as if nobody had ever cared to see her before.

"Okay," he said softly. "You want to turn around? You want me to unzip it?"

He set his cigarette in his mouth and stood, and she turned. His hands rested gently at the top of her neck. Then, as he unzipped, she felt a slow descending coolness. Her knees vibrated. Jack sat down in the chair again and she turned around and lifted the dress. "Oh," he murmured.

She gazed at the floor. Her cheeks and even her forehead blazed.

"Don't take it off right away," he said when she set her hands on the waistband of her pantyhose. He liked to feel her legs through the nylon, although the low crotch on it was mortifying. He liked her in her black bra. It was identical to the starchy white ones, yet the change in shade apparently altered everything.

He stood up, and they kissed. Then they walked together, stumblingly, into the bedroom.

"You bought window shades."

"And I have curtains. We'll look at them later. I hope you like them."

When he stroked her between the legs, his hand under her panties, she groaned.

He smiled, a tender, teasing smile. "You like that," he said softly.

"Yes."

Her vagina hurt when he tried to enter her because he wasn't quite hard. She didn't understand why. It was a personal problem of his. This was the first time they'd had intercourse. Still, at the moment he fully pushed into her an emotion arrived in the room—love was the only word for it, she thought—although almost immediately she felt nothing physically. It was just a sensation of pain and longing, and the hope that this would transform into something pleasurable, or something that had some sort of emotional significance.

Body a slingshot, her feet propped by his ears—Jack had a great many ideas. She'd never known there were so many positions, the possibility for such contortions. She concluded that this was the way a jaded aesthete makes love while questing for a fresh sensation. Her mind had detached itself. She opened her eyes. He was staring at her face. "Do you ever come this way?" he inquired personably.

"No."

"Why?" His tone was perfectly matter-of-fact, as if they were sitting beside one another in a bus.

She shook her head, her face prickling.

Then they lay beside one another. She glanced at the clock. 12:17. A jolt banged through her. "I have to go."

But he wanted to lie with their chests together. He wanted to grow sleepy, the two of them. She felt exceedingly energetic. "I have to go," she repeated, and sprang up from the bed. She put on the jeans and T-shirt she'd crammed into her tote. He moved slowly, groggily, as if purposely resisting her restlessness.

At the train station he held her hand as they waited. She was so anxious to depart that her hand felt like something she could snap off. But then he brushed her hair back from her face, making her skin feel phosphorescent. She listened hard for the faraway train. He was in communication with a spirit submerged in her, over which he had command.

The thing about being kissed well, she decided on the 6 train, pondering the ad of a dermatologist smiling under a rainbow, is that it always surprises, each time. Is it because I never know if he really finds me attractive—is that why so much sensation rushes up, she wondered? Or is it that the mouth itself lives in an amnesiac state and so each kiss is an awakening?

In bed with Jack there was a different sort of kissing, very deep, his tongue entering her mouth. "Does that feel nice?" he'd said, caressing her through her underpants. No, it hadn't. It had felt—transporting, as if he knew a secret about her. Something about her messy, staring childhood self. What she'd felt at that moment was beyond pleasure; pleasure was just the periphery of the experience. And she'd felt he must somehow care for her to give this to her, to do something with so much shame wrapped around it, and to step through the shame and find her. Nice? Is the aim for it to feel *nice*?

No, and what she experienced during intercourse hadn't even been nice. And "intercourse" seemed the accurate term for the gymnastic maneuvers in which they'd engaged. She was so distracted by their different positions that she'd felt numb, as if a part of herself were busy swiveling like an elbow. Then there was that strange thing that happened the instant he entered her. An emotion billowed open in the room. It was a surprising surge that made her want to treasure him and do whatever she could to make him happy.

She gazed at the rainbow doctor, considering. She'd no doubt that emotions could live in parts of the body. This emotion lived in her vagina, obviously. Ina pictured the silver foil emergency blanket that her sister used to take camping. It folded together into a packet the length and width of a deck of playing cards but thin as a pamphlet. The emotion had lived tucked inside her as compactly as that. Then it had gusted open and shimmered overhead. Love. Was that what it was?

She wanted it to suffuse her. She would have to drink quicker, be more inebriated, relax more, quiet her mind because now she couldn't possibly end this thing with Jack—not until they'd had better sex and she'd brought the silvery presence so close it pervaded her.

As long as Simon didn't find out, it didn't matter. And he couldn't find out since the truth was that the affair was somehow a fantasy. Because even though her involvement with Jack had happened, was happening . . . in the most essential way it didn't count. Can somebody find out a secret if you don't tell them? Can they peep in your ear and see the images in your head? No, they certainly cannot, she reassured herself.

She sat back, smiling, and didn't notice that she missed her stop at 42nd Street. She realized only as the train went careening toward 34th. No matter. She'd change at 14th. Where she discovered that although it was long after midnight, partiers crowded the platform. Many were dressed up for Friday night, some in brief rigid skirts like frilled cupcake wrappers and others with hair the extraordinary color of cellophane gobos in the theater, imaginative, pretty outfits which each seemed a gift to the viewer. She wanted to thank them all. Thank you, thank you, was all she wanted to say to everyone.

Chapter 15

In the dim front room, the message button glowed orange. Simon wasn't home yet, thank God. She was massively relieved. You see, it didn't matter what she'd done! He wouldn't know. He was still not back from his evening with Kate—they'd gone to see a classmate's showcase in Alphabet City. Ina didn't bother to turn on the overhead light. Still in her coat, she pushed the button.

"You'll never guess what happened!" came her mother-in-law's cheerful voice.

Ina couldn't imagine.

"We found your pocketbook!"

Ina stood bewildered. How could that be? Hadn't she left it at the truck stop? Weeks ago?

Everything in the room—a bulky old Dell computer, the chunky forms of VHS cassettes with taped performances—lay sheathed in a reflective silver glow from the streetlight, as if bearing impassive witness.

"It was right upstairs in the boys' bedroom," the buoyant voice continued. "You must have brought it there when you went to take a nap. Which is incredible because we looked in that room over and over. Oh, well," she sang, leaping down a note. "You can stop all your worrying now, babe. We have it. Your keys, your wallet—everything."

Hallelujah, thought Ina, shoulders dropping. She was not as out of control as she'd feared. Nothing unfixable had occurred. All were safe. "Great news, Miss Marple!" she said, exultant.

She scooped up the slender cat and twirled with it, kissing its fragrant little head.

But then it occurred to her that the key no longer fit the lock. The checks were mere paper.

Everything of value in the bag had been duplicated and rendered superfluous. Her skin shivered uncomfortably. And she recalled the antique shop where objects seemed to have stolen bits of the personalities of passersby, and the ventriloquist's dummy in its smoking jacket, with its sardonic blue glass eyes. Jack's card! Had her mother-in-law read it? What had she written? Something about squeezed nipples?

Ina pushed the button. "Oh, well!" laughed the older woman, her tone indicating: Such is life!

Mrs. Kirk had never seemed actually to like her. She always behaved as if she were suspicious of Ina's solicitous politeness, as if she could see right through her act. She gave the impression that, if Ina and Simon ever divorced, she'd have plenty to tell Simon about what was wrong with Ina. Might she possibly mail Jack's card to Simon?

Sweating now, she changed into Simon's old green nylon workout pants and took Miss Marple to bed, purposely not turning on the fan she sometimes used for white noise. It seemed important to hear whatever there was to hear. Mostly it was just the smooth susurration of traffic, which gave the impression of masking something, as if the roads had themselves turned into white noise. The apartment door creaked, and she heard Simon's step. When he came in, he began to undress quietly.

"Hi," Ina said softly. "How was your evening?"

Simon paused, stopping his unbuttoning. Did he know about Jack's card with sexual words on it? Had Mrs. Kirk phoned Simon? "Good."

"Oh." Her heart went out to him.

"He has a special quality, that actor from my class. I think he's going to make it. Get known. He deserves to."

"Well, you have a special quality, too."

"Thanks, baby. But you're my wife. You're supposed to think that." In the dark bedroom, he smiled at her, his old, charming Southern smile, which now seemed to have something bittersweet in it.

Simon trailed out, still wearing his unbuttoned shirt. She got up and went and sat beside him on the couch. He looked lost. She so wanted him to believe in his acting; it was central to himself. When they'd lived up in Massachusetts he acted at the Ipswich Playhouse, roaring down the long woodsy roads after a rehearsal got out toward midnight, arriving home nearly laughing with joy at one A.M. He'd been cast as the romantic lead in a community theater production of *Two for the Seesaw*, and, on opening night, despite the clicking of the machine trying valiantly but with limited success to swallow the gusts of cigarette smoke generated by the audience, and the way that his co-star intoned her lines with the dull boom of a grandfather clock, it was obvious he'd won everyone over. There had been something enormously likeable in his performance. It went beyond acting and reminded her of the shy banjo player he'd been when she first met him, open-hearted, a young man who saw the best in others. She recalled his gratitude at the warm applause when he stepped out at the play's conclusion. Still better was the after-party, with Simon in the middle of the group, loose-limbed, drinking jug wine, flushed, laughing, dancing to old rock 'n' roll with the other actors. That's what Ina had always wanted for him, to no longer be lonely. For beneath his affability was someone pining for acceptance.

"I hope you don't mind," he said, "but I feel like being alone right now."

"You know, you really do have a special quality."

"That's what my teacher said. I saw him in the lobby afterwards. He pulled me aside, and said that what Davis has I also have. That I have it in spades."

"Oh! But that's wonderful! That's fantastic! But then why do you seem so unhappy?"

He shrugged. "Can't say."

"Is it that one phase is over and another is beginning? Is that it?"

He smiled painfully. "Maybe. I don't know. Maybe that's it." He looked at her and waited until she left.

Chapter 16

Ina marveled at the different personalities her breasts could assume. They could take on the ebullience of martini glasses or voluptuously accordion into the longitudinal span of a balcony bra, or squash into the defiant circular plates of a Valkyrie, or they could dangle like the dolorous appendages of an octogenarian. She'd been in Victoria's Secret just once before, on the nervous occasion when she'd ended up with the sailor outfit for Simon. The place had seemed tawdry then. Now she found the merchandise to shimmer with delicious suggestion, so much so that she was almost panting. She resolved at last to purchase a matching set of bra and panties in dark morning-glory blue, and a champagne satin bra. Three tiny garments. When the clerk announced the total, she was surprised—$192! But one of the odd principles of life was that the cost of things added up to more than the sum of their parts.

Back at her desk by one o'clock, Ina regarded a cluster of sentences. Something in her was twanging over and over like a rubber band being snapped. She needed to understand this article, an analysis of *Dynamo* performed by puppets. The writer, a scholar at Yale, said that in fact the Japanese master who controlled the figures had brought to them a heightened expressiveness by a subtle working of the strings, and that the effect built on O'Neill's own interest in the ambiguity of masks. Ina had read to this point before, but she couldn't get any further. The sentences jostled. The letters composing the words sat above the paper like water striders. With a sigh, she read the very first sentence again. Then she jumped up, and ran into the next room.

From behind the T-shirts in her bureau she extracted the hidden glossy, crackling peppermint-striped bag. She yanked off her sweatpants and stepped into the morning-glory blue lace panties and hooked the matching bra.

Price tags trembled like pink raindrops. The panties angled up in a dramatic V.

She had an inspiration, and dashed back into her study. She heaved open the bureau's bottom drawer, and dug about until she located a sky-blue satin teddy-top. Bought when she'd married Simon, it had gone unworn for many years. She put it on, and—oh, she thought, what about those tall black strappy heels she'd got on sale years earlier and never worn? And stockings—first she'd put on stockings.

Costumed this way, she clattered back, and set down the toilet lid. She put one high-heeled foot onto it. Up she hoisted, then turned.

Ina stared. The figure in the glass reminded her of someone famous. Where had she seen this body? Where? Ah, yes. She resembled the blown-up photos of women in the lingerie store. How extraordinary. Ina crossed her arms at her waist and lifted off the satin teddy, exposing just the purple-blue bra. Beneath her own familiar face . . . could it be? It was almost too good to be true. She tilted her head down and regarded the floor for several moments, allowing her eyes to lose themselves in the pattern of horizontal and vertical lines.

Then she very swiftly glanced back. It was marvelous. The sexy woman was still there.

Chapter 17

I love that color," he said. "Powder blue."

"Better without the stockings?"

She pulled them down slowly and slid them off, and then inserted her bare feet back into the heels.

"Or without this?" She crossed her arms and lifted off the silky blue scoop-neck top, exposing the bra.

He sat across from her in his piano room, in the squarish low leather chair. "They're all wonderful." Did she want to dance, he inquired.

Yes. Yes, she did. She didn't really know how, but began to sway a little, eyes shut. A greenish light glowed over her, from his MIDI sound system, a closet-sized console of toggles and switches. She felt beautiful.

After a while he said, "You could dance more slowly." He added, "It's more erotic."

She blushed. She tried to do that, to dance slowly. She was full of gratitude that he was looking at her. It was just astonishingly thrilling, revealing layer upon layer of pleasure. She'd felt negligible in a certain way, apparently. As a child, Ina couldn't gain her father's interest. She'd told herself that it didn't matter, that the regard of men in general didn't matter. Wanting their attention was stupid and commonplace, a contemptible weakness of silly women. She was above that. She'd no idea until this moment how intensely she longed to be seen by a man.

"Turn around," he said.

A languid bass melody played, a thick open-throated sound.

"Bend over."

She did, leaning forward to toy with the straps on her shoe. Then she straightened.

He got up and set a cigarette between her lips. "It's sexy," he said, lighting it, then returning to his seat.

She smoked, gazing at him, turning, reaching her arms over her head. She had never actually felt beautiful—and so extraordinarily beautiful—in her life. She had understood always that she might be cute and even pretty, but beautiful was a mature womanly quality she'd never had and never missed because it was entirely out of her range.

He said, "Do you mind if I touch myself?"

"No." This had been part of her fantasy, too, one that entered her mind of its own volition, invented by someone else.

He pulled off his shirt, exposing his chest, which was dark with hair, and then he stood up and stepped out of his pants. He was wearing striped blue flannel boxers. She could see the shape of his penis through them. He had a long, wide penis, marvelously shaped, she thought. She had not known that she could find a penis anything other than either mildly or extremely repulsive. She almost moaned to see him stroking himself through his shorts while he looked at her. And then he took his penis out of his pants, stroking himself. She could hardly keep her eyes open, although it gave her so much pleasure. Her eyes kept drifting shut from embarrassment.

"I haven't been this hard in years," said Jack. "Come over here."

She walked to him through the small dark room. "I like the power dynamic," her mouth said, to her surprise. "I like when you tell me what to do." Her mind spun; how weird. "Do you?"

"Oh jeez, it's the Mount Everest of my sexuality," he said, and he pushed her head down.

After a little while, she lifted her head and told him, "You could smoke while I'm going down on you."

She had never liked going down on a man before. It had seemed dismaying, even revolting. But she loved giving him pleasure like this. She wanted him in her mouth. She'd had no idea about herself, she realized. She even liked the feeling of degradation that was all over her like something hot, as if every part of her were blushing, rejected, demeaned.

She sat back on her heels, and reached for the glass of B&B and took a sip. She kissed him open-mouthed and sat back down again, resting on her heels.

"Do you mind if I use strong language?" he said.

She shook her head, looking up at him. She didn't want to say no to anything.

"Do you want to suck my cock?"

She began to again, wordlessly. He said, "It's so incredible, to have you kneeling at my feet. To think that when you are talking later with someone in the neighborhood on the street— you've had my cock stuffed in your mouth, stuffed in . . . your face." She blushed hard, amazed at the sensation of contempt for her—and yet this too had about it a shocking pleasure she refused to question.

"Do you want me to come on your tits?"

She nodded, not knowing what she wanted, but being radiantly happy to be sexually beautiful. He pulled her up.

When he entered her, it hurt a little. Emotions like gigantic transparent creatures coalesced in the air and attached themselves to her. It surprised her, how that was: gratitude and love arrived with the sensation of his penis.

Later, lying in his bed, she said, "It feels like love to have you inside me."

He cleared his throat. "I have to tell you," he replied, "it isn't the same way for me."

"I know," she said quickly, although she hadn't.

"Maybe it's because of your situation, because you're married—"

"No, it isn't that," she protested before she could understand him. "It's because I'm a woman that I feel things differently. That's all it is."

"You know, sex isn't always a religious experience," he said.

She nodded. She disagreed entirely. She could have kissed his lips and hand and dick as if they were the most sacred things on earth. She believed they were. It didn't matter what he said. Then she started going down on him again. She thought, I don't know where this is going. I don't know where this is going, but I don't want to stop. I don't want to stop.

Part II

Chapter 18

Her father was peering in the wrong direction. He stood on the corner of Isham and Broadway, squinting below a blue Yankees cap. His time-chiseled features appeared anxious in the peroxide light, his mouth slightly pursed. He was wearing his old beige cotton parka, a kind no longer manufactured, restitched by Ina's mother at the cuffs. Ina dashed up beside him. "Oh, Ina!" he cried, turning, his face lit with relief. "How good to see you, darling!"

He clasped her hand between his, which were broad, flat, and smooth, and kissed her on the cheek. "You look wonderful." She wore an electric turquoise puffer coat and scuffed sneakers. She grinned, feeling like an impersonation of the girl she used to be.

"Thank you. Where's Mom?"

Her father lifted his chin toward where Ina's mother sat installed in the green Mercury, her hair freshly colored auburn and set.

Ina called "Mom!" as she neared her. No reaction. Her mother presented a resolute silhouette, unbudging, gazing ahead. Ina tapped her fingernail on the glass. No movement. Her mother was rigid. But after a few moments the window electrically lowered as her mother pressed the button. She remained turned partly way.

"I'm sorry I've been so out of touch," Ina exclaimed. In the past month they'd scarcely spoken. They used to chat almost every night while Ina fixed supper, the receiver clamped between head and shoulder, and the rest of the device clanking behind her across the linoleum like a toy dog. "I've been out a lot with Janie."

Her mother muttered, as if saying an automatic phrase, "Out late and dirty."

"*What*?"

"Haven't you heard that?" She remained averted. "'Out late and dirty.'"

"No! I've never heard that!"

She *felt* dirty, though, and recalled a shaming rhyme about a girl kissed behind a magazine, and a stink and a cork falling from a bottle of ink. Guilt snared her for having vanished from the lives of her elderly parents. But when she did talk to her mother these days, even briefly, she had this peculiar sensation she'd installed a dummy of herself while the real Ina was in the other room. Perhaps this was how gay people felt before coming out, she'd thought. You felt like a fraud. Others spoke to you and it seemed like they were offering up their oblivious humanity even if all they were doing was saying, as the English department secretary had, that morning, "By the way, do you have a cat? We just found out that ours has a kidney condition."

"Poor thing!" Ina had exclaimed. "I do have a cat. It's so sad when they get sick!" But it sounded in her own ears as if she were ridiculing the secretary, as if neither Ina's feeling for cats nor even her liking of the secretary was genuine. Ina could understand why her colleague Muriel had come out to Ina and then, forgetting, had come out to her again. One must be accepted for one's entire self. One's sexuality wasn't something that could be unsnapped like the hood on certain coats. She used to believe it could.

"You've been apologizing a lot lately," her mother observed with the starchiness of offended royalty.

"I've been trying to make some headway with the O'Neill. And then I just need to get out at night."

"Well," her mother said crisply. "It's good you're doing your work."

"I'm finally having breakthroughs, Ma."

Her mother's shoulders sagged with relief. "Really, darling?" she said. "You were just spinning your wheels before. This is great news." After a moment she added, "No one likes to feel like a burden."

"You never are!" Her ears registered how hollow and even ironic her words sounded. Yet she actually meant them!

"Well, get in! Chop chop!"

Warmth enfolded Ina in the sedan's back seat. Opulent afternoon light sank around her, surrounding her with the scent of her mother's Charlie perfume and her hairspray, a familiar combination that invited Ina to collapse into it like a featherbed. The faded yellow-green cloth back seat was pristine except for, on the back ledge, an umbrella from the Bronx Botanical Garden furled tightly around its polished wood handle, and, on the bench itself, a book of maps of Westchester bearing the absurdly low price of $2.95. Ina's parents appeared to her to have shrunk in the past month; the tops of their heads just skimmed the front seat. She felt bad to have fallen hurtfully out of touch. She treasured her mother and had enjoyed speaking with her most evenings. Her mother was canny in ways Ina wasn't. "Why does the *Times* need a whole Home section every single week?" Ina once exclaimed, exasperated.

"Ever notice how thick with ads it is? That's why."

Ina's mother was concerned by low housing starts, the factory explosion in Bhopal. Newspaper stories were real to her in a way that they weren't to Ina. She'd been employed since age fifteen, with forged working papers and an altered name, Roberts, instead of Rabinowitz.

"So, you've made new friends?" her mother asked.

"No." Ina shoved her hair back off her warm forehead. An orange-peaked Howard Johnson's slid by, familiar from childhood. Her father was driving them up to the Wanamaker's at the Cross County Shopping Center. In recent years her parents had become almost excessively generous in their spending on Ina, dramatically different from how they'd been in her childhood.

"Don't overdo."

Ina blinked, impressed by her mother's intuition—even as she knew her mother didn't suspect what she was actually up to.

"How's Simon?" called her father.

"Terrific!" For so he was. In his new scene for class, he played an ambassador in a David Hare play. His teacher was full of praise. And last night Simon had reported that the internet business was suddenly growing by leaps and bounds.

"He's the CEO type," her father said.

Car horns suddenly blared in a chorus. Ina's father flapped his hands. "They don't give you a chance to make up your mind!" he exclaimed. He was sitting under a green light, and, after another moment, continued straight ahead.

He drove with one foot on the gas and the other on the brake. He was the only person she'd ever heard of who had taught himself to drive. His parents—who tended a corner candy store in Brooklyn—couldn't pay for lessons. He'd grown up speaking Yiddish, and, despite having had to find his own way in the world, had miraculously retained a profound gentleness. She'd always fantasized about taking care of him, even when she was so little she had to stand on the bed for him to change her clothes. When you're old I'm going to treat you like a king, she used to secretly vow. And now the future was almost here.

Ina's mother contemplated her daughter in the large bathroom mirror at Wanamaker's as they washed their hands. Ina flashed a smile and glanced away.

"You've lost a lot of weight, Ina."

"Just a little."

"It becomes you."

Ina shrugged, rushing for the door.

On the floor, they perused racks of skirt-suits and dresses, but Ina felt restless, uncontrollably irritable. Had her mother always sprayed the Charlie perfume on so thick? Ina loped off to inspect a rack of blouses. Nothing good. She returned and her mother, while making a point about their neighbor's daughter, Lucy, tapped the back of Ina's hand. Ina jerked away, surprising herself. She immediately walked off, pretending interest in a pair of poly-blend trousers to cover her rude behavior. "Give them here!" declared her mother with mock imperiousness. She held Ina's purse and puffer jacket.

"No, I don't really like them," said Ina brusquely, and returned the hanger to the rack.

She must not have gotten enough sleep last night. Where had this orneriness sprung from? Out of the corner of her eye, a clingy white top arrested her attention. It had a plunging slit collar. Beyond it on the racks hung a short parochial girl-type skirt. Ina forced her attention back to the trousers in front of her, and selected two pairs: a stiff charcoal faux wool threaded with red checks, and a serviceable navy. Fine for teaching. She carried the pants into the dressing room. Her mother accompanied her into the cubicle, and observed from her bench seat. The slacks fit okay, although both pairs were a little boxy at the hip.

"We'll get these and go," Ina said as they left the dressing room.

"That's it?" Her mother stared, surprised.

"I'm sorry. Nothing's grabbing me today." Ina surveyed the racks of button-down office blouses with their squarish shoulders and tendency to gap, the platinum and emerald sateen tops with droopy bows—Misses' clothing that, Ina suddenly thought, made women resemble squat, doleful little men.

"Just a minute," she muttered, and strode away. She snatched up a pink baby-doll cropped tee. "I'll be right back."

Ina flew into the changing room, plucked off her blouse,

and pulled on this minuscule shirt. It clung nonchalantly with the top two buttons splayed. The hem hung just past her bra, dropping from the crest of her nipples. How would Jack react? She opened another button and her breasts seemed to swell, presenting themselves.

"Darling?"

Ina's arms prickled. Her mother stood in the doorway, consternation on her face. "What is that? Pajamas? Something for the beach?"

Ina started to yank it off. "Wrong size," she called, her head trapped in the ludicrous thing. With a savage jerk, she wrenched out in a way that made her feel like her head was about to rip off too.

She tossed the shirt on the floor, and her mother bent. "Just leave it, Ma," Ina growled. "I'll get it." Her mother was smoothing the retrieved garment with her veined hand. "Such a pretty color," she said.

"Come on, Ma!" screamed Ina. "It's obviously the wrong size!"

She snatched the shirt and ran back to where she'd found it and threw it bunched up over the rack, then returned to her parents. She shook her head, unable to speak, and felt like some surly pimply-faced, sour-tempered adolescent, the kind of monstrous girl she'd never been. "Let's just go," she declared.

"You don't want these pants?" asked her mother, lifting up the two poly-blend trousers.

Oh, my dear Lord! The moment somehow broke Ina's heart, as if all her mother's hopes for her were woven into those awful slacks. She shook her head again. "I'm sorry. It was a mistake to come today. My tastes are changing." She turned around and strode toward the plate-glass doors, which wavered like loose Jell-O.

Outside, it was surprisingly hot. Her parents were lagging behind, still in the store. Acres of cracked blacktop reflected the glare of sunlight like a kind of white mineral icing. She plunged toward where the car was parked. It seemed incredibly laborious to traverse the asphalt, the distances distended. She wanted to weep.

She stood beside the car, holding her breath. She had always been close to her parents. Her dignified, loving, rather old-world parents needed and deserved a good daughter. They already had one ill, eruptive daughter. And they were fragile, kind souls somehow unfit for the swiftly changing world. If she remained very still, she told herself—forcing herself to be as absolutely unmoving as she could, not stirring an iota beside the emerald sedan—then her reasonable, kind, reliable self would return, would have to return, for she missed it very much.

The gritty low apartment houses of Yonkers slid past as her father drove. In the growing dark, the buildings clustered more closely together, becoming hard-edged and concentrated. Finally her mother said, "Will you come back to the house, Ina?"

"Yes, thank you," she answered softly, in hopes of salvaging the afternoon.

Back in the Bronx, Ina's father dropped them off. In the green, echoey lobby, Ina's mother checked the mailbox, wordless. She remained quiet in the elevator. They entered the apartment, and Ina went directly into the bathroom and shut the door but then just sat on the pink shag toilet cover. When she and Violet were girls, it was always Violet who'd been overemotional, and Ina had vowed to be nothing like her. Violet exploded in rages, burst into tears, jabbed toward their father once with her grapefruit spoon from where she sat in her dinette chair over supper and declared in a withering tone, "You don't get a period, which is why you can ask that!"

Ina had blanched. All their father had said was, "Do you plan to come to Jones Beach tomorrow or are you going to stay home and study?" What an insane response from Violet! On another occasion their father remarked that a bread Violet had baked seemed a little dry. Violet grabbed the entire loaf and hurled it into the sink, then cranked the tap on high. So there! And often, at dinner for no reason Ina could discern, Violet shoved back hard from the table, her chair legs screeching, her enormous breasts weighing down her body, and then plunged off into their bedroom. She heaved the door shut so hard it boomed like a cannon and plaster sprinkled down from the ceiling. Ina and her parents stared at the tablecloth. Then the younger brother, Stuey, snickered.

Their mother shook her head and Stuey went quiet. Nevertheless, Violet's mood held the whole family hostage. Her mother tiptoed to the refrigerator and fetched the Pyrex cups of canned fruit, and the family ate silently, meditatively, the cool translucent peeled grapes, veined and greenish, like Frankenstein eyeballs, the festively dyed, rose-red snippets of cherry, and the white cubes of icy pear, a sophisticated Parisian flavor which to Ina suggested exotic possibilities. And all the while the problem of the eldest daughter compelled their attention.

Nobody followed Violet. She'd rage even more if pursued. Yet it didn't seem decent to revert to normal conversation—Violet would hear, and think she was forgotten. And so the family sat, sucking the holiday-colored fruit so chilled it resembled sherbet, and spoke in hushed tones about inconsequential matters, contemplating the madwoman behind the door. It had seemed to Ina that Violet's anger was connected to her femininity, which was of a particularly virulent strain, and which Ina associated with the dark line of hair that straggled down from Violet's navel. Violet was a problem child, a rabid daughter, somehow snatching the reins of her parents' love and twisting them so that her galloping parents fell down and were hurt. Ina had never, ever wanted to be like that.

And now she was. She tapped her teeth together, recrossing her legs on the toilet.

"Where's Ina?" she heard her father ask softly after the apartment door creaked.

"In the bathroom." Their hushed voices made Ina feel distinctly more insane. She shook her head in the airless pink room.

"Did she say if she wasn't feeling well? I'd like to feel her forehead."

Then, "Ina!" called her father. "Are you okay?"

"Out in a minute!" she bellowed. This must have been how Violet felt—incomprehensible, plagued, frothing, craving something to smash. She glanced at the spindly crisscrossed wood dowels of the drying rack in the bathtub from which hung a few pairs of her mother's sateen mauve underpants, and then at the small rickety table with its three good legs and one bad one that her mother had found on the pavement and topped with a doily. Cans of Aqua Net hair spray stood on it, along with an ancient hardcover volume in cellophane that her mother had bought at a library sale and had told Ina was a truly wonderful book. It was entitled *The California Diet*, and in it, Ina, knew, her mother had penciled, "I will lose 15 lbs.! I will take pride in myself!" Underneath this volume was a palm-sized notebook on whose cover her mother had written in her neat cursive: "Enjoy yourself! It's later than you think." PERSONAL, it said under this. Oh, Ina wished her mother *would* enjoy herself! The little notebook was bound with a rubber band. Curious, but not wanting to trespass upon her mother's privacy, she didn't open it.

Ina patted her mother's bound little green notebook. She wished her mother was stronger. She didn't want to feel sorry for her anymore. Her friends who didn't feel sorry for their parents seemed to know things about the world she didn't. She was struck again by the fact that her mother had a beauty and frailty quite like that of O'Neill's mother, Ella. Both had lost their father young, to TB. They were linked by a mournfulness around the eyes, an indelible wistfulness. Yet Ella had been a wealthy convent girl while her own mother was the daughter of a peasant seamstress. She'd certainly had the better life, with her great street-smart sturdiness.

Ina got up stiffly from the pink shag-covered toilet, cranked the tap and washed her face in cold water. Then, still feeling abashed, she stepped out.

They all three sat around the dinette table and ate plain Israeli butter cookies that came in a narrow cellophane sheath with a minuscule orange tag the size of a tic-tac, indicating they cost forty-eight cents at the kosher store. Ina and her father drank Maxwell House instant; her mother sipped hot water. Ina's mother described how Ina's niece had auditioned for a youth orchestra, playing her violin behind a curtain, and was chosen to be concertmaster. When Ina's father went to the bathroom her mother instantly swiveled to her.

"Buy that kind of top if that's what you like."

Ina stared at the green vinyl tablecloth. "Thanks, Ma." A chalky pattern charted where a sponge had swept across it, leaving a ghostly swash.

"I'm sure Simon would appreciate it."

"Ma!" she erupted. "Can't you please just leave it alone?"

Silence. Ina's cheeks banged hard from blushing. She could hear the tick of the clock. After a moment, her father returned, the floorboards creaking under him, and she murmured, "I have to be home for Simon."

"Of course," said her father. "It's always so good to see you, darling."

Ina nodded. Her parents walked her to the door, where they stood for a moment under a tiny glittery chandelier that twinkled like Glinda the Good's crown.

"Darling," said her mother emphatically, "you've got to determine your own tastes. That's the way to be in this life." She glared into Ina's eyes with her own Cleopatra green ones.

Ina's father smiled behind her and shrugged in his white button-down shirt as if to say, "What can you do?" His wife had grown up poor in the Bronx, the daughter of immigrants, and at times was adamant, a firebrand.

"Thanks, Ma."

Her mother was right, she knew, but she, Ina, could hardly put her own tastes first, even if she could figure them out. Her mother's pleasures seemed modest. She carried a tote from the Yonkers Philharmonic and attended book discussion groups at two different Bronx branches of the library, and still worked as a stenographer for a patent attorney, and had had four children, who were grown. She had married a man whom she found handsome and deeply compatible. For breakfast she ate a hard-boiled egg with two rye crackers that gouged the roof of the mouth if eaten carelessly, and late in the evening she crunched Rome Beauty apples and read ladies' magazines borrowed from the library, which she returned by the date stamped on the manila card pocket. She loved all holidays except her birthday.

Downstairs, Ina emerged into the still-bright air. As she walked to the corner and happened to glance up, there were her parents on the terrace, looking out for her! "Go inside, you two!" she yelled.

"What?" shouted her father, cupping a hand behind his ear.

"Go inside!"

He shook his head, baffled, and bent his ear even more toward Ina.

Oh, they were impossible! She swung her hand through the air in a "never mind" gesture. She walked away, aware that they were still looking after her, which somehow seemed just the last straw. How could she possibly deserve all their love? She wished she could repay them. She wished she could freight them with a pharaoh's riches, with jewels, furniture, and even servants, everything to equip them for a long afterlife where they would know only happiness and comprehensible children who wanted just decent things, and where all their own longings—whatever they were—would be met.

"It sounds like you felt like you lost your parents today," said Jack, his voice scratchy. She phoned him as soon as she was home. They spoke every day now.

His words made something sag inside her, from sheer gratitude. She said, "I wish there were time to do everything when you and I get together. Talking and everything else."

"Come over tomorrow at one," he said abruptly.

She suddenly felt anxious. She always arrived around five. Pages were due to Marguerite in seven days. "I have to work." Although in truth she could hardly work properly. Her thoughts skittered away.

"Don't be so rigid."

"I need to be."

"I'm surprised you still think that," he said.

Simon arrived home that evening excited. He flung his messenger bag onto the couch. "I just called Kate." His heavy twill trousers sagged at his waist. He'd yanked his tie loose. "I told her to find a different scene partner."

At last. Kate was no favorite of hers. She had a baby-doll voice and wore snug high-waisted jeans and low-cut frilly blouses that accentuated her overripe curves. Simon's acting had improved from working with her, it was true. But you learn different things from different people. This sounded like a really good development, stemming from his teacher saying he had a special quality.

"Have another partner in mind yet?"

"No. I need to focus on my job, Ina."

"What? You *are* focusing."

"Not enough. I'm seeing my moment!" He quit pacing. "Life doesn't have an infinite number."

She'd heard about instances like this. A person finally gets the signal they've long wanted, but then gets spooked and backs away. "I keep thinking about what Mr. Humphries meant about you having a special quality—"

But Simon had stiffened at her presumption. In fact it was the first time that she'd spoken that name; she'd always intuited that Simon wouldn't like it, that for him the teacher's very name had a kind of special significance. But what he said next surprised her.

"It's not about my acting," he said, his tone quieter. "There are things you might not realize. By the time a person's forty, they're at the height of their business career. That's what studies show. If you haven't made director by then, you're probably never will. If you haven't made VP, you won't."

His birthday was in February, three months away. He'd be forty. "I've been thinking about this for months." He resumed striding across the living room to the windows and back. "Keep doing the acting, or go for company director? Tonight I decided."

"I had no idea you were even considering this. Or torn about this." A confused, tingling sensation. Why hadn't he shared this major concern with her? "Did you feel you couldn't tell me?" Guilt rayed through her.

"I wasn't sure," he said curtly. His teeth gleamed. "Anyway, I can come back to acting later."

"Can you?" The main event of his week was Friday scene study, especially if he got to put up a piece. "*Can* you just pick it up again later?"

"Don't undermine me!" he exclaimed.

She patted the couch beside her. His pacing was making her dizzy. Still, he kept looping, head down.

"I'll probably never have this kind of opportunity again to make such a big financial shift. Napster is the thing everyone in the industry was waiting for. A purpose for the speed."

"Although it's stealing, right?"

"The cable company can't change people's behavior. Ina, there are 80 million people on Napster! You wouldn't believe the atmosphere at work."

She seized his arm as he strode past and reeled him in, and he finally sat down onto the couch beside her. "Think about your parents, Ina," he said. "Your father retired late. He's home basically just worrying. My father retired and has dialysis. I don't want that. I want to retire while I'm still healthy enough to enjoy it." He sprang up again, went into the kitchen. But it seemed weird to her that he was already thinking of retiring. It sounded morose.

He removed the foil-covered carcass of a broiled chicken from Key Food, and gouged out a chunk of meat with his fingers and ate it cold. She felt shockingly sad. She'd loved the performer Simon. And she loved even more simply the grand happiness that acting had given him. Once, putting up a scene from *On the Waterfront*, he'd stepped before the class wearing a strapped undershirt. "What are you, the butcher?" called a classmate. Laughing, Simon had gleefully recounted this to Ina. "What are you, the butcher?" had been a refrain of theirs for weeks. It always made Simon grin as if it encapsulated the joy of life itself.

"So, you don't feel like you're giving up?" she asked gently.

"Not really." He dug into the carcass. "I think there's lots of things that could make me happy. What I really want is to be financially independent. My father never had that. He was enslaved to that crummy house with its leaking pipe in the front yard in the middle of winter. He couldn't afford to hire a backhoe. We had to dig with shovels through the freezing mud."

Simon had told her about this. The glazed pool under the hard dirt, the icy digging. At one point his father asked Simon and his stepbrother Gideon to carry a board across the muck. Gideon dropped his end and when Simon asked him why, he answered, "So that you would look like an asshole."

"I don't want that life," said Simon bitterly.

Ina felt a strong desire to sleep. Who would Simon be without his central joy? Still, it was mature of him to make this decision, to be realistic, to ante up. She understood that she herself must have her experiences now, while she still could, before Simon was home more.

The phone rang, jarringly loud at that late hour, and Ina jerked up. Simon wiped his hands and answered. "Hello?" After a moment he put the receiver back in its cradle. "A hang-up." It rang again a few moments later. Simon picked up. Was Jack talking? Her stomach clenched. "Hello?" said Simon again. "Who is this? I hear you there." But then after a moment Simon replaced the receiver and glanced at Ina. He didn't say another word.

Chapter 19

For what seemed an eon, the VCR held the green numbers 1:26. Ina smoked one of his Marlboros. Beyond the dusty glow of the glass, starlings flickered. They swarmed and settled on the limbs of the tree, continually rearranging themselves. She sighed, and blue smoke swirled. No experience had ever been more luxurious. She'd fanned the day open and discovered unsuspected compartments. She and Jack were not touching one another and yet she was aware that any instant they would. It made something happen to her skin and to other parts of her. Her eyes turned to the VCR again. It was still 1:26.

"There's something I have to tell you." Jack sounded concerned.

"Yes?"

She wore the sheer black chiffon skirt he'd requested, tall boots, and a velveteen silver V-neck top inherited from her mother, and she sipped from a paper cup of coffee that came from the bagel place. She was still getting her bearings. Entering his building meant stepping into an altered atmosphere.

"You should know this." He took her hand and led her into the windowless middle room. There he released her and sat on the leather chair, the corners of his mouth drawn down and his eyes gazing at the floor.

"What is it?"

"Tsk." He held up a hand. "Just sit. Do you want to sit on my lap?"

She shook her head, and seated herself in a chair opposite. "My father is famous," he reported. "I'm the son of a famous man." He sounded horrified and depressed. He said his father's last name, then spelled out his first.

She recognized it. It was the name of an actor who starred in a daytime TV show while Ina was growing up, and had then, extraordinarily, made the jump to films. She wanted to make a joke about understanding where Jack got his good looks, but he slouched low in his chair, glum. "There's no getting away from it, from his influence. His name even turns up in crossword puzzles. Or there'll be a movie on in the middle of the night with him in it! I hate that he and I have the same last name. I don't want people to think that any success I might have—if I do—is because of him."

She heard George's voice: *Don't get too close.*

"He keeps offering to try to set things up for me, use his connections, and it just makes me sick. My parents divorced when I was four," he added. "I have almost no memory of them ever living together."

He spoke rapidly, his tone flat, as if it were essential for Ina to know these facts before they could move on. "My brothers and I commuted between their apartments, which were the total opposite of each other. My mother's place was a mess. She drank and was often asleep or just passed out in the afternoon, and she didn't wear enough clothes, she was inappropriately dressed for someone raising children—" Jack opened his eyes. "Is something amusing you? You look like something is amusing you."

Ina shook her head, surprised by his misunderstanding. "No."

He regarded her coolly. Her face stung during the unhurried inspection. Then he nodded. "Why don't you sit here?" He patted the armrest of his chair. She got up and settled herself there.

"In my father's place the cereal was always in the same place and it was never anyplace else on the shelf. Bedtime was at a particular time, never to be diverged from." He contemplated her, then smiled. "You look nice there. Solemn."

He touched her nose with the tip of his index finger. "Are you interested in any of this?"

"Of course." She was extremely interested. She remained still, breathing shallowly. It was as if he were performing a delicate operation—as painstaking as transferring a raw egg to her in a relay race—and it would be easy for her to bungle things.

He said, "It's so quiet here when the air conditioners are on. You'll be amazed."

She smiled to herself. It would be a different season then and she'd no longer be with Jack.

Did she want to see a home movie from a childhood Christmas, he asked. He'd requested his brother send it expressly so he could show her.

"Yes," she said.

When it started to play, Ina relaxed.

In the video, Jack and one of his brothers were young teenagers, lounging in chairs. His mother was a fashionable woman in her thirties, slender, with a bouffant hairdo and white denim hip-huggers with a broad white belt. She looked cut out of *Vogue*. She held an enormous copper tray before her and said, "I made rum balls and pfeffernüsse, and those Italian almond cookies you all like, and also spice cookies and, oh, yeah, M&M cookies. I've been baking and Tupperwaring all damn week. I found a book called *A Hundred and One Christmas Cookies*. A person could go nuts." Ina was taken aback. Jack's mother sounded contemporary and sardonic. Also somewhat unhinged.

Jack's father strolled into the room, tanned and fit, chest hair foaming over the V of his collar. He looked superimposed from another reality, a far more important one. When he sat in the corner, the entire room drew toward him, as if even the coffee table and Christmas tree were mesmerized. "Glad to be of assistance," he offered, and although what he said was absolutely bland, he said it in a way that made it seem charming, imaginative.

"Bring the cookies close!" instructed the cameraman.

"Okay! Norman Rockwell women, watch out!" cried his mother, as she wriggled the platter progressively nearer the camera. She began to sing the strip-tease music from *Gypsy*. Erratically shaped cookies swam closer and closer in the field of vision, spreading, blurring, becoming one central cookie that engulfed the lens, which went blank.

Ina suppressed a laugh. "Intense."

"We had a good time," said Jack.

He asked her if she would mind running some errands with him. She most certainly did not. It was almost too exciting to be alone in his apartment all afternoon. They went shopping at the Rainbow Store for envelopes that Jack needed. They visited a hardware store in whose basement were garbage cans with round lids that flung aloft when you stepped on a lever, and brooms with synthetic pink bristles as smooth as fur. Rounded retro toasters featured four bagel-wide slots. Many of the appliances seemed like life-size cartoons to the almost hallucinogenically happy Ina. She would have liked to burrow under Jack's arm and nestle. The scent of his underarm pleased her, making her feel overtaken by a bloated, drowsy happiness, reminiscent of the rare occasions in childhood when she'd felt aware of her father's love. She trailed Jack from store to store, almost drunk on the number of hours they had available.

"There's something I'd love to try doing with you," murmured Jack late that afternoon. The wash of traffic rose up—the sizzle of tires on the avenue. She hadn't quite been asleep.

She smiled, eyes opening. Tea-colored light radiated through the closed blinds. On the windowsill stood candles they'd burnt on previous evenings, the tops collapsed in, forming thin curled collars around hidden bowls. Each erratic shape seemed perfect in itself, holding an orphic significance. His arm was around her. He pulled her close. She recalled Simon giving up his Friday evening acting class—giving up acting entirely—and had to blink away the moisture that gathered in her eyes.

"The thing is, it might sound morbid."

She listened closely.

"There was this girl I went out with once, this eighteen-year-old. She was very uptight about sex. She wouldn't do more than take her shirt off. But then she started talking about necrophilia—"

A chill fluttered through Ina.

"And I said that, yeah, it actually really turned me on. She wanted to pretend to be dead." He was silent a moment. "She was really good at it, too."

Momentarily jealous of this girl who was good at something, Ina nodded. But there were limits. She thought of cadavers, worms, and decay. Why would anyone want to have sex with a corpse? She'd heard of necrophilia but thought it was just for sickos.

She stumbled against the bedframe, rising. "I'm sorry, I can't." She was possessed by the need to be out alone in the city, among normal people, families, with fresh air on her cheeks. This place was rancid; she could almost smell the rot. "You can stay. You don't need to walk me."

"Ina." He came over to where she was dressing quickly. He touched her arm. "You're making me feel awful," he said softly.

"I just need to think."

"You think too much." He looked into her eyes. "And, you're making me feel like a creep."

"You're not," she said.

But she immediately rushed out. She noticed the cracked, blistered walls of the stairway as she descended. Why hadn't she seen it was really disgusting here before? He'd certainly pointed it out. What was it O'Neill had written to his girlfriend? She'd copied it out just last week. "Experience is the only true test of one's age. Have you reached out for everything, tried everything, hesitated before, 'No, you must not,' realized with joy every new sensation, stripped things of their husk?'"

Well, not everything needed to be tried to know its value.

She walked back to the subway station quickly, and even so there seemed to be tedious blocks added, the sunlight low on the brick walls an unlovely orange soda color, and the bare trees like molded concrete.

Chapter 20

The New Jersey highway divided and redivided. Ina's lane continually disappeared. She was headed to her sister's house, and the drivers to her left often refused to let her in. Once, she was forced to take the exit and then loop all the way back around for several miles to drive over the same dreary frightening passage that she'd just taken. The asphalt was gritty with salt from a past snowstorm. Far ahead, the road merged into an identically hued slate-gray sky. She should be working but she needed to visit her sister. It had been way too long.

Outside Hoboken, Ina found parking near Violet's neat, drab little house. She opened the front door with her own key, balancing a bag of groceries, and called. Silence. The drifting scent of orange pekoe tea arrived. It felt good to be back. The kitchen radio urged, "Don't listen to unbelievers! You have an ability to see what the naysayers can't."

Was it an advice show? Some kind of hypnosis? The speaker had an almost irritating self-confidence. "Never give up!"

Pausing, Ina rested her eyes on the hallway table, which was heaped with magazines and advertising flyers. Below, phone books stood frozen mid-tumble, each balanced on a sharp corner of its spine. Violet had always been a "thing-keeper," to use the Pippi Longstocking term the two sisters had adopted. The problem was, she could no longer stay organized. The place was obviously out-of-control. "Your master, he's waiting," said the soft voice.

Ina spotted a crooked wall hanging—an embroidery of the

Hebrew alphabet, the *aleph* a contrapposto knight, the *shin* a deep-prowed ship with a tall mast—and nudged it straight. Violet had stitched it in high school, when she'd still been an industrious young woman with a level gaze and an absorbent mind. She'd often been Ina's instructress. "That's wrong!" she frequently exclaimed to her.

"Having faith is important," continued the radio voice. "And you can build up your faith the way you can build up your physical strength. Let me teach you how."

Then it came to her. It was a live person, not the radio! She hoisted her grocery bag higher and hurried into the kitchen. And there, with Violet, sat two well-groomed older ladies, one white, one Black, both in below-the-knee dresses, hose, and heeled shoes. They were all mutually absorbed, as if the speaker had taken a long time to arrive at just this point; none acknowledged Ina's presence. "But first you have to understand: He's testing you."

White Corelle teacups sat on the table, brimming with tea—only Violet's cup was drained—and round golden Nilla wafers formed a circle on a plate. "He wants to see can you still believe, no matter what. There's a reason you got what you got."

"Amen," said the Black woman.

"He's given you a special burden. He knows what's best for you."

"I don't think so!" interrupted Ina.

Three faces swiveled. Ina coolly met the women's stare.

"Sister Ina!" called the white woman. "Welcome! Come join us! If you want to put in your opinion, that's fine. We want to hear it. But, girl, don't stand so far away!"

Violet was gazing at Ina with her wide light-blue eyes. "He does know what's best for me."

"No, Violet," said Ina, suddenly near tears.

Her sister continued to regard her. "Maybe He does," she said. "You know sometimes, at night, when I'm laying in bed and saying my prayers,"—it had always been Violet's way to speak intimately and frankly, no matter who was present, but it still surprised Ina—"it occurs to me that maybe if I have this illness other people in my family won't have to."

"It doesn't work that way," said Ina.

The white woman patted the chair beside her. "Come sit."

Ina had the strange feeling that if she did, this woman might persuade her of things she knew better than to believe.

"I'm sorry," Ina said, shaking her head.

"Hate to leave when we're disagreeing," said the Black woman. But the ladies rose, and Ina accompanied them to the door.

"God bless you," the white lady said, at the entrance, and, despite herself, despite her inability to believe—her sense that God himself was a vast non sequitur like a candelabrum unscrewed from the ceiling and parked in a dusty room—Ina murmured, "You, too."

In the kitchen, Violet chewed a Nilla wafer, her eyes fixed on the brochure. A cartoon of a young man as a hippie with bellbottoms and love beads said in a speech balloon: "What's It All About, Man?" How old were these things? Violet appeared to be in a quiet, almost chastened mood. She was a short pale woman with a pageboy haircut and very alert, strikingly blue eyes, wearing a dingy pink sweatshirt that said GO METS across the bust, and dark stretch slacks.

Finally she set the pamphlet aside. "Inalonchikle! What are you wearing?"

Ina looked down at the skirt and gray cotton turtleneck. Her sister was used to the stretched-out sweatpants. "A skirt."

"No, the gook on your face."

Ina's face flushed. "Mascara."

"I thought you were a feminist."

"I am." In fact, she felt guilty to be wearing makeup in front of Violet, who'd never experienced this novel pleasure, and likely never would. Ina clattered a cellophane bag of carrots as big as bananas down on the table. "Let's start."

"It's on very thick."

"Ready?" asked Ina, ignoring her sister's comment.

"I think instead of wearing the makeup, the makeup is wearing you."

Ina smiled painfully. "Could be," she said. "Now do you want to make this salad?"

"A few weeks ago those carrots might actually have been good."

Ina regarded the slightly hairy vegetables sadly. "True."

How impossibly removed she had become from her poor sister. Violet's life was static, or slowly devolving. Ina's was making both more and less sense than before. She hadn't spoken to Jack for a week. Things had to be over with him. But she felt so lonely.

"About the makeup," she exclaimed. "There's a reason." Why not at least try to be closer? Why assume they each must be so extremely isolated? "You see," she said, "I met someone."

Violet gazed, attentive.

"At a party. He's a composer, a musician. He plays the piano."

My gosh, Ina thought, how wonderful if she and Violet could be intimate! Many other sisters were. Had she ever really, truly tried? No, never. "Something woke up in me. Something I didn't know about."

Still Violet didn't speak. She seemed rapt.

"Nothing really happened, of course. We just talked. But it made me realize that I was tired of being invisible."

"None of us should be invisible," replied Violet softly. Her arms were neatly crossed, as if keeping herself warm. "Who is he?"

"Nobody I can have in my life. Actually—and this is sad, Violet—he's kind of a troubled person. Unwell. Mentally."

She'd been wrong to keep so much back! "Even if I weren't with Simon, he wouldn't be someone to get involved with." Wanting to have sex with a corpse!

"You seem to know a great deal about him."

"Only a little, really. But he's not important. What's important is what I learned."

"I wonder if Simon would agree he's unimportant."

Ina's insides crept. "Violet," she said faintly, with growing concern. "I trusted you with a confidence."

"And I'm glad." But she didn't look glad. She looked angry. She said, "Nevertheless, you're not the only person I have a responsibility to in this situation."

Fear prickled through Ina. "I haven't done anything wrong," she said. "A woman is allowed to talk to a man at a party. Even a married woman."

Not that Violet went to many parties. And the ones she currently attended seemed pathetic. A gathering at the synagogue. Friday evening Shabbat dinner in their parents' house. Was it then wrong for Ina to tell her about her life? Was it selfish?

"You're absolutely right," replied Violet. "A person isn't meant to be locked away."

Ina's glance fell on the pamphlet. *What's It All About?* "I'm sorry you are."

"Don't let so much time go by then."

"I'll be more available now."

"And why might that be?"

Ina looked at her sister and wished she could say, "I won't be going back to see that man."

"You look like you're about to cry," said Violet flatly, just as a point of fact.

Ina laughed. "I'm fine."

"Good." But her sister was still regarding her steadily. "Then let me kiss your cheek. Your bright red cheek." She jabbed toward Ina's face—at her rouge? Her embarrassment? Violet smiled wider. "Don't look so scared, tateleh. I know how to keep a secret."

"There's no secret."

"If you say so." Violet bestowed a big smacking kiss.

To brighten the mood, Ina turned the radio on to a soft-rock station, keeping the music low. Ina started on the carrot-raisin salad using the grater. This was an old pyramidal box with tiers of gaping oval mouths. A steady sandpaper rasp rang out over the sound of Madonna singing as orange-colored slivers gathered on the plate.

"That's wrong," said Violet. She pointed. "Too big. After you grate, cut the pieces up."

"Okay." In the implement drawer, Ina found a knife sheathed in canary-yellow cardboard printed with the word "Sabatier" beside the winking face of a chef.

"Money well spent," declared Violet.

"Even though you can't use it much yourself?" For her hands were no longer trustworthy.

"So you take it."

"I wasn't hinting!"

"I didn't think you were. It's a good knife, and shouldn't just lay in a drawer."

She had Ina slide it out of its sheath so they could appreciate how the tang went all the way around.

Ina liked that Violet still derived pleasure from her purchases, even the ones she couldn't use. Back when she still lived with their parents, and had a job at the New York State employment office, Violet had often walked up Seventh Avenue to Macy's. She'd bought a Kitchen-Aide bread mixer and very high thread count sheets. She'd also bought, on different occasions, cocoa powder in a tin from Germany, real white chocolate, pages of edible gold, and saffron from Persia.

She opened the door to the Bronx apartment hot and late.

"What are you wasting your money on now?" her mother yelled. Her plump daughter's sensuality struck her as unseemly.

"Whatever it is, it's mine!" said Violet, marching straight into her bedroom

"It's wonderful," said Ina now. But the dull blade swam across the carrot slivers.

"Make the pieces small."

Ina pressed. It was like cutting with the rim of a soda can.

"Smaller," muttered Violet.

Ina leaned her whole weight down, and a wire suddenly blazed deep in her finger. "Oh, fuck!" she exclaimed. A gash of bright red swelled. Then: "I'm sorry, Violet." She'd never once heard her sister curse. She hurried over to the sink to rinse the pulsing cut, and found a Band-Aid.

Then she bent close to the plate. Her skull was squeezed by a tightening band.

"Do you know what 'smaller' means?"

Ina nodded. She tried hard to drive the knife through the wobbly strands.

"Violet," Ina said this softly. But her voice had come out tense. Under the Band-Aid her finger throbbed. "You always make me feel like a screw-up." She paused. "I can't afford to feel like that anymore."

Silence.

"It costs me," she said with a tight voice. "I didn't used to think that it did. But it does."

Ina glanced up. Her sister's face was going pink and her bottom lip quivered. Regret sank into Ina. Her sister had a terrible illness! "Oh, I'm sorry! That was wrong."

But Violet remained wordless.

"Things keep coming out of me these days—things I don't mean." She laughed, as if this were funny.

Violet's face glistened, the skin taut and shiny. "Do you know how you make *me* feel?"

After a moment, Ina shook her head. "No," she said gently.

"You became so exalted, Ina," said Violet, "with your doctorate. A snob."

Yet Violet had always appeared skeptical of Ina's education! As if it only affirmed Ina's advanced incompetence at life.

"It's just sitzfleisch, Violet. You always say so."

"I have a headache," replied Violet. "I want to lie down."

Ina accompanied her along the corridor. Just past the bathroom, one of Violet's feet stuck. The toes curled under. Last month her sister didn't need help. Now, standing rigidly in place, her legs bounced a little, a muscle tremor. How did Violet manage when she was alone?

Violet flopped down hard when they reached the bed, and Ina helped swing her legs onto the mattress. She unlaced Violet's specially molded space shoes and eased them off. Through the venetian blinds the sun shone as if through yellow algae in a fishtank.

"You always knew so much," said Ina. "I always admired you. The names of the trees, the names of birds. And you could tell a story wonderfully." Ina stopped. "You still do tell a story wonderfully."

Violet's eyes were shut. Her lashes gleamed. "I try to remember."

Ina's throat hurt.

"Why don't you finish the salad. I'm going to stay here."

And so Ina returned to the kitchen. She clasped the little knife. She tried very hard to get the pieces right. And it came to her that even if she sliced the pieces perfectly, even if she cut herself, it would fix nothing; it wouldn't save Violet. Life was unfair. Despite Violet's being good for the Hebrew school teachers; despite her neat handwriting and heartbreaking taut-pulled knee-high socks and all the pain she'd endured being ridiculed for being an overweight girl—she was not exempt. Nothing guaranteed against further suffering. Not intelligence, not virtue, not past suffering.

Ina finished the salad, adding the raisins and almond slivers. She covered it with plastic wrap and set it in the fridge. Then she turned off the radio. Silence entered, a waiting presence.

"It's late," Ina called as she approached her sister's bedroom before leaving. She stopped at the doorsill. Her sister gazed at her with wide-open, blue eyes.

"Are you going now?"

"Yes."

"I'm so glad you came."

Ina was surprised. She knew herself to be massively flawed. Violet really deserved better. Still, she answered: "Me too."

When she stepped over, Violet gave her a big smooch, then stroked Ina's arm as if she were a cat. "My sister," she said.

Ina drove fast in the direction of the Holland Tunnel. Dingy little row houses blurred past. She clasped the steering wheel tight. Her sister's nerves were actually exquisitely tender. She'd always believed that Violet, being blunt, could take bluntness in others. Not so. The imperviousness had been an illusion.

She reminded her of Simon's mother, another woman hiding out in an inner terrain. It was the refusal of contact that infuriated Ina, in Simon's mother's case. The sense of a person sending forth a simulacrum rather than the raw, real live human being. Some people propped up replicas of themselves and acted as if there was something wrong with you if you objected to the rubber kiss, the mechanical hug. Her foot pressed down on the gas.

It was possible to live one's whole life in a calloused, numbed state. She shoved down even harder. A man in a green convertible roared up beside her. He gave her a thumbs-up, smiling like the Sabatier man, and Ina dropped back.

In Manhattan, she dialed from the corner. "Can I come up?"

"Where are you?"

"Here. I want to do that thing."

"Shhh," he said. "What's wrong? Are you coming from your parents?"

"No."

"What happened?"

"Please just let me in."

She ran to his lobby door, and the buzzer was already ringing when she arrived.

Chapter 21

He wouldn't do it right away. First he ordered in supper from the Orange Kitchen—cheddar omelets and toasted rye bread with home fries. They ate while watching a redecorating show on TV. She sat keyed-up, half-frightened.

"Why don't you put on more lipstick?" he asked at last.

She nodded, pleased. Why had she ever believed men were oblivious to how women looked?

"Actually, do you have a brown lipstick? I can't really talk about it, but brown lipstick is good. A certain kind of woman wears brown lipstick."

He liked particular things that were trashy or blatant. She wanted those things. She stepped into the bathroom, fluffed up her hair and then carefully re-outlined her eyes with midnight-blue eye shadow.

In the living room he clasped her by the wrist and drew her into the bedroom. She lay down on his bed, on her stomach, still wearing her street clothes. The only light came from a gooseneck lamp aimed at the wall. "If I try to do anything to you," he said, "you can't make it easier or harder. Your arms should be dead weight. If I kiss you, don't open your mouth."

She nodded. She was breathing very strangely: slowly, deeply.

"Do you mind if I take pictures?"

"I want you to," said the low voice that emerged from her. She added quickly, "But don't save a copy for after I leave." She'd become afraid Simon might somehow end up seeing them. "Promise you won't."

"I do promise. Okay. I'm going to go out of the room now. It might be a little while until I come back."

She heard him walk out and across the apartment. Her rib cage rose and fell as she breathed in what seemed to her an exaggerated fashion, now that she was supposed to be dead. After a while, from across the apartment came the soft thump of his footsteps. She suddenly worried her contact lenses would go dry—she wasn't supposed to open her eyes to blink. The floorboards creaked. He entered the room (she pictured him in his loose sand-colored chinos). Then all got quiet. She felt his warm presence at the foot of the bed. She held her breath as long as she could, aware of the movement of her body when she inhaled. His digital camera clicked—a noise so subtle it seemed internal to his mind, as if she could hear his eyes stripping her substance away. A hand negligently pulled one of her legs apart from the other. The camera snapped.

And then he flung her skirt up above her waist. *Tsk*, a definitive metallic sound. He didn't pull down her tights. He dragged her sideways a few inches and flipped her body over roughly so she lay on her back. Silence. Then came the light knock of his camera as it was set on his windowsill. Her mouth went dry. The bed sank as he got on his hands and knees over her. His mouth on hers was warm, firm. A wet, erotic kiss. She was shocked that he wanted to kiss a girl even if she were passed out or dead. It was a brusque, sloppy, firm kiss. She longed to kiss him back, but focused on letting her lips stay slack. Then he bent and pressed his mouth above her knee. He kissed her thigh, through her stockings.

He ran his tongue up toward her crotch. It dragged on her skin. Everything he did was a revelation because he was doing it *for himself*. Then he lay on top of her and ground into her. He stroked her breasts, but quite soon he said, in a soft but matter-of-fact voice, "That's it. Are you disappointed? Be yourself now. I started missing you."

She opened her eyes, reaching to hug him. "I was surprised that you kissed me."

He shrugged. "Kissing is sex."

"It's always seemed to me like something that only the woman would want."

"That's because of your unusual experience."

She smirked—then caught herself. Ironic skepticism was her old defense.

He ran his hand up from her waist to her throat and then lips. "Was this disappointing?" He looked at her. "I thought I'd want to do more. But then I wanted to see your expression."

They began to kiss again, as their alive selves. After a while of that he became more focused. He stopped and yanked her underpants off entirely. Usually they had sex with her underpants pulled to one side. She wanted to see his face, to be with him if he came. She would glimpse his intimate self—his secret self.

"Would you?" he asked gently, and she went down on him. She hoped he would come, she wanted him to come. Her face started to hurt. She felt as if steel had been wedged in her open jaw. Drool ran down her chin. And then he lay her down on her back and entered her again and again, groaning, and suddenly pulled out and ejaculated on her stomach, the liquid hot, thick, with an acrid ammonia scent. But his face had remained merely clenched, flat. Still, she was radiantly happy.

After a while he reached for a box of tissues and mopped up her stomach. He opened his arms and she crept in. He patted her head and wrapped his arms around her tight. "I love you," she heard herself say—a relief, to say it. "I love you, I love you," she murmured again, like a bottle draining.

He nodded and kissed her hair. He said in a serious, frank voice, "I love you, too."

Chapter 22

She pushed her apartment door open and it emitted a long grating sound, the hinges dry. She must remember to get some WD-40. “Back, back,” she whispered to the cat, its triangular face pressing to slip out.

“What’s going on?” said Simon flatly. He’d clicked off the TV. Her stomach contracted. It was just after 10:00 P.M.

“I visited Violet,” she answered brightly. “Then I went and saw Janie. Weren’t you working late?”

Simon continued to inspect her and she restrained an urge to turn away. Fear hammered in her but she spoke matter-of-factly. “Why?” she asked, “Is something wrong?”

“You tell me.”

She should confess about Jack. But her throat clasped shut. *This* was the real world, the actual black-and-white world, the world with gravity and weight. The rest was a hallucination. To lose her life for that!

“I called Janie,” he said.

“We went out to the Cafe Gitane,” she answered, face pulsing. *Please let Janie not have been home.*

Simon continued to study her. “I left a message.”

“She must not have checked her messages yet.” A drop of perspiration chilled the back of her neck.

“I wonder what I’d see if I followed you around with a video camera,” he said.

“Nothing. I’m doing what I say.”

He said softly, “I think you go out clubbing with Janie.”

"To gay places," she said, purposely looking him in the face. She had done that with Janie in the past. "We just dance. I'm not doing anything wrong, Simon." She marveled at the calm voice coming out of her. But she must not, must not crash their lives. In the future she could sort everything out.

"You might not believe it's wrong," he stated. "Don't make a fool of me." Simon was regarding her coldly, with a bitter look. As if he now understood what she was all about.

Her skin felt icy, as if she'd turned into a lizard.

He stood up. "I'm calling the restaurant."

"They'll never remember us," she said quickly. "We sat at the bar. It was busy."

"Would you swear on the Bible?"

Oh, that broke her heart. She gazed at him, wordless. His faith was central to him, although he rarely spoke of it. She owned a translation of the Old Testament wrapped in yellowing torn paper, a contemporary English version with You for Thou. It was crammed somewhere in among the cookbooks and phone books in the kitchen. To set her hand on it and lie—the idea imparted a sense of decay, teeth rotting. Her own father might even be physically harmed by her doing so, she irrationally felt. He was a believer.

"Forget it," said Simon bitterly. "I don't even know what that means to you."

She was aware of her cigarette-smoke-infused clothing. Still, she stepped over and grabbed Simon's hand—his fingers were limp. He sighed, a pained hollow sigh that seemed to come from someplace ancient. "It's so cold, baby!"

"What do you mean?" She clasped him tight.

"I feel so separate."

"You aren't! Come back!" she moaned, her mouth drawn down, and with her whole being wishing to cure his loneliness. To convince him and her, too, that it didn't exist. But then she suddenly went sick inside with the awareness that of course he was lonely. And that she was at that very moment manipulating him. Treating him as something instrumental to her. Not as an alive, feeling human being. "I'm sorry," she said gently. "Of course you're lonely. I'm gone a lot."

He was looking at her.

"But there's something I'm figuring out." She vowed to herself—yes, she absolutely vowed—that very soon the thing with Jack would be over and she'd have learned what she needed to. Then she could be fully present with Simon.

"After working all day, I need to go out. Be with other people. It's helping me see something in O'Neill. I can't put it into words yet. All I can say is that before this I was looking at just language. Symbols. It was all just cognitive."

He sighed again, and said, "I don't want to ruin your life."

He sounded relieved, even as a heaviness had settled over him. "It will be good for you to finally finish the book. And then publish it. And be home."

She nodded. She allowed herself to believe that she would be able to submit pages to Marguerite in five days.

"It's the currency of the system, publication," he reflected. The atmosphere had shifted. "Mind if I watch some TV?"

"Of course not," she said. And she sat beside him, looking at the talk show party on TV.

Why don't you just leave Simon, Janie had asked her recently. But Simon was essential. He'd been there the evening three years earlier when Violet showed up riding a one-person electric cart saying that one day soon she'd need it. Ina had objected: "Aw, you'll be walking when I'm in a rocking chair!" Violet hatcheted out a laugh that made her bangs fly up. But as Simon and Ina strolled through the Bronx dusk later, he said regretfully, "I know it hurts, but it's better to let yourself see the future."

Was it this that made her cling to Simon? Of course, he took care of the rent. She could never afford this neighborhood;

judges and stockbrokers lived here. He paid Con Ed, and the gas—she didn't even know the name of the company that supplied it, was it KeySpan? She mostly just bought groceries.

But obviously there was something beyond finances. She loved him. And had the sense that if she left him, she'd be fucking up her life. He was her *bashert*, although not Jewish: still, the one God intended for her. If she saw him at the end of the block, looking slightly lost, she urgently went racing toward him.

He turned off the TV. "Come here, my crazy, desperate, unhappy wife." He lifted up her hand and kissed her palm, and then he kissed her on the mouth.

Chapter 23

O'Neill had gone up the mountain to the tuberculosis clinic and had come down a different man. She explained this to Sybille's students the fourth time she met with them. In previous weeks she'd resorted to exercises from Janie's textbook, but she'd gotten tired of that and saw they had too. She could at least share what she knew of the writer who'd changed American theater. Her own pages had been due the week before but it was too alarming to think about. Besides, the only actually important aspects of scholarly work—outweighing all else—were its originality and force, and these were gathering within her. She had no idea of the precise pub date of the monographs and articles she admired. "Get it to me when you can," Marguerite had said, because obviously quality was what counted. No, today she wanted to consider the major event that had altered O'Neill.

As a young man, Ina explained—letting her glance fall on Theodore, the boy who always sat directly opposite her—O'Neill had lived a life of reflexive defiance, and squandered all his chances. His first year at Princeton he brought a prostitute to a school function. He was expelled, and that was the end of his college career. A few years later, he got a woman pregnant and married her, but then ran away to work on a steamer ship bound for Buenos Aires. There he got drunk and slept on benches in the port. When he returned to the U.S., he spent his days soused, and lived in a cell-sized room above a dive bar. He tried to commit suicide. Nothing in him felt worthwhile. Life was crap. And then he got sick with tuberculosis.

At the clinic he went to, the patients slept outside. It was winter, and freezing cold. Some patients lived, lots died. Ina told them about a photo she'd discovered at the Beinecke library that wasn't in any of the biographies: a line of men at the sanitorium, many with sensitive faces. Some smiled, a few looked lost, all wore monochrome clothing—all except one, who was clad in the flashy checked jacket of a bon vivant and who glowered at the camera. He looked like somebody for whom life was a joke that he resented. That was O'Neill. By the time he came down the mountain, he'd changed. He'd survived, and his life was really his own. It didn't belong to someone else. His life mattered, at least to him.

He immediately enrolled in a playwriting class. He would redefine his father's melodramatic theater, make it into a place of truth. He lived by the shore and swam out as far as the sharks, even in winter. The cold had saved his life, and he came to need it. She told the students about another photo she'd found at the Beinecke, also not in any biography, of O'Neill in swim trunks on the beach shortly after he'd returned from the sanitorium. He'd penned directly onto the image that the water was 39 degrees, and he'd circled a patch of snow on the sand. It was New Year's Day, 1914.

"But what if he didn't have writing and he had to come down the mountain anyway?" asked the walleyed boy.

Ina raised her eyebrows, feeling a slight tingle over her entire body that she hadn't felt in years. She only experienced it in classrooms when someone said something brilliant. It was like being powdered with electric rain. "That can be our writing prompt! Lots of us have to come down the mountain and live our ordinary lives without that magic thing. What's it like when you don't have that special thing but you still have to come down the mountain?"

The mountain was Jack's apartment. She didn't want to leave.

But the boy who'd asked the question was trembling. He looked very pale. His leg was bouncing. To Ina's surprise, he abruptly threw his books together, and left.

The class fell quiet. Ina gazed down, stricken. She'd never had a student storm out. She should not have made a writing prompt out of a student's extremely personal question. Perhaps he thought she was mocking him. She opened the textbook, her fingers shaking slightly, to find one of its good, sturdy, classroom-tested prompts.

But hands were moving in notebooks. Several of the students were already at work. They were writing quickly, as if they'd stumbled on something they needed to tell. Aurelia was bent over her diary, her plumed pink pen creaking. The man in a yarmulka leaned so close to his page that his gray eyes were almost on par with the lines themselves. Ina too registered an urge to write, but quelled it, thinking about the impossibility of putting words to what went on with Jack.

"I'm going to have to spank you," he'd said the day before, as they walked to his apartment from the subway.

To Ina's surprise, these silly, boorish words made her limp with excitement. How shocking and even mortifying to be aroused by such a thing. But no, it wasn't aroused: it was momentarily pleasurably paralyzed. Ecstatically subsumed. However, Jack didn't introduce the notion of spanking again that day.

But the day after the creative writing class, when she was still considering Theodore's prompt (for thus she thought about it), Jack said something that had the same effect. She'd met him outside the music school where he taught. Giddy, gleeful, she'd interrupted him several times while he was speaking. He told her: "I want to clamp my hand over your mouth."

She turned away and watched the passing traffic. *Oh.*

And then, a few minutes later, as they were waiting at the bus stop, she said, rather sharply, "I can't come over again tomorrow. This is an unusual week for me. Get it?"

"Did you say, 'Get it'?" he replied. "I see I'm going to have to take a firm hand with you."

Something in her collapsed, swooned. She felt thoroughly wanted and loved. The way a little girl might feel who was cared for by a parent who made her do what was good for her whether she wanted to or not.

That same evening she stood across the room in high heels, a bra and panties, and dark gray pantyhose. There was something mortifying about their opaque girdle-like low crotch. Yet being looked at by him in this shaming garb was puzzlingly erotic. Her knees felt wobbly. What was it about humiliation? She recalled a time when, as a third grader, she'd been changing her clothing in the school bathroom, putting on her costume for a play, and her feet stepped into a cold puddle on the floor, and at that instant the door few open, bringing a gust of laughter from the children in the hall. Indelible! So much shame! She had estranged herself from that little girl. Jack had found her. He'd come back and located her where she was still rigidly stationed decades later, feet chilled in a bathroom puddle that might be urine, chest exposed, the children laughing. He still wanted her, liked her, stepped through her horror at herself and embraced her. How kind!

He sat on his bed; she knelt between his legs. He stroked her hair, tucked a lock of behind her ear, then said, "Your whole job on this earth right now is to suck my cock."

She felt immense relief: she didn't have any other job on earth. She didn't need to be intelligent or return difficult phone calls or hand in chapters or be nice or liked. Her shoulders sank, and she felt she had a new ability to be present exactly where she was on the planet, in this room, doing this. It made no sense, it was probably delusional, but in that moment she felt wanted past any act of volition and therefore fraudulence, wanted in her core self, the way perhaps a parent loves an infant before their first word, for a self beyond even her own knowing. He wanted her for what she was involuntarily, without contrivance, spontaneously, in her bones. Sex now seemed like the pull tab of life. Sex swept you open, flung out your true contents. You didn't know much about yourself until you discovered what you liked sexually. What you hungered for. What made you grateful. Sex was the royal road to the person you were before you cloaked yourself in sentences. It made your personality seem like a costume—tinsel and masks.

"Good girl," said Jack.

"Oh, please say it again."

"When you earn it."

He drew her up on the bed, and she lay down on her stomach. She was feeling a distracting amount of gratitude. He dragged his hand up her leg toward her crotch and she fantasized about the big supper she would buy him at his favorite restaurant, The Wicked Wolf. He'd order chicken parmigiana with a potato and creamed spinach. Or lasagna! Maybe he'd order that. He stroked her and she parted her legs and she had to suck her lips into her mouth so as not to exclaim, "I want to take you to dinner." It reassured her to know soon they would stop; it made her anxious to receive so much.

"Can I tell you something about me?" he murmured, after. They lay under his blanket, on their backs. Paraffin scented the air. A neighbor's door creaked opened, followed by a muffled conversation in the hall, and then the voices moved off. "It has to do with something that happened when I was little. It has to do with voyeurism."

She nodded, and held her breath. She didn't want to distract by the smallest twitch.

At a beach vacation when he was six, he'd glimpsed his

mother's friend changing her clothing. This woman had been slightly younger than his mother, perhaps twenty-five, and was staying with them that week. Jack had been put down for a nap when he heard a noise. He opened his eyes and there, behind a curtained-off portion of his bedroom, was his mother's friend changing out of her swimsuit. A fantastic, extraordinary feeling overcame him.

The next afternoon he purposely lay down on his cot for a nap around the time he thought the woman might be changing her clothes. Through half-shut lids, he gazed. Sensing something, she turned and their eyes met. She stiffened and hastily covered herself. Deeply ashamed, he worried she would tell his mother. He never knew if she did. "You can't imagine the number of hours I've spent standing near my window looking out, hoping to see something."

"Have you ever seen anything?" She felt the poignance of this young man staring into the impassive city.

"Very rarely. But you know, even the pornography I like has an edge of voyeurism in it. I like it to be a real person, who you could actually imagine meeting."

He clasped her hand, and smiled with relief. "It's so nice to tell you. It's weird, standing at the window with binoculars and trying to steal a glimpse of someone who doesn't want to be seen. I thought for sure any woman I told would think I was a monster."

"I don't." His words brought to mind the lonely minotaur—part bull, part human—in its labyrinth.

He drew close to her. "I feel less like a monster," he murmured, "telling you."

She pictured him at the window. What would he see? A person at a table eating with invisible others, door moldings, the poles of floor lamps, a swatch of blue screen facing a vacant-seeming room. It was mostly a world of dead things, unresponsive, that he saw, stationed in his darkened apartment hoping for a glimpse, a visitation, the thrilling sight of a woman's body. Ina understood he was a troubled person with whom she was falling ever more in love.

The next morning, scrubbing off the last smudge of eye shadow at the bathroom sink, she recalled that O'Neill had been obsessed with looking glasses. On his mountaintop when he was sick with TB, his nurse dragged over the heavy mirrored bureau in his room so it faced the bed. She'd noticed that he was always desperately searching for his reflection. A friend, seeing the new furniture arrangement, declared "You're the most vain person I've ever known!"

O'Neill replied, "I just need to make sure I exist."

Ina straightened. O'Neill's mother had been immersed in her drug fog. No wonder he didn't know he was real. Jack's mother had been an alcoholic. Her own mother had been profoundly depressed when Ina was young. She flung the cotton into the trash and hurried to her desk.

Lots of us are attracted to people who are unavailable, she scribbled, or who return us to ourselves shrunken. Then she sat back. Jack was the opposite. He gave Ina a delirious, fantastical experience of herself. Marvelous, thrilling. She struck her notebook with her pen. How to ever leave him? How to free yourself from addiction to a delusion? Well, didn't one become free by discovering a piece of reality that had previously been hidden? She stared out the window at the stark, bare tree branches. Something would be revealed if she stayed the entire night.

That evening she explained to Simon that her friend Patience had invited her to stay at a hotel while driving to her parents' house in Connecticut just before Christmas.

"Sure you want to do that—take even more time from your work?"

"It's a special chance."

He nodded, leaned over and stroked her perspiring brow.

"How is *your* work going these days?" she asked.

"Like gangbusters. You wouldn't believe how good it feels to be offering something people really want, that they can't get fast enough."

"I'm glad. It sounds fulfilling."

He laughed, although she hadn't meant to be sarcastic. "Ina, I made the right decision."

"Of course."

The phone rang just then, and she grabbed it. It was Marguerite, who said, "I'm sorry, my dear."

"Sybille's class?"

"Unfortunately."

"I thought she was back."

"So did we all."

Ina recalled Theodore storming out. The thought of returning made her stomach churn. She didn't know how to teach this class. "Am I not supposed to be on leave?" she asked, although she knew Marguerite could well point out that Ina hadn't submitted her pages.

"Ina," uttered Marguerite in her flat deep voice, as if speaking to someone behaving crazily.

There was simply a finality in her tone.

"All right. Very good," sang Ina with an angry tightening in her chest. "I'll be there."

After she hung up, Simon said, "I wonder if she's losing respect for you."

Chapter 24

Cattails exploded open in erratic shapes amidst the wetlands of New Jersey; the marshland gleamed with wheat-colored grass. Ina's own painted face glimmered against the fields. Half asleep, she gazed at the landscape rushing through her cheeks and mouth. The conductor approached in his dark blue pants and spongey shoes, and she handed him her ticket. He clicked a complicated pattern with his hole punch. Tiny paper snippets rained down.

She probably ought to feel degraded by the things she and Jack did together. The faculty at Quincy would certainly think so. Yesterday she'd hurried up his stairs, almost weak with excitement, in order to stand across from him, nearly naked, wearing just the new black velvet bra and panties. She had put on makeup. In fact, she no longer let him see her without makeup. Which was certainly not good. Cosmetics were a multibillion-dollar industry that depended on making women feel plain if they didn't buy them. And she wanted them. She was enchanted by them. She adored the fashionable black rubbery pouch with crisp white stitching from Sephora that Janie had given her, which now clattered with exquisite objects she enjoyed even just fingering: the swizzle-stick-long brushes with their tipped lobes of fur, the metal chambers of faintly shimmering powders in shades of cocoa and mocha and jade. But how was this not degradation, female abasement? She sighed.

She'd nearly punched a man once on a street in Manhattan years ago who'd said, "Nice tits." He'd been eating a slice of pizza at a counter on the street. Furious, she'd gone straight up to him and shouted, "Stop harassing women!" He'd laughed in her face. She'd resented the radio psychologist observing her when she spun; he seemed like a gross, smug gargoyle king. But it was all different with Jack.

He set a photo of her on his piano, beside the photo of a TV star he said she resembled. He took photos of her legs while she sat on the couch and he was on the floor in front of her. He took her to a discount store on Third Avenue and, blushing, asked her to buy underpants from a certain box. They were three for five dollars, high-waisted, of cheap nylon pastel. It excited him to see her put her hands in the crowded box as she searched for her size. At his apartment he lay on the floor and asked her to walk over him in the underpants.

No, she shouldn't like it. It ought to offend her to be objectified. But that was the thing: it didn't really feel quite like objectification. It felt like being wanted through all her layers, like being permeated by the sun, with nothing gnarly rejected.

She even liked when he showed her pornography. She found it compelling. As a teenager when she'd looked at *Playboy*s while babysitting or, once, with Simon (a woman displaying gigantic jug breasts), she'd only felt curdling disgust. But with Jack it seemed one long intimate secret between them. A woman's lewd face had splayed across his computer monitor, and Ina had felt a sledgehammer slam her chest. The woman's mouth opened wide as she grinned, licking the tip of a penis longer than a prize zucchini and a dark sullen red. The woman's smirking expression indicated *"This is great!"* The man's pubic hair glistened.

Ina liked that the women in Jack's pictures didn't have model-like bodies. She was particularly interested in a white woman with suede-brown breasts which poured straight down like Slinkys. Her aureoles were the size of coasters. That she was attractive to men! That women didn't need to look like the images in *Cosmo*!

"Can I look again?" asked Ina after the picture changed.

Jack showed her which button to push. He held his arms around her while she looked. Part of her shame at being a woman fell away. But she mustn't think about that now.

To clear her mind, she opened the newspaper. She heard the conductor unclasp the compartment door, even as the train was still rattling forward. Cold air rushed in. She tried to attend to what was on the page. It was about Fox News. Newt Gingrich had been hired by the "permanent CEO" of that station, Roger Ailes. She used to assume that Fox News was too fringy to make a difference. But it was growing in viewership. She wondered about its affect on people like Timothy McVeigh, who became convinced the enemy was the federal government.

On the book pages she saw, to her surprise, the review of a work by a rival academic. It was unusual for the paper to cover a book from a university press. But Kakutani thought this book important. The critic praised the scholar's original mind and her verbal incandescence. Ina gazed at the newspaper's serif type, and it was as if a car battery had been dropped into the pond inside her; the envy she felt corroded and bubbled.

"Cherrywood!" the conductor called, striding up the corridor. Ina stood abruptly. Suburban houses flashed past the open door. When the train ground to a stop, screeching, the conductor flung out the stairs, and she descended into the brisk air. The houses here seemed prim—posh center-door colonials, outsized Cape Anns. The December air was bracing.

In the town, Ina stopped by the little grocery store to get a drink. Bubble gum and sawdust perfumed the air. And there, bagging groceries, was a familiar figure: Marguerite's daughter wearing a thick navy wool jumper that draped to her knees, white hose, and Converse sneakers. She set each item carefully into the bag she was packing, "Hello, Tina," said Ina when it was her turn. "I work with your mother." Tina smiled. "It's good to see you."

Tina nodded. "It's good to see you too," she said slowly. She seemed to mean it although she also seemed not to know who Ina was.

He was in class, sitting, as usual, directly opposite her. She dipped her head toward him in salute, but he just sat rigidly. "Thank you for coming back, Theodore," she said softly.

He shrugged.

In his honor, and perhaps to demonstrate to Theodore the virtue of taking a risk, she decided not to assign a prompt from the textbook but to offer a writing prompt directly from her own life, even if she were the only one who knew. "Write about a time you surprised yourself," she said. "When you did something you had no idea you were going to do. You might write about a time you enjoyed something you didn't think you would ever enjoy. Start right now."

Many of the students were still looking at her. "Now, please," she said to Theodore, who seemed to have glazed over with rage, as if he again suspected he was being mocked. Perhaps he thought she was referring to his surprising departure from their last class. But after a moment he too started writing.

For once, Ina decided to jot as well. "First thought, best thought," she told herself, the mantra of freewriting. The words tumbled onto the page, each seeming to extrude the next like segments of a telescope. Ten minutes passed in an instant. "That was nothing," she announced. "Go another five."

But something was amiss. She glanced up. Theodore wasn't writing. "Keep going, please," she urged him.

He sighed heavily, and picked up his pen, which was wide, shaped like a lozenge, and bore the word Prozac. It surprised her that he didn't mind using this pen although other things, to her less personal, had offended him.

When the time was again up, she was surprised by how little seemed to have landed on her page yet how detailed it was.

"Let's hear these," she said, turning to the older woman. "Grace, would you start?"

"I hate to disagree with you, but we don't usually have to read what we've written," said Theodore.

"Is that true," Ina asked pleasantly. "Do you hate to disagree with me?"

He stared.

Something ticked in her throat. She never used to get riled by a challenging student. But in the past she'd been more oblivious.

"You're all going to read. Even though I know that you haven't in the past." She half expected Theodore to leave, but he did not. "Grace, please start."

Grace lifted her paper and described a time she'd fixed a car by herself on a deserted highway. After her, Prudence, who loved Emily Dickinson, read about filling in for the star during a community theater production of *Hello, Dolly!* Aurelia, who had wanted to send Ina her essay about needles, read a beautiful piece about once opening the attic window of her grandmother's house and lying down on the roof when she was depressed, to gaze up at the stars. And Theodore wrote about batting surprisingly well in a baseball game.

"Wonderful," said Ina. "Thank you. So many good discoveries of what really made you happy. Grace, would you distribute your story?"

"Actually, if Sybille writes, she reads," muttered Theodore, but then he looked embarrassed, and gazed down.

"Does she?"

With an apologetic air, Grace nodded.

Ina was about to say that she hadn't realized this—when it occurred to her that this was exactly the position she'd put Theodore in, being forced to share secret work. Everyone looked at her. She glanced at her paper. A soft roar filled her ears, and behind it came the sound of a chair scraping back—in fact all the sounds in the classroom had gotten very loud. Was there any part she could read? It began with her pleasure at being kissed and then described looking at erotic pictures online—the ecstasy on the face of the woman in one of the photos, the cheesy cop outfit of one of the men—how it surprised her that she liked that, too.

"You don't have to," said Grace. "You're the substitute."

Ina glanced at her, grateful. "It surprised me how much I liked to be kissed," she read. Her words were snatched from her throat before she'd half-said them. It seemed to take a long time but finally she was able to reach the paper's conclusion: "I pushed the button again. The woman had runny cheap fluorescent blue mascara and her tits"—for yes, this was the word on the page, the word that seemed most apt while scribbling under pressure—"held up by her hands, offered to the camera, the viewer, were reminiscent of saddlebags, canvas thermos bottles, suede cylinders with nipples—" Ina was nearly gasping. The students in the back, she noticed, had leaned forward. But she couldn't speak any louder. Suddenly, dementedly, it seemed important to say: "—of a beautiful rose pink. All this was beautiful. Things you couldn't imagine beautiful are in fact beautiful."

She thought she might faint. Thank God the Vietnam vet who read Bukowski wasn't here today. Was this what groundbreaking writers felt? Her face throbbed.

Silence in the room.

Then, as if stirring herself out of a trance, Grace exclaimed, "Brava! You really anted up!"

"You anted up!" said Prudence. "That's Sybille's highest praise."

Theodore was staring at her, one eye evasive and the other shocked.

"We'll take a break now," said Ina.

And so the class dispersed. Ina's skin felt charged with frigid electricity. On her way out the door a hand grasped her arm.

It was Aurelia, who had crawled out her grandma's attic window. She wore a grubby-looking sweatshirt stitched with a giant Hello Kitty applique, her ginger hair cropped short in a pageboy. "Thank you," she whispered. Ina nodded and rushed out. She walked hastily in the direction of the student center for a coffee. She could not stop trembling.

Her vision was sharper as she walked downhill toward the train. The world had taken on greater specificity. In the late-afternoon sun, each clot of dried soil cast its own idiosyncratic blue shadow. A bronze leaf twirled. Or was it a bird rotating as if on a trapeze? She stopped for a moment and peered up at the revolving object until she determined that yes, it was a leaf, whereupon it flew off on pointy wings. Grace had distributed pages to the class from a memoir about an abusive marriage, in which the wife has been isolated in a remote house. "Setting's important," Ina had said. "How does being out in the world function in the story compared to the claustrophobia of the house? What details strike you?"

Hands shot up. Students who'd until now been watchful were no longer standoffish. Her own unabashed writing had opened a door. She found herself less judgmental. Student ideas she might have rejected before now seemed neither right nor wrong; they seemed interesting. She'd always been a somewhat harsh teacher, and this stemmed from her harshness with herself. She'd had a clear idea—really, an overly clear idea—of what she wanted the students to learn. Now she could see the limitations of that approach. Now she wanted to leave a space to just notice and listen to what the students found exciting. She was glad Marguerite had asked her to teach Sybille's class. She would write with them again, this time understanding that what she wrote would be shared.

Chapter 25

At Summit Street, where she had to change trains, there were twelve minutes before the local would arrive. The cold made her lungs burn. An outdoor phone was riveted to a steel board. "You've got to hear this headline," she shouted to Jack. "Radiation Ripples from Big Bang Illuminate Geometry of Universe." She laughed. "That's the *Times*, Jack."

She inched her hands up beside the article, which was swept sideways by the wind. "The Hubble is finally up over the earth's distortion field."

She lowered her head to the phone, bracing against the wind. "I'm just not out in the real world enough."

"Come and see me. I'm real."

"I suppose you are," she said gently, momentarily dizzy.

On the express, gazing out at the rushing landscape, she thought about how, before she met Jack, she'd assumed you had to choose between being your actual self and your social self. Other people couldn't really, truly know you. Your real self lived in the intellectual work you did. But perhaps a person could have both—she dragged her finger down the coiled spine of her notebook—could have both lingerie and glittering insight. What was that Greek word for recognition? Amphora? Agora? She tapped the glass beside her.

At Penn Station she phoned Jack again. "I think I found my way ahead. Fast writing. It's the opposite of the yellow stickies. I don't know why I didn't think of it earlier. It's something O'Neill did, at least in his first drafts."

"Tell me in person."

"You're too distracting. Besides, I'm in my teaching clothes."

"Good. I might like them."

And Jack did like those scratchy trousers, the tracing paper sherbet-pink blouse with the blind luminous buttons, the scuffed shoes with the peeling heels, even the old white battalion-nurse bra.

"I want to tell you something." She described reading the review this afternoon, and how envious it had made her feel. It was not a rare feeling, this envy, but she'd never spoken about it to anyone.

Jack patted her: "I'm sure your work is as at least as good as that woman's." She winced. She understood that her work was probably *not* as good. And yet, as Ina leaned into his hairy chest, she felt she had discovered the antidote to envy. At long last! The envy was gone! She was blissfully relieved of the bad feeling. It would be nice if he understood the quality of the other woman's work, yet all that really mattered to her was just being there, that she was the girl in his arms. She asked him what he was thinking about and was surprised at his ability to catch half-ideas and convey them, bevies of associations and visual impressions. And then he asked her what she was thinking about and listened closely.

She told Jack about a time she'd gone sledding with her brothers in Van Cortlandt Park when she was little but had wandered off and gotten lost. Sunset cast a rusty glow across the snow and the chain-link fence. She started singing to herself, tears running down and chafing her cheeks. How lonely and pointless the world seemed. She had always felt this. This was the feeling under everything. A figure was approaching the fence, from the side. He'd bent down in his hooded parka and stepped through a hole in the fence. Her own father! "What are you doing here all by yourself?" he exclaimed. In the car, the heat came on with a whoosh and he poured cocoa from a tin thermos. Then he wrenched off her boots and socks and clasped her icy feet between his hands.

Ina leaned back although it was long past time to go. Yet in the half-darkness in which so much had come into existence, she wanted to talk about Winnicott. Didn't he have a phrase "transitional space"? She recalled another phrase: "The making real of the hallucination." She spoke fast.

Jack laughed, but not unkindly. "You're talking about so many things at once."

"Yes, but Winnicott—"

He nodded and kissed her, without condescension.

"You and I invent things together," she said softly, "but then they're actually real."

"I know. You don't have to explain."

She was surprised. He was there too.

Only Miss Marple was in the apartment. It was nearly 11:00 P.M., the rooms echoing with the sound of a helicopter ratcheting over the river, suspended there as if stuck. Had there been another bridge jumper? Madly, Ina wondered if it was Simon. Had he somehow—impossibly—heard about Jack? She sat at the window, rigid, holding in her hand a notebook in which she meant to write down the short stories she'd be assigning for her spring semester class. But the unmoving thrum of the helicopter filled her mind.

At last she heard a key in the door. "Where were you?" she exclaimed.

Simon looked rumpled, fatigued. It was almost midnight. Ina felt weak with relief.

"After work I went to Kate's. She had a panic attack."

"I didn't know she got those."

"Well, she does."

"Isn't that asking a lot, after you put in a whole day at work?" She hated to think of him stuck in traffic, sitting at lights.

"It's called being a friend, Ina. How was Quincy?"

"Good," she said. "Teaching was good."

He went into the kitchen and drank glass after glass of water. "You were drinking with Kate?" she asked. Wine always made him thirsty.

"Yes. She wanted to, to calm down. Panic attacks are terrible. She said it's like jumping out of your own skin over and over."

"Well, you're a good friend."

"Just an ordinary friend," he said.

Chapter 26

Something was missing when she awoke the next morning. She lay quite still. What was it? Something to do with Simon?

No.

Something in a dream?

Not that, either. She had the feeling that what had vanished had long preceded Simon.

Her old loneliness! Her eyes opened.

It had been so continually present, she had scarcely been aware it even existed—this loneliness. She'd certainly never believed she could lose it.

Above her, the ceiling offered a pattern of lunar craters and dry lakebeds. She followed the outlines, charting unnamed continents. The loneliness—she'd assumed it was merely the sensation of being conscious. She'd once stood beside her high school friend Stella on a wintry Bronx afternoon on a bluff overlooking the Hudson. "Isn't this romantic?" Stella remarked. The pearl-gray river diffused into the moist January air in shades of shale and iron. Pretty, yes. But romantic? Didn't romantic involve a lover? She'd become aware at that moment that Stella possessed an inner authority—a kind of self-companionship—that Ina might never have. Whether or not she had a partner, Stella was unafraid to find an atmosphere romantic. Stella could relish the desolate, gusty blue of the afternoon. The loneliness that Ina had become aware of for an instant that afternoon beside the Hudson was simply the ordinary texture of existence, she'd assumed.

Now that had changed.

"You're intoxicated," said George. "People who are intoxicated are in love with their drug. Outsiders see just a drunk on the sidewalk."

"No, George, I've never been clearer. I'm seeing so much. About envy, for instance—"

"That's just the nature of sex. It makes you think you're having revelations." He continued, musing, "Addicts love to talk about their drug. They find it endlessly fascinating."

Across the street, Ina saw the professor's gold pencil was weaving. "Sex *is* a drug," she conceded. "But that doesn't mean it's not important. Or that you don't learn real things from it."

"Do you hear what you're saying?" George crowed. "It's exactly what I've been telling you for years, Ina. Sex is important."

She felt sick. She said slowly, "Yet for some reason I still find it hard to believe." It was like discovering that the walls of the building you lived in were secretly made of honey.

The professor turned another sheet of yellow legal paper and tucked it under her pad. Ina glanced quickly away.

"I know, darling," said George consolingly. "But make yourself. Because the longer you stay high on your drug, the more danger there is. To others and to yourself."

All the more reason to find out what she needed to by staying over. The piece of reality that would undo the delusion.

The phone rang again the instant that she hung up. "There appears to be a problem," announced the voice of a child pretending to be starchy.

"What, Violet? Look, please just forget what I told you about the guy at the party."

"Marguerite." Her voice was icy.

Ina was mortified to have made the same mistake twice.

"You could come to campus or we could discuss it over the phone. There's been a complaint from a parent."

Ina couldn't breathe for a moment. The broad floorboards themselves seemed unsteady.

Marguerite sighed. "It's alleged that you read pornography aloud in the classroom." Ina saw Theodore. "I assume, Ina, you did not."

"Marguerite, I did not read pornography."

"I need to see what you did read. To prepare a response. Who was the author?"

Cold radiated down from her armpits. "Me, actually."

Marguerite was silent. Then, "Ah, well. That will have to go in your file. We must be responsive to parents these days. That's not news to you, of course."

Ina shut her eyes. If she lost this job, Simon would be so horribly disappointed. And rightly so. And what could she do without a recommendation?

She said, mouth dry, "Marguerite, I wrote *about* pornography."

What an idiot boy!—to confuse the two!

"Alas, nothing is obvious to me these days," said Marguerite flatly.

"Baseball bat penis" was one phrase Ina recalled in the free-write. And, "Legs spread. A woman leering while she stroked herself."

"Marguerite, I really regret the inconvenience this is giving you. But what I wrote was just to share with that class."

There was a pause during which Marguerite seemed to be reading, or taking a note. Then she remarked, "O'Neill treating you well?"

"I've been having breakthroughs."

"So you've said."

There was an awkward pause. "Any news of Sybille?"

"No. I can't imagine what's in her mind. You can't live too erratically and teach young people, you know." She added, "I look forward to reading the writing you shared in class. You'll email it?"

"It's handwritten. But—"

"Fax it. With a copy typed out, please."

Was this even legal? "I'm wondering about the protocol—"

"Ina." Marguerite's voice was steely. "You only have a year-by-year contract, I hate to remind you." Then she ended with: "Let's please try to make this little problem go away, shall we?"

She typed up the piece. It was the most humiliating thing she had ever done. Her eyes resisted the words scrawled on the page. "Tips" she typed, instead of "tits," and had to correct that. "Cylinders" got misspelt in various ways. The gleam of Marguerite's wire-rimmed glasses seemed to flash from her keyboard. Had it been something like this that had made Sybille disappear?

With a kind of dull doggedness, Ina made it to the photo shop. The copy machine was old and cost just ten cents. Ina snatched up the paper that rolled out. The tattered white edges of her original document stood outlined against a dark background, imparting the clinical, even ironic appearance of court evidence.

A woman in a Bo-Peep wig of yellow curls accepted the page. She returned it after a few moments with a slip: *Transmission OK*. Ina trod home even more slowly, her eyes drawn to the tiny sharp green leaves still on the shrubbery although it was December. She had an inkling of why people cut themselves: to bring the sensation elsewhere. At home, she pulled open the big bottom drawer, and buried the pages beneath an apron from her fifth-grade play when she'd played Dolly Madison and a birthday card from her mother with glitter sifting off.

Oprah was giving away Christmas presents when Ina turned on the TV.

Audience members were in tears, jumping up and down. After that came the five o'clock news.

The phone rang at last. "I've written the parent and made

nice," said Marguerite wearily. "Best to be a little circumspect, Ina, yes? Not to let yourself get quite so carried away."

"I understand."

There was a slight pause. Marguerite sighed and said, "Ina, what you read in the classroom was really inappropriate. I can understand why the student was upset."

Ina said nothing. She pressed her hand against her leg to stop her fingers from vibrating.

"Look, I covered for you this time, Ina. But you have to think more clearly about the wellbeing of the students. There have to be boundaries."

"Of course," said Ina, too soon.

Marguerite didn't speak for a moment. It came to Ina that this was a difficult conversation for Marguerite to be having, and that Ina hadn't been hearing her properly. Marguerite said, "The boundaries are there for a reason."

"Yes," said Ina very softly.

She sounded chastised but sensed that again she was missing something important. She'd again answered too soon, as if merely thinking of pleasing Marguerite. "I'll be more aware of maintaining appropriate boundaries going forward. Thank you, Marguerite."

"Fine." Marguerite hung up.

After Ina set the receiver down she sat quite still. It seemed to her that the sweaty heat and smell of the porn woman's body which she'd written about, that it was all over her and that she'd imposed it on Marguerite. George was right: this was an addiction. She was not in control. Oh, she must stop it and get free. She must do it now, as soon as possible, before she fucked up worse.

An idea came to her for a cure, and she rushed to Court Street, where she purchased a yellow-fabric notebook the size of her palm.

"Turn around," she wrote inside, leaning against a light post

on the way back. *"I like this part of you where it starts to get meaty."*

Below that she put, *"But don't you think the most beautiful thing in the world is a woman's body?"*

At her own desk she added, *"'They're so beautiful!'—said when I was taking off my bra."*

Each of these sentences had awoken her for a rapturous moment, rousing her out of a dreary ordinariness. She'd capture their magic. Store them. Then she could open the notebook and experience the awareness he'd brought her, and not need Jack. And she could leave him, at last.

Inside the front cover of the notebook she copied down a passage by Elia Kazan, Tennessee Williams' director: *"Promiscuity for an artist is an education, a great source of confidence and a spur to work."* It was an education, yes.

Under the last of Jack's sentences, she added: *"'You're like a Christmas present I get to unwrap!' said while looking at me in my red silk slip."*

"Do I like to see breasts? Uh, yeah! It's a great feeling. It's like getting to sit down to a steak dinner."

As she transcribed the words, she noticed to her dismay that their force vanished. Set on the page, they didn't impart the delirium they'd had when Jack had said them. Why couldn't the ecstasy of these sentences actually change her? Lots of artists had been aided by drugs—Coleridge, Rimbaud, Allen Ginsberg, William Burroughs, John Lennon, even the cartoonist R. Crumb. Why did some people's epiphanies transform them? She turned to a fresh page. Freewrite, she told herself. As if you're in Sybille's classroom.

I have no respect for drug visions, she wrote.

And that seemed part of the answer.

She noticed, too, that Jack's sentences, separated from their context, seemed stupid and boorish.

She took the little yellow notebook and tucked it into the

bottom of her bureau drawer, beneath the solitary white Girl Scout glove and Betsy Ross apron from her fifth-grade play. She would free herself by staying over and discovering the piece of reality she didn't yet know. She even had a guess of what it might well be.

A week later, on Monday morning she awoke early, the sky still dark. "It will be good to see Patience," she remarked. Patience was a friend from graduate school, now teaching up at Brandeis. They were only occasionally in touch. "You know, she's trying to conceive a baby, taking all kinds of measures." Did her voice sound normal, she wondered.

Simon paused, buttoning his shirt. He turned to her, his shirt still half open. "That would be a good idea for us," he said. He came over and took her hand. "You know, more love makes more love. That's what Ivan said he found out from having kids." He leaned over and kissed her—and she smiled back stiffly. Simon smelled faintly of chlorine.

"I'm going to talk to Atkinson today directly. I need to be responsible for something quantifiable. Some bottom-line output. That's the only way I'm really going to advance."

Ina sat up. "Can you do that? Go over Suzanne's head?" Suzanne was his supervisor. Atkinson was the Senior Vice President in charge. As with the church, hierarchy was sacrosanct. "Won't she go ballistic?"

"Not if she doesn't know." He smiled his impeccable new smile. "Atkinson can be discreet."

His body looked sculpted. He was working out once a week with a weight trainer, which surprised Ina since he'd given up acting. He looked less and less like the shy, lithe Texan he'd been when he first came east.

"He'll make the decision seem like it's hers. I know he respects my work."

"Well, don't say anything negative about Suzanne."

Simon nodded absently.

"Simon!"

"I'm not an idiot. Call me from Patience's."

"Good luck!" she said as he was leaving, but he didn't seem to be listening.

As soon as he left, she took out her little suitcase.

Chapter 27

Snow flickered through the air, blue-gray, juddering like footage in an early movie. It was late afternoon, just after 4:00 P.M. Jack was waiting for her outside the music school, rocking up and back on his toes. "I feel like a character in a novel," he said bitterly, "who gets to be happy for just one day." They headed uptown on Broadway. She hung her head, but then took his hand and he seemed to forgive her for not staying over more than this one night. The Upper West Side shops glowed and the sparse traffic moved ever more silently as the flakes accumulated. Everything seeming more private. The sky was a dingy white. Ina felt almost sick with excitement.

When they passed the ornate gates of the Apthorp, Ina told him that her sister had once lived there. She'd rented a beautiful large, square bedroom in a shared apartment, and lived on cheese, Carr's water crackers, and gold Bosc pears. After work, she sang in a prestigious chorus. Everyone thought Violet was at the beginning of her adult life but she was actually in the middle.

"It's wonderful she had those experiences," said Jack gently, and he seemed to sincerely mean it, although he'd never met Violet.

At the corner, they waited for the bus. The wet, descending flakes were the size of sugar cubes, and yet, as they floated past, she sometimes glimpsed their scissored intricacy. "I have a surprise waiting for you,' said Jack.

"Something we've used before?" She'd worn a see-through bra. He'd bound her wrists with silk ties.

"No."

The bus approaching from a block away was a lit box, almost entirely empty. They boarded, and sat side by side, facing forward. The vehicle crossed the park, gliding past pristine fields, fir trees with crosshatched pagoda boughs caked with white. At Lexington Avenue they at last got off and went into Agata & Valentina. So here's where all the people were! The aisles of the store were crowded. They bought fish and asparagus and a baguette and butter and candied apricots. To Ina's eyes, each thing seemed especially exquisite. The skin of the salmon was an Escher-patterned silver-and-graphite, as smooth as a nectarine. The fish flopped onto the butcher paper with a lush indolence. Homemade marshmallows were fragrant even through their glittering cellophane wrapping. Back on the street, a sifting of snow descended fine as table salt. As they approached Jack's building, she started to wonder about the surprise. Was it crotchless panties? Real handcuffs?

At his door, Jack laughed at her expression. "You look frightened!"

She'd just recalled a photo he'd shown her of a device that chained a woman's arms over her head and forced her legs apart.

He pushed the door open slowly. Then flipped on the light. She saw it immediately.

Large and square, it occupied its own platform in the middle of the room, with wires extending out of it. It resembled a TV. "What does it do?"

"You don't know?" He peered at her. "It's a TV! A new TV, Ina!" he exclaimed. He joggled her arm, grinning. Then he reached down and produced a clicker. "Turn it on. I'm getting a new couch, too."

Yes, of course it was just a TV. It was obviously a TV. She could have laughed at her own obtuseness. How sad that this is what he wanted!

"Well, you needed a new one."

"It's for us," he replied coolly.

She pushed a button and the surface flooded with light. On the screen, human figures looked snipped out of something as clean-edged as aluminum foil. An old movie was showing that featured a family of eccentrics sitting around a Christmas table. Ina pushed the arrow and a biography show came on, blaring, chronicling the life of a 1980s sitcom actress. She clicked again. At each channel, an unfamiliar clarity sprang out, a world without shadows. She frankly missed the old kaleidoscopic blur.

Jack took the remote and turned the TV to jazz music. "There are no commercials on this station. Isn't that great?"

"It is," she said, smiling. "It's wonderful, Jack."

He poured red wine. A resinous, bass sax played. She went into the kitchen and unwrapped the salmon steak. It was so fresh that it had just the faintest, almost sweet aroma. She moved slowly, as if even here she had to accommodate the new television.

At two in the morning, at last, she lay in his bed waiting. He was in the bathroom, brushing his teeth. She breathed deeply, almost panting. The thing she wanted to know was waiting at the end of dawn. The thing that Cavafy knew. The secret about sex. She was going to scrape through the surface of it. At the clank of his belt buckle a moan escaped her. And then at some point later in the night she was groggy and still aroused and nestled into him. The roar of garbage trucks shook the room. It was still dark.

"Is that three nine workers or nine three workers?" he remarked conversationally, in a voice like Elmer Fudd. She opened her eyes. He was deeply asleep. Later he said, "Weren't you going to be wearing a policewoman's uniform?" And then, "Two tickets for an overnight cruise . . ."

So, even in his sleep, he hadn't forgotten her! And he hadn't forgotten sex. She was surprised and felt guilty.

The next time she found herself conscious, the shades had brightened. What was the thing she was waiting to discover? It still hadn't arrived. She purposely slowed her breathing to summon sleep. "One," she counted, and then "one" again, clearing her mind by returning to the same originating number. When she awoke again, the shades were squares of ivory. Sensing that she'd stirred, Jack wrapped his arm around her and pulled her toward him. A crash resounded—glass shattering. An intruder! He jumped up and went running. Her body prickled all over. Silence. After a few minutes he returned. "It was nothing," he said. "You know those boxes I store over the kitchen cabinets? Well, one fell for some reason and knocked a spoon to the floor."

"Oh."

"I'm going to make us some coffee. You stay sleeping."

Knives of light flanked the window shade, standing on point. She felt a great disappointment. It was late morning. She looked into the burning light, liking how it made her eyes sting and then blaze. It felt good to mortify them.

"Would you wait a moment?" she said. "There's something I want to tell you. Nothing bad! It's just that, I really thought . . ." She shut her lids; twin orange spikes stood on a field of green. "If I stayed over, I'd discover something. I thought—and this might make you sad . . . " She opened her eyes and turned to face him. "That I wouldn't need to stay over again."

He nodded, serious.

"But I learned that it isn't like that. I feel like I want to just as much—or more—than before."

"But that's so sad," he said. "That you thought you'd get it out of your system."

She shrugged, and looked again at the piercing beams.

"That's like saying that you thought because you had one meal you wouldn't be hungry anymore. Sex doesn't work like that. It isn't a piece of information. It's a need."

She suddenly understood quite clearly what she'd expected to learn by staying over. It wasn't about sex, really. She thought she'd learn that he was fraudulent, that he had a secret self that was manipulative, oblivious, and cold; this hidden self would be revealed during the unguarded hours of the night. She'd discover that he had a kind of inanimate mechanism deep inside him, that he himself was somehow at his core meretricious, unfeeling, merely serving his own needs. She'd see this and be free of him.

But no, he was for real.

Coffee with half-and-half, cigarettes, a box of bittersweet chocolates, blue Stilton on four whole-wheat biscuits, two big navel oranges—she would like a picture of that table. The radiators clanked and rattled; they were in a tropical country far from the city. She sat in a sheer black bra under a stretchy black camisole, and her underpants. He wore just his flannel boxers.

"This is so wonderful," Ina said, helping herself to a chocolate.

"Isn't it like this for you all the time, at home?"

She was surprised by his naïveté, that he thought married life could be like this—but then she thought, what if he's right and I'm the naïve one?

"This reminds me of my girlfriend Stella's apartment when I was growing up. Her parents had these parties," she remarked. "The best part was the morning after."

Jack smiled, listening.

Would she ever be as happy again as she was now, she wondered.

"I slept on an air mattress next to Stella's bed," she told him. "We'd stumble out, and the family was already sitting around the dining table—her mother and father, her aunt, who was very sophisticated, and Stella's older sister, who had studied art history in Florence.

"The table was laid out with leftovers—usually a runny Brie, and a hunk of Jarlsberg, and Gorgonzola. Potato chips. Garlic dip. Prosciutto. And big round purple grapes. I'd only had green grapes before, those narrow kind of rectangular ones."

"Sounds pretty great."

"It was. Show tunes were playing," said Ina. "It was the first time I heard adults listening to musicals. *Candide. A Little Night Music.* Cole Porter. *Annie Get Your Gun.* I remember sitting with them one morning, when it struck me. I felt, *This is the whole point of being an adult.*"

Jack nodded.

"And now, this feels just like that," said Ina. "It feels like the whole point of being an adult is to get to have this.

"My parents were so cautious," she continued. "They gave you the sense that you were always doing the right thing if you were studying. Whereas Stella's family believed the opposite, that sensual pleasure was not the enemy of life but one of its values. Mrs. Partella had taped a snippet of paper to the fridge: 'The desires of the heart are as crooked as corkscrews.' She'd cut it out of *The New Yorker*. Her message seemed to be that it was worth it to follow all the crooked bends."

Ina recalled being back home from Stella's family, and sitting in silence beside her sister Violet at the white Formica desk. Tomorrow was school. Her stomach hurt. How many hours had she wasted on show tunes?

"I like that time after a party, too," said Jack. "Once I visited friends in the Hamptons and the whole week was like that, with odd bits of fantastic food left around, and people deciding to cook supper in the middle of the night. And I actually thought, 'I'm good at this.'" He laughed, sounding, she thought, like the privileged son of a movie star. "Good at relaxing."

She didn't comment, although what he described seemed to her simply being dissolute. He hadn't grown up fired with the urgent need to work the way she and her brothers and sister had, as if work redeemed one's life and gave it meaning, and so his Hamptons week seemed nothing to be proud of. She remained silent, though; she never concerned herself with traits of his that would bother her if this were not an affair.

"And you're getting much better at relaxing," he said, and straightened the strap of her bra.

In the late afternoon she returned home, and moved numbly around the apartment, putting her clothes in the laundry bag and bathroom cabinet. Miss Marple meowed and meowed. Ina fixed a cup of coffee and then went down to Key Food to shop for supper.

But the door didn't creak open until close to 11:00 P.M. Simon wore a rumpled, blue button-down shirt and loose trousers. "How did your meeting go?" she asked. She went over, but something in his demeanor stopped her from kissing him.

"Fine," he said. "Tell me: how was your trip?"

Ina had showered and changed. "Nice. I'm very tired."

"You didn't leave me a number. I had no way to reach you."

"Didn't I? We were at a Holiday Inn in Meriden."

He watched. "Did you do that on purpose?"

"No, baby." She turned and walked into the kitchen. "Just thoughtless. I'm sorry." She swiveled the oven's control, heard the suction catch. She'd reheat his supper. Her fingertips vibrated, an almost subliminal shiver.

"If you want to be apart, just say so," he said. "I'll pay for your rent for a year—a thousand dollars a month for a studio. After that, you're on your own."

She was shocked and terrified. His words seemed so abrupt. Her bones jammed against one another. She couldn't breathe. There was no space in her stomach or lungs. She kept shaking her head. "I don't want that," she blurted. "I love you, Simon."

"That may well be," he replied.

"I love you and I don't want to be apart." She felt toward

him a great baffling tenderness. It felt lodged in her like a bone in her heart. This was love, she knew, although it was painful. What she felt for Jack was a pure monochrome. When she was with Simon, she pretended that Jack didn't exist, and he seemed not to. But Simon was always real to her and she always felt toward him this great cherishing.

She drew near to kiss him, and when she was very close he jerked back, as if he'd scented something.

"I can't trust you," he said. He rushed into the living room and yanked the big square peach-colored cushions up off the couch, and hauled them into the front room. He threw them down on the floor. "I'm not hungry," he said. "I need to be apart." He shut the door.

In the living room, she sat quite still. She turned the lights off and returned to the stripped, hard coil foundation bench of the couch and sat there, cotton-tongued. She remained there, immobile.

But two hours later he stood in the doorway. He didn't say anything but went back into the front room, leaving the door open. She followed him in and lay down behind him on the couch cushions, his body hot and sweaty in his office shirt. The cushions were wedged into the narrow room, the foam so rigid that it buckled and jutted up at an angle. For a long time she lay clasping him from behind, her eyes open. The streetlight cast a powdery white haze that converted everything to metal—the wood undersurface of the desk, the rolling chair with its circular seat and lozenge-like backrest, and Simon's body, too, the back of his neck and his crumpled white office shirt—all appeared made of steel. There came the tuneless whistling of a man walking outside in the street.

She set her cheek against his back and eventually drifted off. During the night he took her hand. "Oh, Ina," he said, with exhaustion and mournfulness.

She said nothing.

He said, "I want to believe you."

"Then do. Please."

Simon was silent, his head tilted up, looking out toward the building opposite, which was lit by the streetlight's gluey glow. Above that stretched the chalky city sky into which full dark never came. He tapped her hand, acknowledging that he was glad she was holding him.

"What did Atkinson say?" she asked softly.

"Put me back on the rollout. Elana's people will report to me."

"Ha! Wow. Excellent."

"Yeah," he said. "Although," he added, "not to piss off Suzanne, I still have the responsibilities she gave me—the strategic thinking, the communication duties."

"Can you do all that?" She kept her tone level, so he wouldn't feel undermined.

"Atkinson put his confidence in me," he said stiffly, "I'm not going to let him down."

Simon's skin seemed silvery blue, oddly luminous. He was almost as slender now as when they'd first met.

"I'm really proud of you."

He squeezed her hand and nodded.

The room wobbled nauseatingly. She had expected there would be some liberating revelation from staying over, from staying the whole night. She would have cracked sex open and grabbed its message, as if it were a fortune cookie. She would discover that Jack was insincere, manipulative. But that hadn't happened. He was not a fraud.

She no longer had any idea how she could leave him.

Chapter 28

Eye-nah!" sang George, as if wagging a finger at someone playing hooky—although in fact she'd been phoning and leaving messages for him all weekend. It was noon on Tuesday. Across the street, the history professor stood framed in the window, sharpening yellow pencils; she held each aloft before either inserting it back into the machine or setting it aside. "What's the matter?" asked George. "You've been calling so much."

"Things are okay now," she responded. "And in some ways, actually, everything's wonderful—in some ways things are better than wonderful, in fact. But where've you been?"

"Oh, so much happened. I was in a scary place. And I learned so much about myself."

She laughed. "You sound like Dorothy in *The Wizard of Oz.*"

"It wasn't good." His tone was serious. "I was at a place I found online. You know I like to explore erotic geographies—"

"English, please."

He took a breath. "Sometimes I like to be in control. Other times not."

He'd never told her this. "I discovered so much. And isn't that what you're supposed to do when you go to the underworld—come back with a treasure? Remember how Psyche was supposed to retrieve a box of beauty? So she could have Eros back."

The story had a vaguely familiar ring. Ina bent forward. "And did she find what she wanted in the underworld?"

"I don't recall. She got her husband back, though. And you?" he added abruptly. "How are you? Seeing Manhattan?" It seemed clear he didn't want to discuss his own activities further.

"I stayed over. It was beautiful."

"Really?" He did not sound charmed.

"Yes, and I told him all about this family that's always been significant to me, the Partellas. Stella Partella—"

"But Ina, you have to stop! Remember in the beginning you said you'd stay clear—that this would only be a fling? You're being as unclear as possible. You should stop seeing Jack right now and get into therapy."

"I will soon."

"Darling," he said. "Soon is never."

"It's not so simple." She swiveled from the window to eliminate any chance of seeing the professor, whose fault this whole entire situation seemed suddenly, ridiculously, to be. "I can't put my reasons into words yet."

"Hm. What I hate," George continued, "is all your sneaking around, and that Simon gets to be the pristine one. I hate how he sticks it all on you. It took two of you to make this problem."

Ina sighed, unable to see how the current situation was Simon's fault. Nor what exactly he'd stuck on Ina. And yet in fact there did seem to be something clinging to her, something dark and sticky pressed sneakily onto her back.

After she hung up, Ina searched until she located her battered copy of *The Hero with a Thousand Faces*. It was in the corner, under a pile of books. She brushed off a skein of blue dust that wafted like a goat's beard. Surprisingly, there was nothing in the volume about Psyche. Ina brought her laptop into the living room, the wires dragging clumps of spidery lint. She needed to know if Psyche got her underworld beauty.

Beneath the bright winter windows, she read that Psyche and her husband Eros lived a marvelous life in the dark. Psyche had agreed never to see her mate. But one night she lit a candle and glimpsed his celestial beauty for an instant before a drop of wax scalded him awake, and he fled. To find him, Psyche had to go to the underworld to fetch beauty, as George had told her, in return for which her mother-in-law would reveal Eros' location. Psyche did get the box of underworld beauty, Ina discovered. But she made a mistake. She looked inside. The container actually held a deathly sleep, to which the girl succumbed. At long last Eros awoke her with a touch of his arrow. Ina raised her eyebrows. Paging Dr. Freud.

But what is underworld beauty, Ina wondered. Surely not a benumbed sleep, whatever the stories say.

She read on and discovered that, as the reward for her quest, Psyche was given a drink—the ambrosia that renders humans immortal.

She typed in a word. The screen answered: "Chartreuse was invented by a 16th century alchemist as an attempt to create *aqua vitae*. Its color comes from the plant's chlorophyll, and it's made by the Carthusian monks near Grenoble, France."

So, Jack had been right. It was a monastery drink. The cat bounded up, her spine protruding, and her coat slightly greasy, sticking out in spatulate clumps. Ina would need to cut those. She gave the creature a kiss on the head, and read:

"*Aqua vitae* was believed to restore the youth of the aged, endow animation to the dead, and be a key ingredient in the creation of the philosopher's stone. The monks intended their liqueur to be used as a medicine."

She submitted a final inquiry, in honor of Mrs. Partella, who celebrated those intoxicated by life.

The familiar line assembled. But the words on the screen gave her a surprise. Wasn't the speaker a merry Bacchus?

Apparently not. The poem was emblazed with the title: "Death's Echo." It wasn't at all a joyful god who was calling the tune.

The desires of the heart are as crooked as corkscrews,
Not to be born is the best for man;
The second-best is a formal order,
The dance's pattern; dance while you can.

Dance, dance, for the figure is easy,
The tune is catching and will not stop;
Dance till the stars come down from the rafters;
Dance, dance, dance till you drop.

Chapter 29

Every day she went over earlier. Four o'clock. Three. Riding the train to Jack, she read in the newspaper that on a mountaintop in Arizona a cult was celebrating the end of the world, all the sanctified souls ascending. The Nasdaq had climbed a miraculous 85 percent in the past year, exceeding the record for any index in the history of the stock market. Opposite her, a man with boots that tapered past the toes to the width of butter knives wore a black paper top hat. A girl napped against his shoulder, her silver harlequin mask imparting a look both generic and mystical. On Third Avenue a bare-chested man in a green plastic lei raced past Ina, hooting, pursued by three female demons in rhinestone tiaras.

On the train back, panic gouged up in her. She tried to stifle the awareness that her life had become desperate and mechanical, a matter of racing between apartments. She must not live this way in the new century. The morning before Christmas she went into her study and dug out the little yellow notebook that contained sentences of Jack's. If only she could determine how to let this book free her. Why were Jack's words so transporting when he said them but inane and dead when set on the page? Why must she keep going back? Her eyes fell on a sentence: "I have no respect for drug visions."

Ha! That sounded like Violet: curmudgeonly, severe. "How judgey," as Aurelia or even Theodore might say. Yet they were Ina's very own words. She recalled writing them. She found a pen on her desk and inquired again why some people are capable of being transformed by their epiphanies.

They believe in the value of what they see, her hand explained. *They accept the validity of marmalade skies and kaleidoscope eyes, the pleasure dome and cavernous rivers that run measureless to man, the pennywhistle of the modem inviting you to go out and dance.*

How to believe in the virtue of her own intoxicated visions? How to believe in the value of distortion? Shaking her head, she buried the book back in the drawer.

On Christmas Day, she went to church with Simon. She liked the service, its comprehensibility and length and direct talk of love, and the music that sounded like shafts of God's majesty resonating. Simon's family had never exchanged gifts at Christmas. His father used to lead the boys on silent walks; that had seemed to him a fit way to celebrate the birth of the Lord—appreciating what God had created. She and Simon rode the 63 bus to Prospect Park and quietly pointed out things they wanted the other to notice: a nest balanced high in the branches, a green wood bench with a plaque on it honoring someone who had loved this meadow, and even, when it arrived for their journey back, the 63 bus itself, which had only the driver inside.

On New Year's Eve, she and Simon ate dried pineapple chunks and salted cashews, sitting in their living room. She wore green glitter glasses in the shape of 2000. On TV, two million people thronged Times Square.

As the countdown began, Simon held the protesting cat, Miss Marple.

"Are you worried?" asked Simon. His white work shirt hung loose. He was very slender and muscular, with anxiety in his eyes.

She wasn't really.

"I'm not! Don't you be!" she said. "We'll bring Miss Marple

with us to the other side! You, me, and Miss Marple in space suits!" Simon laughed. The giant second-hand of a clock was creeping upward to meet the small hand already stuck on midnight. The catastrophe would happen soon. She wanted life to change. She wanted to step into the unknowable, with everything wiped clean.

She took the perplexed cat, and Simon held her in his arms. They stood in front of the TV.

"Ten, nine, eight . . ." She breathed shallowly. At midnight all might go dark. Explosions could blast. A chill ran over her skin, as if it were being painted with rubbing alcohol. She wondered if, absurdly, the building they were standing in might itself crack and fall.

Three, two—Simon clenched her hard, and she clenched him hard back—one, Happy New Year! In the distance, muffled fireworks thumped, remote popping and crackles. Simon and Ina kissed. Everywhere car horns blared, a sustained chorus, dissonant, half-moaning, as if celebrating and protesting the new year at once. There had been no roaring bombs. All was as it had been before. On TV the crowd danced. In the morning, *The New York Times* had a single banner headline: 1/1/00.

She was still in her life.

Chapter 30

Sylvia, do you remember inviting a movie star?" Her father lifted his spatula as if in benediction. He stood in front of the electric broiler in her parents' tiny kitchen.

Ina's face prickled. She turned away and walked to the foyer closet. Visiting her parents had become difficult but she was trying to still do the important things.

"When did you do your hair?" asked her mother.

"It's just a few highlights. Last week," boomed her voice, for she'd stuck her head into the closet as she hung up her jacket. This new jacket was excessively lightweight. It was of a silvery synthetic with stylish bold lapels and a tapered waist, with something of David Bowie's futurism about it. Jack loved it. She would have felt deceitful, continuing to wear her old grubby turquoise puffer to her parents; it now seemed like a costume. She'd bought this new jacket in Chinatown, where she'd sat with her hair folded into innumerable foil packets, and emerged with her hair streaked a fashionable blonde.

Her parents were still staring when she returned. "It suits you wonderfully," said her father. He regarded her with warm, unabashed scrutiny. "Although, I don't know, this makeup—it's a harder look."

She nodded, ducking her face.

"You never used to be interested in your appearance," said her mother.

She shrugged. She felt as if she'd grown unseemingly large,

sitting at her old familial table. Here she was, a big, sturdy, life-devouring daughter.

"Maybe it's that you finally have the time." Ina's mother sounded unconvinced.

Over supper Ina's mother mentioned that she had been forced to take one day a week off, a cost-reducing measure for the business. As a result she was home more, and had put on weight.

"I didn't know your hours were cut back."

"You're never home so we don't talk as much." Her mother's tone was factual.

"You're staring, Ma!" Ina exclaimed.

"How is your work coming?" her mother replied.

"Fine."

"I always wanted you to go to law school," she said with a wistful smile.

"Maybe I should have," Ina conceded for the first time in her life. "I could have supported myself more definitely. Academia is iffy unless you get tenure."

"But you have Simon to take care of you!" came her father's voice. He was carrying over a plate of butter pinwheel cookies with crusted jelly-dab centers. He'd poured himself a cup of tea.

"A woman has got to be able to support herself," said her mother. "There are no guarantees." She clasped Ina's hand with one whose fingerprints had worn down. "You're still young."

"Finish your book," declared her father. "If you can't manage it, let Simon have a crack. He's really a Renaissance man. Some of the best ideas in that article you wrote about that Jesuit poet—they had the ring of Simon's mind."

Ina smiled, exasperated. She could still recall the long winter afternoons when she studied Gerard Manley Hopkins, during which even the grim apartment in which they then lived seemed infused with the grandeur of God. It seemed detectable in the sound of their parakeet, Gabriel, splitting a seed, the blue graphite sheen of the blunt-tipped pencil in her hand, the gray sky lowering over Chicago, and even the dressmaker's dummy rising primly in the ground-floor window of the building opposite like a diva drawing herself up before breaking into song.

"Simon's mind!" said Ina. "Don't you think I have ideas, Dad?"

"Sure," said her father. "But Simon's got a certain originality in his thinking."

"I do too."

"Don't go out so much, then," said her mother. "Stay home." Her mother's eyes widened and her face went white.

Something caught in Ina's throat, and she said hurriedly, "Simon isn't a scholar." Her mother ignored her.

Her father had gotten up and was starting to wrap some of the cookies in wax paper.

"Please come in here a moment," said her mother abruptly. Her chair scraped as she stood. She walked ahead of Ina across the apartment and into her bedroom, which had been the girls' room. It was painted a cheerful yellow, its windows decorated with puffy white tulle curtains. It held two narrow beds from Ina's own girlhood.

"Darling," said her mother. "You're making a terrible mistake."

"What?"

Her mother lifted her fingertips, and Ina blushed to the roots of her hair. Her mother was almost eighty. She had a different view of things.

"It came to me just now," she said in a tone of wonder. "Simon is such a good man. Decent, caring. He's like a son."

"Don't, Ma," urged Ina. She got on one knee on the rug before her mother, and yet a sensation of relief went through her—her mother knew! Ina felt more real, more whole, and yet guilt-stricken for paining her mother. Still, if her father heard, he'd feel horrified, and it would get back to Simon. "Please don't worry. Everything's fine."

"It isn't fine," said her mother bitterly. "I've seen more of life."

Ina hung her head but forced herself to say: "Ma, this doesn't concern you."

"I love you so much, darling," exclaimed her mother. "You're the only healthy daughter I've got. The only one with a chance for happiness." She shook her head. "In my office, Ina, there are many divorced women. Diane. Inga. They're lonely. And it's hard making ends meet."

"I'm not divorcing Simon!"

Her mother gazed at Ina. "He'll divorce you."

"He won't, Ma."

"Ever in dreamland. Your best chance is to stop now. Oh," her mother said, "how could I be happy knowing I didn't persuade you? How could I be happy if you ruin your life? Please, tell me you won't see him again."

"Well," Ina began evenhandedly.

Her mother got up swiftly and walked out of the room, leaving the door open wide. Ina felt exposed and ashamed, kneeling in front of the bed on the thin green-yellow carpet. She rose slowly, stiffly, and went into the living room.

"What's wrong?" asked Ina's father.

"Nothing!" said Ina. She said to her mother: "You might be right."

Her mother quirked up a corner of her mouth. "Of course I'm right." Ina viewed her as one of the shrewd, street-smart empresses of the Bronx, the last of that generation who grew up poor, with survivors' grit in their soul and Yiddish swirling in their ears, and who strode out to meet life on its own terms.

But her mother's terms were not her own. She didn't want the older woman's judgment. She would miss talking to her mother, she decided twenty minutes later, the chill wind reaching down her back as she waited for the 7 bus, rocking from foot to foot. She drew her thin silver jacket close, shivering, and the thought came to her, with a spasm of worry, that this was precisely what addicted people did: separate from loved ones who disagreed with them, telling themselves the others didn't understand.

A few weeks later the new semester began, and a familiar voice arrested her on the stairwell, calling her name.

"Marguerite!" Ina said, swiveling, "I'm late to class!"

"I know you are."

The department chair stood far below. She resembled a battered king on a chess board in her drab columnar coat and pompommed hat. "And I'm leaving the building. But I want to talk. Please tell your students to wait five minutes."

As promised, Marguerite had arranged for her to teach just two courses, back to back, two sections of a Gen. Ed. class called simply "The Interpretation of Literature." When the students asked if they could submit a creative response instead of an analytical paper, she gave an emphatic no. She arrived five minutes late and held them an extra five, blaming the railroad schedule. She'd hoped to avoid Marguerite.

In her office, the chairwoman regarded Ina. She wore gray cat's-eye glasses beneath a hairstyle fixed with pins that clasped her hair tightly to her head and that looked painful to slide in. On the corner of her somewhat messy desk stood a rick-racked can stuffed with pens and magic markers, and, behind her on a shelf, the little TV. "Are you well?" inquired Marguerite.

"I'm fine, thank you."

Ina was aware she'd grown thin. She was now a size zero. In fact, her new slenderness imbued her with joy. She felt guilty that Marguerite misunderstood.

"Because I want you to know there's no shame if you're not."

In Ina's peripheral vision stood the office chair on which Marguerite's daughter often sat. Misshapen as an old baseball mitt, it had been repaired with gray and silver tape, and sagged to the side.

Marguerite mused: "It would have been better if Sybille had come to me outright."

"I'm okay," said Ina.

Marguerite smiled as if it pained her. "Ina, we both know it's not my job to worry about you or to press you. It's your responsibility, whether or not you do your work."

"True." Ina shifted onto her other foot. The shoe seemed to be driving a spike into her heel, and, when she shifted, the bottom of her foot was slick.

"It's just that I hate wasted opportunities. It seems so unnecessary considering how much went into getting this far."

Ina stared. Could she seriously think that Ina wouldn't ultimately deliver?

"I need your work by April 1. That's the very last date I can give you. April 1, understand? Otherwise I won't be able to read it in time. This is just reality."

Ina smiled in gratitude. "Of course! Thank you!" she exclaimed. It was actually fantastic. All could still be well. Marguerite's confidence in her had been seriously eroded by her missing two deadlines but she would redeem herself.

The chairwoman stood up and pressed Ina's wrist, which seemed even more intimate than shaking her hand. Marguerite's hand was very warm, almost moist. And then Marguerite did an odd thing. She ducked her head to look at Ina straight in the eyes, as if to step beyond their roles into something more intimate. "April 1." To Ina's surprise, she added the word, "Please."

"I will," said Ina hoarsely, before rushing off.

Chapter 31

Yet still she saw him. Although a change happened the next time Ina visited. It began when Jack played "Isn't That the Life?"—a duet between the lead and the little boy in *Goodbye, Columbus* who's obsessed with Gauguin's paintings. "Mangoes and cherries, with plenty to share," sang Jack, the piano ringing out high Polynesian harmonies. "Some bright morning I shall fly away there!"

Ina echoed "I shall fly away there." She was thinking of Violet. In Violet's dreams, was she free of her body's restrictions?

He came over and attempted to tuck himself beside her in the chair, squeezing in affectionately. "Such a beautiful melody," she said, then added, "I'm sorry that I have to leave in twenty-five minutes." He shook his head as if he had water in his ears. Then he jumped up and crossed the room, getting away. Mystified, she followed.

"I feel like I don't know what's really going on!"

"What?" She grabbed his hand, which he pulled away.

"When you're going, when you're coming back. What's really happening. I'm not in the loop. The other person isn't in the loop, either. You're the only one in the loop."

But she'd been being *kind*! Allowing him to enjoy the immersive pleasure of their afternoon together. Sparing him the anxiety of watching the minutes tick away. How had he not understood? "I didn't want you to be upset," she explained.

"I'm allowed to be upset," he replied. "And angry too.

I'm allowed my reaction. That's no justification for hiding the truth."

Oh.

The awareness came that she'd been condescending. Creating a fantasy for him.

"You need to be a whole lot more forthcoming."

She saw his point, although it frightened her. Even the objects in the room seemed to acquire a new relationship to one another. "You're right," she slowly agreed.

And in the days that followed, the stolid days of February, she began to train herself. She explored ways to tell a difficult truth. She discovered that it was possible to shut a certain psychic door, shift the atmosphere in the antechamber thus created, and then fling open the inner door behind which the truth stood. She just had to brace herself a moment before the cold honest statement was revealed. Then she and Jack could walk around the statement as if it were an ice sculpture. Before them stood the simple truth, which they could now share. She must resist the impulse to dissolve into apology. Apology confused her and tempted her to deny reality.

Sometimes when Jack sighed or sat disconsolate, a spasm of fury blazed through her. The uncharitable feeling she had was, *I had to deal with it; you should too. Buck up!*

At other times, seeing Jack woebegone, hunched in his chair, she was saturated with sadness, and stood in his doorway feeling as if she could sob until she was shredded.

By a strange synchronicity, at this time of greater honesty with Jack, Simon seemed to be watching her more closely, as if he sensed something was different. He surveyed her from the kitchen doorway in the dark early morning as she steamed brussels sprouts or cauliflower. The droplets of humidity swelling on the glass pot lid seemed also to be on her hot, feverish neck. She despised this self-consciousness, this guilt, this feeling of being surveilled. She resolved to be home by 6:00 P.M. each day.

That meant leaving Jack's no later than five—or even earlier, to beat the stuck and slow trains of rush hour. Her afternoons with Jack got shorter. In this more restricted time period, it felt as if some itchy spiderweb of self-consciousness clung to her. She couldn't lose herself. A clock had moved into her head. One night, impulsively, she told Simon that she was going to attend the regional MLA conference in Philadelphia and stay overnight. She had not thought she would attend this year since she wasn't presenting, she told him, but had changed her mind. She should go to keep up her academic connections.

Still, her stomach quivered during the allocated evening at Jack's apartment. At a door slamming, she jumped. She announced, "This has got to be the last time I'm staying over."

"But why?" His voice was raspy with mournfulness.

"It makes me too anxious." She sucked in her lips so as not to apologize. In her head she counted to five.

"But that's so sad."

"It is what it is," she stated flatly—a phrase of Simon's she'd never liked before but now appreciated for its syllogistic beauty.

Jack was still asleep when she awoke the next morning at 10:00 A.M. She got up quietly and pulled on her skirt and cotton turtleneck. Downstairs, she bought a coffee at the bagel shop and seated herself. The mirror beside her reflected a banquet of pastries and smoked fish. She turned so as get away from the figure in the glass, a sleepy slender woman sipping coffee—herself. Young mothers pushed strollers with spokes that glittered like roulette wheels.

She was thinking about Simon with a perspective previously impossible. If she went back to bed the thoughts would vanish. For how long hadn't things been right between them?

Once, early in their courtship, Simon had been a pale lean figure hurrying along Houston Street while she—a suddenly squat-feeling woman—lumbered behind. He'd been nineteen.

He was excited by the city, and rushed up the Greenwich Village sidewalk farther and farther ahead of her. Tired and frustrated, she finally sat down on a bench at a city bus stop and watched. Two-thirds of the way up the block, he stopped. Then pivoted around. He ran back, calling, "Are you okay?"

"You're in your own world."

"I'm not!" he exclaimed. "I was totally aware of your being with me—but then you weren't!"

She'd laughed—he could always make her laugh—and they'd gone into a pizza joint where he ate slice after slice, sitting in a plastic-walled pavilion on MacDougal. She'd wanted him to have a treat before the long subway ride to her parents' apartment. The pavilion offered a blurry view of the city, the orange oil dripping from the pizza onto the paper, making it translucent, his knee bobbing, and the pavilion glowing from lit yellow cabs as if the walls themselves were grease paper.

She'd felt essential to him but unremarkable, like a person's own arm. She'd known this all along but hadn't allowed herself to register it. There was much she hadn't let herself register. She had been like the plastic of the pavilion, bleary with running colors, unable to let any image draw into focus. And yet all that while Ina had wanted to be seen. She knew this now from her time with Jack.

Ina scribbled fast, freewriting in her notebook. Out of the corner of her eye she glimpsed something ugly: herself as an ample-cheeked girl with a gob of yellow hair. Weird, because Ina was actually thinner than she'd ever been. And yet, the mirror world figure was all appetitive girth. Dismayed, Ina clamped her fingers underneath the chair and, with a savage yank, swung her body away from the shining surface.

After Simon had come to live with her in Chicago the second year of her program, she had much less time for herself. To tide him over until he got an engineering job, he DJed for a local small country-music radio station, sitting close to the mic and speaking confidingly to it, using all his voices. Mostly he played early bluegrass, and sometimes, after spinning a record, just for the fun of it, he did his own rendition, with his own banjo picking. She tuned in when she could, hoping to hear his beautiful, often melancholic tunes, and, when he did perform, it amazed her to think of all the other women and men in the city hearing his intimate playing. But the gig was just a few hours in the evening, and the rest of the time he was around, waiting for her. She found that she couldn't think deeply unless she was alone in the apartment.

One Saturday morning when she had a paper due that Monday, desperate to have the place to herself so she could work, she wept in the bathroom. He tapped on the door. "What's wrong?" She told him, and he became frantic. "I'm not welcome in my own home!" he cried out. He threw things into a valise and rushed off, clasping the fabric suitcase, dressed in an old plaid shirt, his skin greenish. Pangs of love went through her like blows to her chest. She set off after him and ultimately tracked him down in front of a peeling, scuffed tan building. He had been investigating renting an apartment there. But this couldn't possibly be right, she'd felt. He couldn't possibly be meant to live by himself in this sad moldy building!

"Please, Simon," she said, hugging his slack body. "I'm sorry. Come home."

"I can't. It's all wrong."

And they'd wandered the streets together. At last Ina promised that she would be better, although even at the time she didn't quite know what "better" meant. And so she'd lived in a kind of muddle-headedness, smiling, trying to be pleasing, trying not to hurt his feelings, truly loving to be with him but also feeling as if she were somewhat mechanized, not quite there.

The ramshackle depressive moldering abode resembled Simon's parents' house, she became aware, gazing out at First Avenue. The linoleum house stood in his past. She was trying to rescue him from what had already happened, the sadness and sense of abandonment already inside him.

"Come *on*!" exclaimed a woman attempting to sidle past. She was balancing a tray with coffees and sandwiches.

Ina grimaced an apology. She clasped the seat of her chair and made a swinging lurch. The creature in the mirror flew at her—fleshy-cheeked, lank-haired, surging, greedy. Violet! With her rages and mammoth breasts and her violent torrents of tears. The gorgon she'd vowed never to be.

Her pages were covered in messy writing. Ink splotches shone like dark stars. She didn't want to return to being the frightened, morose girl tracking after Simon. If this meant being like the woman in the glass, so be it. She shut the book and tucked it under her arm, satisfied for the first time in months by a morning's work.

"Where were you?" groaned Jack.

"Downstairs at the bagel shop."

"Did you bring me anything?"

She lifted up a crackling brown bag, and unpacked a burnished gold smoked whitefish the size of an opera purse. Smoked salmon rolled onto white glazed paper. Salty creamy squares of Muenster cheese with edges a crosshatched orange, and a tub of Tastee cream cheese. Four bagels, still warm, and a jelly-centered Linzer cookie glowing like stained glass.

"What were you doing downstairs for so long?"

"Thinking."

"You take a long time to think."

"I have a new thought once every fifteen years."

"Aw, you have lots of good thoughts, Ina."

She smiled. When she was fifteen she'd discovered studying, and when she was twenty-eight she'd married Simon, and at forty-one she met Jack. At this rate, if she was lucky, she might have three or four more new ideas in her life, and it would be a good life.

Chapter 32

The playwright's mouth drooped at the corners. His soulful, forceful dark eyes were in shadow under his protruding brow. He looked truculent, standing on the sunstruck beach, arms crossed in a way that made his biceps bulge, a man in his early thirties who'd already won a Pulitzer. Ina studied him, her leg bouncing. This is what it looks like to be committed to telling your truth. He wasn't actually sure of himself. He was uneasy. She found it unexpectedly reassuring.

Ina let the biography fall shut. Then she left her study, stepped into the hallway, and quietly opened the door to the bedroom. Simon lay on sheets yellow as marigolds and marked with a grid of big dark squares resembling plant cells. So dear! He said her name, and turned toward her.

"Could we talk a little?" she asked. She leaned against the wall by the door.

"What's going on?" Simon sat up groggily.

On the pillow beside him, the cat looked hot and lank as a worn fur hat, settled within herself. Ina felt slightly delirious, and nauseated.

"Honey," she said, "I want to tell you some things I've been feeling. And you could tell me what's going on with you, Simon. For just an hour, say. Just until eleven." She jutted her chin toward the VCR clock. Surely they didn't need to be afraid of just one hour?

Simon was watching her. He was fully awake.

"It's just that . . . " And here her voice snagged. "It's that when I see that woman downstairs being kissed by her boyfriend, I feel bad. I feel like her boyfriend finds her sexy. I don't feel like you really like to kiss." She gazed at him, nearly hyperventilating.

"But I do." He shoved the pillows behind him.

If she could just tell him, the situation would change, would *have* to change! Feeling reckless, somewhat out of her mind, she continued, "I've felt so ugly, Simon. I've felt like I'm missing an important part of life. Like I'm not actually alive."

He gave an abrupt nod. "Come over here." He swept his arm out from his side, to indicate a place where she'd be cozy, a warm nest.

"Not yet." She leaned against the wall. "If I lie down next to you, I won't tell you."

What dizzy relief there was in flinging out the truth! Some piece of her—the censoring part—was anesthetized. She could say anything, now that she'd begun. "And it's lonely without you knowing. It's awful."

"*Are* you lonely?" He glanced at her.

"Yes."

Once she said it, she knew it was true. Jack said he loved her, but he didn't really know her. Not really. What she yearned for was to be close to Simon, who actually knew her, who had known her for years.

A plane rumbled overhead; the windows rattled and then stilled. He looked at her, not moving. Why didn't he say anything else? The plane had become a distant murmur. "Once, years ago," she said, "I heard a man call, 'Hey beautiful!' It was right here on Hicks Street, in the late afternoon. I was going off to see Janie. And, Simon, I thought the man was talking to me! But then this woman ahead of me smiled and waved back. I remember she had a pink bracelet around her wrist. I envied her so much. It had been years since I'd felt attractive to anyone."

He held himself quite rigid, and was staring at her fixedly.

She bit her lips, but, after a moment, stopped biting them. Still he remained silent.

The cat slowly extended a paw, and settled her small triangular face onto the crook of her arm. Downstairs a door screeched open. After a pause, it thumped shut. There was the clatter of a key. She pressed her tongue against her teeth.

"Simon, if you don't give me any reaction . . . " Her words came slowly; she was piecing out her understanding. "It's almost as if I haven't told you. As if I haven't said anything. I start to feel unreal."

"I don't want you to feel unreal," came his voice.

His face had acquired its old dejected expression, the thin mouth, the eyes sunk morosely in their sockets. A bolt of something—fury, perhaps cruelty—passed through her.

"As unreasonable as this is, can you try not to look so sad?"

He laughed sardonically. Then shoved the pillow behind him. "I'm allowed to let my face assume whatever expression it wants. It's just a little too controlling of you to tell me how my face should look."

"True."

Out the window, a corner of the fire escape glittered. Its black paint had cracked and buckled all over; the resulting curved segments were lit with orange rust. She exclaimed: "You've always been so disinterested in clothing. When I put on that rhinestone skirt, you make no response—"

"I feel like you're studying me for my reaction. As if you're trying to trick something out of me, to script me." He gazed at the blank TV. "That it's really not about communicating. Look, the women's magazines are full of information about how to appeal to a man. I miss sex too," he said, which surprised her although of course it shouldn't have. Since she'd been with Jack, she'd avoided sex with Simon. "I'd like us to be intimate," he added mournfully. "But you've rejected me so many times I can't do the reaching out." Yes, it was true that there were times she'd pushed his hand away from her breasts.

She didn't reply but again glanced out the window, at the dusty black paint on the fire escape, shattered into veins of orange rust.

"Why don't you just come over here?" He patted the bed and then swung his arm wide.

She did want to hug him, to hold him. "Okay."

They kissed on the lips and she crept under his arm. His body radiated heat. He hugged her, making her feel snug, tucked in. She became more and more tired. Her skin blurred into the surrounding air, a sensation of diffusion, a languid surrender to an old sweet sadness.

Alarmed, she bit the inside of her lip. She'd been falling asleep. "Let's get up."

She didn't want to drift into somnolence. She had a sudden impulse to pinch him, as if he were an insensate being or someone who out of sheer perversity withheld his reactions, hoarded them away. "Let's not sleep," she said. "Let's go out."

The original city huddled across the East River. A storybook kingdom with copper green spires, it lay dwarfed by soaring towers whose mirrored walls looked made of cloud and sky. The farther out Ina and Simon walked over the Manhattan Bridge, the louder the wind blew. Soon they trod along without speaking a word, faces buried in their lapels. A Q train came thundering by, its windows juddering as it passed. Inside, the passengers looked zoned out, music siphoning into their ears, dulled expressions on their faces. She had an impulse to scream through the glass: "Wake up! Look! React!" The train grew deafening, then abruptly flung itself away into a murmurous distance. She and Simon kept walking. About ten feet before the bridge ended, the wind ceased.

Crumbling red brick buildings appeared, sooty tenements

whose windows stood an arm's reach of the bridge. Chinatown. Empty red clay flowerpots stood stacked on one fire escape. On another, plastic clothespins clasped children's underthings. Mighty Mouse flew skyward on royal blue underpants, so close anyone on the bridge could swipe them. So, people lived normal family lives even this close to a jostling thoroughfare. They had futures, goals. Perhaps it was ludicrous, but she envied them.

"Isn't this fun that we're out?" asked Simon, nodding encouragingly as they turned onto a bustling street. On the sidewalk, wind-up plastic ducks and toy monsters clattered in a thrumming swarm in front of discount shops that also sold handbags, shopping carts, day-glo delivery man vests, tourist T-shirts.

"It's nice." She felt far from her body, which seemed made out of something paper thin, battered by the elements. It was a raw February afternoon, the sky silvery gray, the dissolved sun apparently quite low, and the pebbly surface of the buildings casting shadows in the eroded bricks, tiny blue nooks and crannies.

At Joe's Shanghai they were seated at a shared big round table of other couples and small family groups. The red type from the menu floated before her, the font expanding as her eyes seeped.

Soon a waiter thumped a reed basket down on their table. Ina held the shallow ceramic spoon to her lips and bit gently, careful not to let the hot liquid scald. The crabmeat inside the soup dumplings had a luxurious complex flavor. "How's your food?" she asked.

Simon bobbed his head, widening his eyes and smiling around his soupspoon, miming delight. The skin of her face felt drawn tight. Ina set down her implement. Several dumplings remained, but they had congealed, appearing sluglike on the lettuce leaf.

Right after lunch, she said she wanted to return home. This

time they took the subway, boarding at Canal Street. It was a tedious, dreary trip. When they climbed to the sidewalk back in Brooklyn she trudged up the street, drunk with drowsiness. He strode briskly ahead of her as he often did. She watched his green-blue chinos and white sneakers move up the pavement. He seemed in his own world. "Wait, Simon!" she called.

"I thought you were in a hurry to get home."

"You don't always have to give an excuse."

"Not an excuse. An explanation."

"Oh," she said, bewildered. "Sometimes it feels as if the first thing you do is defend yourself. I feel fended off."

"Whatever," he replied. But he made a point of walking beside her, exaggeratedly matching her step. He made an extremely scowly mouth, and she couldn't help laughing.

"See?" he said with a wink. "I'm not so terrible."

It was only dusk when they reached home, but she lay down right away on their bed. Simon unlaced her shoes and wrenched them off. As she drowsed and then woke and drowsed again, she was aware of Simon at the very end of the apartment, listening to a TV program that featured horns and Vegas gongs. It seemed peculiar that nothing had changed. No, that wasn't right. Now she was without hope, flat and empty.

Chapter 33

The days grew brighter and longer, swelling open. On the mornings Ina wasn't teaching, she woke, washed, and went to Jack's. She felt herself in the grip of a delirious nightmare. Sometimes he was asleep when she arrived, a sweaty, heavy, almost walrus-like creature in the bed, unwilling to wake up, saying, "Soon, soon," and hugging his pillow. She was wearing makeup; she was wearing a tight skirt. It was eleven o'clock in the morning. She sat on his couch listening to the beeps of the trucks going in reverse, entering the garage adjacent to his living room. On the limbs of the tree, still as bare of leaves and even bark as if it had been scraped, the starlings hopped about, creatures on amphetamines. Ina regarded the small shelf of dusty books on his wall. How had she become involved with someone who read so little? Yet when he did wake up, he was grateful she was there. At such times it seemed mean of her to judge his bookshelf. Music was his language, of course.

She left his apartment at the hour when schoolchildren flooded the streets. She followed gum-chewing parochial-school girls whose pleated plaid skirts flapped at their knees, or, on a few of them, their thighs, and boys with obviously expensive haircuts in russet blazers and ironed gray trousers, released from their elite academies on the Upper East Side. She loved to overhear them, even when what they said was rude. That was normal for their age. One day a woman with her arms full of drycleaning preceded her, and the translucent wrapping cast a ghostly, radiant shadow on the sidewalk, billowing, doubling, as if the spirit realm was close. The buds on the shrubbery had become visible, green starlike packets printed with the secrets of nature. It seemed to her strange now that she'd never been interested in astronomy or even the names of trees, as Violet had been. As a child, Ina had thought Violet foolish and even deluded for studying botanical guides and for learning about classical music, all of which had sounded alike to elementary school Ina: dull, depressing.

Ina had in many ways been a backward child, she now saw, even as she read far above her grade-school level. She had receded into a world of make-believe that was, to her apparent luck, validated by those in authority. The letters and words in books had been her friends. In the inky blue-black gleam of print on the page she caught reflections of the actual world over her shoulder. These days sometimes on her walk to the subway a kind of terror overcame her.

One afternoon at the start of March, she noticed an elderly Asian woman trudging behind a shopping wagon that was empty except for a one-gallon jug of water. The woman wore sneakers and black stretch slacks. She had a hard time drawing breath. Several paces behind her followed a middle-aged woman with a similar face, who was keeping an eye on her. Ina suddenly missed her parents, whom she had stopped visiting. She missed the way her mother rushed out into the building's gold-wallpapered corridor and actually cried out "Goody goody!" when Ina stepped off the elevator, missed the way her father patted her hand with his broad flat cool one, saying, "So wonderful to see you, darling." And she missed as well, more than this, learning things about them that they shared only now, late in life—that her father used to go horseback riding at a stables in Queens after work when he was in his twenties, or that her mother had called herself Maryanne when *New York Times* employment ads specified "Only Christians Need Apply."

"Well, I can't save them," she muttered, and heard herself.

The next afternoon, Ina took the A train and then the 24 bus the long journey to her parents' door, where she let herself in with her key.

Her mother was sitting in the living room. She looked up, startled, and shut her book. It was an old library volume, a Best Short Stories anthology from the 1940s in crackling yellow cellophane. She occupied a low square-backed, green-gold velvet chair, faintly regal. A forest of houseplants, mostly spikey iron plants with mottled thick leaves like spears, rose behind her. Ina's father was out.

"I've ended it," announced Ina, lying. She somehow felt she had a right to now. She was an adult, entitled to her own private life.

Her mother jumped up and came over quickly. Ina was surprised again by what a small person her mother had become, as if condensing into an emblem of herself.

The old woman's body trembled as they hugged. Then her mother pulled back. An ashy hint of yesterday's mascara blurred her wet eyes. "I'm so proud of you, darling. You did right."

They walked over to the dinette and sat below the murky sconce chandelier with its asterisk stars and its pear-colored light, her mother not releasing Ina's hand.

"I felt like I was sitting shiva," said her mother. "Life was so much emptier."

"Yes, emptier." But the way that Ina said these words, as if reminded of something else, made her mother glance up. She looked penetratingly at her daughter, taking her time. Blood rose to Ina's cheeks. She felt as if the skin of her cheeks would curl back, revealing something ugly. She wished she could protect her mother from knowing about her ill-sorted, compromised life; her mother deserved better. Nevertheless, she suppressed an impulse to look away.

Her mother suddenly smiled sardonically. Bitterly. After a long moment she said, "Well. I suppose you know what's best for you."

"Yes." Ina lifted her mother's hand, on which blue rivers meandered, and kissed it.

Her mother disregarded this. Her hand lay cool and moist in Ina's. "It's your life."

Again, she sounded cynical, soured, as if she were seeing Ina in a new way and didn't like the corrupted girl she saw.

"Ma, it is."

Her mother shook her head sadly. She sighed.

"But I know you want what's best for me."

"Fat lot of good that does," but then her mother laughed. When Ina's father came home from grocery shopping, the two women were sitting near one another, splitting a can of diet Shasta ginger ale and eating Stella D'Oro "S" cookies, each puffy plain cookie like a giant toggle switch.

After supper, Ina and her parents unfolded lawn chairs on the apartment terrace and surveyed Johnson Avenue. They sat three floors up. Her father had carried out a packet of early cherries from Key Food, which they ate. They watched a man in a champagne-colored SUV try to maneuver into a deceptively small spot—one that Ina and her parents had often seen drivers try to park in. It was between a fire hydrant and a driveway, so looked ample. But if you left enough space for the fire hydrant, you usually jutted into the driveway.

The SUV driver parallel parked into the spot three times, no four. Then he emerged and slammed the door with a wallop. The SUV blocked the driveway by several feet.

The driver was a bulky man in a flap cap, and Ina could hear the jingle of his keys as he strolled off swinging them like Greek worry beads. He passed a teen in an electric-pink fur vest walking a gleaming sealskin dog. The dog sprang up on him and the man shoved it off hard, hurling it. The animal squawked. The man raised his fist as if he'd punch. "Stop it, you nut job!" yelled the girl.

"Let it touch me again and it's dead!" shouted the man.

Ina's mother sighed. "Usually the father walks it. He's a music critic. Always with earphones. But he holds the leash tight. The dog's inside all day, it has excess energy. And that girl is always daydreaming. She allows the dog too much leash. Oh look, it's the Asian couple!" Her mother jerked her chin up, her expression affectionate. "Home early."

The perspective from the terrace had a pleasant theatrical quality, Ina noticed. She sipped her instant coffee.

"What are you doing for your birthday," her father asked. "Taking a trip?"

"No. I feel like staying put."

Ina's mother shifted.

"The River Café is always nice," said Ina's father.

"I don't feel the need to do anything so fancy these days."

Ina's mother sighed.

Crossing the street toward them was Mrs. Leonard, with a gray scarf tied snugly under her chin, her head thrust forward and trembling as if balanced on the tip of a cane. She was the mother of Ina's girlhood pal Lucy; they lived in the apartment next door. Lucy had once been engaged to marry when she was in her thirties, and had even bought a big white dress, but canceled at the last minute. She didn't want to abandon her widowed mother, Ina secretly believed.

Ina watched Lucy's spindly mom pick her way quickly along the pavement with her little fabric shopping bag coiled over her arm, her back hunched and her hair sprayed a lacquered black, a solitary figure radiating a percussive energy. There was a time when Ina had resented this woman. She'd abruptly concluded every visit of Ina's with the declaration "Lucy, ask your friend to go home now. Every good thing must come to an end." *Why must every good thing come to an end?*, Ina had wondered, irritated. Now she felt only sorry for this trembling figure making her way up the sidewalk.

"There's the man who collects cans," observed her father. "I have some for him." He went inside, the screen door slapping behind him.

Ina remarked, "I like the perspective from here."

"You see the whole street," said Ina's mother. "I wish the woman who lives in that first-floor apartment there would get a boyfriend. She had someone over once but it didn't take. Everyone needs someone to love. I don't want her to miss out."

"Why don't you tell her?"

Her mother harrumphed with a smile. She helped herself to another cherry.

"Ma, why were you so sad when I was little?"

Her mother turned her face away. "You remember that time?"

"Of course." Ina had been a toddler, but it had lasted a few years.

Her mother tilted her face more fully away, towards the relatively new, tall, red brick Independent Living building that occupied a far corner. "Nobody's in there. Do they think there are so many old people who want to move? It's going to stand mostly empty." She said this with a kind of vicious pride. "Look, it's been open half a year and you can see it's mostly empty."

"Ma, would you tell me about that time now?"

Her mother sighed. "Who wants to revisit the past? It's too painful."

"I do. I promise not to bring it up again."

"You and your promises."

Ina said nothing. She too turned toward the new brick edifice, eighteen stories tall. She too took pleasure in the obvious emptiness of most of the rooms, all the curtains hanging in exactly the same way, and past them, the empty gray spaces.

"They're going to lose a lot of money on that," her mother said. "In this neighborhood, people want to stay living in their own apartments."

Ina remained quiet.

"After you, I got pregnant again," said her mother. "Because the obstetrician wouldn't tie my tubes when I asked."

Ina sat very still, listening hard. She'd had no idea.

"Abortion was illegal, you know. We were going to fly to Cuba. But finally your father got a doctor to say that I would lose my mind if I had to bear this child. And so I got an abortion. But I was depressed after. So they gave me electroshock."

"Oh, Ma, I'm so sorry."

Her mother held up her hand. Don't.

"You wouldn't believe how horrible. The gray ball they put in your mouth so you don't swallow your tongue. The terror of the volts. And all these sad sack people zonked out, lolling in wheelchairs down the corridor as they're rolling you toward the room."

Ina half laughed, and tried to take her mother's hand, but her mother shook her away as if she were a fly. "Was that the worst part?"

"That was not the worst part."

Ina's mother seemed to be trying to peer into the vacant rooms of the Assisted Living Place. She was squinting hard in that direction. "It might surprise you, what the worst part was. Maybe it doesn't sound so terrible. The shock treatment would take away some of your memories. That was the most frightening part. You didn't know what would be taken, or how much. The doctors insisted they would all come back." Her mother shrugged expressively; one of her great themes was the idiocy of certain authorities.

"And did they?" asked Ina, the world going glassy a moment. She wiped her eyes, thinking of the thin gray woman she recalled sitting in their blue kitchen in the Bronx, seeming lost inside herself, searching for something, with this needy child at her feet.

Ina's mother turned toward her, smiling as if incredulous

of Ina's naïveté. Ina was struck again by her mother's beauty. She looked like a Russian aristocrat, with her fair skin and high cheekbones. "Darling," she said, regarding Ina with her beautiful blue-green eyes. "The doctors were telling us a fairy tale. Maybe it was the same one that some of them were telling themselves. No, what was lost stayed lost."

Something twitched in one of the windows across the street. A nurse's hand, pulling wide the curtains. And there was a woman in a wheelchair sitting with her back to the window.

Ina started to cry. She tried to take her mother's hand. "I'm so sorry."

Again her mother swept her hand through the air as if dispelling a fly. "Now you know."

Now she did. They sat in silence for the few minutes until Ina's father returned.

The empty soda cans were in a small white plastic bag tied securely shut. "Here they come!" he yelled to the man downstairs, who'd been patiently waiting all this time, before her father flung the bag. The man caught it, saluted, and called "Thank you, papi!"

"They haven't raised the return price for those cans in decades," said her father. "It's still five cents a can. It's really wrong." Together they watched the can collector walk off, his big bag hoisted over his shoulder. It was nice to sit with her mother and father.

Later, her father walked her to the bus stop. His khaki pants bagged loosely below the knee and hung absolutely flat in back. His shoes had a spongey base. It amazed her to recall the old feeling of terror and incapacity he used to induce. He'd sat her down for an important conversation when she was a high school senior. He told her he'd been thinking for a long time about Ina's future, and had concluded that she ought to apply to the Cornell School of Labor Relations because the male-female ratio there was 50 to 1. There would be no trouble finding a husband. He'd sent away for the promotional materials and application, which he handed her. They were pristine and heavy. She felt she ought to want this pragmatic, reasonable way of life—labor relations—rather than what she did want, which was to enter more deeply into the world of English literature. What she wanted seemed both childishly impractical and impossible to convey. Her desire had to do with the joys of poetry and novels, but he read only the newspaper. She hadn't even tried to explain herself. Now however, as they descended past the hardware store toward the bus stop, she found his recommendation about college touching: he'd been born in 1921 and he was a factory manager. That was who he was. He was trying to bring her into the world he knew.

He went up to the blue metal sign riveted to the pole and examined the numbers printed on the metal in tiny white, then turned his wrist and looked at his watch. "Eight minutes." It surprised her that he believed in the schedule. A million things could go wrong and did go wrong concerning street traffic. How did he survive without being endlessly disappointed?

"Two more minutes," said her father later, and Ina sighed.

"One minute."

She shook her head.

But to her surprise, the bus loomed, large and blue, cresting the hill at the very minute that the schedule had specified.

Once in her seat she watched until he turned around in his white button-down shirt, which clung slightly to his back—it was hot out—and he began slowly to walk away.

Chapter 34

The next morning, Ina lugged a red-topped card table down to the basement of her brownstone. She had awoken thinking about the view from the terrace. She had realized something. She swiveled the vinyl-covered square and shot out the rickety legs, then fetched a yellow legal pad and pen—no laptop, only a few notes. The furnace's oily aroma permeated the space. The walls were constructed of rocks the size of cannonballs, and the air held a mineral tang.

She wrote briskly, at last having a clear idea of where she was going. Her topic was the double vantage point, a perspective that was at the core of how the audience experiences tragedy. She should have understood it earlier. Athenians entered the theater knowing Oedipus's fate. They were gods seated on a terraced mountainside savoring the bittersweetness of dramatic irony. But they were also humans subsumed by the action. As it happened, this twinned sense of detachment and immersion was exactly how O'Neill experienced his life. He wrote about it in play after play—the pressures of social convention and the self that, like a jack-in-the-box, leaps out. "Forget I said that! I must have been crazy! I was just pulling your leg!"

That was the kind of thing his characters often claimed.

But beyond this was another layer. The playwright wanted to haunt, to possess. He wanted to produce in you an experience you couldn't resolve. After Edith Wharton saw *The Emperor Jones*, she accused O'Neill of practicing voodoo. When Ina saw the play, she'd been so overcome she didn't want to talk for hours after. Her body throbbed with the inescapable drums and the footsteps of the terrified man running for his life.

Across from Ina leaned an upended sofa whose bungeed innards gaped. It looked like a giant, expressive puppet, an Easter Island head. After the original performance in the ancient theater of Dionysus, she recalled, the masks were carried up the hill and hung in the temple. There, the empty eyes and open mouths drank lunar light. She pictured the giant, gaping faces glowing on their pegs.

She wanted to examine O'Neill's appeal to the irrational. That's why she'd been drawn to these weird plays, really, she now saw. It wasn't only to understand her mother that she'd studied O'Neill. It was to find something stifled in herself.

In her book, she would analyze how the master manipulated the vantage point and used the plastic arts (trance rhythm; choreographed, robotic movement) to haunt the audience. Ina flipped to a fresh sheet, and sketched a chapter outline. Then she set down a title. *The Erotics of Theater: Methods and Mystery in Mid-Career O'Neill.* She would focus on how O'Neill used what she thought of as the iconography of the unconscious—she scratched down the phrase—to reach beyond the defenses of the logical mind. O'Neill used emphatically stylized methods to connect with audiences, much like the German expressionists he admired. These distorted and symbolic images spoke directly to the psyche of the viewer, slipping through gaps in the fence of logic. O'Neill had been on the lookout for these gaps in the fence. Few scholars had studied this aspect of his work outright.

She flipped to a fresh page and began. She started with the frantically conventional mother in *The Great God Brown*. Instead of analyzing the meaning of the words on the page, though, she focused on the cadences of the character's language on the ears of the audience, the mother's particular music. She'd finally found her organizing idea. It seemed to be as on schedule as her father's bus.

A phone was ringing. As soon as she stepped out of the basement, where she had been writing all morning, she heard it, faint, far above. She climbed quickly. At each floor it grew louder: her own phone. She started to run, to catch it before the call jumped to voicemail. Jack wouldn't leave a message.

"Have you heard the news?" whispered Simon.

"What?" He sounded weird.

"We're ruined. The company's ruined. Tech stocks are cratering."

Ina's knees felt rubbery. "What?"

"The value's collapsing. The entire tech index."

She was overcome by a great sense of sorrow for Simon, and terror for them both. What was all that work of his worth? His giving up acting. She replied, "Maybe the stock value will come back?"

"Nobody here thinks so," he said, sounding frightened. "Things were overvalued. And the company's in hock. So that we could do the fiber rollout. The value has gone away. It's like money is vanishing. Millions and millions of dollars are just gone." His voice was faint. "There'll have to be layoffs."

She had been living her life and he had not. He'd been saving up his life. "I'm so sorry."

"Everyone is walking around like they saw a ghost."

"Can you come home now?"

But without even seeming to realize it, he'd hung up.

That evening they sat on the couch and watched the news. Simon could not eat. They looked at footage of the stock exchange, men with expressions of shock on their faces staring silently at monitors, tickertape on the floor as if it were the grim morning after a parade. Ina's mother phoned and said, "Ina, dear, let me speak to Simon." She immediately put him on. He listened, and said, "Thanks, Mom," a few times. And then: "I appreciate that. It won't be necessary. But thank you. Yes, I feel the same way about you."

Her mother spoke further, and Simon listened. Ina could hear the exhorting, cheering tone that her mother employed and yet it seemed, paradoxically, that the longer she spoke the more discouraged he became. His very shirt and suit trousers seemed to wilt, hanging in a looser, slack way.

"It was nice of her to call," he said after he hung up.

Simon's own parents didn't.

After Simon left the next day, Ina returned to her manuscript. If Simon couldn't support them, she must try. It was enormously fortunate that she'd found her thesis. "You were right," she looked forward to telling Marguerite. "The deadline has actually been good for me."

By midafternoon her arm muscles ached and she had to stop often and shake her fingers out. She sipped coffee from a jam jar and ate pretzel rods. The writing came fast. In the evening Simon returned home looking weary but with a wisp of hope. His company sold internet hardware; there was a chance its value would build back. In the meantime, there was no place to go. No one was hiring. Over a quiet late supper she asked him what it was like for him at the job. "There's a reason they call it work," he said grimly. He didn't want to elaborate.

"What you're doing is so hard."

He shrugged.

She made the 7Up cake he liked. She brought him the cat to hold. She bought a record of Earl Scruggs that Simon played over and over. She showed him her table of contents and said she was now fairly certain she could get her book published. "I'll be able to take some of the pressure off of you."

"Thanks, Ina," he said, tapping her hand, half-wincing as he smiled, as if he had a toothache.

One afternoon a bell clanged in the street. In the past, Ina had always ignored the sound. Now she found Violet's Sabatier knife and she raced with it downstairs toward the squarish blue truck parked at the corner, its body crudely painted with saws, axes, and cleavers—an emissary from the time of ice wagons.

Two customers were already on line. The first was a woman in a blue housedress. Behind her, the history professor cradled a brown paper bag.

"How's your work going?" Ina asked. She felt foolish but knew this was a sensation the professor typically induced.

"Good." The professor craned her head to peer inside the truck. She wore black pedal pushers, a T-shirt, and white tennis shoes, her hair as sleek as Audrey Hepburn's. From inside came the shrill whirr of the whetstone.

"What are you writing about these days?" Ina pursued.

"Moscow. The ways it destabilized the Weimar regime."

The customer before them collected her single knife and walked away. The professor handed her paper bag to the dour, scruffy, middle-aged man in the doorway. He vanished with it into the truck. "After my parents passed away, I cleaned out their apartment," she said. "The blades of my parents' knives were thinner than aluminum foil. From years and years of sharpening."

"Ah." Naturally the history professor's parents maintained their possessions with Teutonic discipline. "I've always wondered, if you don't mind my asking, why you decided to study the Weimar Republic. You emigrated from Germany? Was your family there involved with the government? Or the arts?"

The professor stared. "I'm a Jewish girl from Queens. My parents were Litvaks."

"Really!"

"My father was a housepainter. My mother was a seamstress."

Ina was tilted her head in surprise.

"We were always struggling. It was very hand-to-mouth. One day when I was a girl I saw a movie at the Loew's Paradise. The men were in tuxedos and the women wore gowns. It was so romantic, so beautiful. I fell in love. I wanted to enter that era. It turned out to be the Weimar Republic."

The wheel, which had been silent, started humming and singing, scraping, keening, from deep within the truck.

"And in a way I have gotten to live in it. I've never stopped loving that time." The professor shrugged. "Few people ask."

After a few minutes the man with dark stubble appeared in the truck's doorway, frowning. It was two dollars a knife, so the total, he told the professor, was ten. The professor paid with singles she drew one after another from her pocket. The grinder held out a brown paper bag, holding it at both the bottom and the top. "Careful!"

"Of course," replied the professor.

Ina watched her step away lightly in her white Keds. So, a serious life's work could be built on an early passion. Such a love could be valid enough to establish a whole significant life upon. How little she had understood.

"Goodbye!" she called, but the professor didn't respond.

It didn't take long for Ina's own knife to be sharpened. Then she returned to her writing. She posted her chapters to Marguerite on March 27, pleased to finally make a deadline, and almost danced all the way home.

Chapter 35

Along with her package to Marguerite, Ina seemed to have dispatched her last remaining restraint. Sex with Jack got wilder. She surrendered to the shameful rapture of obliging. In a short black slip like a maid's outfit, she lay on her stomach on his piano bench, legs splayed, and he took photos. She went down on him until drool sleeked her face. He said, "You did a good job." To reward her, he fucked her hard while she lay on her stomach, a pillow under her hips. One sultry day late in May, Jack turned on his air conditioner. She was still here.

She loved when he threw her arms impatiently over her head, and when he clasped the bars of the headboard while thrusting into her or even yanked her hair. She had the paradoxical sensation that this wasn't an obliteration of her personality but rather the purest acceptance of it. Once, she eased him deep into her mouth, bringing him farther in than she'd thought possible, her whole self a tube, a conduit, her eyes streaming, glory. Sandpaper abruptly rasped her throat. A salty stench arose. Oh God, she thought, overcome by humiliation. Vomit lay on his crotch. She quickly wiped him off with an edge of the sheet and turned her face away.

"What is it?"

She whispered, "I'm embarrassed."

"I'll tell you when to be embarrassed," he said.

Shame vanished. It seemed the kindest thing anyone ever told her. Basking, she returned to her task, aware at the periphery of consciousness that his words had made her feel entirely accepted—no need for shame!—although they sounded like an order.

She left Jack that afternoon at 3:00 P.M. It had been sunny and clear before but now the air was dark and cold, full of stinging raindrops. She was due to meet her sister across town in twenty minutes. She should have left earlier.

Yellow cabs stood bumper-to-bumper, a few of them honking. Down the block, a crosstown bus swerved to the curb at 76th Street and she ran for it. There was a line. She joined it and climbed aboard—she even got a seat. And then they were off. The bus heaved across the avenue but then stopped. Ina stared through the vast windshield at the stalled traffic. She hated to make her sister wait. The windshield wiper kicked upward, askew, a spindly insect leg, then subsided. All was clear, then the colors oozed and ran like wax before the wiper kicked again. Her last class of the semester had been on Tuesday. She just had exam papers left to grade. They were stowed in the tote she was carrying. She'd put *King Lear* on the syllabus, a first for her, and had asked the students to select one of either the maddened old monarch's or the supposedly berserk Edgar's speeches to analyze. Demanding, exquisite stuff! Turning from the windshield, she gently extracted a blue book, and tried to read. This proved impossible. It was too upsetting that the bus scarcely advanced.

Poor Violet, to be in town on such a day! But it was finally the day of her appointment to discuss the beta interferon treatment. She had waited seven months. The bus at last finished laboring across Lexington. Then it traversed Madison, Park, and Fifth Avenue. She couldn't bear to look at the time. At the corner of Central Park West, Ina bolted off although she knew it was a stop too soon, and ran.

When she finally reached Amsterdam, she turned the corner and there was Violet. Erect, she stood with her hands resting on her walker, stationed beside the flight of broad red steps of Sarabeth's. "Why aren't you inside?" yelled Ina.

Violet seemed not to hear. She wore a blond fuzzy wool coat that Ina knew she'd bought on a stopover in Iceland years ago. It had been a splurge. The rain shimmered beautifully in the weave of the bodice, although it drooped sodden and dark toward the hem.

"Why aren't you inside?" Ina repeated when she grew close.

Violet regarded her with curiosity, as if the answer was obvious. Her face was shining and wet in the tight, triangular hood. Her eyes were a startling navy blue.

"I wanted to feel it."

"But it's so cold! And loud!" Cars had started honking.

Violet shrugged.

"And the aide left you?"

"I expected you any minute."

Ina kissed her sister's chilled, wet check and helped lift the walker. Violet rested her two feet on each step. Her stalwart, unsmiling manner suggested that the doctor's visit hadn't gone well.

It was quiet inside, after the street. Exquisitely groomed mothers, their hair pulled sleekly back, tiny earrings glinting, sat over tea with daughters and a few sons in school uniforms.

"And?" asked Ina, after the waitress took their order.

Her sister shrugged. Her eyes looked glassy.

"You're not a candidate." Ina felt a terrible pang. Others had benefited from the new treatment; why couldn't her sister be allowed to?

"No need to look so tragic," said Violet loudly. "I haven't lost anything. I just haven't gained. No change."

Ina reached for her sister's hand across the table.

Violet grimaced. "Stop. No Sarah Bernhardt."

The soup and salad arrived but Ina had no appetite. Across from her, Violet ate methodically. She sawed her giant popover in half. It revealed cavernous pockets in the middle, from which steam escaped. Violet generously buttered and swiped raspberry jam across it.

"You're poor company, Ina," she observed.

"Sorry."

"You look like you've had more beauty treatments. You got your eyebrows tweezed. And your hair's got streaks."

Ina shifted in her seat.

Violet scooped a lump of jam into her tea. She stirred it, still scrutinizing Ina. Then her expression softened. She smiled, raising her spoon as if conducting an orchestra. "It looks good."

Ina smiled.

"Just because I'm not playing around with makeup," said Violet, "doesn't mean I don't want you to."

"Violet, what exactly did the doctor say?"

"My disease has progressed to the point where the treatment wouldn't help. Maybe it could have helped me years ago, I don't know." Violet took another bite of her popover. She chewed with determination.

"Shouldn't we ask another neurologist?"

"I want to hear about the makeup," said Violet abruptly. "Please don't leave me behind."

Ina looked down at her plate. "Well, cosmetics always seemed archaic to me, before. Embarrassing. Sexist. And I didn't want to call attention to myself, I guess. I preferred to be judged by my thinking."

Violet smiled. "You're seeing that man."

Ina's heart paused an instant. The sounds in the restaurant seemed to grow louder, as if someone had spun a dial.

"You don't have to admit it," said Violet. "That's okay. But I want to tell you something." Violet dabbed her lips. Her beautiful blue eyes were cool and lucid. "You should use me as an alibi. Say you're staying with me. Get all the happiness you can. Don't look so worried. You don't have to acknowledge anything. Just say, 'thank you.'"

"Well," said Ina, surprised and grateful—how dear of Violet!—"thank you for being so kind."

"We're sisters."

They finished their giant, eggy popovers—Ina, too—eating with their fingers, dabbing on more jam so it reached the corners. They seemed to be in agreement now about the importance of pleasure. But was Violet really happy? Ina saw her smile wobble while she chewed. And she couldn't help herself from already thinking of the pleasure of staying over another whole night at Jack's.

"You were given a raw deal," she blurted. Two women at the next table glanced over because she'd spoken with such vehemence.

Violet set down her knife. Then she reached into her handbag and produced a pen, which she handed to Ina. It was white plastic with shining gold letters that spelled out, *This is the day which the Lord hath made. Thou shalt rejoice and be glad in it.*

"There was an ad in the back of a magazine. You send in the message and they print it up. $19.99."

"Well, it's terrific, Violet," she said, her throat sore. The incised print held the overhead light in tiny tunnels.

"Keep it. It's for you."

Outside the café windows the air was now an even cobalt blue. The rain had stopped. A young woman stepped past on the sidewalk incongruously holding ice skates over her shoulder, her yellow hair glowing.

"I wanted a baby sister and then you showed up," said Violet. She'd often said this when they were children; it had frightened Ina, as if Violet had a mortal claim.

Her sister pulled from her pocketbook an enormous linen kerchief printed with red roses. She tied it tightly under her chin. It had the effect of making her eyes look even larger and more innocent.

"Thanks for asking for me," said Ina.

The air felt fresh and cool when they stepped out. The worst of rush hour had passed. Ina walked to the curb and held up her hand. A cab finally stopped, and once her sister was inside, Ina remained on the pavement, watching, not ready to leave. She looked until her sister's cab melded into the necklace of red lights.

At home, the mailbox held a single envelope. The Quincy seal decorated its upper corner, with Marguerite's initials inked above. Something wrenched in her gut. Ina's fingers felt clumsily thick as she opened the envelope. *Thank you for your contributions.* The air in the vestibule was suddenly quite thin. Her contract was not being renewed.

Marguerite's signature was set neatly across the bottom. How could this be? She'd submitted work—quite excellent work, she was confident, providing a detailed overview of the entire book and three strong chapters, with another cursorily sketched. She'd spent such a great deal of time preparing to do the actual writing that the references had come quickly to her. She regarded the seal at the top of the page. The emblem had once seemed to her preposterously pompous, an Oz imprint, when she'd first been hired. Now it seemed the sign of her last foothold on a life that made sense. The letter was dated May 10. *Good luck in all your future endeavors.*

She made her way up the stairs, her legs heavy with wet sand. Upstairs, still in her coat, she dialed the chairwoman's number. Marguerite often worked late. No answer. She sat rigidly at the table, chastising herself, her hands clasped over her waist. Many people who lost an academic position never found another, or not in a place they and their partner would want to live. She sat quite still, as if to belatedly demonstrate how entirely in command of herself she was, how calmly disciplined. Outside the rain began again. She hoped Violet had made it home. She was still sitting at the kitchen table when Simon arrived after eight.

He turned pale when she told him. "Call her at home," he said. "Now. Give her a series of 'by when' dates."

"She wouldn't want to be called at home."

"Oh, Ina, this matters." He shook his head in frustration and disappointment, and then dragged back the seat beside her and sat down. "How could this happen?"

She shook her head, hot with guilt. "I don't know. I submitted work."

"Not good enough. You should have been in better touch with Marguerite. You should have been tracking this whole thing more. Frankly this whole year you've been acting weird. You weren't paying attention."

She said softly: "I was."

"You took too much for granted. You didn't see it through."

She was silent.

He slapped his hands down hard on the table, and everything jumped. Then he just seemed to sag within himself.

Something banged the window; she realized there had actually been banging for a while now—buckshots of rain, illuminated by the streetlight into handfuls of mercury beads, which seemed to be lodged inside Ina's stomach, indigestible, sharp.

"I'll call her tomorrow. Let's not overreact," said Ina to herself as much as to Simon. Marguerite had a strong sense of justice, having experienced so much injustice herself. Ina would trust herself to that.

CHAPTER 36

After a sleepless night, Ina sat by the telephone at 9:00 A.M. She waited a few minutes, and then dialed Marguerite's number. No answer. She allowed herself to call once every hour, each time holding her breath as the phone rang, afraid and hopeful that Marguerite would pick up. Everything in the apartment seemed askew: the rug on the living room floor, the giant framed print of Lautrec's skeptical black cat with bristling eyebrows, the screen in the window which was in fact tilted, and which she'd never been able to pull straight. Now she found a hammer and tapped the rim of the screen, working it down steadily by sixteenths of an inch. She swept under the couch, exposing dusty cat-toy jingle balls and a sock that appeared molded from lint. Every time she finished with one task, she found another. There were things in the freezer that should have been thrown out ages ago. A packet of turbot that had for some reason gone orange. It was hard as a mosaic, crystallized with ice. Dated a year earlier. It wasn't until late afternoon that the department chair answered.

"But Ina, your courses have already been assigned to someone else," she said. "This can't have come as a surprise."

"Actually, Marguerite, it did. Didn't you get my manuscript? I sent it on March 27, from the post office itself."

"I did receive a package from you."

"Oh, good," Ina said, although the information frightened her. "I know this might sound arrogant, but I believe I'm making a significant contribution in my field. Shouldn't we ask authorities in my area to assess the work? I could propose names."

"That won't be necessary."

"But you told me from the beginning that there was a strong possibility of a tenure track job. You certainly led me to believe that." The cat leapt onto her legs and she pushed it off, its claws scratching in a way that felt oddly bracing.

"Ina, you have no book contract."

Ina was set aback. She set her fingertips lightly on the tabletop. Something was wrong with the room. "But we never agreed I'd submit that."

"It should have been obvious."

Silence hung between them. Then Ina spoke slowly, putting energy into being quite clear. There had obviously been some kind of miscommunication that needed to be rectified. "I believe I can get that. The editor of the drama series at Chicago told me to reach out when I had a manuscript to show him. And *The Eugene O'Neill Review* has already published two of my articles, when I was only a graduate student. So I have good reason to believe they'll want a chapter, which would help get the book taken by a top-tier press."

What a joy it would be to return immediately to the underground yellow light so conducive to writing, as if saturated with ideas!

But Marguerite was saying, "Professionalism, Ina. It's a given that we expect faculty to do excellent scholarship. But they also have to be people who can be relied upon to display sound judgment." She paused. "I don't know if that seems plebian to you."

The back of Ina's neck prickled.

"It doesn't." She didn't repeat the word "plebian"; it might sound sarcastic. In some way Marguerite seemed to be alleging that Ina exempted herself from the humdrum world of Marguerite.

"I showed up on those days you wanted me to," she protested.

"You did. And we appreciated that."

"I set my work aside. And I took a risk—I did creative writing."

"Quite."

The faxed pages. Ina felt as if she'd swallowed a gallon of sea. And that she was caught in a riptide hauling her far from where other people were. She recalled Grace saying, "You're just the substitute." That had rankled her. She should simply have said, "Yes, I am," and foregone the urge to read.

"Perhaps I exercised poor judgment."

Marguerite said nothing.

"Of course there is a role for restraint." She was clutching the receiver, which had become slippery with sweat. "If I had it to do over, I wouldn't have read that to the students. It was just my first time."

"Do-overs are nice," replied Marguerite.

There wasn't much more to say other than the usual pleasantries, and shortly thereafter, they hung up. Her job was truly over.

Ina lifted her head and took a swig from a bottle of Bartles & Jaymes. It had a cloying taste, dull, almost metallic. The apple-green punch had been the only thing in Jack's refrigerator. She had gone straight over. On the subway into Manhattan she thought about how she'd tell Simon about her conversation with Marguerite. Tomorrow afternoon they were scheduled to see his old scene partner, Kate, in an acting showcase. Ina marveled that ordinary life continually went on despite private calamity. She knew that no matter what, Simon wouldn't want to disappoint Kate.

"Slow down!" said Jack when she brought a fresh bottle back to bed. "It'll be okay, Ina."

"I know," said her mouth. Outside, it looked like it would soon rain. She took another sip, and warmth swam through her. This second bottle still had all its sprightly carbonation, and reassured her that there was a secret interlocking-geared system, a wise system, behind things. This system had been guiding her all this while, and would keep her safe. Even as she knew this impression was merely an effect of the alcohol, it still seemed valid. She found it pleasant to drink the Bartles & Jaymes fast; in fact, the sweet-sour liquid was, clearly, designed to be drunk in just this way.

"You don't have to feel so desperate," said Jack, trying to pull her close.

"I know." She didn't want to be distracted. She put on her T-shirt and went over to the window. The traffic on First Avenue stood bumper-to-bumper, just like yesterday, the yellow cabs glowing beneath the darkening skies. A car honked and then others joined in, horns blaring in enraged affirmation. People walked tilted forward. She envied all the people hurrying, having a place where they were expected.

"You're better than a lectureship, anyway."

She wished he would not talk.

"I mean, you have a doctorate. You ought to apply for jobs here in the city. At NYU or Hunter. Or Columbia."

"I need to publish a book." Rubberiness inflected the *p*s and *b*s of the word publish. "With a reputable press."

"I think Marguerite was very unfair."

Ina liked the tingle of the drink. An effusive, joyful sparkle filled her mouth with each sip. "She wasn't, actually," said Ina. "Judgment is part of what they hire you for. And producing,"

"You're writing your book. She should have gotten that. And you have good judgment."

As if to disprove him, Ina gulped her drink. She wiped her mouth with her wrist. "There was this boy in the writing class, and I wanted to show him that I wouldn't be ashamed. I think that was it. From the moment I walked into the classroom, he was disagreeing with me. Disrespecting me. I wanted to prove that I was one of them."

"But you weren't."

The cacophony from the street rose again, car honks blooming inside one another, a megaphone cone unfurling from inside a megaphone cone. She set the empty bottle down on the floor beside the bed and climbed in. "Is it going to rain soon?"

"I don't think so."

A jangle of keys rang in the hallway. Jack set a finger on his lips and said, "Shhh." He always wanted her silent when a neighbor spoke in the hallway or opened their door. She didn't know if it was that he didn't want to be overheard or that he wanted to overhear. It was one of the many traits of his from which she removed judgment. She rested her head on the pillow and let the voices in the hallway drift. And then the next thing she knew it was quiet. Jack was absolutely still. He was turned toward the window. The room was utterly dark. How many minutes had gone by? She grabbed the clock and swiveled it. 1:14. The clock must have been mis-set! She got up and rushed into the kitchen. The microwave also said, almost incomprehensibly, 1:14. She returned to the bedroom. "Jack," she said, shaking him. "It's so late!"

He groaned, his arm lank, his body heavy.

She wouldn't arrive home before two, if that. How could she have slept so long?

She carried Jack's brick-like phone into the bathroom. There was no answer at her house. Simon must be asleep in the bedroom with the door shut. "I'm at Violet's, honey," she said to the answering machine. "I went to visit her this evening, and we stayed up late, talking, and then I fell asleep."

She shut her eyes so that she wouldn't see the distracting pile of *Wired* magazines stacked on the windowsill, the pressed chocolate squares of his new plastic shower curtain. Thank

God her sister had invited her to do this. "I'm going to stay overnight. But please don't call because I don't want to wake Violet. I'll come home in the morning."

Then she set her finger down on the bar of the receiver and got a new dial tone. The phone rang five times and then there was a clatter. Her sister's groggy voice said flatly, "Hello?"

"It's me. I'm with him."

"I dreamed you were coming over, and then the phone rang. Isn't that strange?"

"Yes." Ina was washed through with sadness. "That is strange."

Her sister hung up before Ina could even say thank you.

Still, she was uneasy all night long. The bed was a hard plank. She wished she could come home right now without it raising questions.

Ina was surprised by the radiant spring light that swept over the street in the early morning when she stepped out. What a silly worrywart she'd been! How good life was, she felt, as she swung her legs down the sidewalk. She wondered if Janie, circling a stupa in Nepal as the sun arose, had considered how light itself expressed a mystic value. She had told Ina about the hundreds of people who walked around and around the tall pavilion, clattering the prayer-wheels, accruing merit, seemingly hoisting the sun aloft every morning.

Yellow forsythia bloomed in a ten-foot geyser in a shopwindow on Madison Avenue. On Park, a doorman in a snug blue Russian-style coat with brass buttons stepped smartly across the pavement, a chrome whistle between his lips. The apartment buildings themselves, massive and trim, resembled yachts anchored in perfect alignment. The acting showcase where she was to meet Simon was in a church on a side street near here, a short stroll away. She had yet to tell Simon about the fact her job was definitely lost, but the world itself seemed to be arguing for an amplitude of opportunities. In the window of a French pastry shop, each apple tart pinwheeled a perfect sunflower of slices under a glimmering aspic sheen.

She turned onto 75th Street, and the chocolate-brown canopy of the Carlyle Hotel appeared, the name in swirling white letters. The hotel had private phone booths, she recalled. A doorman swung open the door. An opulent hush enfolded her. There were the booths, just where she'd remembered. Art Nouveau mahogany carvings framed the glass, slender curving branches and leaves. She would tell Simon now about the conversation with Marguerite. She slid into the booth and dialed, thinking that even a bad thing could become something good.

"Where are you?" asked Simon.

"In town! I decided to come straight in for Kate's play. Do you want to come meet me now? Why don't you leave right away? It's fantastic out."

"Where were you last night?"

"What?" She touched the phone cord. "Didn't you get my message? I stayed over with Violet."

"No, you didn't. Violet called me. She was worried about you."

A loud humming commenced in her ears. "She called me before seven," said Simon. "She said you were supposed to come over last night. She said she'd woken up during the night and remembered. She didn't know where you were. She was very worried."

Ina stared at the metal shelf beneath the phone. She immediately regretted not saying that she'd stayed over with Janie. Was it too late to say that now? There was no air in this little booth. What sentence would change everything back? Surely there was one, if she could just think of it. There had always been before. Where was it now? But the magic sentence wouldn't come. The black-and-white tile of the corridor floor seemed to float above itself.

"Where were you?"

She shook her head as if he could see.

"Baby, you're having an affair and now I know it," he said softly.

She began to cry, and then so did he. Hers were dry gasping sobs at the idea of his sadness, the pain he must be in. To think that he'd been alone for two hours not knowing where she was, guessing she was with a different man.

"Come home right now," he moaned.

And then she was running through the lobby.

Outside, it was shockingly bright. A doorman in a blue jacket held a taxi door open for her. She slid in, feeling soiled and ashamed. During the whole ride she leaned forward, her back aching while she clasped the little leather ring tacked to the plexiglass divider, as if somehow the cramped clench in her back helped the cab along.

The on-ramp to the Brooklyn Bridge was backed up, metal car roofs gleaming. She let her eyelids fall shut. A sickening darkness surged, and her eyes opened. The Hudson River glittered with soporific monotony. Each sharp glint tapped like a dental pick. She couldn't tell which was worse, seeing or not seeing. She held her eyes open, blinking only when her eyes started to blaze, the river fold upon fold of painful brightness.

Part III

Chapter 37

Dr. Morris's office was in a short brick Federalist house on Twelfth Street. A narrow staircase led up to a refinished attic with stalwart, ageless-looking houseplants and a sea-green sofa facing an armchair upon whose ottoman Dr. Morris rested her sizeable calves. She was a stocky woman with oversized glasses and a ducklike lisp, and yet for years she had been, appearances notwithstanding, the chairperson of a department at Cornell-Weill, and a psychiatrist and psychoanalyst highly recommended by George.

"So?" she began, as if they were family.

Ina explained that she'd had an affair and Simon had discovered it. It had been a week since he found out. She fell silent, wondering what else she could possibly say. Everything seemed unspeakable. The very breath seemed to be being suctioned out of her mouth even as she'd said those few sentences. Simon sat beside her on the couch, doleful, silent, holding himself rigid, as if resisting broken edges within. They both seemed to tacitly agree that since she was the one who'd fucked up, it was her job to clean the mess, so she'd begun, but almost instantly ran out of words.

"Babetude is crucial," volunteered the doctor.

"Babetude?" Ina was surprised by the silly word.

"Feeling attractive. Like a babe. Especially at this point in your life, as you're entering middle age."

Ina had an impulse to sigh. It sounded like a truism from a woman's magazine. Ina wanted the kind of therapist who said unexpected, profoundly illuminating things. Time was of the essence. Simon was hurting terribly, she herself was often numb.

And yet something in Dr. Morris's words made Simon shift toward Ina and ask, "Did you go on long dates with him?"

She shook her head, intensely sad for Simon, although at the same time terror seeped into her stomach, sharp edged.

"How did you meet?" he asked.

"At a party that Janie took me to."

"So Janie knows." He stared at her, eyes flat with rage.

For a moment, she was incredulous; this seemed such a distraction from the main issue. "Yes, Janie knows."

"Did she set you up?"

"No."

"Where does he live?"

"The Upper East Side."

"So he's rich. He makes more money than me."

Ina shook her head.

All this while the therapist sat with her pencil pressed against her cheek. A spasm of annoyance went through Ina at the useless-seeming round face whose gaze traveled from one to the other.

"He doesn't," said Ina. "He actually lives in a pretty crummy apartment."

But Simon continued to glare at her, infuriated, then he looked away. These answers hadn't changed anything. A prism strung from the knob of the window flashed a hint of rainbow across the wall, and it occurred to Ina that this had once been a girl's room, now remodeled. Dr. Morris's daughter, probably off to college. A car honked, its sound echoing off the bricks like an invitation to follow into the distance, into the angles and crevices of the air.

"You made a fool of me," muttered Simon.

"No," said Ina. "I made a fool of myself."

The therapist crossed her legs. "Neither of you is a fool. There are always important reasons within reasons. And maybe ways to get things moving in a good direction again."

She turned a crackly page in the big book that she had balanced on her lap. It had floppy vinyl covers and seemed like it would be difficult to write in. Ina stared at her as if she were a moron. Dr. Morris lifted her pencil and said, "I'd like to hear about the first moments of your relationship. You know, what draws one person to another is often very significant. It can carry meaning for the whole course of the relationship. Simon, could you tell me what first attracted you to Ina?"

My gosh, did they actually have time for this? thought Ina. She and Simon needed someone brilliant, not plodding—someone who could illuminate the hidden structure of things and at the same time cast a kind of optimistic magic upon it. Still, she was surprised by what Simon said:

"Ina seemed so alive, and so smart. She seemed like a kind of diamond in the rough."

For the first time since they'd walked in, the therapist made a note.

The day he found out, he was standing in front of their building in Brooklyn Heights when she arrived home in the cab. He looked haggard and pale.

As soon as he saw her, his body began to shake. She got out and put her arms around him and hugged him hard, aware she smelled of Jack's cigarettes. "It's nothing," she said urgently. "It isn't worth being so hurt over."

"Oh, Ina," he groaned. After a few moments he proposed that they walk over to the promenade, away from their own street. He wasn't wearing socks, having dressed in haste, and his bare feet pulled up from his shoes while he walked, exposing the reddish place where the back of the foot scraped.

"What do you want to do?" he asked her as soon as they'd sat. He looked away.

"Stay together."

"I don't see how we can. Oh, I don't know what to do." He was almost rocking back and forth with grief.

"We can, Simon," she said, for she wanted to. She loved him. She had always loved him. Jack seemed an absolute chimera. Of course, that was actually part of the problem, she knew—that he seemed to exist in a separate reality, a nonreality.

She clasped Simon's hand tightly, and then smoothed the fingers out on the bench, and the whole time his hand and fingers were inert. She was disgusted with herself. She'd played a game with another person's existence. She was still doing it.

And then he said, "I'm exhausted, and I'd like to be alone. I'm going to go up to the hotel." It was a Marriott on Tillary Street where they'd sometimes swum or sat in the bar playing Scrabble. He asked her to pack his suitcase. He didn't want to go into their apartment. He didn't want to be where they'd lived together.

He remained downstairs on the pavement until she returned holding his overnight bag. "May I walk with you?" she said.

He nodded. He was still in too much pain to ask any questions. Tillary Street, when they reached it, was nearly empty, its four wide lanes carrying only a coarse, gritty wind. Sharp-edged particles swept through the air. They crossed the old, industrial thoroughfare and trudged two dull blocks until they saw the bright brass doors of the hotel.

"Please don't come any further."

He passed through the doors and vanished. The afternoon sky was Brillo-pad gray. He'd told her he was going to sit in the hot tub and she was glad. She crossed back over the empty windy plaza and found a phone booth.

"The other person knows," she told Jack. She caught that childish locution. "My husband knows. Simon knows."

"Oh, I'm so sorry."

She wanted to be out of touch for a month, she explained. She needed to figure out how she felt about her marriage. She couldn't know while she was still seeing or even talking to Jack. His presence acted as an anodyne.

"My great charm," he responded, his tone dry.

She shifted her weight, and the segmented metal phone cord clattered like heavy jewelry, something grotesque reticulated like the tail of a rat.

"We won't talk for a whole month then, Ina?"

"Yes."

"Fine. Let's figure out the exact date."

He fetched a calendar, and they did so. And then he explained that if, when they spoke again, she wasn't making plans to get a divorce, he needed to end things. He sounded different: regretful, detached.

She bent her head. The sidewalk's pattern of pebbly shards had an intricacy that her eyes wanted to lose themselves tracing. Escapism, again. She straightened her spine and watched the traffic slip past.

"I understand," she said, already craving to see him again with every cell of her skin.

That afternoon in her apartment, sitting alone on the couch, the hours merged, yellow and strange. To think was pain. Her mind seemed something that needed to crouch very still. She felt shatteringly bad for Simon. Sighing, she dialed the phone.

"You're okay!" her sister exclaimed. "Thank God! Where were you?"

"Don't you know?"

"How could I? Even Simon didn't know where you were."

"I wish you hadn't called him."

"But you were supposed to visit. Of course I was worried. I woke up frantic. You can't let yourself just disappear like that!"

"Violet."

The older sister was silent. Ina swallowed; her throat hurt.

And then Violet said, "Oh." She sounded rueful, abashed. "I'm sorry. I'm so sorry. I got confused."

Ina said nothing. Then whispered, "I shouldn't have phoned you so late."

Her poor sister.

"You sound funny. Are you sure you're all right?"

Ina laughed. She actually laughed! "Yes. But I don't want to talk any more."

And after another moment they hung up. What did it matter if Violet had done it on purpose or not? She had wished to help Ina more than she could.

Simon called from the hotel that evening. "Come here."

She went running down the street, thankful, wishing she could already be there. Hurry, she told herself, hurry. Shadows stretched flat along the pavement, baby carriages as high as houses, dust-filled light-posts the size of towers. Her chest ached, as if a string had been tightened across it. Get to him. On Joralemon, above the Thai restaurant, a neon sign flashed in an upper window, advertising a diet doctor. There was a fat red man and then a skinny green man inside him.

Simon turned the knob on the hotel room door and stepped back, receding. He crossed the room and sat far away in a squarish leather chair. She sat in a nearby chair.

"Are you in love with him?"

It didn't seem possible that the same word could apply to both Simon and Jack. And so she said no. She was aware of herself temporizing.

"Then why did you stay over?" Simon asked. "That's the part I don't understand."

"It was too late to come home." That was true, at least.

"Promise me you won't see him again."

"I won't. I promise you."

"How can I believe you?" he moaned. "You lied to me. That was the worst. To hear a lie from your mouth, to hear you lie in the same voice that tells me everything else." And then he asked: "Why did you do it?"

She pronounced flatly, but with a sense of release, "I needed to feel attractive to someone."

He remained quiet. And then he said, softly, "Oh, I'm so sorry."

Ina was swept with a wild gladness. A thrilling, strange, novel hopefulness overcame her. There was so much he didn't know! She wished it was possible to tell him everything, even what it felt like to be with Jack, so that he could know that too about her.

He said, "I don't know why, but I haven't been attracted to you for two years."

Her heart stopped. "Oh, I'm glad you're telling me," she exclaimed. "Because I felt it. I felt it in my bones. I felt you weren't attracted to me." She added reflectively, "It felt so cold."

She was momentarily oriented and sane. What a gift his words were! How kind he was to confirm what she'd sensed. She came over and sat down on the floor, hugging him at the knees.

She wished she could think of something more to say, to further this strangely wonderful conversation. They were being honest with one another for the first time in years. "You know when I went to Victoria's Secret last spring? I told myself that if you saw me in a sexy outfit you'd get excited and want to have sex with me. You just said 'I hope you enjoyed buying that.'"

"I'm so sorry."

"Thank you." After a moment she added, "But, you know, I should have asked you about it, gotten you to talk about what was going on with you, with us. I shouldn't have let it go. I should have told you about me and heard about you."

He was in the black chair and she sat embracing his legs, holding him. All sorts of things might be possible, now that they'd begun. The very next day, she looked for a therapist, hoping that more of that strange joy awaited them.

*

Ina was insulted in that first session to hear that she'd seemed like a diamond in the rough to Simon, that he'd actually liked that about her. Sitting on the sea-green couch, gazing at the exasperatingly obtuse face of the therapist, it sounded to her as if Simon had felt he could take advantage of the collegiate Ina, a girl ignorant of her own worth. But then she pictured herself in the baggy white painter's pants she'd favored, barefoot, using toilet paper for bookmarks, living on toast and Swiss cheese, poring over each last footnote in the assigned reading for some valuable clue to life even if it was the size of the hole in a sequin. She *had* been something in the rough, although she wouldn't call herself a diamond.

"And you, Ina?" said the doctor, learning forward. "What attracted you to Simon?"

"He was a fantastic storyteller and really just the best company I'd ever met. I don't know that I'd ever met anybody actually like Simon. He described things in a way that showed incredible sensitivity. I felt so lucky to be the person he was talking to."

Dr. Morris nodded. She had a thatch of russet hair that was likely dyed and sat atop her head like a tiny pile of pretty leaves, and she wore no jewelry other than a big watch. She was clear-eyed. Ina needed someone beyond clear-eyed; she needed a therapist who possessed the equivalent of x-ray vision, who provided canny and even uncanny interpretations that helped resolve matters, the way Freud's did.

"So you saw yourself as an audience?" said the therapist.

Ina shifted. "I suppose," she answered, although she'd never consciously considered herself that. She saw the young man singing beneath her window, bringing her pot brownies he'd baked, taking her on bike rides to hidden glens, telling her about the nice, kind people in the little town he'd grown up in in Texas when all her friends at the time viewed their neighbors as members of a rather doltish bourgeoisie.

"The question is," said the therapist, "how can you make things hot again?"

"I don't feel like I can reach out," said Simon, not looking at Ina. "I need for Ina to reach out."

She nodded, awash with scalding guilt.

"I miss intimacy with Ina," continued Simon.

Mournfulness engulfed her. She didn't believe she could do the reaching out sexually and have it work. She was turned on by something else.

"I'm so sorry," she murmured, understanding how lonely he must have been these past months. She didn't know if she could make love with him again at all, after Jack. Her insides were sagging and dissolving; it was an alarming sensation. She was going to have diarrhea. "One moment. Excuse me." She stood up, and inadvertently met the eyes of the therapist with her oversized glasses and steady, implacable, inquisitive, somehow reassuring gaze, and at that instant a piece of information arrived. She knew the nature of this terrible old feeling inside her—a feeling she'd spent her adult life avoiding. It was fear. Just fear. Fear accounted for why she'd zoned out all these years. It was nothing fancy. She heard her father's authoritative voice recommending the Cornell School of Labor Relations. Dr. Morris said, "Are you okay?"

"Yes. Yes, I am." Her insides still in turmoil, as if filled with gooey raw bread stuffing, she sat back down. Simon was regarding her quizzically. "I just got scared. I got scared that we can't fix what's broken between us."

"Don't you think we can?" Simon's face looked eager, greenish, anxious.

The terrible feeling surged. Fear.

She said: "I wish I could say yes, I wish I could make it all better."

"Nobody's asking you to do that," said Dr. Morris. "It's not your job."

"I wonder why you thought it was," said Simon.

"A terrific question," said the therapist. "In any case, I'm glad you decided to stay in the room."

With a heave, however, the therapist rose to her feet, the notebook tucked under her arm, and the pink headlights that had been her knees disappeared.

Their evenings were quiet. Once Ina walked in on Simon crying. Often he just wanted to sleep, his thin body tucked in on itself. Ina held him, looking out the dark window toward where a sky hung over lower New Jersey like blurred wax. In the morning, after Simon went to work, she could think her thoughts and feel her feelings again. They seeped back. At night she felt vacant, vigilantly focused on Simon. She was waiting for the next therapy hour. Just two sessions remained before the therapist went on vacation and she needed to give her answer to Jack.

"You seem to carry the weight of the world on your shoulders," Dr. Morris said to Simon at the start of the second session. "I just get a really crushingly sad vibe from you."

"I've hurt Simon so much," Ina explained.

"I don't think it's just that," said the therapist. "I think it precedes you."

"How could you know? You just met Simon."

"Experience."

Ina lifted her eyebrows. Still, it was true that Simon's parents had not protected him from his bullying stepbrother, a troubled child who collected knives.

"You felt abandoned by your parents," said Dr. Morris. "Given your past, it makes sense that it wouldn't take much for you to feel attacked. You have a history of abuse."

Simon and Ina exchanged an exasperated glance.

A gust of moist air swept in the open window at that instant, pushing up the short white curtain with its knobby tassels. How melodramatic, thought Ina, to declare that Simon had experienced abuse. The window-glass glittered with pretty raindrops. They trembled, a hundred scattered jewels, as if demonstrating that truth was actually diffuse. But Ina suddenly understood that it was characteristic of her to resist coming to a conclusion. Clarity itself seemed a distortion. She atomized the truth so that, like the droplets shimmering on the window, each reflecting a tiny therapist's office and a tiny Ina and Simon, reality seemed inaccessible, dispersed, nothing you could do anything about.

She turned to him. "You certainly didn't get what you needed at home, really. You liked school because it was a place where adults saw you."

"I did like school," he said, perking up, turning back to the therapist, looking relieved to find something easy to talk about. "The teachers and I could have conversations." His favorite day of elementary school was the last day of the year because the teachers always said, "I love all of you." One year his teacher didn't say it, and he still remembered that. He'd been shocked and hurt.

Ina was surprised that Simon was telling all this to Dr. Morris, with her large gray glasses and pragmatic, no-nonsense manner. He seemed at ease with her. Perhaps in some way she reminded him of the placid-seeming ladies of his Texas town.

"We all need acknowledgement," said Dr. Morris, again stating what Ina thought was obvious. Yet it no longer bothered her.

"You certainly deserved more from your parents," said Ina.

"They did their best," he replied.

"Not the point," said Ina. His parents refused to give him praise. They didn't want him to get a swelled head. They shrugged at his report cards with their lines of As. Which may have been part of why he came east. When he met Ina, he'd had a waifish, bedraggled charm with his thin cotton snap-front shirts and purplish circles under his eyes because he never put himself to bed before dawn, even when he had an early class.

Dr. Morris flipped a page in her big notebook. "Being with Ina gave you a kind of stability," she said. "And now it's gone."

"Yes."

"I'm so sorry. But in some ways it's a mixed blessing, the way crises often are. 'Don't waste a good crisis,' isn't that something they say in business?"

Without a smile, Simon agreed that it was.

Ina took his hand, which had the desolate feel of an empty glove. She used to be so afraid of him saying "You're ruining the whole day!" if she brought up something unpleasant, and so she didn't. He deserved to feel happy. Simon had been supporting her financially, managing a high-stress job, and she'd felt obliged to make sure his weekends were sweet. This allowed her to feel generous—a grand emotional benefactor!—even as she lied about her feelings, creating a fantasy reality for him. "I'm glad we're talking now," said Ina.

He smiled. "Yes."

After that, a single session remained before she needed to give her answer to Jack. Restless, she wandered the city. Air conditioners jingled, their razored backs resembling the unevenly cut pages of a thousand metal books, the streets a library flipped inside out. It was a dream metropolis. Everyone who could go away had. In the early morning came the thrum of engines skimming low. Airplanes sprayed the streets against West Nile virus. The bureau and bedside table thrashed, as did the bones of her chest. Outside, powder thick as pulverized lime coated abandoned cars. The white sun deprived everything of a shadow. Ina trod for hours, past mangoes starting to ferment in sidewalk stalls, past overgrown kittens leaning against grimy pet-shop windows and presenting a wall of flattened, bored adolescent flesh. The heat of the sidewalk came up through her sneakers. She thought of Janie circumambulating a stupa at daybreak every morning, the rattle of brass prayer wheels in her ears, the sun sharpening as she walked with hundreds of other people around and around, until the light was bright and ordinary, full of dust. She'd told Ina that she'd seen things that she didn't think she'd ever forget. Banks of candles whose plentiful smoke drifted like yards of silvery silk vanishing into the morning air, saying *Evanescent.* You felt the heat as you passed. Buddhist nuns bringing soup in a cauldron to whoever was hungry. A man who, instead of walking, did a full prostration on bandaged knees and hands, over and over, and each time he collapsed down his whole body transmitted the utter faith, "Now I will receive enlightenment." Ina stopped. Wasn't that worth traveling across the earth for? Why had she been so mystified by Janie's journey? She wanted to feel alive in her life. It was going too fast, Janie had said. Ina had wanted to feel alive too, hadn't she? She used to live as if life could be put on hold, saved up for later. She inhaled a nail-polish scent. An odd excitement possessed her. Her knees registered something before her mind did. She looked up and—strange not to have realized this sooner—saw that her feet had carried her to Jack's.

Dizzy suddenly, she touched the brick wall beside her to steady herself. Oh, mad joy! She could just cross the street. Be up in his apartment inside the languid warmth of his room. The tan sheets around them. His arm under her back. His face lowering itself to her chest. How fantastic to be together, with the late afternoon glowing off the walls. Her heart seemed to be beating in her arms. At that very moment, a familiar bulky figure descended the stairs. Good Lord, what luck! She felt herself begin to grin. He wore jeans. A ball cap shoved back on his head. She could already see the smile that would break out on his face. He was about to be so happy, so surprised! The door of the lobby swung out. But no, no, the man she was looking at was broader, with blond hair.

Not Jack.

She found herself walking across the street, standing outside the smudged glass door of his building. Here were the buzzers, a double row. His was 4B. The sight of his button made her head light. It had something of his own identity in it, that button in its familiar place, bottom left on the grid. She had, she realized, a crazy feeling of affection toward that button! She lifted her hand to touch its friendly roundness—then stopped. And dropped her hand. What the hell was she doing?

If she pressed the button and went upstairs, all the forward momentum would stop. She would return to the old painful stasis. They all would. For despite the apparent indirection in the sessions, in these two weeks she and Simon had gained something. They were both better able to admit reality, even if it scared them. She herself was learning to zone out less, not to leave the room in the various internal ways she did. This would end if she reverted to Jack. A figure started coming down the stairs. Quickly, she turned and walked away, imagining Jack's eyes on her back, half-hoping his voice would call out to her. But it did not.

Five days. She counted again. Five. Something significant might yet change, must change.

"Keep?" asked Ina.

"No," said Violet, at almost every book or magazine Ina held aloft.

Ina clamped newsletters into jagged-toothed binders and toted stacks of mysteries to the local library. She sifted through bulletins from the ACLU and Common Cause, the NAACP and Planned Parenthood and Children's Catholic Charities. She had always known that her sister donated to worthwhile organizations; it was just Violet being Violet. But now, discovering that her sister continued to contribute even though she had practically no income, Ina saw the strength of her character.

And she was glad to notice this because it mitigated some of her hard feelings toward her sister. "You set a good example," Ina murmured as she tucked a new Channel 13 card into Violet's wallet.

"Instead of thinking about me, it would be better for you to be working on your O'Neill."

Ina grimaced, lifting up—with yellow plastic gloves—a ball-like structure of paper strips and yellowing housing insulation. A mouse nest. "This has waited long enough."

Her sister harrumphed. Ina set the thing into her black garbage bag along with the gloves. She returned to the crowded bookshelf. Violet was sitting on the small old orange-and-yellow couch, and Ina stood with various bags and boxes at her feet: a paper bag for the recycling, one box for the library, and another for Goodwill.

"Keep," said Violet, smiling at the object in Ina's palm. A wooden horse as tiny as a spool of thread, painted orange, purchased from the Lillian Vernon catalogue when they were girls and Violet was going to go galloping off everywhere. "Our niece might like that. Out," she said of three old *Reader's Digests*. "You clean when you can't sit still."

"Lucky for you."

"How are you doing?"

Ina pulled gingerly on the cord of some implement wedged at the back of a shelf, and an unwieldy object came hurling down. It slammed into Ina's toe (she gasped) and then walloped the floor, hurling water.

"Careful!" she heard Violet shout in her head. But for once Violet had not actually admonished her. She was sitting silently.

A clothing steamer with a yellow body still full of liquid had been stored wrong. Now it lay askew, puddling.

"Simon and I are in therapy," said Ina, limping into the kitchen. "It's good for us," she called. "It's very good."

"Is it?" called Violet.

"Yeah. We're talking to one another."

"About your feelings?"

Ina returned with a roll of paper towels. Who did Violet have to discuss her feelings with? There was a tremendous amount with which she was alone. "Yes. Although when you put it like that, it sounds like a luxury."

"I don't think it's a luxury," said Violet, and Ina's throat tightened with sadness.

The steamer had gouged the wood floor. Ina sopped up the mess, waiting for her sister to comment on the damage. But she did not. Instead, Violet said, "Cherry. Not practical."

"Well, it's beautiful."

And Violet did not sardonically say *was*. She said: "Beauty is important. You should take the steamer. That too." She pointed to a red tin Swee-Touch-Nee tea chest the size of a card deck.

"But it's so charming! And you can keep little things in it. Stamps. Matches."

"There's something in there already. Look."

The lid was clasped shut with tiny claws. Inside was a curious object the size of her thumb: a sharp pencil-point sprouting an eraser, the body of the implement having been used up but the tip still good. "That's the Depression you're looking at. Don't waste anything. It's from Mom's father. The watch repairer." He'd died when their mother was two. And their mother had saved this funny two-sided item all her life, a scrap of inheritance.

"You should keep it," said Ina.

"Won't have any place for it soon."

Ina laughed. "You're getting more space by the minute, Violet!"

"But I want you to have it. It can remind you of how valuable even a pencil was once. And how rich you are now. No matter what happens. If you ever feel poor, hold it. I've done that."

"Have you?" said Ina, but her sister was looking away, and didn't answer.

After a moment, Ina set the tin beside the doorway, with the other oddments her sister had given her.

"Not that you should settle," said Violet loudly. "You're still young."

Ina was about to object—she certainly didn't feel young—but compared to her sister, whose life was so restricted, she supposed she was.

"It'll be nice when you get back to your work," said Violet. "You'll be less of a sad sack."

"I've noticed you keep giving me pencils."

Violet smiled. "It was nice of you to propose doing this. You must know why I agreed."

"The aides got fed up?"

"I'm moving to a nursing home."

"Violet." Ina felt scooped empty inside. She needed to sit. She sat down right on the wood floor.

"As you know, I prefer to deal in realities. And I'm sorry, I really am, Ina, that sometimes I force other people to deal with them too."

Ina smiled, but her mouth twitched. Was this an apology? It no longer seemed necessary.

Violet said softly, "It will be easier for people to take care of me. And life will go on inside the nursing home, too."

Ina felt a terrible pressure in her chest. After a moment she said, "You're an inspiration. You really are."

"A nice consolation prize." Violet spoke with her usual sourness.

But then she added, "Come here. Thank you for this week. You're a good sister."

Ina said nothing; she felt like a louse. She came over and her sister pulled her down onto the couch and set a wet smack on her cheeks, stinging and loud.

"Things will work out for you," said Violet.

Ina grimaced, trying to smile, but her throat was tight.

"Keep," Violet said flatly as she set her hand on Ina's arm.

"It was as if I was taken over," said Ina. They had reached the end of the last session before she had to give her answer to Jack. It was also the last session before Dr. Morris left for a month. "I used to find it hard to believe in the reality of that person having the affair. I told myself it wasn't the real me. I didn't know who it was."

"Absolutely typical." Dr. Morris took off her oversized gray plastic glasses and rubbed her eyes. Her face looked naked and much older. Ina was glad that Dr. Morris would get to have a vacation. "I can't tell you the number of times I've heard a person in a committed relationship who's had an affair say, 'It felt like someone else was doing all this. I felt propelled forward. I didn't recognize the person doing these things.'" She set the glasses back on her face.

Beside Ina, Simon sat mute, gazing down disconsolately.

"But it's the primary relationship itself that's created this unrecognizable person," said Dr. Morris. "Your relationship was in trouble, it was unhealthy, which is why the affair happened."

Dr. Morris stood, as did Simon. Out the window, over the chimneys toward the horizon, the night air held the bioluminescent green of pond scum. The summer stretched ahead. Tomorrow Ina must give her answer. Ina said, "The unrecognizable person—does she ever go away?"

For that unrecognizable figure still seemed a plague, an evil haunting spirit.

"What do you think?"

Ina contemplated the therapist's unpretentious, practical, friendly face, and was aware of Simon standing in her peripheral vision. "If you acknowledge her, I suppose, then yes. If you accept her and take her in, whatever that means. Then she changes into something else."

Dr. Morris nodded.

And then Ina and Simon were walking down the steep stairway. When they arrived at the front doorway, he reached around her and flung it open, to her surprise, pushing hard and letting her precede him out. The slate sidewalk held up shallow bowls of milk, reflections of the streetlight in the slick gray surface. "Careful as you step," said Simon, and he stuck out his elbow so that she could grab hold of it to steady herself as they walked to their car.

CHAPTER 38

It was a drenching night that gave way to a drizzly morning. The grass across the street glowed preternaturally bright through the mist; the tulips were a weird electric yellow. Ina slipped the sex diary in which she'd inscribed Jack's statements into the pocket of her raincoat. She walked to a coffeeshop on Montague Street, purchased a coffee, and brought it to her table. She took out the book, but didn't read it. She simply lay her hand upon it, as if it were a kind of bible. It was 8:40 A.M. At nine, she would phone. The tarmac shimmered out the window, reflecting the shop opposite and the orangey-yellow sign that flashed: Sleep-eze. Sleep-eze. In the gutter, glistening blue moisture lengthened the neon letters to the size of subway grates. She drank another coffee and then made her way home through the haze.

The phone rang once, twice, and then his voice answered, abrupt, as if he'd been interrupted. "Hello?"

"It's Ina."

"Hi."

"How are you?" she asked warmly. "I missed you so much. It's so good to hear your voice."

Jack remained silent.

She stared at the wood floor. Still, he didn't speak. She blurted, "Jack, I'm not leaving my marriage. Not now." Her tone was flat and dull, although her heart jabbed in her chest.

"I'm such an idiot," he said.

She pressed the phone to her ear.

"I feel like crying right now."

She wanted to say "I'm so sorry," but it seemed obvious, and even invasive.

And then somehow they began talking about her decision-making process, the way she sometimes hid hard truths from herself. The fact that he was continuing to talk to her surprised her. She'd thought that they would have to cease speaking instantly. It just seemed very strange that they could keep talking, and she felt at that moment that he really did love her. "Things aren't real to you that should be," he said. "You go into a dream state. You de-realize things."

"You're right. I'm trying to do that less."

"You're like a cat that has to go to the vet and hides under the bed, Ina. I wish I could just scoop you up and carry you over here. But I can't put any more pressure on you than I have. Even the amount I've put on you makes me feel disgusted with myself."

She didn't answer.

"You could move in here," he said. "I could pay our expenses."

"That's very nice," she replied, but she was thinking, *Absurd!* What about her boxes of papers, her closet of clothes and winter coats, two computers, a printer, lamps, snow boots—

She stopped. Could she seriously imagine actually living with Jack? She'd always dismissed from her mind her objections to the ways Jack was, allowing herself to remain untroubled by a certain depressive insularity of his, as well as by his comments about women with short hair, his love of porn, the weird hours he kept. But no, this wasn't the real reason she couldn't move in with him. If she left Simon now, she would spend the days fraught, weeping, worried about Simon, sick with fear that she'd made a catastrophic mistake. She'd drag the phone into the bathroom to talk to Simon, and feel angry at Jack—rigid, resentful—if he pressured her not to. A mess for all concerned.

Because there was something of herself still lost inside Simon and maybe something of Simon still lost in her.

She recalled crossing the street to Jack in her black dress, feeling beautiful, feeling that she was a beautiful woman for the first time in her life. "Move on," she told him now. She sat back against the wall, drained of energy.

"I will," he said gruffly.

"That's good, Jack."

Neither of them spoke. Outside her window, the aspen tree shook its round green leaves as if it had caught a chill.

"Ina, I don't know what you're waiting for," he burst out. "Except maybe for things to seem real to you—for your previous unhappiness in your marriage to seem real. But you're fiddling while Rome burns. When we hang up, I'm going to try to begin to forget about you."

She pressed her fingernails into her palms until they pulsed. She pictured him removing from his bed the red silk slip of hers he slept beside, and getting rid of the blue plastic necklace on his piano, the few sets of stockings in his drawer. "I made a big change myself," said Jack. "I haven't had a cigarette for four weeks. I didn't want to live in such an unhealthy way anymore. I went cold turkey."

"Did you? That's wonderful." It touched her that he continued to share with her.

"Whatever." Apparently it wasn't for Ina to comment on any longer. "I walked all over Manhattan. Wore out the leather of my shoes. I couldn't sit still."

She saw his apartment, all the rooms vacant the afternoon she'd stood under his window.

"You want to hear something surprising? I didn't have any physical urge to smoke. None at all. But I felt sad all the time. The only thing that helped was walking. You know, I've smoked since I was fourteen."

"Are you breathing better?"

"No," he said with a laugh. "But I'm glad I gave it up."

"That's really good, Jack." And then: "How is *Goodbye, Columbus* going?"

"Not great," he said immediately. Something was different. He no longer spoke with the pause of him plucking a cigarette from his mouth, that meditative moment. "Still have the final number to work out, with the Tahitians and Short Hills people waving. One of the producers didn't like what I had. Still, there are a few really hooky numbers, I think. Well, it's what one of the singers said."

"You rehearsed it already?"

"With four of the actors. At the BMI offices."

She could just see him heading out in his winter jacket, tapping his pocket for his wallet, grabbing his keys from the little shelf under the mirror where he kept them, taking his neat folder of impeccably organized sheet music, stopping a moment at the door, head down, to make sure he had everything. He must have been lonely when he got home, having been through that big experience by himself.

"And now, Ina, I'm going to go to singles gatherings." He spoke with a new, frank coolness. "Get on Match.com JDate. I'm going to get out there."

"Good."

Her face and throat hurt, and it seemed to her that everything she was looking at had been emptied of inner contents; all that was left were casings. Yet it would be good to no longer feel guilt on Jack's behalf, to no longer feel she was taking advantage of him. That aspect of her life, at least, would be clean.

"Ina," he said softly, "I wish you the best."

"Thank you," she said. "You, too. I wish you the best too, Jack."

That evening she plugged in the George Foreman grill and

poured water from the Brita pitcher into a big pot. This is good, this is good, she reassured herself as she rinsed under the tap first one and then the other of the trout she'd bought. They had slippery, dense bodies, each with a sharp cartilaginous fin and staring crumpled-gold-foil eyes. It was important to be efficient and to get lots of things done.

She cranked the radio up and briskly scrubbed several big lumpy Idaho potatoes with a stiff-bristled brush, a gift from her mother-in-law. She selected a plump, squat tomato and took pleasure in observing the evenness of the slices into which she cut it, each section a uniform eighth of an inch. "It's important to have the right implement," she explained to Miss Marple, who watched from the doorway. "See, a knife like this, wide and sharp, is what you need. It's worth spending extra for it."

She was doing fine. She was doing great, she told herself. The microwave hummed while the potatoes trundled around, and although she shouldn't have—she could blow a fuse—she shoved the plug of the grill into the wall. The device, as it heated, began to emit loud pops, like joints cracking. She'd gone months infected by a kind of lassitude. It was grand to finally be effective again! Blue flames curled up around the edge of the big pot. She rinsed the blue-green broccoli heads. They were tight, fragrant. She chopped, and each bouquet unclasped a shower of florets. A low tone crooned, "Need to be with you, baby," a glorious voice infusing the air, and, oh, she felt herself sinking to the linoleum. Her knees had given way! She shut her eyes and recalled she and Jack dancing slowly, in his living room. He had one arm around her, the other slightly raised. He looked at her kindly, seriously.

"What's burning?" inquired Simon. He stood in the kitchen doorway. She jerked from the wall and got up clumsily. "Is something wrong?"

"Oh, my God!" Ina yelled, and yanked the cord from the

socket. A blaze of jagged blue-white forked through the air and sparks cascaded. "I'm such an idiot!"

She pulled open the grill, but there was only one trout, which lay scorched, blackened. She looked around the counter for the other. Then down at the floor, and then *behind* the grill (could it have slid out?) and then once more stared inside the device. A fish can't just vanish! How do things go missing? The top of the grill was quite heavy. She squatted and looked up, and there was the charred fish clinging to the lid in a state of levitation. "I'm so stupid," she muttered, and then laughed. Even she could see the absurdity of the situation.

Barry White sang, "You're the first, my last, my everything." She clicked off the radio.

Simon regarded her from the doorway. He wore rumpled blue trousers that had fallen to his hips and a perspiration-soaked wrinkled white shirt. "Don't worry about it. Did something bad happen today?"

"Some days are just like this."

He smiled sympathetically. "I have days like that too. We can go out to dinner if you want."

"I'll make something else."

He kissed her, then walked off into the bedroom to change his clothes. His kiss was irritatingly light. Ina wiped her mouth hard with the back of her hand. She bit her upper lip. The pain of her teeth shoving into her lip felt horribly pleasing. She could see how people made a habit of self-cutting. She forced her mouth to unhinge and remain open as her lip throbbed.

And then she focused on the supper, which was, surprisingly, quite salvageable. The fish had just acquired a smoky flavor, reported Simon, who ate his and then half of hers.

A pebble had been inserted between the layers of her skin, she discovered when she awoke on Saturday morning. She could not stop being irritable with Simon. Alarmed, she sequestered herself in her office, working on a chapter about the use of island music in *The Moon of the Caribbees*. But when she emerged in the late afternoon, she was ornery again. That evening they took the train to Upper Broadway for a free church concert of Bach that Simon had seen listed in *Time Out*. As they strolled up Broadway toward the venue, she spoke about Marguerite, considering how bifurcated at times the department chair's life might feel. She was one of only two Black people in the Quincy English department. Simon jangled the change in his pocket and perused the shopwindows they passed. Offended, Ina quit talking and simply walked beside him.

At the concert, the singers' voices echoed in the alcoves of the little stone building, resonating and blending in the clerestory. Violet had once sung here. She'd gone to Music and Art High School, and performed here in a chorus, one of many girls standing on tiers of benches, wearing a white shirt and dark skirt, ranks of angels. Ina had been too young to appreciate what Violet was doing. She was eleven when Violet was seventeen. She'd been impatient and bored, wondering why the singers made such pompous faces, miming surprise and awe, lifting their brows high, flipping the pages of their scores with a self-important air. People considered Ina mature for her age but in fact she was the opposite—a limited child. She merely had a high reading level. In fact, that turned out to be a liability.

"What a nice concert," said Simon, at the end.

"It was. Thanks for finding it."

He smiled and winked at Ina, as if to say, *That's what I do.*

They walked down Broadway, past a large discount store whose open door emanated the acrid scent of glazed fabrics and then a few tiny shops still hanging on, a bakery, a shoe repair. "I wonder if Violet misses singing," said Ina. "I wonder if she sings to herself."

"Hm."

"It used to be so important to her."

He nodded but seemed not to be listening.

Simon walked with his hands in his pockets and seemed almost to be humming to himself as he glanced into the shopwindows. Ina stopped talking. A small crowd of high-schoolers from a Jewish day school rushed past, uproarious, in the opposite direction, the girls in gray knee-length dresses, the boys in yarmulkas and identical thick black shoes. Ina had been in this neighborhood once with Jack. They'd met in the late afternoon at a trendy bar with purplish light, where all the women had stick-straight hair Ina had marveled at. She had an impulse to grab Simon's hand to make him walk slower, but didn't. She was wearing screw-on earrings of blue glass that were hurting her ears, so she plucked them off. It no longer mattered how she looked. An old man in dusty wingtip shoes and an undershirt shuffled up to a garbage can on the corner and started sorting through it.

Simon seemed not to have noticed she'd ceased talking. I'll tell George on Monday morning, she told herself, for she had reverted to her habit of sharing her experiences with her old friend, but her body was shaking, shivering, although it was a hot sticky night. She crossed her arms tightly. At the corner Simon waited, turned back, and smiled at her. She smiled back, enraged, depressed. The old feeling from the year before came to her: there was no point in being alive. Then he set off again. Laughter came from a side street: two preppy young men in blazers, leaving a bar. The moon illuminated the scattered wispy clouds. She felt perfectly ordinary trailing Simon. She felt as unremarkable as the lamp posts they passed, the grimy bricks. She dug her hands deep in her pockets.

Simon stopped at a small restaurant a few steps down from the street. "Want to have supper here?" It was a crowded pizza place. Its glass door was framed in orange paint, and a paper menu was taped on a side panel. The restaurant itself was as brightly lit as the inside of a refrigerator.

"They have eggplant and ricotta pizza," he said. "You like that."

She smiled.

"What's wrong?"

"I'll talk about it later."

"No, tell me now."

She replied stiffly, in acid tones, "When you don't seem interested in what I'm saying, I feel less like talking."

"But I *was* interested."

She nodded.

He blurted, "Oh, Ina. I'm sorry. Isn't it ironic: you hate when something is done to you, and then you end up doing it to someone else."

Her heart eased. It was true that his parents had deprived him. "Thank you."

"Tell me again about Violet. Tell me what you were going to tell me before."

"Okay. Inside."

And she told him over supper. She managed to tell some of it. He looked at her intently. At the end, he said, "I bet she sings to herself all the time. That isn't a thing a person stops doing. I don't think Violet is ever going to stop singing."

But the next day they argued again, and it was worse. Driving back from visiting friends in Connecticut, Simon asked her which route she thought they should take. Often in the past they'd hit bad traffic. She proposed a route, and they made good time. She couldn't help asking, "Simon, aren't you happy that the way I suggested worked out?"

"It's fortunate it worked," he replied. "Although we don't know if we would have hit a jam going over the Whitestone. That might have worked out, too."

She couldn't let it go. Impossible. Something was clawing at her. She couldn't bear to be slimed again—for his refusing to acknowledge her successful suggestion felt like being slimed. "Why can't you just say, 'That was a good call'?"

"Oh, my God, Ina," he screamed, his face flushed. "I feel like driving off the side of the road and crashing the car!"

She shut her eyes.

"I'm criticized all week long," he said, "and I really can't bear to hear more. The way I am has got to basically be okay."

Her heart jumped. Was he right? Couldn't he change?

In the apartment he went immediately into the bedroom and shut the door. This was new. She stood in the living room, then stepped into the kitchen and drank a glass of water. Ten minutes, fifteen minutes passed. She went to the bedroom door and asked, "May I come in?"

His voice came back. "Okay."

He lay in the dark.

"How are you?" she asked softly.

He didn't answer immediately. She stood silent. "I feel so shut down," he said after a while. And he looked horribly depressed—as he hadn't looked really since the first days after he found out about her affair. "What's behind the bad mood you've been in all weekend?"

"I feel far away from you," she replied. "I don't feel loved by you, Simon. It feels to me that to live with you is to feel unloved."

"Oh, sweetie," he said sadly. And then he put his arms around her and clasped her. "It's not true. I do love you."

"I feel like your sidekick when we're together."

She could identify the feeling, now that she had a basis of comparison.

"In my mind it's connected to your having had an affair," he said. "I can't reach out to you because I don't know if you're making a fool of me."

"If I were seeing someone else," she said, feeling the truth of the statement, "I wouldn't be feeling so lonely. I feel this way because I'm not seeing anyone else. I'm just alone here. And I felt this way for a long time before that man. Only I couldn't name it. I didn't know what was wrong."

He nodded, clasping her again, but his arms felt bony, rigid, as if they were sticks and he had never learned how to use them to hug. Still, it was good lying with him in the dark, talking. They fell asleep hugging one another.

And then, a pillar loomed. Simon was calling her up to the mercury-bright surface of consciousness. Up and up she swam through the heavy dark water. Finally, she broke through to the air. He was standing beside the bed. "I'm sorry, I need to tell you something."

A frightening expression was on his face—his skin pallid, with eyes that were staring and huge.

She sat up, so groggy she felt drunk. "Say it," she said quickly.

"I swore I'd never tell you, but something happened this evening—your saying that you don't feel loved by me—that made me realize I have to tell you. It's the only chance."

She watched him. She could hardly breathe, and yet she felt quite calm.

"A long time ago, when I was taking acting courses"—last year, then—"I had an affair." He began to weep. "I'm so sorry."

"Oh," she said, instantly sick.

"I was so afraid to tell you," he said, in a voice wrenched out of his gut. "I thought you'd leave me."

So she wasn't crazy. He *had* withdrawn. He *had* been locked away from her. "I'm so glad you're telling me," she said, although she felt bizarre, a thousand miles distant, and also obscurely enraged. She recalled the evenings at the Barnes & Noble, examining books about self-cutting and bulimia, wondering how it was that people had affairs because she almost felt she wanted to have one, and the afternoons of listening to the radio psychologist. "Was it that red-haired actress on Long Island?"

"Please don't guess. It's not important."

"But it was someone in your acting class?"

"Yes."

"Simon, was it a man?" Maybe this was the truth, at last.

He smiled sadly. "No. I'm not gay."

His face shone, metallic. He was an eerie stranger.

"Let's go into the living room," she said, for it had become unbearable to remain in the bedroom, which was claustrophobically overheated, and where everything seemed distorted, with Simon's attenuated figure hanging in the air. She got up and they went into the living room. It was cooler here. How pale he appeared.

Simon said: "It broke my heart before when you said you felt lonely, living with me. I felt so sorry for you." He added: "I planned on taking this secret to the grave."

"That sounds so macabre," she moaned.

Then she asked, "How long did the affair go on?"

"I don't want to say."

"But it was longer than a weekend? Did it go on for months?"

"It lasted a little while."

She nodded. "And *why* did you do it?" She added, "Did she make you feel good about yourself in a way I didn't?"

"No. I don't know why I did it. It was like I was coiled up inside. I don't know more than that."

She yearned for him to say more. She felt almost outraged at his reticence. Still, she dropped the inquiry.

He looked distinctly different to her now, younger and lighter. It was striking, how unburdening himself had transformed him. He looked like the man he had been when she first met him, when he was twenty, shyly advancing with his banjo to accompany the soloist.

"Was it Kate?" she exclaimed.

He was obviously wretched. "It's not important."

"But you still see her!"

"The relationship changed," he said swiftly. "It morphed into a friendship."

They sat there in silence, and then Ina said, "Would you mind if I slept a little more?" For it felt suddenly almost like extortion for him to keep her awake.

In the bedroom, he piled the blankets on top of her, making her cozy.

And then he kissed her deeply, over and over, and ran his hand down her breasts, and she was shocked to find herself excited, panting, aroused by him.

"Oh," she said, happily disoriented, staring up at him.

He smiled down at her. "Good?"

"Yes."

After Simon left for work the next day, Ina looked up pictures of Kate. She had an hourglass figure, and favored snug, lowcut shirts. She often wore a pink straw cowboy hat with both sides of the brim angled up. She had big emerald eyes and a valentine-shaped mouth. Ina knew from Simon that she was an actress of considerable force. The idea of Simon with her made Ina feel ill. She had to turn off the computer to make herself stop staring at photos of Kate.

"To think he was so indignant with you!" exclaimed George. "And you were—what is that word to describe the way slaves are?—abject!"

Ina glimpsed an italicized capital letter *I* stalking down the street, with a hunched gnomish lowercase a trailing.

"You carried all his secret shit."

What did that even mean? She supposed it meant the parts of oneself one didn't want to know about and so somehow foisted on the other. Most likely all people in couples carried a bit of one another's "secret shit." Simon surely carried much of hers. "In any case, it was Simon who took the risk and told the truth. It's the most wonderful thing."

"Is it?" said George stickily.

"Yes."

For with his news, a change had happened. In the evening, she and Simon sat over dinner and found themselves smiling at each other. Simon seemed both younger and sunnier than he'd been in ages. He kissed her a lot. He told jokes and shyly watched her laugh. In part because it made Ina happy, he called Violet and played the banjo for her, a high-flying lighthearted tune, and Violet held up the phone so that others could hear, the nurse who brought medications, the mute roommate in her bed. After Simon wished Violet good night and hung up, he and Ina sat quietly. She felt closer to him than she had in years. She didn't tell George about these evenings. She no longer wanted to describe to him her time with her husband.

"You seemed so happy when you were acting," she said to Simon one evening as they strolled along the promenade, holding hands. The city twinkled across the river, the windows with their brittle lights. "Do you miss it?"

"Not really."

"But you seemed so alive then, so excited." She'd thought perhaps it was the joy of acting which had inspired the affair, the teacher graduating him class upon class, and him feeling his new powers.

He shrugged. "The acting was a wonderful thing to have done."

"Did the affair make you happy?"

"No," he said sharply. "It was like living a nightmare. I was horrified by myself. And I missed you so much. It was like I couldn't get at my love for you."

"But you were too afraid to leave me."

"I never considered leaving you." He added: "When I found out about your affair, I thought it was payback for what I'd done."

She shook her head. Her affair was not payback.

The dark trees lining the walk seemed to be tossing something amongst themselves. It was shaped like a jigsaw puzzle piece and seemed to leap from tree to tree, alive as a monkey. She squinted, trying to see what it was. All at once she recalled that what had been missing in their marriage had been missing long before Simon had had his affair. That was the truth. Even when they'd lived together in Chicago, an aspect had been missing, and she'd kept shuffling this knowledge away from herself, hoping it wasn't real. Even sitting together in a late-night jazz club on Chicago's South Side, she'd felt isolated and lonely, hearing the marvelous music, noticing a man in a blue blazer sipping brandy, a signet ring on his pinky—she still remembered that chunky signet ring. Things seemed too innocent with Simon, even then. Antiseptic. And there was a sadness to them. Ina lifted her hand now as they walked along the promenade. She was holding Simon's hand. She slid one of his knuckles into her mouth. "Oh, really?" he said, as if she'd asked a humorous question. "Is that so?"

In answer, she slid in his entire index finger. She slowly drew her head back, his finger glistening, leaving a salty taste in her mouth, and she looked him in the eye, refusing to be ashamed of this weird thing she'd done.

"You don't say!" he said, and then he pulled her to him and they kissed under one of the antique lamps. She inhaled when they kissed. She loved the scent of Simon.

The next morning, although she had stopped sharing with George what was going on inside her marriage, she made an exception. "I'm going to wear the red bodice for Simon. It's strapless, sleeveless." Jack couldn't keep his hands off her when she wore it. "I've never worn anything like it for him."

"Then he's in for a surprise."

"And maybe I am, too."

Chapter 39

For once Ina took the initiative, scanning the entertainment notices and ordering tickets. A cabaret singer who was a favorite of theirs would be performing Sinatra. He was in his forties, a fine lyric tenor who made each song sound as if he'd lived it. Admission was first come, first served, so they got ready early, at five o'clock in the late afternoon on Saturday. It was almost July, and the days stretched long. Simon put on a blazer and a silvery gray shirt that brought out his eyes He looked elegant, the planes in his face prominent. Ina sat on the bed while he dressed, then, when he was finished, asked him to step out.

Alone in the bedroom, she donned the red bodice. Its fabric stretched across vertical wire boning that flared up from her waist. It gave her the torso of a superwoman while exposing the very top half inch of her breasts. She zipped the black skirt and slid her feet into her high-heeled ankle boots. Then she ran her hands through her hair, brushing it back. Her pulse banged in her wrists. Finally, she stepped out of the bedroom, feeling more nude than if she were naked.

Simon, standing at the apartment door, grinned. "Va-va-va-voom!" He made his eyes big and rubbed the air in front of her breasts as if polishing headlights. She laughed, coloring.

They walked down Remsen Street over the brightly lit sidewalk. It seemed somehow to her that they were striding too loosely, as if they weren't in fancy clothing at all. "Slow down, please," she asked. He pantomimed railroad wheels after the brakes have been applied, elbows bent, hands circling and coming to rest. Then he stepped beside her carefully down Remsen. They rode the R train to 49th, and emerged on a Midtown side street of dusty restaurant awnings. In the high afternoon light, the sunstruck russet cloth over the doorways was threadbare and bleached yellow. Individual stitches extruded like tiny nubbles of braille.

"I think the company might actually come out of this whole situation okay," remarked Simon. "Cable still has the advantage over dial-up."

"Oh, that's so good to hear." What a relief. It seemed almost a reward for his determinedly continuing on, the fates behaving fairly for once. He really was magnificent in his grit and good cheer, and his truly bone-deep kindness. It was what had drawn her to him in the first place. When they saw Dr. Morris again, she'd tell her this. It was this, too, not just his storytelling. She took his hand and held it, her handsome husband, with whom she was out on a date. Maybe it would work out for them.

On 51st Street, they waited for the light to change at a corner. Glittering ice chips and sawdust had been dumped in the gutter. Empty cabs rolled past, followed by one transporting an elaborately made up woman, leaning forward to direct the driver, her beautiful pearl-colored nails resting on the plexiglass, her face pleased and confident.

"You're early!" called the host. He was a glamorous young man with backswept blond hair. He led them along a corridor and into a vast, well air-conditioned room. Only two other people were present: a couple midway through their supper, facing one another across a long banquet table. The host seated Ina and Simon directly beside them, and they turned—an older pair in their sixties. The wife wore a boxy blue paisley dress; the husband's blue jacket hung loosely from sunken shoulders.

"Hello there!" The wife thrust out her hand. "Good to get here early! You know, we just love Sinatra! Jerome here plays piano in our town: Corning. Upstate."

"Guilty as charged!" said the husband.

"We're culture vultures," the wife continued. "Come to the city every chance we get. This time we've seen, what Jerome? Three shows? No, four. We saw *Forbidden Broadway Strikes Back*, *Jekyll & Hyde*, *Les Miz*, which of course we've seen before. And what else?" She paused. "Oh, I'm already counting *this*!" She laughed.

Simon said, "My wife writes about the theater. She's working on a book about Eugene O'Neill right now. She just got her doctorate from Chicago, which has the best graduate English department in the country."

"Oh my, a professor!" said the wife, looking a little uncertain.

Ina shot Simon a look, self-conscious that he'd boasted about her.

"O'Neill. Very grim," added the husband.

Ina laughed. "True." She lifted her big tasseled menu, trying to convey by her intent expression that she and her husband wanted some privacy. To her consternation though, Simon leaned toward the wife and remarked, "You've sure been busy, seeing all those shows. No moss on you!"

"That's right. Now young folks like you, it's a surprise you like Sinatra."

"He's actually appreciated by lots of younger people," said Simon.

Ina took a long time studying the various dishes, holding the menu even higher. But Simon just glanced and immediately flapped his menu shut, then launched into questions of the Corning people. How often did they get down to New York? Where did they like to stay, when they visited?

Ina stroked her hair forward, over her cheek. The longer Simon chatted, the more ludicrously fleshy and exposed she felt in her revealing top. Couldn't he quit talking to them? Well, Simon couldn't help being polite; they probably reminded him of his Texas hometown, where it was considered just regular good manners to be convivial to strangers. But wasn't it possible to be friendly and not give away their special evening?

Each time there was a chance to let the conversation peter out, Simon stoked it. When the woman said she'd recently taken a course in calligraphy at the local high school, Simon volunteered: "Ina and I took a very good course at our local high school, too, when we lived up in Connecticut. It was on music history—taught by a man who always brought a gigantic suitcase of records. You should have seen it!"

What was Simon doing? She addressed him softly, pointedly, looking at him as if peering directly down a hallway, as if to say, *Let's act like it's just the two of us*: "How's your chicken?"

"It's fine."

She bent closer to him. She murmured, "It's good?"

"Mm-hmm." He glanced at her neck; the place where he looked felt hot, as if he'd pressed with his thumbs.

"The food here *is* pretty good, isn't it?" the wife volunteered. "And you really never know what it's going to be like at a show. But this place actually gives you value for money, which is rare in the Big Apple."

Simon swiveled his chair even more fully towards them, smiling with interest.

What the hell? Ina reached out and took his hand. Just us, she tried to signal. She was sweating, although the room was overly air-conditioned, and she worried that her skin gleamed. She felt obscurely mocked, the tops of her breasts toppling this way and that, two chiffon pies. When Simon asked them, "Do you know about Zagat?" Ina stood up abruptly. "I have a headache. I'm going to get aspirin."

Simon glanced at her, surprised.

She quickly walked out of the vast room and down the brick corridor. Outside, in the hot bright air, one of the horse-drawn buggies from Central Park trotted past, jingling, garlanded, the animal's hooves clanging on the stones. Its stable must be around here. A slender man in a black vest said to her, "What's wrong? You made yourself so pretty. What happened?"

Her eyes stupidly filled with tears. "Thank you," she muttered. She went back inside to get away from the man and his kindness. The vestibule bar was now crowded with men in dinner jackets waiting for drinks. She stood near the beige-tinted mirror that lined one wall, watching them, letting time pass.

When she returned, Simon looked at her with concern. "You okay?"

"Yup. Thanks." She assiduously did not turn her face toward the Corning people.

"I think there are two h's in Southampton," the wife said.

"Not the Southampton in Massachusetts," said Simon.

Ina crumpled her napkin in her hand. What was the use? Ashamed, she put on her black cotton jacket and firmly zipped it up.

Simon made an unhappy face, and it became a momentary childish tussle between them; he tried to tug the zipper back down, she shook her head and pulled it up to just under her chin. He let go. The gold tab, the size of a flip-top, dangled like a ludicrous miniature necktie.

A convivial hubbub was filling the room. Most of the seats in the large hall were now taken. The lights went down, and finally their neighbors turned toward the stage. But then the young blond man who had ushered them to their seats came out and announced that there would be a substitute replacing the star, who was sick. Ina sighed.

The music began, and a performer who looked about twenty stepped from behind the curtain—he had a sunny, smooth voice with a swagger in it, and clean gleaming eyes. A toothpaste smile. After that, a woman with platinum Lana Turner hair strolled out. She wore a snug tan satin 1940s gown and delivered her tunes in a smoldering manner, hands placed firmly together on one hip, professionally saucy. Ina glanced at the playbill and counted how many songs remained, disappointed, waiting for the program simply to be done.

On the street afterwards, Simon said, "Did the aspirin work?"

"I didn't buy any! I just wanted to get away from those people."

He contemplated her, a look of distress on his face.

"Why did you keep talking to them?" she asked. "They were so rude!"

"*You* were rude."

"'How many h's in Southampton!' 'Culture vultures!'" She knew she was acting poorly, but she was so disappointed.

"Stop it."

"Why couldn't they leave us alone! How many hints does it take? We were on a *date*! And why did you keep talking to them?" Had he purposely wanted to shame her?

"Ina, I can't believe the behavior you allow yourself," he replied. "I'm just so . . . so extremely disappointed in you."

And he looked it—gravely disappointed.

They had arrived at the stairs down to the subway. "I don't want to be with you right now," he said.

He had on other occasions stalked off in the midst of an argument. It always had a punitive, icy edge. She couldn't bear to see him turn away from her now. And so it was she who swung away and went quickly down the stairs, blinking rapidly and clasping the banister to hold herself upright in her high heels.

Once in the apartment, she wrenched off the skirt and stockings. The bodice, as she yanked it over her head, seemed like a geriatric support garment, hot, stretched out, reeking of her. She chucked it onto the dresser, but it slid off onto the floor. It lay half-underneath the dresser.

She stared at it, then rushed over and snatched up the repulsive, crumpled thing with the urge to rip it apart. Blue gardenias of dust clung to it. She began to squeeze, pressing so hard her arms trembled and the garment crammed down to the size of an egg. Then she stopped. If she didn't put it back on, she'd never wear it again. That whole aspect of her life would be finished. She swept her hand brusquely along the cloth, cleaning it—gray dust floated up. Gently she straightened the wires, trying to restore their shape.

Then, holding her breath, she eased the clinging red garment back on.

Chapter 40

It was late evening when Ina heard the press of Simon's feet on the stairs. She sat up straight from where she'd been bent over the little café table in the living room. Her book was now so firmly cast in her mind that she could compose it right through, regardless of mood. She examined each mid-career play, and only after she'd looked at all other aspects did she consider the logic of the words. The theater was a viewing space. The body had a story to tell. Hers did, wearing this silly bodice.

The air outside was a gauzy black. Apartments across the street had their curtains drawn, except where the bare-chested guitar player sat in the window of his unfurnished living room and, above, on the top floor, where the history professor studied an open book. When O'Neill came down the mountain, he knew that death was real. Ina had never understood this about death, which is why she'd lived her life so dreamily. Witnessing the truth of death had allowed O'Neill to seize control of his life. He'd touched base with cold reality. It pierced through his adolescent sullenness, his reflexive defiance of authority, his peevish need to ruin his own life, all his ploys. Up on the mountain, he'd seen something. It didn't make him a good person. He was a terrible father and often a selfish husband. But he wasn't playing games any more with his life. She herself still lived in a land of make-believe, as if her time was infinite. All this came to her in a flash, hearing Simon's keys jangle outside the door.

The bolt turned, and Simon entered, looking fatigued in his rumpled silvery-gray shirt. He glanced toward where she sat, and then turned and shut the apartment door behind him with extreme gentleness, as if not wanting to upset the equanimity of a madwoman. Something in her flared. She held her breath and counted slowly. One, two, three, four, a pounding beating through her like the tolling of a gong. Still, he looked so defeated, so downhearted. She called softly, "How was your evening?"

He turned, and his face assumed a look of surprise, perhaps at seeing her still in that strange red garment. "Fine."

How sad and tired he seemed! "What did you do?"

"Walked." He shrugged. "Ended up walking all the way to the Starbucks at the City Hall station. Read *Robinson Crusoe* there."

"Weren't your feet sore in those shoes?"

He shrugged again.

"Did you eat anything?"

"A decaf. A monkey bowl of fruit."

She smiled, tears springing into her eyes. A funny, endearing word that: monkey bowl. "How's *Crusoe*?"

"Good." He set on the side table the paperback with its spindly, occasionally chipped print, its pages tinted apricot by time; it had been bought at a used book store. She liked that he persevered with the old, close-set lines of type in secondhand books.

"You were working?" He tilted his chin toward her legal pad.

"Yes. It's all ready to come out, all the ideas."

"Uh-huh."

"Uh-huh," she repeated to her own surprise, suddenly angry again at his response. How fascinatingly ugly it sounded! She wanted to hear it again. "Uh-huh, uh-huh," she repeated, reveling in the loping, ungainly vowels.

"I'm out of here," he said in a clipped voice. "Nothing's changed." His hand rose toward the lock.

"Oh, please don't go," she said softly, in a rush. "That *was* rude. I'm sorry. Forgive me. Please. It's just that I'm so unhappy. I was so disappointed tonight."

She looked at Simon's hand on the door of the apartment, a white door with a shiny, gummy surface. Years of paint coats—innumerable gloopy glazes—had imparted a rubberiness to it. She had an abrupt impulse to drive her fingernails into that springy, nursery texture, pierce down to the wood, make contact. "Please let's not go back to each of us living in our own world. It's horrible."

He nodded slowly, and she noticed the gray in his hair. Then he walked back into the living room and sat down on the couch, looking dispirited. She came over and sat near him, in the wicker chair. He was still wearing the dark blazer and gray slacks. Poignant, sad clothing, it seemed—unbreathing, sweaty, too tight.

Up until now she'd been frightened to acknowledge her response to Simon's appearance. Another woman would see him differently and she should be that woman. But now, she thought, I'm responding normally. And even if I weren't normal, this would be my genuine response.

She sat forward and said, "I had the feeling you were purposely trying to shut me down before. To humiliate me for wearing this top. Although you might not be aware of it."

"No."

She laughed, an ugly laugh. She was allowing herself to be ugly! "No?"

Outside the window the streetlamp illuminated a handful of metallic, olive-colored leaves.

"You asked me not to leave, so I won't," said Simon, giving her a level gaze. "But how is this getting us anywhere?"

She bit back the impulse to blurt, "Right! Let's just shut up and stow our feelings!" Instead, she shook her head. "Shouldn't we talk? Not go back to the old way?"

She had a sudden awareness of how ludicrous she appeared in her red bodice—fat and sweaty, with a pucker of flesh like an extra lip tucked in her underarm. Jack had actually kissed her there, shutting his eyes and then running his mouth across the tucked-away skin; he'd said, with awe, "It's so soft," and she'd blushed, shocked. She said now, gently, "You don't really like me in this, do you?"

"It feels like an attempt at manipulation."

Ina's chest felt scraped by a Brillo pad. "Simon, that feels mean to me.

"Those two out-of-towners," she continued, "did they really need you? I started to feel so inappropriate. So sexually excessive. As if it was easier for you to be the good son than respond to me."

He was looking at the floor, an expression of intense disappointment on his face.

She had to go on, though. She feared that if she didn't—if she didn't expel all of it—they would get nowhere, they would always be stuck.

"I feel turned into your mother sometimes. I think she was overwhelming." A phrase floated to her ears: *a peanut in a peanut shell.* "She could be withering."

He was looking out the window, at the sky beyond. "Whatever."

A smile rose to her lips. "You know, when you say that, it's like you've just stepped aside. And it leaves me isolated. Feeling ugly."

Simon glanced back up at her, a pained look on his face. "I'm sorry. I don't mean that."

Something eased in her too, with a wince, like relaxing onto a knife blade. Oh, he was good. He really was a good man.

He got up and reached over, brushing the hair back from

her face, and for some reason she felt even more embarrassed. Her lips tilted up in a smile, and she worried again if her teeth were yellow. With Jack, she didn't worry about yellow teeth.

"You look very nice," he said, breaking her heart somehow. "I was thinking that this evening." But something was missing. His tone was consoling.

She gave a frustrated, jagged laugh. No, she didn't like the new, unpleasant, ghoulish, enraged Ina who—it came to her—seemed to believe that if she asked for something specifically enough she would get it. How blind. She glanced out the window. To her surprise, the history professor was staring across at her with an expression of astonishment. Ina had always assumed she was invisible to her neighbors. But of course they could see her—the girl in the ridiculously stretched-out lavender pants, and now the woman in the red bodice.

She bowed her head at her neighbor in acknowledgment. She liked that history professor! The woman looked startled, a form had been broken, but then, after a moment, she lowered her head in a nod back. Ina's eyes stung.

"The truth is, I was embarrassed for you tonight," said Simon.

"Because I wanted to have a date with my husband?"

"That isn't what I mean."

"I think it is."

"Stop pathologizing me, Ina. Please grant me the dignity of assuming I actually know what I mean. You behaved poorly. Selfishly."

Oh, he was right! And she was behaving poorly and selfishly now. It felt good. It was necessary. She looked out at the building across the street, each apartment a different diorama, most with their curtains shut. "We're monsters," Violet had once said. She'd been looking down at her own yellowish, spreading legs, covered in scraggly dark hairs. Ina had objected—it was heartbreaking, how Violet saw herself—but in fact Violet had *seemed* monstrous to Ina, volatile, demanding. All her life Ina had thought of women who were like that—appetitive, unbudging—as nightmare figures. But she'd envied them. They were doing something right. "This is what feminism looks like," she told Simon. "What I'm doing right now."

But then she stopped, for the history professor seemed still to be studying her.

No. Ina was just taking the easy way out again. She sighed.

It had simply felt good to rage. Righteous. Powerful. It infused her with a sense that she was correct. Behind the professor, the blue-black landscape was running with moisture, with silvery fire escapes and swollen water-towers. "No, it's not. It isn't feminism."

"You sound like a character in O'Neill." Simon smiled wryly despite the awfulness of the evening.

"Taking back what I just said?"

"Yes."

"It's true. They do that, don't they?" She smiled into his dear face. Oh, she still loved Simon. "But I just saw something I hadn't. Being nasty isn't liberation. Although I suppose sometimes you have to say ugly things to get at the truth." That was part of O'Neill's message, wasn't it?

"Do you?" he said. Simon didn't. Simon didn't say ugly things to reach the truth.

She saw him talking to the old people, being kind to the out-of-towners. Across the table sat his glowering wife in a tight red sleeveless top like the cover of a steamy romance novel. Good heavens! She'd been unfair to him. She'd been unfair to him for years. She'd acted as if he was some Santa Claus, able to produce what she wanted simply because she'd asked. As if, if she asked for a certain kind of kiss, one that aroused her in the way she wished, he could give it to her. And that if he didn't, it was because he was being mean, withholding. She acted as if he had all that she yearned for hidden away in a great big sack of presents tucked behind a door. She simply hadn't seen him, the actual Simon. She'd been mad at him for years, really, with spikes of irritation she'd fled from knowing, and a saturating disappointment from which she'd also estranged herself. Not facing up. "Ever in dreamland!" as her mother once said.

The cat had settled on Simon's legs, regarding Ina with burning gold eyes. "You know, I hated how you left sometimes when we were having an argument," she said. "But I usually left even before that, before we even started arguing. I didn't talk about what wasn't working between us, what wasn't right."

How sad he looked.

"Has it been lonely for you," she asked, "living like this? How has it been?"

He shrugged, lifted his hand and dropped it. "It's been okay. I didn't know that you felt that way, Ina, so disappointed." He looked grievously hurt. He'd believed her! He'd believed all her playacting! She was shocked. He'd been alone even before she met Jack, and hadn't known it. Although on some level he must have. He must have known it but perhaps it simply felt normal to him. At least it felt safe.

"Neither of us talked about what we were missing. We were afraid of hurting each other. I'm so sorry, Simon. I should have told you."

But Simon had shut his eyes. His arms lay at his sides. He was like a man wedged in a metal tube; everything she said was a bombardment against its exterior walls. He was locked away, a solitary soldier enduring explosions against the deep-space rocket ship in which he was lodged.

"Please don't let it all just wash over you," she said. "Would you open your eyes please?"

He opened his eyes and looked at her, and she blushed.

He was so handsome. Maybe he was going to say what she needed to hear. That he was deeply turned onto her, that he'd been missing passionate sex, that he wanted them to find a way to break through to one another, whatever it took.

"I don't believe I can give you what you want," he said.

She felt sick to her stomach.

"I'm forty years old," he said. "I don't think I'm going to change a whole lot."

She came over and kissed his brow. She could not go back to their old prim way, with its stiffness, its loneliness. Nor her frustration and envy of other couples.

"Oh, I don't think you can give me what I want. And I'm too unhappy without it."

His eyes were wet. "It's so sad."

"Yes. But it would be sadder to lose any more time. We've settled for too little and pretended it was enough."

"So you're going back to him?"

She thought, and shook her head. "No. No, I'm not." How lightweight and implausible Jack seemed now! A decidedly idiosyncratic, unlikely person. With none of the gravitas and adulthood that someone like Simon possessed. She had sinned against Jack, too, really. Made use of him. Maybe that's what people do in affairs, even if they love each other. She needed to grow up. She saw herself in a small apartment in Astoria, shared with a housemate, but with a bedroom of her own, tired at the end of a long workday in the city but paying her own way and knowing the reality of things. "I need to be on my own." At least for a while. So she could discover how to quit bamboozling.

She got up, and picked up the cat and kissed her on the mouth—the cat held a paw up and she kissed the paw, too—and then went into her bedroom and found at the back of the closet an old dusty canvas wheelie-bag and heaved it onto the bed and unzipped it. An aroma of the sea flung itself up, and she began to pack.

At the front door, he hugged her hard and they stood in the doorway, both weeping. Then he opened his arms. "Goodbye, darling," he said.

She kissed him on the cheek. Then she descended the stairs, her bag striking hard against her calf at each step as she passed the pallid pink wallpaper roses like swollen, hothouse blossoms, soaked and dissolving. With the meaty part of her arm she shoved open the heavy lobby door. Just at that moment, from far at the top of the stairs, came the soft bang of their own apartment door as it fell shut. She staggered, her knees jelly. The cool air on the pavement seemed to pull her out into it. The rain had stopped.

Across the street, the super was sweeping the front steps of polynoses, the broom rasping, leaving a wet gray shimmer. Ina started to walk. The wheels of her bag clattered, spraying the bit of moisture that lay on the street. An orange macaw stood miraculously on a branch, but then she saw it was just a patch of brilliant leaves, already turned, their sugars frozen early.

"Have a good trip," called the Asian man from across the street, walking with his son, who was in blue pajamas and flip-flops. The little boy waved. "Good trip!"

In the temple-front Bossert Hotel, in the basement dining room, row after row of women in blocky dresses and men in starched white shirts ate canned fruit off of sturdy thick white plates and sipped from sturdy thick white cups. They were the Jehovah's Witnesses who owned the building. Evangelists had been good to Violet. They'd visited her when others had not. She gave a silent nod of homage to the Witnesses in their orderly ranks. Ina was leaving this neighborhood. She'd almost certainly never be able to afford it again. In fact, she had never been able to afford it at all herself.

It was late in life, but not too late.

In the subway station Ina set down her suitcase and swiped her MetroCard. She'd go to Janie's apartment in Washington

Heights for the night, see tomorrow about a Craigslist share. Janie knew a copyeditor at *Business Week*. Maybe they had work. And she would register immediately at office temp agencies. When she finished her book, she wouldn't do a national job search. She would stay local to be with Violet. Luckily, there were many schools in New York. In her shared room, Violet was glad to have the bed by the window, which overlooked the inner courtyard, gray, but full of light. Ina would take the subway up to her in a few days, and tell her what was going on.

Descending the subway stairs, she thought of how often she'd hurried down these very steps, going to Jack, caught up in her whirlwind.

The rumble of a train came from the lower tracks, the noise reverberating. In the station, all the seats on the wood bench were occupied. She stood on the platform, and beside her a man with a British accent crooned into the ears of an infant he clasped, "We'll be there soon, love. Soon, soon, soon." Almost immediately there came a rattling circular rush echoing from the tunnel, a sound like maracas being spun.

New York seemed to swivel around her, and she pictured the blind horse and its pacifying donkey companion underground in the middle of New York turning the Central Park carousel, cranking its fairy tale beauty. The tumbling sound grew louder, and then the air in the station suspended itself an instant. The train came bellowing in.

Fulton Street, Chambers, the ancient places where it was possible to cross the island in just a few steps. Dr. Zizmor gazed down under his rainbow, advertising chemical peels, unblemished skin. His sad, kind eyes brimmed with understanding. *You want to be beautiful. I want that for you, too,* said his eyes. *And I know you actually are beautiful. Yes, even you. I see it. There is hope for you.* He transmitted this to every person in the city, smiling beneath his rainbow. Violet herself had bought a book of his, long ago before he was famous, long before she was ill.

The train started to thunder toward the 72nd Street platform, and Ina thought, I can step out. Cab across town to Jack's. Her fingers rested on the roller-bag handle. In the station, the doors sprang open.

She remained in her seat. A gust of the scent from Jack's pillow rose up. She shut her eyes. Warm air flooded in. The doors stood wide apart, waiting for the local. But still she sat. She could not go to Jack now. He seemed like something poisoned, verboten. He was the means by which she'd harmed Simon. But, further than that, going to him would be like propounding a lie. He was not the reason she was leaving Simon. Could she ever go to him, eventually?

She and Jack had known each other in a particular, extraordinary way, understanding both more and less about one another than anyone she'd ever been close to. He saw her in makeup, and she'd felt fantastic, unmasked, some hallucinated inner part of herself sprung free. But he didn't know the rest of her, the bookish Ina, the everyday Ina. She couldn't imagine introducing him to her parents, to Violet. Still, it had been perfect the way it was. Let him be the last unknown intimate.

The doors jolted shut and the train continued. In the cracked glass of the window beside her swirled the light of passing stations.

The train accelerated and the walls pressed close and got louder, and Ina watched the gray concrete fly past and so saw the precise moment when the train lofted out of the darkness at 184th Street into the treetops and air of upper Manhattan. All the little bright apartments flying! Their curtains shook. Glimpses of TVs and kitchen plates and empty flowerpots and illegal cable lines raced past. All the various lives, flashing a gleam. Life was full of people semaphoring across seas, snatching the sun with their bit of mirror and flinging the shine in an attempt to declare themselves, the self they also wanted to keep secret, the self they craved to discover is real. A thousand hostages longing to stand revealed, as she had been that night when she drank the Chartreuse from which she could not wake up because she was already awake. She stood, hoisted her bag, and then stepped off the train onto the platform and into the night city glowing with its thousand upon thousand lights.

Acknowledgments

I am indebted to the following novelists for the perspectives and insight they provided: Alice Elliott Dark, Marina Budhos, Elizabeth Evans, Alexandra Enders, Rachel Basch, Yona McDonough, and Gary Glickman. I am grateful, too, to Sal Randolph for years of inspiration and friendship, and without whose magical kindness this novel might have taken far longer to find a home.

Priscilla Sneff, Ann McCutchan, Alexandra Shelley, and the members of the thrilling Grove Street Gang sustained my vision and soul during the years of composition. Eugene O'Neill scholar Alexander Pettit offered intellectual companionship concerning the titan of American theater who so compels my protagonist.

I am deeply grateful to Christopher Potter, who worked with me at both the conceptual and sentence level. His insights made this novel much better than it otherwise would have been. Edoardo Andreoni, my editor, and the entire extraordinary team at Europa were a privilege to work with. Malaga Baldi, my agent, has been a grand advocate.

Paul Meltzer, my husband, endured years of conversation about the structure and method of this novel as well as more weeks apart than he would have wished while I redrafted this manuscript, and inspired me to keep believing in the value of my work. It's true that writing is a solitary endeavor but it is sustained, if one is lucky, by a great circle of beloveds.

About the Author

Bonnie Friedman is the author of the bestselling *Writing Past Dark*, named one of the Essential Books for Writers by The Center for Fiction and *Poets & Writers*. She is also the author of *The Thief of Happiness* and *Surrendering Oz*, which was a finalist for the PEN/Diamonstein-Spielvogel Award for the Art of the Essay. Her work has appeared in *The New York Times*, *Ploughshares* and many other literary journals, and she has been named a notable essayist four times in *The Best American Essays*. She has taught writing at the University of Iowa, Dartmouth, NYU, and the University of North Texas. *Don't Stop* is her first novel.